Dani Collins

More than a Convenient Marriage?

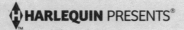

If you purchased this book without a cover you should be aware that this book is stolen property. It was reported as "unsold and destroyed" to the publisher, and neither the author nor the publisher has received any payment for this "stripped book."

Recycling programs
for this product may
not exist in your area.

ISBN-13: 978-0-373-13206-5

First North American Publication 2013

MORE THAN A CONVENIENT MARRIAGE?
Copyright © 2013 by Dani Collins

NO LONGER FORBIDDEN?
Copyright © 2012 by Dani Collins

All rights reserved. Except for use in any review, the reproduction or utilization of this work in whole or in part in any form by any electronic, mechanical or other means, now known or hereafter invented, including xerography, photocopying and recording, or in any information storage or retrieval system, is forbidden without the written permission of the publisher, Harlequin Enterprises Limited, 225 Duncan Mill Road, Don Mills, Ontario M3B 3K9, Canada.

This is a work of fiction. Names, characters, places and incidents are either the product of the author's imagination or are used fictitiously, and any resemblance to actual persons, living or dead, business establishments, events or locales is entirely coincidental.

This edition published by arrangement with Harlequin Books S.A.

For questions and comments about the quality of this book, please contact us at CustomerService@Harlequin.com.

® and TM are trademarks of Harlequin Enterprises Limited or its corporate affiliates. Trademarks indicated with ® are registered in the United States Patent and Trademark Office, the Canadian Trade Marks Office and in other countries.

Printed in U.S.A.

CONTENTS

For my sisters, 'cause they live far away and I miss 'em.

More than a Convenient Marriage?

CHAPTER ONE

GIDEON VOZARAS USED all his discipline to keep his foot
light on the accelerator as he followed the rented car, forcing himself to maintain an unhurried pace along the narrow
island road while he gripped the wheel in white-knuckled
fists. When the other car parked outside the palatial gate
of an estate, he pulled his own rental onto the shoulder
a discreet distance back then stayed in his vehicle to see
if the other driver noticed. As he cut the engine, the AC
stopped. Heat enveloped him.

Welcome to hell.

He hated Greece at the best of times and today was
predicted to be one of the hottest on record. The air shim-
mered under the relentless sun and it wasn't even ten
o'clock yet. But the weather was barely worth noticing.

The gates of the estate were open. The other car could
have driven straight through and up to the house, but stayed
parked outside. He watched the female driver emerge and
take a moment to consider the unguarded entrance. Her
shoulders gave a lift and drop as though she screwed up
her courage before she took action and walked in.

As she disappeared between imposing brick posts,
Gideon left his own car and followed at a measured pace,
gut knotting with every step. Outrage stung his veins.

He wanted to believe that wasn't his wife, but there was

no mistaking Adara Vozaras. Not for him. Maybe her tourist clothes of flip-flops, jeans chopped above the knees, a sleeveless top and a pair of pigtails didn't fit her usual professional élan, but he knew that backside. The tug it caused in his blood was indisputable. No other woman made an immediate sexual fire crackle awake in him like this. His relentless hunger for Adara had always been his cross to bear and today it was particularly unwelcome.

Spending the week with her mother. This ain't Chatham, sweetheart.

He paused as he came alongside her car, glancing inside to see a map of the island on the passenger seat. A logo in its corner matched the hotel he'd been told she was booked into. And now she was advising her lover where to meet her? Walking bold as you please up his million-dollar driveway to his billion-dollar house? The only clue to the estate's ownership, the shields welded to the gate, were turned back against the brick wall that fenced the estate from the road.

Gideon's entire body twitched with an urge to slip his reins of control. He was not a poor man. He'd got past envying other men their wealth once he'd acquired a certain level of his own. Nevertheless, a niggle of his dock-rat inferiority complex wormed to life as he took in what he could see of the shoreline property that rolled into a vineyard and orange grove. The towering stone house, three stories with turrets on each corner, belonged on an English estate, not a Greek island. It was twenty bedrooms minimum. If this was the owner's weekend retreat, he was an obscenely rich man.

Not that Adara needed a rich man. She had grown up wanting for nothing. She had a fortune in her own right plus half of Gideon's, so what was the attraction here?

Sex.

The insidious whisper formed a knot of betrayal behind his breastbone. Was this why she hadn't shared that stacked body of hers with him for weeks? His hands curled into fists as he tried to swallow back his gall.

Dreading what he might see as he looked to the front door, he shifted for a full view. Adara had paused halfway to the house to speak with a gardener. A truck overflowing with landscaping tools was parked midway up the driveway and workers were crawling like bees over the blooming gardens.

The sun seared the back of Gideon's neck, strong enough to burn through his shirt to his shoulders, making sweat pool between his shoulder blades and trickle annoyingly down his spine.

They had arrived early this morning, Adara off the ferry, Gideon following in a powerboat he was "test-piloting." She'd been driving a car she'd rented in Athens. His rental had been negotiated at the marina, but the island was small. It hadn't surprised him when she'd driven right past the nose of his car as he had turned onto the main road.

No, the surprise had been the call thirty-six hours previously when their travel agent had dialed his mobile by mistake. Ever the survivor, Gideon had thought quickly. He'd mentioned that he'd like to surprise his wife by joining her and within seconds, Gideon had had all the details of Adara's clandestine trip.

Well, not all. He didn't know whom she was here to see or how she'd met her mystery man. *Why was she doing this when he gave her everything she asked for?*

He watched Adara's slender neck bow in disappointment. Ha. The bastard wasn't home. Grimly satisfied, Gideon folded his arms and waited for his wife.

Adara averted her gaze from the end of the driveway where the sun was glancing off her rented car and piercing straight into her eyes.

The grounds of this estate were an infinitely more beautiful place to look anyway. Groomed lawn gently rolled into vineyards, and a white sand beach gleamed below. The dew was off the grass, the air moving hotly up from the water with a tang of salt on it. Everything was brilliant and elevating.

Perhaps that was just her frame of mind, but it was a refreshing change from depression and anxiety and rejection. She paused to savor the first optimistic moment she'd had in weeks. Looking out on the horizon where Mediterranean blue met cloudless sky, she sighed in contentment. She hadn't felt so relaxed since… Since ever. Early childhood maybe. Very early childhood.

And it wouldn't last. A sick ache opened in her belly as she remembered Gideon. And his PA.

Not yet, she reminded herself. This week was hers. She was stealing it for herself and her brother. If he returned. The gardener had said a few days, but Adara's research had put Nico on this island all week, so he obviously changed his schedule rapidly. Hopefully he'd return as suddenly as he'd left.

Just call him, she cajoled herself, but after this many years she wasn't sure he'd know who she was or want to hear from her. He'd never picked up the telephone himself. If he refused to speak to her, well, a throb of hurt pulsed in her throat as she contemplated that. She swallowed it back. She just wanted to see him, look into his eyes and learn why he'd never come home or spoken to her or her younger brothers again.

Another cleansing breath, but this one a little more troubled as she turned toward her car again. She was crestfallen Nico wasn't here, not that she'd meant to come like this to his house, first thing on arrival, but her room at the hotel hadn't been ready. On impulse she'd decided to at least find the estate, and then the gates had been open and she'd been drawn in. Now she had to wait—

"Lover boy not home?"

The familiar male voice stopped her heart and jerked her gaze up from the chevron pattern in the cobblestones to the magnificence that was her husband. Swift, fierce attraction sliced through her, sharp and disarming as always.

Not a day passed that she didn't wonder how she'd landed such a smoking-hot man. He was shamelessly handsome, his features even and just hard enough to be undeniably masculine. He rarely smiled, but he didn't have to charm when his sophistication and intelligence commanded such respect. The sheer physical presence of him quieted a room. She always thought of him as a purebred stallion, outwardly still and disciplined, but with an invisible energy and power that warned he could explode any second.

Don't overlook resourceful, she thought acridly. How else had he turned up half a world from where she'd thought he would be, when she'd taken pains to keep her whereabouts strictly confidential?

Fortunately, Adara had a lot of experience hiding visceral reactions like instant animal attraction and guilty alarm. She kept her sunglasses on and willed her pulse to slow, keeping her limbs loose and her body language unreadable.

"What are you doing here?" she asked with a composed lift of her chin. "Lexi said you would be in Chile." Lexi's tone still grated, so proprietary over Gideon's schedule, so pitying as she had looked upon the ignorant wife who not only failed as a woman biologically, but no longer interested her husband sexually. Adara had wanted to erase the woman's superior smile with a swipe of her manicured nails.

"Let's turn that question around, shall we?" Gideon strolled with deadly negligence around the front of her car.

Adara had never been afraid of him, not physically, not the way she had been of her father, but somewhere along the line Gideon had developed the power to hurt her with a look or a word, without even trying, and that scared her. She steeled herself against him, but her nerves fried with the urge to flee.

She made herself stand her ground and find the reliable armor of civility she'd grown as self-defense long ago. It had always served her well in her dealings with this man, even allowing her to engage with him intimately without losing herself. Still, she wanted higher, thicker invisible walls. Her reasons for coming to Greece were too private to share, carrying as they did such a heavy risk of rejection. That's why she hadn't told him or anyone else where she was going. Having him turn up like this put her on edge, internally windmilling her arms as she tried to hang on to unaffected nonchalance.

"I'm here on personal business," she said in a dismissive tone that didn't invite discussion.

He, in turn, should have given her his polite nod of acknowledgment that always drove home how supremely indifferent he was to what happened in her world. It might hurt a little, but far better to have her trials and triumphs disregarded than dissected and diminished.

While she, as was her habit, wouldn't bother repeating a question he had ignored, even though she really did want to know how and why he'd followed her.

No use changing tactics now, she thought. With a little adherence to form they could end this relationship as dispassionately as they'd started it.

That gave her quite a pang and oddly, even though his body language was as neutral as always, and his expres-

sion remained impassive as he squinted against the bright-
ness of the day, she again had the sense of that coiled
force drawing more tightly inside him. When he spoke, his
words were even, yet she sensed an underlying ferocity.

"I can see how personal it is. Who is he?"

Her heart gave a kick. Gideon rarely got angry and even
more rarely showed it. He certainly never directed dark
energy at her, but his accusation made her unaccountably
defensive.

She told herself not to let his jab pierce her shell, but
his charge was a shock and she couldn't believe his gall.
The man was banging his secretary in the most clichéd
of affairs, yet he had the nerve to dog her all the way to
Greece to accuse *her* of cheating?

Fortunately, she knew from experience you didn't pro-
voke a man in a temper. Hiding her indignation behind
cool disdain, she calmly corrected his assumption. "*He*
has a wife and new baby—"

Gideon's drawled sarcasm cut her off. "Cheating on one
spouse wasn't enough, you have to go for two and ruin the
life of a child into the mix?"

Since when do you care about children?

She bit back the question, but a fierce burn flared behind her eyes, completely unwanted right now when she
needed to keep her head. The back of her throat stung,
making her voice thick. She hoped he'd put it down to ire,
not heartbreak.

"As I said, Lexi assured me you had appointments in
Chile. '*We* will be flying into Valparaiso,' she told me.
'*We* will be staying in the family suite at the Makricosta
Grand.'" Adara impassively pronounced what Lexi hadn't
said, but what had been in the woman's eyes and super-
cilious smile. "'*We* will be wrecking your bed and calling

your staff for breakfast in the morning.' Who is cheating on whom?"

She was proud of her aloof delivery, but her underlying resentment was still more emotion than she'd ever dared reveal around him. She couldn't help it. His adultery was a blow she hadn't seen coming and she was always on guard for unearned strikes. Always. Somehow she'd convinced herself she could trust him and if she was angry with anyone, it was with herself for being so blindly oblivious. She was so furious she was having a hard time hiding that she was trembling, but she ground her teeth and willed her muscles to let go of the tension and her blood to stop boiling.

He didn't react. If she fought a daily battle to keep her emotions in reserve, his inner thoughts and feelings were downright nonexistent. His voice was crisp and glacial when he said, "Lexi did not say that because it's not true. And why would you care if she did? *We* aren't wrecking any beds, are we?"

Ask me why, she wanted to charge, but the words and the reason stayed bottled so deep and hard inside her she couldn't speak.

Grief threatened to overtake her then. Hopelessness crept in and defeat struck like a gong. It sent an arctic chill into her, blessed ice that let her freeze out the pain and ignore the humiliation. She wanted it all to go away.

"I want a divorce," she stated, heart throbbing in her throat.

For a second, the world stood still. She wasn't sure if she'd actually said it aloud and he didn't move, as though he either hadn't heard, or couldn't comprehend.

Then he drew in a long, sharp inhale. His shoulders pulled back and he stood taller.

Oh, God. Everything in her screamed, *Retreat*. Sh
ducked her head and circled him, aiming for her car door.

He put out a hand and her blood gave a betraying leap.
She quickly tamped down the hunger and yearning, embracing hatred instead.

"Don't think for a minute I'll let you touch me," she
warned in a voice that grated.

"Right. Touching is off limits. I keep forgetting."

A stab of compunction, of incredible sadness and longing to be understood, went through her. Gideon was becoming so good at pressing on the bruises closest to her
soul and all he had to do was speak the truth.

"Goodbye, Gideon." Without looking at him again, she
threw herself into her car and pulled away.

CHAPTER TWO

THE FERRY WAS gone so Adara couldn't leave the island. She drove through a blur of goat-tracked hills and tree-lined boulevards. Expansive olive branches cast rippling shadows across bobbing heads of yellow and purple wildflowers between scrupulously groomed estates and bleached-white mansions. When she happened upon a lookout, she quickly parked and tried to walk off her trembles.

She'd done it. She'd asked for a divorce.

The word cleaved her in two. She didn't want her marriage to be over. It wasn't just the failure it represented. Gideon was her husband. She wasn't a possessive person. She tried not to get too attached to anything or anyone, but until his affair had come to light, she had believed her claim on him was incontestable. That had meant something to her. She had never been allowed to have anything. Not the job she wanted, not the money in her trust fund, not the family she had briefly had as a child or the one she longed for as an adult.

Gideon was a prize coveted by every woman around her. Being his wife had given her a deep sense of pride, but he'd gone behind her back and even managed to make her writhe with self-blame that it was her fault.

She hadn't made love with him in weeks. It was true.

She'd taken care of his needs, though. When he was home. Did he realize he hadn't been home for more than one night at a stretch in months?

Pacing between guilt and virtue, she couldn't escape the position she'd put herself in. Her marriage was over. The marriage she had arranged so her father would stop trying to sell her off to bullies like himself.

Her heart compressed under the weight of remembering how she'd taken such care to ask Gideon for only what seemed reasonable to expect from a marriage: respect and fidelity. That's all. She hadn't asked for love. She barely believed in it, not when her mother still loved the man who had abused her and her children, raising his hand often enough Adara flinched just thinking about it.

No, Adara had been as practical and realistic as she could be—strengths she'd honed razor sharp out of necessity. She had found a man whose wealth was on a level with her father's fortune. She had picked one who exhibited incredible control over his emotions, trying to avoid spending her adult life ducking outbursts and negotiating emotional land mines. She had accommodated Gideon in every way, from the very fair prenup to learning how to please him in bed. She had never asked for romance or signs of affection, not even flowers when she was in hospital recovering from a miscarriage.

Her hand went instinctively to her empty womb. After the first one, she'd tried not to bother him much at all, informing him without involving him, not even telling him about the last one. Her entire being pulsated like an open wound as she recalled the silent weeks of waiting and hoping, then the first stain of blood and the painful, isolated hours that had followed.

While Gideon had been in Barcelona, faithful bitch Lexi at his side.

She had learned nothing from her mother, Adara realized with a spasm in her chest. Being complacent didn't earn you anything but a cheating husband. Her marriage was over and it left a jagged burn in her like a bolt of lightning was stuck inside her, buzzing and shorting and trying to escape.

A new life awaited though, unfurling like a rolled carpet before her. She made herself look at it, standing tall under the challenge, extending her spine to its fullest. She concentrated on hardening her resolve, staring with determination across the vista of scalloped waves to distant islands formed from granite. That's what she was now, alone, but strong and rooted.

She'd look for a new home while she was here, she decided. Greece had always been a place where she'd felt hopeful and happy. Her new life started today. Now.

After discovering his room wasn't ready, Gideon went to the patio restaurant attached to the hotel and ordered a beer. He took care of one piece of pressing business on his mobile before he sat back and brooded on what had happened with Adara.

He had never cheated on her.

But for the last year he had spent more time with his PA than his wife.

Adara had known this would be a brutal year though. They both had. Several large projects were coming online at once. He ought to be in Valparaiso right now, opening his new terminal there. It was the ticking off of another item on their five-year plan, something they had mapped out in the first months of their marriage. That plan was pulling them in different directions, her father's death last year and her mother's sinking health not helping. They were rarely in the same room, let alone the same bed, so to be fair it wasn't strictly her fault they weren't tearing up the sheets.

And there had been Lexi, guarding his time so carefully and keeping him on schedule, mentioning that her latest relationship had fallen apart because she was traveling so much, offering with artless innocence to stay in his suite with him so she could be available at any hour.

She had been offering all right, and perhaps he hadn't outright encouraged or accepted, but he was guilty of keeping his options open. Abstinence, or more specifically, Adara's avoidance of wholehearted lovemaking, had made him restless and dissatisfied. He'd begun thinking Adara wouldn't care if he had an affair. She was getting everything she wanted from this marriage: her position as CEO of her father's hotel chain, a husband who kept all the dates she put in his calendar. The penthouse in Manhattan and by the end of the year, a newly built mansion in the Hamptons.

While he'd ceased getting the primary thing *he* wanted out of their marriage: her.

So he had looked at his alternatives. The fact was, though, as easy as Lexi would be, as physically attractive as she was, he wasn't interested in her. She was too much of an opportunist. She'd obviously read into his "I'll think about it" response enough to imagine she had a claim on him.

That couldn't be what had precipitated Adara running here to Greece and another man, though. The Valparaiso arrangements had only been finalized recently. Adara wasn't that impulsive. She would have been thinking about this for a long time before taking action.

His inner core burned. A scrapper in his youth, Gideon had found other ways to channel his aggression when he'd reinvented himself as a coolheaded executive, but the basic street-life survival skill of fighting to keep what was his had never left him. Every territorial instinct he possessed was aroused by her deceit and the threat it represented to all he'd gained.

The sound of a checked footstep and a barely audible gasp lifted his gaze. He took a hit of sexual energy like he'd swallowed two-hundred-proof whiskey, while Adara lost a few shades of color behind her sunglasses. Because she could read the barely contained fury in him? Or because she was still feeling guilty at being caught out?

She gathered herself to flee, but before she could pivot away, he rose with a menacing scrape of his chair leg on the paving stones. Drawing out the chair off the corner of his table, he kept a steady gaze on her to indicate he would come after her if she chose to run. He wanted to know everything about the man who thought he could steal from him.

So he could quietly destroy him.

"The rooms aren't ready," he told her.

"So they've just informed me again." Adara's mouth firmed to a resistant angle, but she moved forward. If there was one thing he could say about her, it was that she wasn't a coward. She met confrontation with a quiet dignity that disconcerted him every time, somehow making him feel like an executioner of an innocent even though he'd never so much as raised his voice at her.

She'd never given him reason to.

Until today.

With the collected poise he found both admirable and frustrating, she set her purse to the side and lowered herself gracefully into the chair he held. He had learned early that passionate women were scene-makers and he didn't care to draw attention to himself. Adara had been a wallflower with a ton of potential, blooming with subtle brilliance as they had made their mark on the social scene in New York, London and Athens, always keeping things understated.

Which meant she didn't wear short-shorts or low-cut tops, but the way her denim cutoffs clung all the way down her toned thighs and the way the crisp cotton of her loose shirt angled over the thrust of her firm breasts was erotic in its own way.

Unwanted male hunger paced with purpose inside him. How could he still want her? He was furious with her.

Without removing her sunglasses or even looking at him as he took his seat, she opened the menu he'd been given. She didn't put it down until the server arrived, then ordered a souvlaki with salad and a glass of the house white.

"The same," Gideon said dismissively.

"You won't speak Greek even to a native in his own country?" Adara murmured in an askance tone as the man walked away.

"Did I use English? I didn't notice," Gideon lied and sensed her gaze staying on him even though she didn't challenge his assertion. Another thing he could count on with his wife: she never pushed for answers he wouldn't give.

Nevertheless, he found himself waiting for her to speak, willing her almost, which wasn't like him. He liked their quiet meals that didn't beleaguer him with small talk.

He wasn't waiting for, "How's the weather," however. He wanted answers.

Her attention lifted to the greenery forming the canopy above them, providing shade against the persistent sun. Blue pots of pink flowers and feathery palms offered a privacy barrier between their table and the empty one next to them. A colorful mosaic on the exterior wall of the restaurant held her attention for a very long time.

He realized she didn't intend to speak at all.

"Adara," he said with quiet warning.

"Yes?" Her voice was steady and thick with calm reason, but he could see her pulse racing in her throat.

She wasn't comfortable and that was a much-needed satisfaction for him since he was having a hard time keeping his balance. Maybe the comfortable routine of their marriage had grown a bit stale for both of them, but that didn't mean you threw it away and ran off to meet another man. None of this gelled with the woman he'd always seen as ethical, coolheaded and highly averse to risk.

"Tell me why." He ground out the words, resenting the instability of this storm she'd thrown him into and the fact he wasn't weathering it up to his usual standard.

Her mouth pursed in distaste. "From the outset I made it clear that I would rather be divorced than put up with infidelity."

"And yet you sneaked away to have an affair," he charged, angry because he'd been blindsided.

"That's not—" A convulsive flinch contracted her features, half hidden by her bug-eyed glasses, but the flash of great pain was unmistakable before she smoothed her expression and tone, appearing unaffected in a familiar way that he suddenly realized was completely fake.

His fury shorted out into confusion. What else did she hide behind that serene expression of hers?

"I'm not having an affair," she said without inflection.

"No?" Gideon pressed, sitting forward, more disturbed by his stunning insight and her revelation of deep emotion than by her claim. Her anguish lifted a host of unexpected feelings in him. It roused an immediate masculine need in him to shield and protect. Something like concern or threat roiled in him, but not combat-ready threat. Something he wasn't sure how to interpret. Adara was like him, unaffected by life. If something was piercing her shell, it had to be bad and that filled him with apprehensive tension.

"Who did you come to see then?" he prodded, unconsciously bracing.

A slight hesitation, then, with her chin still tucked into her neck, she admitted, "My brother."

His tension bled away in a drain of caustic disappointment. As he fell back in his chair, he laced his Greek endearment with sarcasm. "Nice try, *matia mou*. Your brothers don't earn enough to build a castle like the one we saw today."

Her head came up and her shoulders went back. With the no-nonsense civility he so valued in her, she removed her sunglasses, folded the arms and set them beside her purse before looking him in the eye.

The golden-brown irises were practically a stranger's, he realized with a kick of unease. When was the last time she'd looked right at him? he wondered distantly, while at the same time feeling the tightening inside him that drew on the eye contact as a sexual signal. Like the rest of her, her eyes were understated yet surprisingly attractive when a man took the time to notice. Almond-shaped. Clear. Flecked with sparks of heat.

"I'm referring to my older brother."

Her words left a discordant ring in his ears, dragging him from the dangerous precipice of falling into her eyes.

The server brought their wine. Gideon kept his attention fully focused on Adara's composed expression and contentiously set chin.

"You're the eldest," he stated.

She only lifted her wine to sip while a hollow shadow drifted behind her gaze, giving him a thump of uncertainty, even though he *knew* she only had two brothers, both younger than her twenty-eight years. One was an antisocial accountant who traveled the circuit of their father's hotel chain auditing ledgers, the other a hellion with a taste for big engines and fast women, chasing skirt the way their father had.

Given her father's peccadilloes, he shouldn't be surprised a half sibling had turned up, but older? It didn't make sense and he wasn't ready to let go of his suspicions about an affair.

"How did you find out about him? Was there something in the estate papers after your father passed?"

"I've always known about him." She set aside her wine with a frown of distaste. "I think that's off."

"Always?" Gideon repeated. "You've never mentioned him."

"We don't talk, do we?" Golden orbs came back, charged with electric energy that made him jolt as though she'd touched a cattle prod to his internal organs.

No. They didn't talk. He preferred it that way.

Their server arrived with their meals. Gideon asked for Adara's wine to be changed out. With much bowing and apologies, a fresh glass was produced. Adara tried it and stated it was fine.

As the server walked away, Adara set down her glass with another grimace.

"Still no good?" Gideon tried it. It was fine, perhaps not as dry as she usually liked, but he asked, "Try again?"

"No. I feel foolish that you sent back the first one."

That was so like her to not want to make a fuss, but he considered calling back the waiter all the same. Stating that they didn't talk was an acknowledgment of an elephant. It was the first knock on a door he didn't want opened.

At the same time, he wanted to know more about this supposed brother of hers. Sharing was a two-way street though and hypocrite that he was, he'd prefer backstory to flow only one way. He glanced at the offending wine, ready to seize it as an excuse to keep things inconsequential between them.

And yet, as Adara picked up her fork and hovered it over her rice, she gave him the impression of being utterly without hope. Forlorn. The hairs rose all over his body as he picked up signals of sadness that he'd never caught an inkling of before.

"Do you want to talk about him?" he asked carefully.

She lifted her shoulder. "I've never been allowed to before so I don't suppose one more day of silence matters." It was her conciliatory tone, the one that put everything right and allowed them to move past the slightest hiccup in their marriage.

What marriage? She wanted a divorce, he reminded himself.

Instinct warned him this was dangerous ground, but he also sensed he'd never have another chance to understand if he didn't seize this one. "Who wouldn't let you talk about him?" he asked gruffly.

A swift glance gave him the answer. Her father, of course. He'd been a hard man of strong opinions and ancient views. His daughter could run a household, but her husband would control the hotels. Her share of the family fortune wasn't hers to squander as her brothers might, but left in a trust doled out by tightly worded language, the bulk of the money to be held for her children. The male ones.

Gideon frowned, refusing to let himself be sidetracked by the painful subject of heirs.

"I assume this brother was the product of an affair? Something your father didn't want to be reminded of?"

"He was my mother's indiscretion." Adara frowned at her plate, her voice very soft, her expression disturbingly young and bewildered. "He lived with us until he left for school." She lifted anxious eyes, words pouring out of her in a rush as if she'd held on to them for decades. "My aunt explained years later that my father didn't know at first that Nico wasn't his. When he found out, he had him sent to boarding school. It was awful. That's all they'd tell me, that he'd gone to school. I knew I was starting the next year and I was terrified I'd be forgotten the same way."

A stitch pulled in his chest. His childhood predisposed him to hate the thought of any child frightened by anything. He *felt* her confusion and fear at losing her brother mixed with the terror of not knowing what would happen to herself. It made him nauseous.

Her expression eased into something poignant. "But then we saw him at my aunt's in Katarini over the summer. He was fine. He told me about his school and I couldn't wait to go myself, to be away from the angry man my father had turned into, make new friends..." Her gaze faded to somewhere in the distance. "But I was sent to day school in New York and we saw Nico only a few more times after that. One day I asked if we would see him, and my father—"

Gideon wouldn't have known what she failed to say aloud if he hadn't been watching her so intently, reading her lips because he could barely hear her. Her tongue touched the corner of her mouth where a hairline scar was sometimes visible between her morning shower and her daily application of makeup. She'd told him it had come from a childhood mishap.

A wrecking ball hit him in the middle of his chest. "He hit you?"

Her silence and embarrassed bite of her lip spoke volumes.

His torso felt as if it split open and his teeth clenched

so hard he thought they'd crack. His scalp prickled and his blood turned to battery acid.

"I didn't ask again," she said in her quick, sweep-it-under-the-rug way. "I didn't let the boys say his name. I let it go. I learned to let a lot of things go."

Like equal rights. Like bad decisions with the hotel chain that were only now being repaired after her father was dead. Like the fact that her brothers were still boys because they'd been raised by a child: her.

Gideon had seen the dysfunction, the alcoholic mother and the overbearing father, the youngest son who earned his father's criticism, and the older children who hadn't, but received plenty of it anyway. Adara had always managed the volatile dynamics with equanimity, so Gideon hadn't tried to stir up change. If he had suspected physical abuse was the underbelly of it all...

His fist clenched. "You should have told me," he said.

Another slicing glance repeated the obvious. *We don't talk.*

His guts turned to water. No, they didn't and because of that he'd let her down. If there was one thing his wife had never asked of Gideon, but that he'd regarded as his sacred duty, it was his responsibility to protect her. Adara was average height and kept herself toned and in good shape, but she was undeniably female. Her bones were smaller, her muscles not as thick as a man's. She was preordained by nature to be vulnerable to a male's greater strength. Given what had happened to his own mother, he'd lay down his life for any woman, especially one who depended on him.

"At any time since I've known you," he forced himself to ask, "did he—"

"No," she answered bluntly, but her tone was tired. "I learned, Gideon."

It wasn't any sort of comfort.

How had he not seen this? He'd always assumed she was reserved because she had been raised by strict parents. She was ambitious and focused on material gain because most immigrant families to America were. *He* was.

And compliant? Well, it was just her nature.

But no, it was because she had been abused.

He couldn't help staring at her, reeling in disbelief. Not disbelieving she had been mistreated, but that he hadn't known. What else did he not know about her? he wondered uneasily.

Adara forced herself to eat as though nothing was wrong, even though Gideon's X-ray stare made her so nervous she felt as if her bones were developing radiation blisters. Why had she told him? And why did it upset her that he knew what she'd taken such pains to hide from the entire world? She had nothing to be ashamed of. Her father's abuse wasn't her fault.

Sharing her past made her squirm all the same. It was such a dark secret. So close to the heart. Shameful because she had never taken action against her father, trying instead to do everything in her power to keep what remained of her family intact. And she'd been so young.

Her eyebrows were trying to pull into a worried frown. She habitually noted the tension and concentrated on relaxing her facial muscles, hiding her turmoil. Taking a subtle breath, she begged the constriction in her throat to ease.

"He went by his father's name," she told Gideon, taking up the subject of her brother as the less volatile one and using it to distract his intense focus from her. "I found his blogs at one point, but since he had never tried to contact us I didn't know if he'd want to hear from me. I couldn't reach out anyway," she dismissed with a shrug. "Not while my father was alive." She had feared, quite genuinely, that he would kill her. "But as soon as Papa died, I started thinking about coming here."

"But never told me."

She flinched, always sensitive to censure.

Her reaction earned a short sigh.

She wasn't going to state the obvious again though, and it wasn't as if she was laying blame. The fact they didn't talk was as much her fault as his, she knew that. Talking about personal things was difficult for her. She'd grown up in silence, never acknowledging the unpleasant, always avoiding points of conflict so they didn't escalate into physical altercations. Out of self-defense she had turned into a thinker who never revealed what she wanted until she had pondered the best approach and was sure she could get it without raising waves.

"I didn't tell anyone I was coming here, not even my brothers. I didn't want anyone talking me out of it." It was a thin line in the sand. She wouldn't be persuaded to leave until she'd seen her brother. She needed Gideon to recognize that.

He didn't argue and they finished their meals with a thick cloud of tension between them. The bouzouki music from the speakers sounded overly loud as sultry heat layered the hot air into claustrophobic blankets around them.

The minute the server removed their plates, Adara stood and gathered her things, grasping at a chance to draw a full breath. "Thank you for lunch. Goodbye, Gideon."

His hand snaked out to fasten around her wrist.

Her heart gave a thump, his touch always making her pulse leap. She glared at the strong, sun-browned fingers. It wasn't a hard grip. It was warm and familiar and she hated herself for liking it. That gave her the strength to say what she had to.

"Will you contact Halbert or shall I?" She ignored the

spear of anguish that pierced her as she mentioned their lawyer's name.

"I fired Lexi."

"Really." She gave her best attempt at blithe lack of interest, but her arteries constricted so each beat of her heart was like a hammer blow inside her.

He shifted his grip ever so slightly, lining up his fingertips on her wrist, no doubt able to feel the way her pulse became ferocious and strong. Not that he gave anything away. His fiercely handsome features were as watchful as a predator's, his eyes hidden behind his mirrored aviators.

"She had no right to speak to you as she did." His assertive tone came across as almost protective. "Implying things that weren't true. I haven't cheated on you, Adara. There's no reason for us to divorce."

As a spasm of agitated panic ran through her, Adara realized she'd grasped Lexi as a timely excuse. Thoughts of divorce had been floating through her mind for weeks, maybe even from the day she had realized she was pregnant again. *If I lose this one, I'll leave him and never have to go through this again.*

"Actually, Gideon," she said with a jagged edge to her hushed voice, "there's no reason for us to stay married. Let me go, please."

CHAPTER THREE

No REASON TO stay married?

Gideon's head nearly exploded as Adara walked away. How about the luxury cruise ship they were launching next year? The ultimate merger of his shipbuilding corporation and her hotel chain, it wasn't just a crown jewel for both entities, it was a tying together of the two enterprises in a way that wouldn't be easy to untangle. They couldn't divorce at this stage of that project.

Gideon hung back to scratch his name on the bill while tension flooded back into him, returning him to a state of deep aggravation. Neither of them had cheated, but she still wanted a divorce. Why? Did she not believe him?

It was too hot to race after her, and his stride was long enough that he closed in easily as she climbed the road behind the marina shops. Resentment that he was following her at all filled him with gall. He was not a man who chased after women begging for another chance. He didn't have to.

But the fact that Adara saw no reason to continue their marriage gave him a deep sense of ignorance. They had ample financial reasons. What else did she want from the union? More communication? Fine, they could start talking.

Even as he considered it, however, resistance rose in

him. And at that exact moment, as he'd almost caught up to Adara, the stench of rotting garbage came up off a restaurant Dumpster, carried on a breeze flavored with the dank smells of the marina: tidal flats, diesel exhaust and fried foods. It put him squarely back in his childhood, searching for a safe place to sleep while his mother worked the docks in Athens.

Adara didn't even know who she was married to. Divorce would mean court papers, identification, paparazzi... Marrying under an assumed name had been tricky enough and he lived a much higher profile now. He couldn't risk divorce. But if he wasn't legally married to her, did he have a right to keep her tied to him?

His clothes began to feel tight. "Adara, you'll get sunstroke. Come back to the hotel," he ordered.

She seemed to flinch at the sound of his voice. Pausing, she turned to face him, her defensive tension obvious in her stiff posture.

"Gideon—" She seemed to search for words around her feet, or perhaps she was looking for stones to scare him away. "Look, I've taken this time as vacation." She flicked her thick plait back over her shoulder. "The gardener said my brother will be back in a few days. I'm staying until I meet him. In the meantime, I might as well see the sights. There's a historical viewpoint up here. You can go back to New York or on to Valparaiso as scheduled. Legal can work out the details. I'm not going to contest anything. Neither of us will be bothered by any of this."

Not bothered? He *wished*. He was shaken to the bone by what she'd revealed, not the least bit comfortable with the fact he'd been so oblivious. It gave him new eyes on her and them and yes, he could see that they'd foundered a bit, but this wasn't so bad you abandoned ship and let it sink.

Apparently Adara was prepared to, offering up one of

her patented sweep, fold, tuck maneuvers that tidied away all conflicts. *Mama's asking about Christmas. We can take two cars if you like, so you can stay in the city?*

Her accommodating nature was suddenly irritating in the extreme, partly because he knew he *should* get back to work rather than standing here in the middle of the road in the middle of the Mediterranean watching her walk away. She might have lightened her workload in anticipation of coming here, but he hadn't. Myriad to-dos ballooned in his mind while ahead of him Adara's pert backside sashayed up the incline of the deserted street.

He wasn't stupid enough to court heat exhaustion to keep a woman, but the reality was only a very dense man would let that beautiful asset walk away from him without at least trying to coax her to stay. Admiring her round butt, he recollected it was the first thing he'd noticed about her before she'd turned around with an expression of cool composure that had assured him she was all calm water and consistent breeze.

The rest of the pieces had fallen into place like predetermined magic. Their dealings with each other had been simple and straightforward. Adara was untainted by the volatile emotions other women were prone to. Perhaps the smooth sailing of their marriage was something he'd taken for granted, but she must know that he valued it and her.

Or did she? He was about as good at expressing his feelings as he was at arranging flowers.

Disquiet nudged at him as he contemplated how to convince her to continue their marriage. He knew how to physically seduce a woman, but emotional persuasion was beyond his knowledge base.

Why in hell couldn't they just go back to the way things had been?

Not fully understanding why he did it, he caught up

to her at the viewpoint. It was little more than a cross-piece of weathered wood in dry, trampled grass. A sign in English identified it as a spot from which ships had been sighted during an ancient war. It also warned about legal action should tourists attempt to climb down to the beach below. A sign in Greek cautioned the locals to swim at their own risk.

Adara shaded her eyes, but he had the sense she was shielding herself from him as much as the sun. Her breasts rose and fell with exertion and her face glowed with light perspiration, but also with mild impatience. She didn't really give a damn about old ships and history, did she? This was just an excuse to get away from him.

He experienced a pinch of compunction that he'd never bothered to find out *what* she gave a damn about. She was quiet. He liked that about her, but it bothered him that he couldn't tell what she was thinking right now. If he didn't know what she was thinking, how would he talk her round to *his* way of thinking?

Her beauty always distracted him. That was the truth of it. She was oddly youthful today with her face clean of makeup and her hair in pigtails like a schoolgirl, but dressed down or to the nines, she always stirred a twist of possessive desire in his groin.

That was why he didn't want a divorce.

His clamoring libido was a weakness that governed him where she was concerned. The sex had always been good, but not exactly a place where they met as equals. In the beginning he'd been favored with more experience. The leader. He wasn't hampered by shyness or other emotions that women attached to intimacy. He'd tutored her and loved it.

Adara had maintained a certain reserve in the bedroom that she had never completely allowed to let slide away, however. While the sex had always been intense and satisfying, the power had subtly shifted over time into her favor. She decided when and how much and *if*.

Resentment churned in him, bringing on a scowl. He didn't like that she was threatening him on so many levels. Yanking the rug on sex was bad enough. Now all that he'd built was on a shaky foundation.

Why? Did it have to do with her fear of her father? Did she fear him? Blame him? Apprehension kept him from asking.

And Adara gave no clue to her thoughts, acting preoccupied with reading the signage, ignoring him, aggravating him further.

She peered over the edge of the steep slope to where a rope was tied to the base of the wooden crosspiece and, without a word, looped the thin strap of her purse over her head and shoulder then maneuvered to the edge of the cliff. Taking up the rope, she clung to it as she began a very steep, backward descent.

Gideon was taken aback. "What the hell are you doing?"

She paused. Uncertainty made her bottom lip flinch before she firmed it. "Going swimming."

"Like hell you are." Who *was* this woman?

The anxiety that spasmed across her features transitioned through uncertainty before being overcome by quiet defiance. "I always did as I was told because I was scared my father would punish me. Unless you intend to take up controlling my behavior with violence, I'm doing what I want from now on."

The pit of his belly was still a hard knot over her revelations about her childhood. He would never hurt her or threaten to and was now even more inclined to treat her with kid gloves. At the same time, everything in him clamored to exert control over her, get what he wanted and put an end to this nonsense. The conflicting feelings, too deep for comfort, left him standing there voicelessly glaring his frustration.

Despite her bold dare, there was something incredibly vulnerable in her stance of toughness though. An air of quiet desperation surrounded her as tangibly as the hardened determination she was trying to project.

She wanted to prove something. He didn't know what it was, but bullying her into going back to the hotel wasn't the way to find out. It wouldn't earn him any points toward keeping their marriage intact either.

"It's fine, Gideon. You can go," she said in her self-possessed way. *Papa doesn't think the Paris upgrade is necessary. I'll find my own way home after our meeting.*

"And leave you to break your neck? No," he said gruffly.

The way she angled a look up at him seemed to indicate suspicion. Maybe it was deserved. He was chivalrous, always picked up her heavy bags, but neither of them were demonstrative. Maybe he'd never acted so protective before, but she'd never tried to do anything so perilous.

"I won't break my neck," she dismissed and craned it to watch as she tentatively sought a step backward.

A completely foreign clench of terror squeezed his lungs. Did she not see how dangerous this was? He skimmed his hand over his sweat-dampened hair.

"Adara, I won't hurt you, but I will get physical if you don't stop right there and at least let me get behind you so I can catch you if you slip."

She stared, mouth pursing in mutiny. "I don't have to ask your permission to live my life, Gideon." *Not anymore*, was the silent punctuation to that.

"Well, I won't ask your permission to save it. Stay put until I get behind you."

He sensed her wariness as he took his time inspecting

the rope, approving its marine grade, noting it was fairly new and in good repair, as was the upright it was tied to. Assured they weren't going to plunge to their deaths, he let his loose grip slide along the rope until his hand met Adara's.

She stiffened as he brushed past her, making him clench his teeth. When had his touch become toxic?

Ask, he chided himself, but things were discordant enough. His assumptions about her were turned on their heads, her predictability completely blown out of the water. He didn't know what to say or what to expect next, so he picked his way down the slope in grim silence, arriving safely on to the pocket of sand between monolithic gray boulders.

The tide was receding, but the cove was steep enough it was still a short beach into a deep pool. It was the type of place young lovers would tryst, and his mind immediately turned that way. Adara wasn't even looking at him, though.

Adara shrugged against the sting of sweat and the disturbing persistence Gideon was showing. She thought they had an unspoken agreement to back off when things got personal, but even though she'd spilled way more of her family history than she'd ever meant to, he was sticking like humidity.

She didn't know how to react to that. And should she thank him for his uncharacteristic show of consideration in accompanying her down here? Or tell him again to shove off? He was so hard to be around sometimes, so unsettling. He was shorting out a brain that was already melting in the heat. She desperately wanted to cool off so she could think straight again, but she hadn't brought a bathing suit and—

Oh, to heck with it. She kicked off her flip-flops and began unbuttoning her shirt.

"Really?" he said, not hiding the startled uptick in his tone.

She didn't let herself waver. Maybe this was out of character, but this was her new life. She was tossing off fear of reprisal, embracing the freedom to follow impulse.

"I miss Greece. My aunt let us run wild here. In Katarini, not this island, but we'd do exactly this: tramp along the beach until we got hot then we'd strip to our underthings and jump in."

"Your aunt was a nudist?" he surmised.

"A free spirit. She never married, never had children—" Here Adara faltered briefly. "I intend to emulate her from now on."

She shed her shorts and ran into the water in her bra and panties, feeling terribly exposed as she left her decision to never have children evaporating on the sizzling sand.

The clear, cool water rose to her waist within a few splashing steps. She fell forward and ducked under, arrowing deep into the silken blur filled with the muted cacophony of creaks and taps and swishing currents.

When her lungs were ready to burst, she shot up for air, blinking the water from her eyes and licking the salt from her lips, baptized into a new version of herself. The campy phrase *the first day of the rest of your life* came to her with a pang of wistful anticipation.

Gideon's head appeared beside her, his broad shoulders flexing as he splayed out his arms to keep himself afloat. His dark lashes were matted and glinting, his thick hair sleeked back off his face, exposing his angular bone structure and taking her breath with his action-star handsomeness. The relief of being in the cool water relaxed his expression, while his innate confidence around the water—in any situation, really—made him incredibly compelling.

She would miss that sense of reliability, she acknowledged with a hitch of loss.

"I've never tried to curb your independence," he asserted. "Marrying me gained you your freedom."

They'd never spoken so bluntly about her motives. She'd only stated in the beginning that she'd like to keep working until they had a family, but he knew her better after her confession today. He was looking at her as though he could see right into her.

It made her uncomfortable.

"Marrying at all was a gamble," she acknowledged with a tentative honesty that caused her veins to sting with apprehension. "But you're right. I was fairly sure I'd have more control over my life living with you than I had with my father."

She squinted against the glare off the water as she silently acknowledged that she'd learned to use Gideon to some extent, pitting him against her father when she wanted something for herself. Not often and not aggressively, just with a quiet comment that *Gideon* would prefer this or that.

"You had women working for you in high-level positions," she noted, remembering all the minute details that had added up to a risk worth taking. "You were shocked that I didn't know how to drive. You fired that man who was harassing your receptionist. I was reasonably certain my life with you would be better than it was with my father so I took a chance." She glanced at him, wondering if he judged her harshly for advancing her interests through him.

"So what's changed?" he challenged. "I taught you to drive. I put you in charge of the hotels. Do you want more responsibility? Less? Tell me. I'm not trying to hem you in."

No, Gideon wasn't a tyrant. He was ever so reasonable.

She'd always liked that about him, but today that quality put her on edge. "Lexi—"

"—is a nonissue," he stated curtly. "Nothing happened and do you know why? Because I thought *you* were having an affair and got myself on a plane and chased you down. I didn't even think twice about it. Why didn't *you* do that? Why didn't you confront me? Why didn't you ask me why I'd even consider letting another woman throw herself under me?"

"You don't have to be so crude about it!" She instinctively propelled herself backward, pushing space between herself and the unbearable thought of him sleeping with another woman. She hadn't been able to face it herself, let along confront him, not with everything else that had happened.

"You said we don't talk," he said with pointed aggression. "Let's. You left me twisting with sexual frustration. Having an affair started to look like a viable option. If you didn't want me going elsewhere, why weren't you meeting my needs at home?"

"I did! I—"

"Going down isn't good enough, Adara."

His vulgarity was bad enough, but it almost sounded like a critique and she resented that. She tried hard to please him and could tell that he liked what she did, so why did he have to be so disparaging about it?

Unbearably hurt, she kicked toward shore, barely turning her head to defend, "I was pregnant. What else could I do?"

How he reacted to that news she didn't care. She just wanted to be away from him, but as her toes found cold, thick sand, she halted. Leaving the water suddenly seemed a horribly exposing thing to do. How stupid to think she could become a new person by shedding a few stitches of clothing. She was the same old worthless Adara who couldn't even keep a baby in her womb.

The sun seared across her shoulders. Her wet hair hung in her eyes and she kept her arms folded tightly across her chest, trying to hold in the agony.

She felt ridiculous, climbing down to this silly beach that was impossible to leave, revealing things that were intensely personal to her and wouldn't matter at all to him.

"What did you say?" He was too close. She flinched, feeling the sharpness of his voice like the tip of a flicking whip.

"You heard me," she managed to say even though her throat was clogging. She clenched her eyes shut, silently begging him to do what he always did. Say nothing and give her space. She didn't want to do this. She never, ever wanted to do this again.

"You *were* pregnant?" His voice moved in front of her.

She turned her head to the side, hating him for cutting off her escape to the beach, hating herself for lacking the courage to take it when she'd had the chance.

Keeping her eyes tightly closed, she dug her fingers into her arms, her whole body aching with tension. "It doesn't matter," she insisted through her teeth. "It's over and I just want a divorce."

Gideon was distantly aware of the sea trying to pull him out with the tide. His entire being was numb enough that he had to concentrate on keeping his feet rooted as he stared at Adara. She was a knot of torment. For the first time he could see her suffering and it made his heart clench. When had she started to care about the miscarriages? The last one had been called into him from across the globe, his offer to come home dismissed as unnecessary.

"Tell me—"

"What is there to tell, Gideon?" Her eyes opening into

pits of hopeless fury. Her face creased with sharp lines of grief. "It was the same as every other one. I did the test and held my breath, terrified to so much as bump my hip on the edge of my desk. And just when I let myself believe this time might be different, the backache started and the spotting appeared and then it was twenty-four hours of medieval torture until I was spat out in hell with nothing to show for it. At least I didn't have the humiliation of being assaulted by the people in white coats this time."

She took a step to the side, thinking to circle him and leave the water, but he shifted into her path, his hand reaching to stop her. His expression was appalled. "What do you mean about being assaulted?"

She cringed from his touch, her recoil like a knee into his belly. Gideon clenched his abdominal muscles and curled his fingers into his palm, forcing his hand to his side under the water even though he wanted to grip her with all his strength and squeeze the answers out of her. She couldn't possibly be saying what he thought she was saying.

"What people in white coats?" he demanded, but the words sounded far away. "Are you telling me you didn't go to the hospital?" Intense, fearful dread hollowed out his chest as he watched her mask fear and compunction with a defiant thrust of her chin.

"Do you know what they do to you after you've had a miscarriage? No, you don't. But I do and I'm sick of it. So, no, I didn't go," she declared with bitter rebelliousness.

Horror washed through him in freezing waves.

"We need to get you to a doctor." He flew his gaze to the cliff, terror tightening in him. What the hell had he been thinking, letting her descend to this impossible place?

"It was three weeks ago, Gideon. If it was going to kill me, it would have by now."

"It could have," he retorted, helplessness making him brutal. "You could have bled to death."

She shrugged that off with false bravado, eyes glossy and red. "At the time that looked like a—what's the expression you used? A viable option?"

It was a vicious slap that he deserved. While he'd been contemplating an affair, she'd been losing the battle to keep their baby. Again. And she'd been filled with such dejection she'd refused medical care and courted death.

The fact she'd let herself brush elbows with the Grim Reaper made him so agitated, he clipped out a string of foul Greek curses. "Don't talk like that. Damn it, you should have told me."

"Why?" she lashed out in uncharacteristic confrontation. "Do you think I enjoy telling you what a failure I am? It's not like you care. You just go back to work while I sit there screaming inside." She struck a fist onto the surface of the water. "I hate it. I can't go on like this. I won't. *I want a divorce.*"

She splashed clumsily from the surf, her wet underpants see-through, her staggered steps so uncoordinated and indicative of her distress it made him want to reach out for her, but he was rooted in the water, aghast.

He cared. Maybe he'd never told her, but each lost baby had scored his heart. This one, knowing he could have walked into the penthouse and found both of them dead, lanced him with such deep horror he could barely acknowledge it.

She was the one who had appeared not to care. The fact she'd been so distraught she hadn't sought medical attention told him how far past the end of her rope she had been, but she'd never let him see any of that.

He followed her on heavy feet, pausing where they'd left their clothes.

She gave him a stark look, her gaze filling with apprehension as she took in that he was completely naked. Her fingers hurried to button her blouse.

Hell. He wasn't trying to come on to her.

"Adara." A throb of tender empathy caught in him like a barbed hook. He reached out to cup her neck, her hair a weight on his wrist.

She stiffened, but he didn't let her pull away. He carefully took her shoulder in his opposite hand and made her face him, for once driven by a need deeper than sexual to touch her.

"I'm sorry," he said with deep sincerity. "Sorry we lost another baby, sorry you felt you couldn't tell me. I do care. You've always been stoic about it and I've followed your lead. How could I know it was devastating you like this if you didn't say?"

She shivered despite the heat. Her blink released a single tear from the corner of her eye. Her plump mouth trembled with vulnerability, and a need to comfort overwhelmed him.

Gideon gathered her in. She seemed so delicate and breakable. He touched his mouth to hers, wanting to reassure, to console.

It wasn't meant to be a pass, but she felt so good. The kiss was a soft press of a juicy fruit to the mouth of a starved man. He couldn't help opening his lips on hers, sliding his tongue along the seam then pressing in for a deep lick of her personal flavor. Involuntarily, his arms tightened while greed swelled in him. Everything in him expanded in one hard kick. His erection pulled to attention in a rush of heat, fed by the erotically familiar scent of his wife.

The feathery touch of her hands whispered from his

ribs to his shoulder blades. A needy sob emanated from her throat, encouraging him.

Here. Now. His brain shorted into the most basic thoughts as his carnal instincts took over. He skimmed his hand to the wet underpants covering her backside, starting to slide them down even as he deepened the kiss and began to ease them both to the sand.

Adara's knees softened for one heartbeat, almost succumbing, then she broke away from their kiss with a ragged moan, stumbling backward a few steps as she shoved from him with near violence. Her flush of arousal dissolved into a bewildered glare of accusation and betrayal.

That wounded look bludgeoned him like a club.

Without speaking, face white, she gathered her things and moved to the bottom of the rope where she tried to force her wet legs into her denim shorts.

Gideon pinched the bridge of his nose, ears rushing with the blood still pumping hotly through his system, deeply aware that the distance had been closed until he'd forgotten that he was trying to comfort, not seduce. But the sexual attraction between them was something he couldn't help. He wished he could. The fact that he couldn't entirely control his hunger for her bothered him no end.

His thoughts were dark as they returned to the hotel, a fresh sweat on his salted skin as they came through the front doors, with not a word exchanged since the beach. The life he'd created with Adara, so easy on the surface, had grown choppy, teaming with undercurrents. She'd stirred up more emotion in him with this bolt to Greece than he'd suffered in years and he didn't like it.

Part of him wanted to cut and run, but it was impossible now he understood what was driving her request for a divorce: grief. He understood that frame of mind better than she would suspect. He'd even bolted across the ocean in the very same way, more than once, but he was able to think more clearly this time. Losing the baby was heart-rending, but he wasn't left alone. He still had her. They needed to stick together. With careful navigation, they'd be back on course and sailing smoothly. When she came out the other side, she'd appreciate that he hadn't let her do anything rash.

He hoped.

Adara blinked as they entered the artificial light of the hotel foyer. The temperature change hit her between the eyes like a blow. The boutique accommodation was the best the island offered, but nothing like the luxury service she took for granted in her thousand-room high-rise hotels. Still, she liked the coziness of this small, out-of-the-way place. She'd give serious thought to developing some hideaways like this herself, she decided.

Another time. Right now she felt like one giant blister, hot and raw, skin so thin she could be nicked open by the tiniest harsh word.

Desire had almost overwhelmed her on the beach. Gideon's kiss had been an oasis in a desert of too many empty days and untouched nights. His heartfelt words, the way he'd enfolded her as if he could make the whole world right again, had filled her with hope and relief. For a few seconds she had felt cherished, even when his kiss had turned from tenderness to hunger. It had all been balm to her injured soul, right up until he'd begun to tilt them to the sand.

Then fear of pregnancy had undercut her arousal. Her next instinct had been to at least give him pleasure. She *liked* making him lose control, but then she'd remembered *it wasn't good enough*.

It had all crashed into her as a busload of confusing emotions: shattered confidence, anger at her own weakness and a sense of being tricked and teased with a promise that would be broken. If she had had other men, perhaps she wouldn't be so susceptible to him, but she was a neophyte where men were concerned, even after five years of marriage. She needed distance from him, to get her head straightened out and her heart put back together.

Gideon was given a room card at the same time she was.

As they departed the front desk for the elevators, she said in a ferocious undertone, "You did not get yourself added to my room." They might share a suite, but never a room. She would *die*.

"I booked my own," he said stiffly, the reserve in his voice making her feel as if she'd done something wrong. She hadn't! Had she? Should she have been more open about the miscarriages?

She shook off guilt she didn't want to feel. "Gideon—" she began to protest.

"What? You're allowed a vacation, but I'm not?"

She tilted her head in disgruntlement. That was not what she was driving at. She wanted distance from him.

"Would you like to eat here tonight or try somewhere else?" he said in a continuation of assumptions that were making her crazy.

"It's been a lot of travel getting here and already a long day. I'm going to shower and rest, possibly sleep through dinner," she asserted, silently thinking, *Go away*. Her feelings toward him were infinitely easier to bear when half a globe separated them.

"I'll email you when I get hungry then. If you're up, you can join me. If not, I won't disturb you."

She eyed him, suspicious of yet another display of ultraconsideration, especially when he walked her to her room. At the last second, he turned to insert his card in the door across from hers.

Her heart gave a nervous jump. So close. Immediately,

a jangle went through her system, eagerness and fretfulness tying her into knots. She locked herself into her room, worried that he'd badger her into spending time with him that would roll into rolling around with him. She couldn't do it. She didn't have it in her to risk pregnancy and go through another miscarriage.

Even though she ached rather desperately to feel his strong, naked body moving over and into hers.

Craving and humiliation tormented her through her shower and stayed with her when she crawled into bed. She wanted him so much. It made her bury her head under her pillow. She couldn't live with a man she had no defenses against.

Steadfast to his word, Gideon didn't disturb her. Adara woke to fading light beyond her closed curtains, startled she'd fallen asleep at all, head fuzzy from a hard four-hour nap.

Like an adolescent desperate for a hint of being popular, she checked her email before rising from bed, scrolling past the work ones that were piling up and honing in on Gideon's.

Brief and veiled as all his communications tended to be, the message was nevertheless maddeningly effective at driving her into fresh clothes and across the hall.

Your brother called. Dinner?

CHAPTER FOUR

ADARA WAS SO anxious, she blurted out her questions before Gideon fully opened his door. "What did he say? Is he coming here?"

The swipe of her tongue over her dry lips, however, was more to do with Gideon's bare chest beneath the open buttons of his white shirt than nerves at the thought of seeing her brother. Why had he brought those wretched jeans that were more white than blue, so old they clung to his hips and thighs like a second skin? No shoes either, she noted. The man was so unconsciously sexy she couldn't handle it. She'd never known how to handle it.

It didn't help that he looked at her like he could see into the depths of her soul. All that she'd told him today, the way he'd reacted, rushed back to strip her defenses down to the bare minimum.

"He won't be back to the island for a couple of days," he said, holding his door wider. "I had a table set on my balcony. They have our order, I only need to call down to let them know we're ready for it."

Adara folded her arms across the bodice of her crinkled white sundress, grossly uncomfortable as she watched him move to the hotel phone, his buttocks positively seductive in that devoted denim.

"I'd rather go down to the restaurant," she said, stomach fluttering as she struggled to assert herself.

"It's booked. And we can talk more privately here." He projected equanimity, but he sent her an assessing glance that warned her he wasn't one hundred percent pleased by this new argumentative Adara.

She swallowed, not at ease in this skin either, but she couldn't go on the old way. At the same time, she couldn't help wondering what had transpired in his conversation with her brother that they needed privacy. Nico lived here on the island, she reminded herself. It wouldn't be fair to bandy about his private business in public.

Out of consideration to him, she stepped cautiously into Gideon's room. The layout was a mirror of her executive room with a king-size bed, lounge area and workstation. Gideon had a better view, but she had taken what they had offered, not asking for upgrades. He, on the other hand, demanded the best.

Moving into the velvety night air of his balcony, she listened to him finalize their dinner then come up behind her to pour two glasses of wine. The sunset turned the golden liquid pink as he offered her a glass.

"To improved communication," he said, touching the rim of his glass to hers.

Adara couldn't resist a facetious "Really? And how long do you intend to make me wait to hear all that you and my brother said to each other?"

"I'll tell you now and you can leave before the meals arrive, if you're going to be so suspicious." He sounded insulted.

Adara pressed the curve of her glass to her flat mouth, a tiny bit ashamed of herself. She lowered the glass without wetting her lips. "You can't deny you used his call like some kind of bait-and-switch technique."

"Only because I genuinely want to salvage this marriage. We can't do that if we don't see each other." The sincerity in his gaze made her heart trip with an unsteady thump.

Why would he want to stay married? She was giving up on children. They both had enough money of their own without needing any of each other's. She tilted her glass, sipping the chilled wine that rolled across her tongue in a tart, cool wave that... *Bleh.* An acrid stain coated her mouth.

Stress, she thought. Rather than being someone who drank her troubles away, she avoided alcohol when she was keyed up. The way her mother had drowned in booze, and the cruelty it had brought out in her father, had always kept Adara cautious of the stuff. Her body was telling her this was one of those times she should leave it alone.

Setting her glass on the table, she leaned her elbows on the balcony railing and said, "Would you please tell me what happened with Nico?"

"He called asking for us. The front desk tried my room first and I told him you were resting."

"How did he even know we were here?" she asked with surprise.

"Ah. Now, *that's* amusing." He didn't sound amused. He turned his back on the sunset and his cheeks hollowed as he contemplated some scowl-inducing inner thought. "I assumed he had a crack security team, but he has something far more sophisticated—an island grapevine. You didn't tell the gardener you were related to him, so a strange woman asking about him set off speculation, enough that he got a call from a well-meaning neighbor and logged in to his gate camera. He recognized you and I guess he's kept tabs on you over the years, too, because he knew your married name. The island only has four hotels, so it was quick work to track us to this one. He invited us to stay at his villa until he gets home."

"Really?" Adara rotated to Gideon like a flower to the sun, buoyed by what Nico's interest and invitation represented. *He wanted to see her.*

A thought occurred, making her clench her hand on the railing. Gideon was a very private person who kept himself removed from all but the most formal of social contact. He wouldn't want to stay in a stranger's house full of unfamiliar staff.

An excruciating pang of loss ambushed her. She would have to continue her journey alone, her request for independence and divorce granted even as her husband's desire for reconciliation hung in the air. As cavalier as she wanted to be about leaving him, it wasn't painless or easy. Her heart started to shrivel as she looked to the emptiness that was her future.

"I told him I would leave it up to you to decide," Gideon continued. "But that I expected we'd move over there tomorrow because you're eager to renew ties." He took another healthy draw from his wine.

Adara blinked, shocked that Gideon would make such a concession. It made everything he said about salvaging their marriage earnest and powerful.

"You said that?" She reached out instinctively, setting her free hand on his sleeve so he would look at her, then feeling awkward when he only stared at her narrow hand on his tense forearm. She pulled her hand away. "I didn't expect you to understand."

"I'm not an idiot. I've got the message that there's more going on than you've let me see." Now his gaze came up and his dark-chocolate irises were intensely black in the fading light. "I want you to quit keeping so much to yourself, Adara."

Longing speared into her, but so did fear. The words *I can't* lodged in her throat. She never shared, never asked for help. She didn't know how.

A knock at the door heralded room service. Gideon moved to let the server in and stood back as the meals were set out. Gideon's knowledge of her tastes and his desire to please were well at the forefront. He'd ordered prawn soup, fried calamari, and baked fish fillets on rice with eggplant. Delicious scents of scorched ouzo and tangy mint made her mouth water. Their climb to the beach, coupled with the time change, had her stomach trying to eat itself. Much as she knew it would be better not to encourage either of them that their marriage had a chance, she couldn't help sinking into the chair he held.

Winking lights bobbed on the water, live music drifted from the restaurant below and the warm evening air stroked her skin with a sensual breeze. The server closed the door on his way out and the big bed stood with inviting significance just inside the room.

And then there was the man, still barefoot, still with his shirt hanging open off his shoulders, the pattern of hair across his chest and abdomen accentuating his firm pecs and six-pack stomach. How he managed casual elegance with such a disreputable outfit, she didn't know, but the woman in her not only responded, but melted into a puddle of sexual craving.

She was in very real danger of being seduced by nothing more than his presence.

Frightened of herself, she stole a furtive glance into his face and found him watching her closely, not smug, but his gaze was sharp with awareness that she was reacting to him. Her cheeks heated with embarrassment at not being able to help this interminable attraction to him.

Gideon couldn't remember ever being so tuned to a

woman, not out of bed anyway, and even at that he and Adara had fallen into certain patterns. Now that he was beginning to see how much she disguised behind a placid expression or level tone, he was determined to pick up every cue. The fact he'd just caught her lusting after him in her reserved way pleased him intensely, but her reluctance to let nature take its course confused him.

"I've been faithful to you, Adara. I hope you believe that."

She stopped chewing for a thoughtful moment. Her brows came together in a frown he couldn't interpret. Worry? Misery? Defeat?

"I do," she finally said, but her tone seemed to qualify the statement.

"But?" he prompted.

"It doesn't change the fact that one of the major reasons we married…" Her brows pulled again and this time it was pure pain, like something deeply embedded was being wrenched out of her.

He tensed, knowing what was coming and not liking the way it penetrated his walls either.

"Obviously I'm not able to give you children," she said with strained composure. "I won't even try. Not anymore."

The bitter acceptance he read beneath her mask of self-possession, her trounced distress, was so tangible, he reached across to cover her shaking hand where she gripped her knife. Her knuckles felt sharp as barnacles where they poked against his palm.

He would give anything to spare her this anguish.

"Having children was a condition that came from your side of the table. It's not a deal-breaker for me," he reassured her.

If anything, she grew more distraught. "You never wanted children?"

Tread lightly, he cautioned himself, touching a thoughtful tongue to his bottom lip. "It's not that I never wanted them. If that were true, I'd be a real monster for putting you through all you've suffered in trying to have one. I'm very—" *Disappointed* wasn't a strong enough word.

"I'm sad," he admitted, drawing his hand back as he took the uncharacteristic step of admitting to feelings. He'd been powerless at sea in a storm once and hadn't felt as helpless and vulnerable as he had each time she'd miscarried. This one he'd learned about today was the worst yet, filling him with visions of coming upon her dead. It was too horrifying a thing to happen to a person even once in a lifetime and he'd been through it twice already. He couldn't stomach thinking of finding her lifeless and white.

Then there was the bereft sense of loss that he'd known nothing about the baby before it was gone. He hated having no control over the situation, hated being unable to give her something she wanted that seemed as if it should be so simple. He hated how the whole thing stirred up old grief. He ought to be over forming deep attachments. He'd certainly fought against developing any. But he wished he'd known those babies and felt cheated that he hadn't been given the chance.

He swiped his clammy palm down his thigh.

"I'm sad, too," she whispered thickly, gaze fixed on her sweating glass of ice water. "I wanted a family. A real one, not a broken one like I had."

"So, it wasn't just pressure from your father to give him the heir your brothers weren't providing?"

She made a motion of negation, mouth pouted into sorrow.

Damn, he swore silently, thinking his version of her as merely ticking *children* off the list with everything else would have been so much easier to navigate.

"I thought you were like my father, not really wanting a family, but determined to have an heir. A boy." *Of course,* her tiny shrug added silently.

He could see wary shadows in her eyes as she confessed what had been in her mind. She wasn't any more comfortable with being honest than he was. He sure as hell didn't enjoy hearing her unflattering assessment of his attitude toward progeny.

"I wasn't taking it that lightly," he said, voice so tight she tensed. "But I didn't know how much it meant to you."

Any other time in his life he would have swiftly put an end to such a deeply personal conversation, but right now, unpleasant as it was, he had to allow Adara to see she wasn't the only one hurt by this. She wasn't the only one with misconceptions.

"I never knew my father, so that gave me certain reservations about what kind of parent I'd make. You're not anything like my mother, which is a very good thing in most ways, but she did have a strong maternal instinct. I never saw you take an interest in other people's children. Your family isn't the warmest. Frankly, I expected you to schedule a C-section, hire a nanny and mark that task 'done.'"

He'd seen this look on Adara's face before, after a particularly offside, cutting remark from her father. Her lashes swept down, her brow tensed and her nostrils pinched ever so slightly with a slow, indrawn breath. He'd always assumed she was gathering her patience, but today he saw it differently. She was absorbing a blow.

One that he had delivered. His heart clutched in his chest. *Don't put me in the same category as that man.*

"I'm just telling you how it looked, Adara." His voice was gruff enough to make her flinch.

"Like you're some kind of open book, letting me see your thoughts and feelings?" She pushed her plate away with hands that trembled. "I've told you more about myself today than I've ever shared with anyone and all I've heard back is that you're sad I miscarried. Well, I should damn well hope so! They were your babies too."

She rose and tried to escape, but he was faster, his haste sending his chair tumbling with a clatter, his hands too rough on her when he pulled her to stand in front of him, but her challenge made him slip the leash on his control.

"What do you want me to say? That I hadn't believed in God for years, but when I took you to the hospital that first time, I gave praying a shot and felt completely betrayed when He took that baby anyway? That I got drunk so I wouldn't cry? *Every time.* Damn it, I haven't been able to close my eyes since the beach without imagining walking into your bathroom and finding you dead in a pool of blood." He gave her a little shake. "Is that the kind of sharing you need to hear?"

Her shattered gaze was more than he could bear, the searching light in them pouring over his very soul, picking out every flaw and secret he hid from the rest of the world. It was painful in the extreme and even though he would never want to inflict more suffering on her, he was relieved when she crumpled with anguish and buried her face in her hands.

He pulled her into his chest, the feel of her fragile curves a pleasure-pain sting. She stiffened as he pinned her to him, but he only dug his fingers into her loose hair, massaging her scalp and pressing his lips to her crown, forcing the embrace because he needed it as much as she did.

"It's okay, I'm not going to mess it up this time." His body was reacting to her scent and softness, always did, but he ignored it and hoped she would too. "I'm sorry we keep losing babies, Adara. I'm sorry I didn't let you see it affects me."

"I can't try anymore, Gideon." Her voice was small and thick with finality, buried in his chest.

"I know." He rubbed his chin on the silk of her hair, distantly aware how odd this was to hold her like this, not as a prelude to sex, not because they were dancing, but to reassure her. "I don't expect you to try. That's what I'm saying. We don't have to divorce over this. We can stay married."

She lifted her face, her expression devastated beyond tears, and murmured a baffled "I don't even know why you want to."

Under her searching gaze, his inner defenses instinctively locked into place. Practicalities and hard facts leaped to his lips, covering up deeper, less understood motivations. "We're five years into merging our fortunes," he pointed out.

Adara dropped her chin and gathered herself, pressing for freedom.

His answer hadn't been good enough.

His muscles flexed, reluctant to let her go, but he had to. *Feelings,* he thought, and scowled with displeasure. What was she looking for? A declaration of love? That had never been part of their bargain and it wasn't a step he was willing to take. Losing babies he hadn't known was bad enough. Caring deeply for Adara would make him too vulnerable.

He reached to right his chair, nodding at her seat when she only watched him. "Sit down, let's keep talking about this."

"What's the point?" she asked despairingly.

The coward in him wanted to agree and let this madness blow away like dead ashes from a fire. If he were a gentleman, he supposed he'd spare her this torturous raking of nearly extinguished coals. Something deeply internal and indefinable pushed him to forge ahead despite how unpleasant it was. Somehow, giving up looked bleaker than this.

"You don't salvage an agreement by walking away. You stay in the same room and hammer it out," he managed to say.

"What is there to salvage?" Adara charged with a pained throb in her voice. Her heart was lodged behind her collarbone like a sharp rock. Didn't he understand? Everything she'd brought to the table was gone.

Gideon only nodded at her chair, his expression shuttered yet insistent.

Adara dropped into her chair out of emotional exhaustion. For a few seconds she just sat there with her hands steepled before her face, eyes closed, drowning in despair.

"What do you *want,* Adara?"

She opened her eyes to find him statue hard across from her, expression unreceptive despite his demand she confide.

He was afraid it was something he couldn't give, she realized. Like love?

A barbed clamp snapped hard around her heart. She wasn't brave enough to give up that particular organ and had never fooled herself into dreaming a man could love her back, so no, she wouldn't ask him for love. She settled on part of the truth.

"I want to quit feeling so useless," she confessed, suffering the sensation of being stripped naked by the admission. "I'm predisposed to insecurity because of my upbringing, I know that. I'm not worthless, but I feel that way in this marriage. Now I can't even bring children into it. I can't live with this feeling of inadequacy, Gideon."

He stared hard at her for a long moment before letting out a snort of soul-crushing amusement.

Adara couldn't help her sharp exhale as she absorbed that strike. She tried to rise.

Gideon clamped his hand on her arm. "No. Listen. God, Adara…" He shook his head in bemusement, brow furrowed with frustration. "When you asked me to marry you—"

"Oh, don't!" she gasped, feeling her face flood with abashed color.

He tightened his grip on her wrist, keeping her at the table. "Why does that embarrass you? It's the truth. You came to me with the offer."

"I *know*. Which only reminds me how pathetically desperate I must have seemed. You didn't want me and wouldn't have chosen me if I hadn't more or less bribed you."

"Desperate?" he repeated with disbelief. "I was the desperate one, coming hat in hand to your father with a proposition I knew he'd laugh out of the room. All I had going for me was nerve."

"Someone else would have taken up the chance to invest with you, Gideon. It was a sound opportunity, which Papa saw after he got over being stubborn and shortsighted."

"After you worked on him."

She shook that off in a dismissive shrug, instantly self-conscious of the way she'd stood up for a man she'd barely known simply because she'd been intrigued by him. It had been quite a balancing act, truth be told.

"Don't pretend you didn't have anything to do with it." He sat forward. "Because this is what I'm trying to tell you. You came to me with things I didn't have. Your father's partnership. Entrée into the tightest and most influential Greek cartels in New York and Athens. I needed that, I wanted it, and I had no real belief I could actually get it."

"Well, I didn't have much else to offer, did I?" she pointed out in a remembered sense of inadequacy.

"Your virginity springs to mind, but we'll revisit that another time," he rasped, making her lock her gaze with his in shocked incredulity.

Suddenly, very involuntarily, she flashed back to her wedding night and the feel of his fingers touching her intimately, his mouth roaming from her lips to her neck to her breast and back as he teased her into wanting an even thicker penetration. She hadn't understood how his incredibly hard thrust could hurt and feel so good at the same time. Instead of being intimidated by his strength and weight, she'd basked in the sense of belonging as his solid presence moved above her, on her, and within her so smoothly, bringing such a fine tension into every cell of her being. His hard arms had surrounded and braced her, yet shielded her from all harm, making her feel safer than she'd ever felt in her life, so that when she'd shattered, she'd known he'd catch her.

Her body clenched in remembered ecstasy even as she was distantly aware of his hold on her gentling. He caressed her bare forearm and his voice lowered to the smoky tone he'd used when he'd told her how lovely she'd felt to him then. *So hot and sweet. So good.*

"Try to understand what it meant for me to form a connection to you."

Her scattered faculties couldn't tell if he was talking about her deflowering or the marriage in general. She shivered with latent arousal, pulling herself away from his touch to ground herself in the now.

"People knew I came from nothing," he said. "You want to know why I only speak Greek when I absolutely have to? Because my accent gives me away as the bottom class sailor that I am."

"It does not," she protested distractedly.

He reached to tuck a tendril of hair behind her ear, his touch lingering to trace lightly beneath her jaw. "If you want me to talk, you're going to have to listen. People respect you, Adara. Not because your father owned the company, not because of your wealth, but because of the way you conduct yourself. Everyone knew your father's faults and could see that you were above his habits of lashing out and making hasty decisions. They knew you were intelligent and fair and had influence with him."

"Now I know you're lying." She drew back, out of his reach.

"He didn't sway easily, that's true." He dropped his hands to his thighs. "But if anyone could change his mind, it was you. Everyone knew that, from the chambermaids to the suits in the boardroom. And people also knew that you were being very choosy about finding a husband. *Very* choosy."

He sat back, his demeanor solidifying into the man who headed so many boardroom tables, sharp and firm. Not someone you argued with.

"I didn't appreciate what that choosiness meant until I was by your side and suddenly I was being looked at like I had superpowers because you'd picked me. Maybe it sounds weak to say my ego needed that, but it did. I went from being an upstart no one trusted to a legitimate businessman. I had had some success before I met you, but once I married you, *I* had self-worth because *you* gave it to me."

"But—" Her heart moved into her throat. She wanted to believe him, her inner being urgently needed to believe him, but it was so far from the way she perceived herself. "You're exaggerating."

"No, I'm telling you why I'm fighting to keep you."

"But people respect you. That won't go away if we divorce."

"*Now* they respect me. And perhaps that wouldn't go away overnight, although I can guarantee I'd be painted the villain if we split. People would pin the blame on me because you're nice and I'm not, but I'm not saying I want to stay married so I can continue using this knighthood you've unconsciously bestowed on me. It comes down to loyalty and gratitude and my own self-respect. I *like* being your husband. I want to keep the position."

"It's not a job." She'd tried to treat Husband and Wife like spots on an organizational chart and it wasn't that simple. Having a gorgeous body in a tux to escort her to fundraisers wasn't enough. She needed someone she could call when her world was crashing in on her and she thought she was dying.

That unexpected thought disturbed her. She had learned very young to guard her feelings, never show her loneliness, be self-sufficient and never, ever imagine her needs were important enough to be met. Wanting to rely on Gideon was a foreign concept, but it was there.

Gideon was watching her like a cat, ready to react, but what would he have done if he'd come home to find her sobbing her heart out? He'd have tried to ship her into the sterile care of stiff beds and objectifying instruments.

And yet, if she had found the courage to ask, would he have stayed with her and held her hand at the hospital? Would it have made a difference if he had?

It would have made a huge difference.

Deeply conflicted, she pushed back her chair, fingers knotting into the napkin on her lap. She didn't like feeling so tempted to try when there were so many other things wrong between them. "You make it sound so easy and it's not, Gideon."

"We have a few days before your brother shows up," he cut in with quick assertion. A muscle pulsed in his jaw. "I've cleared my schedule to the end of the week. We'll spend time together and set a new course. Turn this ship around."

She wanted to quirk a smile at the shipbuilder's oh-so-typical nautical reference, but her system was flooded with adrenaline, filling her with caution.

"What if—" She stopped herself, not wanting to admit she was terrified that spending time with him would increase her feelings for him. He was trying to make her feel special and it was working, softening her toward him. That scared her. If she knew anything about her husband, and she didn't know nearly enough, she knew he wasn't the least bit sentimental. She could develop feelings for him, but they'd never be returned.

What was his real reason for wanting to stay married?

"Look how much we've weathered and worked through since this morning," he reasoned with quiet persistence, showcasing exactly how he'd pushed a struggling shipyard into a dominant global enterprise in less than a decade. "We can make this marriage work for us, Adara. Give me a few days to prove it."

Days that were going to be excruciating even without a replay of today.

Nerves accosted her each time she thought of seeing Nico again and in the end, her consideration of Gideon's demand sprang from that. She would prefer to have him with her when she met Nico again. She couldn't explain it, but so many things, from social events to family dinners, were easier to face when Gideon was with her. She'd always felt that little bit more safe and confident when he was beside her, as if he had her back.

"You'd really move over to my brother's house with me?" she asked tentatively.

"Of course."

There was no "of course" about it. He showed up for the events in his calendar because it was their deal, not because he wanted to be there for her.

At least, that was her perception, but she hadn't really asked for anything more than that, had she? He'd offered to come to the hospital each time she'd told him about another miscarriage. She was the one who'd rebuffed the suggestion, hiding her feelings, not only holding him at a distance but pushing him away, too fearful of being vulnerable to even try to rely on him.

Which hadn't made her less vulnerable, just more bereft.

She couldn't stomach feeling that isolated again, not when she had so much of herself on the line. Still, she wasn't sure how to open herself up to help either.

"If you really want to, then okay. That's fine. But no guarantees," she cautioned. "I'm not making any promises."

He flinched slightly, but nodded in cool acceptance of her terms.

CHAPTER FIVE

GIDEON WAS A bastard, in the old-fashioned sense of the word and quite openly in the contemporary sense. When he wanted something, he found a way to get it. He wasn't always fair about it. His "bastard" moniker was even, at times, prefaced with words like *ruthless, self-serving,* and *heartless.*

When it came to other men trying to exercise power over him, he absolutely was all of those things. He fought dirty when he had to and without compunction.

He had a functioning conscience, however, especially when it came to women and kids. When it came to his wife, he was completely sincere in wanting to protect her in every way.

Except if it meant shielding her from himself. When Adara's brother, "Nic," he had called himself, had invited them to take a room at his house, that was exactly what Gideon had heard. *A* room. *One* bed.

Normally he would never take up such an offer. Given the unsavory elements in his background, he kept to himself whenever possible. He liked his privacy and was also a man who liked his own personal space. Even at home in New York, he and Adara slept in separate beds in separate bedrooms. He visited hers; she never came to his.

When she rose to shower after their lovemaking, he took his cue and left.

That had always grated, the way she disappeared before the sweat had dried on his skin, but it was the price of autonomy so he paid it.

Had paid it. He was becoming damn restless for entry into the space Adara occupied—willing to do whatever it took to invade it, even put himself into the inferior position of accepting a favor from a stranger.

Irritated by these unwanted adjustments to his rigidly organized life, he listened with half an ear to the vineyard manager's wife babble about housekeepers on vacation and stocked refrigerators, trying not to betray his impatience for her to get the hell out and leave them alone.

The nervous woman insisted on orienting them in the house, which looked from the outside like an Old English rabbit warren. Once inside, however, the floor plan opened up. Half the interior walls had been knocked out, some had been left as archways and pony walls, and the exterior ones along the back had been replaced by floor-to-ceiling windows. The remodeling, skilled as it was, was obvious to Gideon's sharp eye, but he approved. The revised floor plan let the stunning view of grounds, beach and sea become the wallpaper for the airy main-floor living space.

"The code for the guest wireless is on the desk in here," the woman prattled on as she led them up the stairs and pressed open a pair of double doors.

Gideon glanced into a modern office of sleek equipment, comfortable workspaces and a stylish, old-fashioned wet bar. A frosted crest was subtly carved into the mirrored wall behind it. In the back of his mind, he heard again the male voice identifying himself when he had called the hotel, the modulated voice vaguely familiar.

It's Nic...Makricosta. I'm looking for my sister, Adara.

Gideon had put the tiny hesitation down to anything from nerves to distraction.

Now, as he recognized the crest, he put two and two together and came up with C-4 explosive. A curse escaped him.

Both women turned startled gazes to where he lingered in the office doorway.

"You told me your brother had changed his name. I didn't realize to what," Gideon said, trying for dry and wry, but his throat had become a wasteland in the face of serious danger to his invented identity.

"Oh," Adara said with ingenuous humor. "I didn't realize I never..." A tiny smile of sheepish pride crept across her lips. "He's kind of a big deal, isn't he? It's one of the reasons I hesitated to get in touch. I thought he might dismiss me as a crackpot, or as someone trying to get money out of him."

Kind of a big deal? Nicodemus Marcussen was the owner and president of the world's largest media empire, not to mention a celebrated journalist in his own right. His work these days tended toward in-depth analysis of third-world coup d'état stuff, but he was no stranger to political exposés and other investigative reporting in print or on camera. Running a background check would be something he did between pouring his morning coffee and taking his first sip.

Gideon reassured himself Nic had no reason to do it, but tension still crawled though him as they continued their tour.

"My number is on the speed dial," the woman said to Adara. "Please call if you need anything. The Kyrios was most emphatic that you be looked after. He's hurrying his business in Athens as best he can, but it will be a couple of days before he's able to join you." She made the statement as she led them into a regal guest room brimming with fresh flowers, wine, a fruit basket, a private balcony with cushioned wicker furniture and a massive sleigh bed with a puffy white cover. "I trust you'll be comfortable?"

Gideon watched Adara count the number of beds in the room and become almost as pale as the pristine quilt. She looked to him, clearly expecting him to ask for a second room. Any day previous to this one he would have, without hesitation. Today he remained stubbornly silent.

Color crept under her skin as the silence stretched and she realized if anyone made an alteration to these arrangements, it would have to be her. He watched subtle, uncomfortable tension invade her posture and almost willed her to do it. He wanted to share her bed, but he suddenly saw exactly how hard it was for her to stand up for herself.

She gave a jerky little smile at the woman and said, "It's fine, thank you," and Gideon felt a pang of disappointment directed at himself. He should have made this easy for her. *But he didn't want to.*

The woman left. As the distant sound of the front door closing echoed through the quiet house, Adara looked to him as if he'd let her down.

"Do we just take another room?" A white line outlined her pursed mouth.

"Why would we need to?" he challenged lightly.

"We're not sharing a bed, Gideon." Hard and implacable, not like her at all.

"Why not?" he asked with a matching belligerence, exactly like himself because this issue was riling him right down to the cells at the very center of his being.

Her gaze became wild-eyed and full of angry anxiety. "Have you listened to me at all in the last twenty-four hours? *I don't want to get pregnant!*"

"People have felt that way for centuries. That's why they

invented condoms," he retorted with equal ire. "I bought some before we left the hotel. Do you have an allergy to latex that I don't know about?"

She took a step back, her anger falling away so completely it took him aback. "I didn't think of that." Her brows came together in consternation. "You really wouldn't mind wearing one?"

He stood there flummoxed, utterly amazed. "You really didn't think of asking me to use them?"

"Well, you never have the whole time we've been married. I wasn't with anyone else before you. They're not exactly on my radar." She gave a defensive shrug of her shoulders, averting her gaze while a flush of embarrassment stained her cheekbones.

Innocent, he thought, and was reminded of another time when they'd stood in a bedroom, her nervous tension palpable while he was drowning in sexual hunger.

Anticipation was like a bed of nails in his back, pushing him toward her. On that first occasion, she had worn a blush-pink negligee and a cloak of reserve he'd enjoyed peeling away very, very slowly.

Don't screw this up, he'd told himself then, and reiterated it to himself today. The first night of their marriage, he'd had one chance to get their intimate relationship off on the right foot. He had one chance to press the reset button now.

The primal mate in him wanted to move across the room, kiss her into receptiveness and fall on the bed in a familiar act of simple, much-needed release.

But it wouldn't be enough. He saw it in the way her lashes flicked to his expression and she read the direction of his thoughts. Rather than coloring in the pretty way he so enjoyed watching when he suggested a visit to her room, she paled a little and her lips trembled before she bit them together.

"You don't…" Licking her lips, she looked to him with huge eyes that nearly brimmed with defensiveness. "You don't expect me to fall into bed with you just because you've got a condom, do you?"

Expect it? The animal in him howled, *Yes*.

"It's always been good, hasn't it?" He bit out the words, perhaps a little too confrontational, but his confidence was unexpectedly deserting him.

She crossed her arms, shoulders so tight he thought she'd snap herself in half. "It's always been fine."

"Fine?" he charged, gutted by the faint praise.

She sent him a helpless look that made him feel like a bully.

"I can hardly deny that I've enjoyed it, can I?" she said, but the undertone of something like embarrassment or shame stole all the excitement he might have felt if she'd said it another way. "I just…"

"Don't trust me." He ground out the words with realization. It was an unexpectedly harsh blow. "Come on," he said, holding out his hand before he lost what was left of his fraying self-control.

She stilled with guardedness. "What? Where?"

"Anywhere but this room or I'll be all over you and you're obviously not ready for that."

A funny little frisson went through Adara as she took in the rugged, intimidating presence that was her husband. He held out a commanding hand, as imperious and inscrutable as ever, but his words had an undercurrent of…was it compassion?

Whatever it was, it did things to her, softening her, but it scared her at the same time. She was already too susceptible to him.

And his desire for her was a seduction in itself. Her insecurity as a woman had been ramped to maximum with everything that had happened, but things had shifted in the last twenty-four hours. She was looking at him, hearing him. His sexual hunger wasn't an act. She knew the signs of interest and excitement in him. His chiseled features were tense with focus. A light flush stained his cheekbones—almost a flag of temper if not for the line of his mouth softened into a hungry, feral near smile.

Her body responded the way it always did, skin prickling with a yearning to be stroked, breasts tightening, loins clenching in longing for him.

Oh, God. If she stayed in this room, she'd *beg* him to be all over her, and where would that lead beyond a great orgasm? She didn't know what sort of relationship she wanted with Gideon, but knew unequivocally she couldn't go back to great sex and nothing else.

She moved to the door, not expecting him to fall in beside her and take her hand. A *zing* of excitement went through her as he enveloped her narrow fingers in his strong grasp. Stark defenselessness flared and she wanted to pull herself away. Why?

"It's not that I distrust you," she said, trying to convince herself as much as him while they walked down the stairs, her hand like a disembodied limb she was so aware of it in his. "I know you'd never hurt me. You can be stubborn and bossy, but you're not cruel." It still felt strange to speak her mind so openly, increasing her sense of vulnerability and risk. Her heart tremored.

"But you don't trust me with who you *are*," he goaded lightly.

Her hand betrayed her, wriggling self-consciously in his firm grip. He eyed her knowingly as he reached with his free hand to slide open the glass door on the back of the house.

An outdoor kitchen was tucked to the side of a lounge area. A free-form pool glittered a few steps away, half in the sun, the rest in the shadow of the house. The paving stones dwindled past it to a meandering path down the lawn to the beach. The grounds were bordered on one side by the vineyard and by an orange grove on the other.

"Swim?" he suggested as they stood at the edge of the pool staring into the hypnotic stillness of the turquoise water.

Working up her courage, she asked softly, "Do you trust *me*, Gideon?"

His hold on her loosened slightly and his mouth twitched with dismay. "I don't wholly trust anyone," he admitted gruffly. "It's not because I don't think you're trustworthy. It's me. The way I'm made."

"The "it's not you, it's me" brush-off. There's a firm foundation." Disgruntled, she would have walked away, but he tightened his hold on her hand and followed her into the sunshine toward the orange grove.

"Would it help to know that I've been more open with you than I've been with anyone else in my life? Ever? Perhaps you learned to keep your feelings to yourself because you were afraid of how your father would react, but after my mother died, no one responded to what I wanted or needed. Even when she was alive, she was hardly there. Not her fault, but I've had to be completely self-sufficient most of my life. It shocks me every time you appear to genuinely care what I'm thinking or feeling."

The sheer lonesomeness of what he was saying gouged a furrow into her heart. She might have a stilted relationship with her younger brothers, but they would be there if she absolutely needed them. She unconsciously tightened her hand on his and saw a subtle shift in his stony expression, as if her instinctive need to comfort him had the opposite effect, making him uncomfortable.

"You never talk about your mom. She was a single mother? Constantly working to make ends meet?"

His face became marble hard. "A child. I have a memory of asking her how old she was and she said twenty-one. That doesn't penetrate when you're young. It sounds ancient, but if I can remember it, I was probably five or six, which puts her pregnant at fifteen or sixteen. I suspect she was a runaway, but I've never tried to investigate. I don't think I'd like any of the answers."

She understood. At best, his mother might have been shunned by her family for a teen pregnancy, forcing her to leave her home; at worst, he could be the product of rape.

A little chill went through her before she asked, "What happened after you lost her? Where did you go?"

His mouth pressed tight.

Her heart fell. This was one of those times he wouldn't answer.

He surprised her by saying gruffly, "There was a sailor who was decent to me."

"A kindly old salt?" she asked, starting to smile.

"The furthest thing from it. My palms would be wet with broken blisters and all he'd say was, 'There's no room for crybabies on a ship,' and send me back to work."

She gasped in horror, checking her footstep to pause and look at him.

He shook his head at her concern. "It's true. It wasn't a cruise liner. If you're not crew, you're cargo and cargo has to pay. If he hadn't pushed me, I wouldn't be where I am today. He taught me the ropes—that's not a pun. Everything from casting off to switching out the bilge pump.

He taught me how to hang on to my money, not drink or gamble it away. Even how to fight. Solid life skills."

"Does he know where you are today? What you've made of yourself?"

"No." His stoic expression flinched and his tone went flat. "He died. He was mugged on a dock for twenty American dollars. Stabbed and left to bleed to death. I came back too late to help him."

"Oh, Gideon." She wanted to bring his hand to her aching heart. Of course he was reticent and hard-edged with that sort of pain in his background. Questions bubbled in her mind. How old had he been? What had he done next?

She bit back pressing him. Baby steps, she reminded herself, but baby steps toward what? Their marriage was broken because *they* were broken.

She frowned. The future they'd mapped out with such simplistic determination five years ago had mostly gone according to plan. When it came to goal achievement in a materialistic sense, they were an unstoppable force. A really great team.

But what use was a mansion if no patter of tiny feet filled it? Without her father goading for expansion, she was content to slow the pace and concentrate on fine-tuning what they had.

She wasn't sure what she wanted from her marriage, only knew she couldn't be what Gideon seemed to expect her to be.

Where could they go from here?

The sweet scent of orange blossoms coated the air as they wandered in silence between the rows of trees. Gideon lazily reached up to steal a flower from a branch and brought it to his nose. A bemused smile tugged at his lips.

"Your hair smelled like this on our wedding night."

Adara's abdomen contracted in a purely sensual kick

of anticipation, stunning her with the wash of acute hunger his single statement provoked. She swallowed, trying to hide how such a little thing as him recalling that could affect her so deeply.

"I wore a crown of them," she said, trying to sound light and unaffected.

"I remember." He looked at her in a way that swelled the words with meaning, even though she wasn't sure what the meaning was.

A flood of pleasure and self-consciousness brimmed up in her.

"That almost sounds sentimental, but the night can only be memorable for how awkward I was," she dismissed, accosted anew by embarrassment at how gauche and inexperienced she'd been.

"Nervous," he corrected. "As nervous as you are now." He halted her and stood in front of her to drift the petal of the flower down her cheek, leaving a tickling, perfumed path. "So was I."

"I'm sure," she scoffed, lips coming alive under the feathery stroke of the blossom. She licked the sensation away. "What are you doing?"

"Seducing you. It'd be nice if you noticed."

She might have smiled, but he distracted her by brushing the flower under her chin. She lifted to escape the disturbing tickle and he stole a kiss.

It was a tender press of his mouth over hers, not demanding and possessive as she'd come to expect from him. This was more like those first kisses they'd shared a lifetime ago, during their short engagement. Brief and exploratory. Patient.

Sweet but frustrating. She was too schooled in how delicious it was to give in to passion to go back to chaste premarital nuzzling.

He drew back and looked into her eyes through a hooded gaze. "I remember every single thing about that night. How soft your skin was." The blossom dropped away as he stroked the back of his bent fingers down her cheek and into the crook of her neck. His gaze went lower and his hand followed. "I remember how I had to learn to be careful with your nipples because they're so sensitive."

They were. Sensitive and responsive. Tightening now so they poked against the dual layers of bra and shirt, standing out visibly and seeming to throb as he lightly traced a finger around the point of one. A whimper of hungry distress escaped her.

"I remember that most especially." The timbre of his voice became very low and intense. "The little noises of pleasure you made that got me so hot because it meant you liked what I was doing to you. I almost lost it the first time you came. Then you fell apart again when I was inside you and you were so tight—"

"Gideon, stop!" She grasped the hand that had drifted to the button at the waistband of her shorts. Her lungs felt as if all the air in them had evaporated and a distinctive throb pulsed between her thighs.

"I don't want to stop," he growled with masculine ferocity. "The only thing hotter than our first time together has been every time since."

She wanted to believe that, but yesterday...

Gideon watched Adara withdraw and knew he was losing her. He'd come on too strong, but hunger for her was like a wolf in him, snapping and predatory from starvation.

"What's wrong?" he demanded, then swore silently at himself when he saw that his roughened tone made her flinch. He wasn't enjoying these heart-to-hearts any more than she was, but they were necessary. He accepted that, but it was hard. He was the type to attack, not expose his throat.

Adara flicked him a wary glance and stepped back, arms crossing her chest in the way he was beginning to hate because it shut him out so effectively. She chewed her bottom lip for a few seconds before cutting him another careful glance.

"Yesterday you said… Maybe I'm being oversensitive, but what you said when we were swimming really hurt, Gideon. About me not being good enough. I *try* to give you as much pleasure as you give me—"

He cut her off with a string of Greek epithets that should have curled the leaves off the surrounding trees. "Yesterday was a completely different era in this relationship. What I said—" The chill of frustration gripped his vital organs. How could he explain that his appetite for her went beyond what even seemed human? He understood now why she'd confined their relations to oral sex, but it didn't change the fact that he ached constantly for release inside her. "I felt managed, Adara. I don't say that with blame. I'm only telling you how it seemed from what I knew then. I want you. Not other women. Not tarts like Lexi. *You.* Having you hold yourself back from me made me nuts. I need you to be as caught up as I am. To want me. It's the only way I can cope with how intense my need for you is."

She blinked at him in shock.

He rubbed a hand down his face, wishing he could wipe away his blurted confession. "If that scares the hell out of you, then I'm sorry. I probably shouldn't have told you."

"No," she breathed, head shaking in befuddlement. "But I find it hard to believe you feel like that. I'm not a siren. You're the one with all the experience, the one who thinks about using condoms because you've used them before."

"Yes, I have," he said with forcible bluntness, not liking how defensive he felt for having a sexual history when she'd come to him pristine and pure. "But you know when the last time I used one was? The night before we met. I don't remember much about the woman I was dating then, only that the next evening she left me because I asked her if she knew anything about you. Pretty crass, I know. I couldn't stop thinking about you."

Her searching gaze made him extremely uncomfortable. He jerked his chin.

"Let's keep walking."

"And talking? Because it's such fun?" Adara bent to retrieve the blossom he'd dropped and twirled it beneath her nose as they continued deeper into the orange grove. His revelations were disturbing on so many levels, most especially because they were creating emotional intimacy, something that was completely foreign to their marriage. Nevertheless, as painful as it was to dredge up her hurts, she was learning that it was cathartic to acknowledge them. Letting him explain his side lessened the hurt.

She glanced at him as they walked, no longer touching.

"I hate thinking of you with other women." The confession felt like a barbed hook dragged all the way from the center of her heart across the back of her throat. "Infidelity destroyed our family. We were quite normal at first, then Nico was sent away and it was awful. Both my parents drank. My father fooled around and made sure my mother knew about it. She was devastated. So much yelling and crying and fighting. I never wanted anything like that to happen to me."

"It won't," he assured her, reaching across with light fingers to smooth her hair off her shoulder so he could tuck his hand under the fall of loose tresses and cup the back of her neck. "But tell me you were jealous of Lexi anyway. My ego needs it."

"I felt insecure and useless," she said flatly.

He checked his step and a spasm of pain flashed across his face before he seared her with a look. "Exactly how I felt when I saw you walk up the driveway here. Like I'd been rejected because I wasn't good enough."

She bit her lips together in compunction while her heart quivered in her chest, shimmering with the kind of pain a seed must feel before the first shoot breaks through its shell. She wanted to cry and throw herself into him and run away and protect herself.

"We're never going to be able to make this work, Gideon. I don't want the power to hurt you any more than I want you to be able to hurt me. This is a mess. We're messing each other up and it's going to be—"

"Messy?" he prompted dryly. "Just take it one day at a time, Adara. That's all we can do."

She drew in and released a shaken breath, nodding tightly as they kept walking. Their steps made soft crunches in the dry grass while cicadas chirped in accompaniment. No breeze stirred beneath the trees and the heat clutched the air in a tight grip.

"Should we go back and swim?" she suggested.

"If you like."

It didn't matter what they did, she realized. They were filling time until her brother returned, distracting themselves while sexual attraction struggled for supremacy over hurt and misgivings. They should give in. Sex would take the edge off their tension and God knew she wanted him. Lovemaking with Gideon was a transcendent experience as far as she was concerned.

But she'd never felt this vulnerable with him before. It made physical intimacy seem that much more *intimate*. Her normal defenses were a trampled mess. The idea of letting him touch her and watch her lose control was terrifying. He'd see how much he meant to her and that was too much to bear.

Twenty minutes later they were in the pool. His laps were a purposeful crawl with flip turns and patterned breathing, hers a less disciplined breaststroke that made one lap to his four. Tiring, she moved to sit on one of the long tile stairs in the shallow end, half out of the water as she watched him. The pool was fully shaded now, leaving her quite comfortable watching his athletic build cut through the water.

When he stopped and joined her on the step, he was breathing heavily, probably having swum a mile though she'd lost count ages ago, distracted by the steady thrust of his arms into the water and the tight curve of his buttocks as he kicked. She really couldn't fathom what a sexy, virile man like him was doing with mousy, boring her.

And even though he'd pushed himself with thirty minutes of hard swimming, his gaze moved restlessly, as if he was looking for the next challenge.

"You're not comfortable with downtime, are you?" she said.

He glanced questioningly at her while diamond droplets glittered on his face and chest hair.

"You're driven," she expounded. "I keep thinking of all those plans we made, but what does it matter if we have a floating hotel? I know it's top-notch, but who cares? We don't need the money and the world doesn't need another behemoth cruise ship."

"It matters to the people we've employed and the ones who invested with us. But you're right, I suppose. Wealth isn't something either of us really needs. Not anymore. It's a habit I've fallen into, I guess."

"You worked hard to get here and now you don't know how to stop," she paraphrased.

He made a noise of agreement.

"If we don't have children, what would we fill our lives with? More hotels and boats?" Involuntarily, her ears strained to hear the words *each other*.

They didn't come. After a long moment he said, "Our last five-year plan took months to mold. This one can, too. There's no rush."

"There is," she insisted. "I feel like if we don't have everything sorted out before we sleep together again, our marriage will go back to the way it was and I'll be stuck in it." There. She'd said it. Her worst fear had blurted out of her.

He stared at her for a long minute, absorbing her outburst, then he chuckled softly and shook his head. "And I can't think of anything but making love to you again. New plans?" He shook his head as if she was speaking another language. "We're at quite an impasse."

He wasn't being dismissive, just blatantly honest. Her heart constricted as she absorbed that this was what he'd meant about trusting him. Somehow she had to dredge up the faith to believe he'd continue working on their marriage along with the courage to surrender herself to him. The potential for pain was enormous.

While the yearning to feel close to him was unbearable.

She looked up to where the afternoon sun had bleached the clear sky to nearly white. Not even close to evening or bedtime. She hadn't brought either her green-light or red-light nightgown. How else could she possibly signal to him that she was receptive to his advances?

Oh, Adara, quit being such a priss. They were learning to *communicate,* weren't they?

Her internal lecture didn't stop her heart from beating frantically in her throat as she set tentative fingertips on his wrist where it rested on his thigh. Leaning toward him, she shielded her eyes with a swoop of her lashes and watched his lips part slightly in surprise before she pressed hers to them.

Heat flooded into her. The very best kind of heat that had nothing to do with Greek sunshine and everything to do with this man's chemistry interacting with hers. He didn't move, letting her control the pressure and deepening of their kiss, but he responded with a muted groan of approval and drew on her tongue with gentle suction.

Runnels of sexual hunger poured through her system, spreading out in delicate fingers that excited her senses and made her want to tip into his lap.

Shakily she pulled back and licked the taste of him off her lips before she gripped the railing in slippery fingers and forced her weak knees to take her weight as she stood.

"Will you, um, give me a minute to shower before you come up?" The question was so uncouched and blatant she felt as though she'd stripped herself naked here in public.

"I'll use the shower in the cabana and be up in ten," he replied gruffly, eyes like lasers that peeled her bathing suit from her body.

Adara wrapped a towel around herself and went to their room.

CHAPTER SIX

THE PARALLEL TO their first time kept ringing in Gideon's skull. He was just as keyed up as he'd been then, his masculine need to possess twitching in him like an electric wire, while his ego inched out onto that wire, precarious as a tightrope walker.

No room for false moves. The message pulsed as a current, back and forth within him.

He climbed the stairs as though pulled by an invisible force. No matter how many times he told himself it was ridiculous to place so much importance on this—he'd done this before. *They* had. It didn't matter. This meant something. The last time he'd felt this sense of magnitude, Adara's initiation to sexual maturity had been on the line. He'd felt a massive responsibility to make it good for her, especially as he'd been selfishly determined he would be her only lover for the rest of their lives. The pressure to ensure they were both satisfied with that exclusivity had been enormous.

Without being too egotistical, he believed they had been. He certainly had. Her subtle beauty had flourished into his own private land of enchantment.

This ought to be a visit to the familiar, he told himself as he turned the handle on the door and pressed into their room. It wasn't. This was uncharted territory and the initiation this time was happening to both of them, moving them into some kind of emotional maturity he would have rather avoided. The tightrope he was walking didn't even feel as if it was there anymore. He was walking across thin air, reminding himself not to look down or he'd be tumbling into a bottomless crevasse.

As he leaned on the door until it clicked, she opened the bathroom door and emerged wearing one of his T-shirts. The soft white cotton clung to her damp curves and naked breasts before falling to the tops of her thighs. He couldn't tell if she wore underpants and couldn't wait to find out.

"I didn't bring anything sexy," she murmured apologetically, her eyes bigger than the black plums in the basket. Her apprehension was unmistakable.

"You look edible," he said, voice originating somewhere deep in his chest. He moved across to her. "I didn't shave." He took her hand and rubbed the heel across his jaw where a hint of stubble was coming in.

"It's okay," she murmured and pulled her hand back then wrung it with her other one. "I'm sorry. I don't know why I'm so terrified. This is silly."

A swell of tenderness rose in him. He took her hands and kissed each palm. "It's okay. I'll take it slow. As slow as the first time. I want to savor every second."

Her smile trembled. "I know it will be good, but my body seems to think we're strangers. I keep reminding myself I know everything about you. The important things, anyway."

His blood stopped in his arteries as he thought about what she didn't know about him. Important things, but so was this. He needed to cement their connection before he could even contemplate stressing it with a full exposure of who he was. And wasn't.

Adara cupped the sides of his head, trembling with

nerves and anticipation, wanting the kiss that would erase all her angst and drown her in the sea of erotic sensations he always delivered.

Gideon wasn't moving, seeming to have slipped behind a veil of some kind.

"What's wrong?" she asked as doubts began to intrude.

"Nothing," he said gruffly and set his mouth on hers.

The first contact was just that, contact. Like finding the edge of the pool when your eyes were closed and head submerged and your lungs ready to give up. Relief poured through her as the familiar shape and give of his full lips compressed her own.

And then he opened his mouth in a familiar signal that she do the same and she nearly melted into a puddle of homecoming joy. His arms slid around her and pulled her into a hard embrace against his shirtless chest, muscles bulging with such strength it was almost uncomfortably hard against her tender breasts, but so welcome.

Adara curled her arms around the back of his neck and clung, kissing him unreservedly as her senses absorbed every delicious thing about him. His shoulders and back were gloriously smooth and naked, scented with body wash and rippling hotly as he moved his hands on her, awakening every nerve in her body.

The wide plant of his strong legs let her feel the brush of his hairy legs against the smoothness of her thighs. She wriggled closer, wanting to feel the hard muscle that told her he liked the feel of her against him. Her body craved contact with that gorgeous erection and she arched herself into firm pressure against the ridge she could feel behind the fly of his shorts.

"This isn't slow," he growled, straightening and grasping a handful of T-shirt between her shoulder blades.

The soft fabric stretched across the round thrust of her

breasts. Her nipples stood out prominently. Eagerly. He leaned to take one in his mouth, suckling her through the fabric until she let out a keening moan of distress at the pleasure-pain. He pulled back to examine the wet stain that turned the cotton invisible, clearly revealing the sharp pink tip and shaded areola of her breast.

Adara gasped at how flagrantly erotic this was, but couldn't help arching a little in pride when she could see how excited he was by the sight. He smiled tightly before bending to do the same to her other nipple, bringing her up on her toes the sensation was so ferociously strong. A ripple of near ecstasy quavered in her abdomen, making her weak and mindless. She clung to him as if he was a life raft.

"I've always liked that, too," he said with satisfaction.

"What?" she asked breathily.

"The way you dig your kitten claws into me when you're about to come."

The heat that suffused her nearly burned her alive. "I'm not," she said in a near strangle.

"No?" A light of determination flared behind the liquid heat that had turned his dark eyes black.

Her heart skipped in alarm, but his superior strength easily backed her to the bed and levered her into the poofy cloud of the duvet. He took a moment to admire the purple undies she was wearing, the prettiest pair she'd brought, before he drew them down her legs in a deliberately slow tease of satin against skin.

The unfettered daylight and proprietary touch of his strong hands on her legs made her thighs quiver.

"Gideon," she protested.

"You're so close, *matia mou,*" he cajoled, thumb stroking into her wet folds to search out the knot of sensation that was undeniably eager for his touch. She instinctively lifted her hips off the bed at the first contact. He bent and chuckled softly against her inner thigh, kissing his way to where her entire world was centered.

Latent modesty curled her fingers into his hair and she moaned indecisively, wanting badly to give in to what he offered, but she felt like such a wanton. She tossed her head back and forth, tugged on his hair, then felt the hot lick of his tongue and nearly screamed with delight. Need ravaged through her and she encouraged him, nearly begged him with the rock of her hips and clench of her fist in his hair and then—

Release seared through her like a white-hot blade, blinding in its intensity. Sensations racked her on waves of unadulterated pleasure that gripped her for an eternity, exquisite and joyous.

She came back on a sobbing pant of gratification. Aftershocks trembled through her as she became aware of Gideon kissing his way up her torso, pushing aside the T-shirt. He lifted onto an elbow to admire the quivering breasts he'd bared, then slowly lifted his gaze to her face.

Adara felt utterly defenseless and he made it worse when he said, "Now imagine how you would feel if I left you right now."

The way she had been leaving him in exactly this state for weeks.

He began to roll away and her world crashed in. "Don't!" she cried.

He showed her the condom he'd reached for. "I can't," he said with a near-bitter fatalism. He opened his shorts and pushed them down, kicking his shorts free.

The thrust of his erection was as powerfully intimidating as ever, but she positively melted with anticipation. "Can I—" She tried to help him with the condom.

"Next time, Adara. For God's sake, just let me get inside you."

He lifted to cover her, his weight a sweet dominance as he pushed into her, filling her with the heat of his length and rocking his hips so he was seated as deeply as possible. Then he weaved his fingers into her hair and nuzzled light kisses on her brow and cheekbones, giving her time to adjust to his penetration.

"You don't know what it's been like," he grumbled.

She had an idea. Her body was barely hers, responding to the feel of him so strongly that just the thick stretch of him inside her and the faint friction of their tiniest movement was setting off another detonation. It would have been humiliating if it wasn't so amazingly, sweetly incredible.

"Oh, God, Gideon. I'm sorry," she moaned and scratched at his rib cage as she tilted her hips for more pressure and shuddered into ecstasy beneath his weight.

"Oh, babe," he said consolingly against her lips, rocking lightly to increase the sensations, forcing and prolonging her climax. "You missed this, too."

She shattered, unable to stop herself gasping in joy

"Don't be arrogant," she warned a minute later, turning her face to the side in discomfiture as she tried to catch her breath.

"I'm not, I swear I'm not." His breath was hot on her ear before his tongue painted wet patterns on her nape.

"You don't seem quite as swept away as I am," she said pointedly, pressing against the wall of his chest.

"I'm barely hanging on. Can't you feel me shaking? If I was naked, I'd have been lost on the first thrust. Being inside you is so good, babe. I never want to leave. It's always like this, like I'm in heaven."

Her heart seemed to flower open to him and her hands

moved on him of their own volition, absorbing that he was, indeed, trembling with strain.

"I thought I was the one shivering," she confessed softly.

"I live for this, Adara. The feel of you under me, the way you smell, the heat and the insane pleasure of feeling you around me." He pressed deep as he spoke, sparking a flare of need in her for another and another of those fiercely possessive thrusts.

"Don't stop," she begged. "It feels too good."

With an avid groan, he took her mouth in a deep soul kiss and thrust in a purposeful, primal rhythm. The sensations were nearly too much for her, but she couldn't let him go, couldn't give it up. Her legs locked around him and her heels urged him to heavier, harder slams of his hips into hers. This wasn't a man initiating a virgin; it was too halves trying to meld into a whole. The sensations were acute and glorious and feral.

And when the culmination arrived, it was a simultaneous crescendo that burst from the energy between them, surrounding and sealing them in a halo of shimmering joy as they clung tightly to the only thing left in the universe. Each other.

Gideon left Adara at a complete and utter loss. She always left the bed first, hitting the shower so she could recover her defenses after letting them fall away during sex. Lovemaking always made her feel vulnerable, and after acting so greedily and helpless to her desire for him, she needed alone time more than ever. She'd never felt so peeled down to the core in her life

But Gideon disappeared into the bathroom, stealing her favorite line of escape. She sat up, thinking to dress, but then go where?

The toilet flushed and she flicked the corner of the duvet

over her nudity, not sure where to look when he came out of the bathroom. He struck a pose in the doorway with elbows braced and a near belligerence in his naked stance.

"What's wrong?" she asked, unnerved by his intense stare.

"Nothing. You?" He seemed almost confrontational and it got her back up.

"No. Of course not." Except that she'd pretty much exploded in his arms and didn't know how to handle facing down this tough guy who didn't seem to have a shred of tenderness in him anymore. She slid a foot to the edge of the bed. "I'll, um, just have a quick shower—"

"Why?" he challenged. "You just had one."

True, but where else did one ever have complete privacy except the bathroom? She'd figured that one out in grade school. It was one of her coping strategies to this day. She set her chin, trying to think up a suitable way to insist.

"I hate it when you run away after sex," he said, coming toward the bed in a stealthy, pantherlike stride. "Unless you're inviting me to join you in the shower, stay exactly where you are."

Her heart skipped, reacting to both his looming presence and the shock of his words.

"You're the one who started it, running out like you had a train to catch the first night of our honeymoon. I thought that's how we did this," she defended, going hot with indignation. "When we're done, we're done."

"Our first night was your first *time*. If I hadn't left you, I'd have made love to you all night and I didn't want to hurt you any more than I already had." He leaned over her as he spoke, forcing her onto her back.

She pressed a hand to his chest, warding him off. "Well, I didn't know that, did I? You walked out on me and I didn't like it, so I made it a habit to be the first to leave every other time."

He hung over her on straight arms, his eyes narrowed hawkishly. "So you're not running away to wash the feel of me off your skin?"

"No." That was absurd. She loved the feel and smell of him lingering on her. "Sometimes I run the shower but don't get in," she admitted sheepishly.

He muttered a curse of soft, frustrated amusement. "Then why…?"

"You make me feel like I can't resist you! Like all you have to do is look at me or say a word and I'll melt onto my back. That's not a comfortable feeling."

"That's exactly how I want you to be. I want you here, under me. I want to make love to you until we're so weak we can't lift our heads. I've never been comfortable with how insatiable I am for you. At least if we're in the same boat, I can stand it."

She almost told him then that sometimes she woke in the middle of the night and ached for him to come to her. Shyness stopped her, but she overcame it enough to reach up to the back of his head and urge him down to kiss her. She stayed on her back, under him, and moaned in welcome as he settled his hot weight on her.

He groaned in gratification.

Moonlight allowed Adara to find his T-shirt on the floor. The doors were still open and the air had cooled off to a velvety warmth that caressed her nudity. She took a moment to savor the feel of her sensitive skin stroked by the night air. It was an uncharacteristic moment of sensuality for her.

She glanced at her naked form in the mirror. The woman staring back at her through the shadows was a bit of a stranger. The dark marks of Gideon's fingerprints spotted her buttocks and thighs. They'd got a little wild at times through the afternoon and evening, definitely more voracious than either had ever revealed to the other before.

Her abdomen fluttered in speculative delight. His focus on her had shored up places inside her that had been unsteady and ready to collapse. Her footing felt stronger now, even if the rest of her still swayed and trembled.

Yes, there were still places inside her that were sensitive and vulnerable, places very close to her heart. In some ways, she was even more terrified than she'd been before they'd come up here and thrown themselves at each other, but she was glad they'd made love. Very glad.

A whisper of movement drew her glance to the bed. Gideon's arm swept her space on the bed. The covers had long been thrown off and the bottom sheet was loose from the corners. They had indisputably wrecked this bed.

The body facedown upon it, however, was exquisitely crafted to withstand the demands he'd made upon it. Adara took a mental photo of his form in the bluish light: his muscled shoulders, the slope of his spine, the taut globes of his buttocks, his lean legs, one crooking toward her vacant spot as he came up on an elbow.

His expression relaxed as he spotted her in the middle of the room. She tightened her grasp on the T-shirt she clutched to her front.

"Get back here."

The smoky timbre of his voice was a rough caress all its own, while his imperious demand made her want to grin. Despite being a naturally dominant male, he usually phrased his commands as requests when he spoke to her. That was all part of the distance between them, she realized. Part of both of them not letting the other see the real person. She ought to be affronted by his true, domineering and dictatorial colors, but she liked that he wasn't quelling that piece of his personality around her anymore.

She liked even more that she wasn't afraid of this side of him. He wasn't an easy man to resist on any level, but she wasn't afraid to stand up to him.

Even if he still made her feel inordinately shy.

"I'm thirsty. And I want to see what's in these baskets." She turned away, prickles of awareness telling her he studied her back and bottom exactly as proprietarily as she'd looked at him before he'd woken. She shrugged his T-shirt over herself.

"That's the first thing I noticed about you and I hardly ever get to see it naked."

"My bum?" Her buttocks tightened beneath the light graze of his T-shirt and she felt herself heat. She turned to bring the basket along with the wineglasses to the bed, not bothering with the wine itself. She was after the sparkling water in the green bottle.

As she placed the basket on the bed and knelt across from him, she caught a look of disgruntlement on his face.

"All of you," he clarified. "You're gorgeous and I like looking at you."

She didn't know what to say. She was flattered, but only half believed him.

Tucking her loose hair behind her ear, she confided, "I've never felt confident about the way I look. Showing any hint of trying to be sexy while my father was alive would have been a one-way ticket to hell. And I never really trusted any man enough to flirt." She gave him the bottle of water to open for her then poured two glasses, drinking greedily only to make herself hiccup.

She giggled and covered her wet lips, but sobered as she saw Gideon glowering into his glass.

"Men who hit women make me insane. I know it's not

right to answer violence with violence, but if your father were still alive, the police would be involved right now, one way or another." He took a deep slug of his water, eyes remaining hooded, not meeting her shocked gaze.

His vehemence was disturbing, prompting an odd need to comfort him. She reached across to stroke his tense arm. "Gideon, it's in the past. It's okay."

"No, it's not," he said sharply, but when he looked at her, his expression softened a little. "But right now isn't the time to think about it. Get rid of that," he ordered with a jerk of his chin at the T-shirt.

"What am I? Your sex slave now?" She did feel a little enslaved, but she wasn't as resentful as she ought to be about it.

"No. You're my wife. You ought to be comfortable letting me see you naked." He set aside his glass to reach for an orange.

She finished her own water and set it aside before easing the shirt off her body and setting it aside while she continued to kneel demurely, feet alongside her buttock, arm twitching to cover her breasts. To distract herself, she watched Gideon efficiently section the orange and bring a piece to his mouth.

He clutched it in his teeth and looked at her. "Bite," he said around it.

Her heart did a somersault. "Why?" The defensive question came automatically, but then she thought, *Just do it,* and leaned down to close her mouth on the fruit.

They bit it in half at the same time. Tangy juice exploded in her mouth. At the same time, his firm lips moved on hers in an erotic, openmouthed kiss. When she would have pulled away in surprise, he set a hand behind her head and kept her close enough to enjoy the messy, sweet, thorough act of sinful wickedness.

When he finally let her pull away to finish chewing and swallow, he grinned. "You flirt just fine, Mrs. Vozaras."

"Do it again," she blurted, making herself be assertive so she'd quit letting habits of inhibition hold her back from what she wanted.

A flicker of surprise flashed in his eyes before his eyelids grew heavy and his gaze sexily watchful. In her periphery, she was aware of him growing hard and her mouth watered for that too, but she took another bite of orange and splayed her hand on his chest, leaning into him to enjoy the sticky, tart kiss.

The last shreds of her inhibitions fell away and they didn't get back to the orange for a long, long time.

"You're going to burn," Gideon said as he returned from the waves to see the sun had moved and the backs of Adara's legs were exposed to the intense rays.

She stayed on her stomach on the blanket, unmoved and unmoving, only blinking her eyes open sleepily, as if she didn't have an ounce of energy in her. Forty-eight hours of unfettered lovemaking, impulsive napping and abject laziness were taking a toll on both of them. His own ambition had frittered into an *I'll look at it later* attitude. He'd left his phone and tablet up at the house, bringing only his sunglasses and wife to the beach.

"I like being on vacation," she told him, still not moving.

He adjusted the umbrella so she was fully in the shade then flopped down beside her. "So do I. We should definitely do this more often."

A shadow passed behind her eyes before she lowered her lashes to hide it. She shifted to rest her chin on her stacked fists, the circumspect silence making him aware of all the things they'd avoided while enriching their knowledge of each other's capacity for physical pleasure. Suddenly they were back in the pool, he couldn't think beyond his sexual hunger, and she was telling him that she needed to know where their relationship was going.

Restless frustration moved through him. He didn't know what to tell her. This was perfect. Wasn't it? He couldn't think of one thing they needed besides warm sand, the reassuring swish of a calm sea, each other's heated breath while they—

A faint noise lifted his head and a preternatural tingle went through him as he noticed a speck appear in the distant sky. They hadn't been tracking time, neither of them particularly interested in a return to reality, but apparently it was descending whether they were ready for it or not.

"Babe? I think your brother's here."

CHAPTER SEVEN

GIVEN HOW THEIR trip to Greece had started, Gideon supposed he shouldn't be surprised by Adara's reaction, but the way she paled and panicked startled him. She took herself back to the house as if her skin was on fire. In their room, she pulled on a sundress and revealed a level of agitation he'd never seen as the thwack of chopper blades became loud enough to make the house hum.

He dragged on shorts and a collared shirt, concerned by the way her hand shook as she tried to apply makeup.

"Adara, you look great," he reassured her, even though her lips were bloodless and her eyes pools of anxiety.

Coming back from a place of dark thoughts, she gripped his forearm with a clammy hand. "Thank you for being here with me. I don't know if I could have done this alone."

Shaken by the reliance and trust her statement represented, he wanted to pull her into his arms and assure her he'd always be here, but she was already pulling away from him. She had been waiting for this a long time and he could see she was both eager and filled with trepidation. Not knowing her brother or how this would go for her filled him with his own anxiety, wanting to shield her yet knowing he had to let whatever happened happen. He could only accompany her outside where the sound of the chopper blades faded to desultory pulses.

Walking out a side door, they stood on the steps, Adara's fingernails digging into his biceps as she gripped his arm.

They watched Nic Marcussen help a woman with crutches from the helicopter. Rowan Davidson was vaguely familiar to him as a moderately famous child actress who'd had a flirtation with notoriety among the euro-trash social elite. She seemed surprisingly down to earth now as she spun with lithe grace on one foot, accepting her second crutch while trying to take a bag from her husband at the same time.

Nic shouldered the bag's strap and reached back into the chopper for one more thing: an infant carrier.

As the couple made their way across the lawn toward them, Gideon felt the slicing gaze of the media magnate take his measure.

It wasn't often that Gideon met a man he considered his equal. Standing on the man's stoop didn't exactly put him on an even playing field and he might have been more uncomfortable with that if a severe expression of anguish hadn't twisted Nic's expression when he transferred his gaze to Adara.

Her tense profile barely contained the emotions Gideon sensed rising off her as viscerally as if they were his own. Everything in him wanted to pull her close and screen her from what was obviously a very painful moment. But he had to stand helplessly waiting out the silence as Nic paused at the bottom of the steps and the siblings were held in a type of stasis, staring at each other.

Like a burst of rainbows into a rainy afternoon, Rowan smiled and stepped forward. "We're so glad you came," she said in a warm Irish accent. Hitching up the steps on her crutches, she embraced Adara with one arm, kissing her cheek. "I'm Rowan. It's my fault we're late. And you're Gideon?"

She hopped over to hug him as if they were long-lost relatives, and for once Gideon didn't take offense at an unexpected familiarity, accepting her kiss on his cheek, still focused on his wife who seemed to be in a kind of trance.

Slowly Nic set down the baby carrier and let the bag slide off his shoulder on his other side. He took a step forward and Adara tipped forward off the stoop, landing in the open arms of her brother. It was beautiful and heart-rending, the reunion so intense it could only be the result of long, intense suffering apart.

"We should give them a minute," Rowan said huskily, her eyes visibly wet as she dragged her gaze from the pair. "Would you be an absolute hero and bring Evie into the house for me?"

Gideon didn't like leaving Adara, but followed Rowan to the kitchen where she began preparing a bottle. The baby craned her neck and followed Rowan with her Oriental eyes, beginning to strain against the confines of her seat, whimpering with impatience.

"I know, you're completely out of sorts, aren't you?" Rowan murmured as she released the baby while the bottle warmed. Cuddling the infant, she nuzzled her cheek and patted her back, soothing the fussing girl.

"We were supposed to be here all summer just enjoying being a family," she said to Gideon. "Then it came up that I could have a few pins taken out of my leg. I wanted to put it off, but Nic said no, he could handle Evie for a couple of nights while I was in hospital. But Evie decided to cut a tooth and bellow nonstop. He didn't get a wink of sleep. Then he found out Adara had come looking for him. He didn't know which way to turn. Here, do you mind?" she said as a *ping* sounded from the cylindrical bottle warmer.

She held out the infant and Gideon had no choice but to take her so Rowan could retrieve the baby's bottle.

He held the sturdy little girl's rib cage between his palms. Her dangling legs wriggled and her tiny hands scratch-tickled his forearms while her doll's face craned to keep Rowan in view. She was the smallest, most fragile creature he'd ever held and fear that he'd break her made him want to hurriedly hand her back, but Rowan was occupied tipping the bottle to spray milk on her wrist then licking it off.

"I've used crutches so many times I can do a full tea service on them without spilling, but I haven't mastered juggling a baby. Yet." She smiled cheekily and hopped over to him. "Just rest her in the crook of your arm and—yes, I know you want that. You're hungry, aren't you? Uncle's going to feed you."

No, I'm not, Gideon thought, but found himself with a weight of soft warmth snuggled onto his forearm. As little Evie got the nipple in her mouth and relaxed, he did too. Her charcoal eyes gazed up at him trustingly and he felt a tug near his heart. Her foot tapped lightly onto his breastbone while she swallowed and breathed heavily with audible greediness. He felt like a superhero, making sure she wasn't going hungry.

"Shall we sit outside? I hope you've been comfortable here?" Rowan led him out of the kitchen to the patio.

"Very," he assured her, sincere. "You'll have to let us return the hospitality when our cruise ship launches next year. Now, how do we do this? Do you want to sit and take her—?"

A noise inside the house snapped Rowan's head around like a guard dog hearing a footstep. "That was Adara into the ladies' room. I'll just— Do you mind? I want to make sure Nic…" She *was* good on crutches, swooping away like a gull, a telling thread of concern in her tone as she disappeared into the house.

He snorted in bemusement, thinking that Nic Marcussen seemed the least likely man in the universe to require a mother hen for a wife, but apparently he had one.

While Gideon was literally left holding the baby.

He looked down at the girl, surprised to see how much of the bottle she'd drained. As her bright gaze caught his, Evie broke away from the teat to give him an ear-to-ear milky grin of joy and gratitude and trust.

A laugh curled upward from deep in his chest, surprising him with how instant and genuine his humor was. Little minx. They learned early how to disarm a man, didn't they? He was in very real danger of falling in love at first sight.

Adara wiped at her still-leaking eyes and tried to pull herself together so Gideon wouldn't worry. He had been right. It was okay. Nico was and always had been her big brother in every way that counted. Nevertheless, her heart was cracking open under the pressure of deep feeling. She desperately craved the arms of her husband to cushion her from the sensation of rawness.

As she went in search of him outside, she saw him settling into a chair at the patio table, his back to her. Biting her lips together, she tried not to burst into happy tears as she stepped through the door and moved to his side—

—where she found him holding a baby, smiling indulgently at the infant as if the tot was the most precious thing in the world.

The kick of pain blindsided her. For a second she was paralyzed by the crash back to the reality of their imperfect life, winded so much she wasn't able to move, let alone retreat, before Gideon glanced up and saw the devastated expression on her face.

If he'd been caught with Lexi in flagrante delicto, he

couldn't have looked more culpable. *It wouldn't have hurt this badly.*

"She's on crutches. The baby was hungry. I couldn't say no," he defended quickly while his arm moved in the most subtly protective way to draw the baby closer to his chest. In the way of a natural father sheltering his young.

At the same time, his free hand shot out to take Adara's arm in an unbreakable grip.

"You look like you're going to fall down. Sit." He half rose, used one foot to angle a chair for her and maneuvered her into it.

Adara's legs gave out as she sank into the chair. She buried her face in her hands and frantically reminded herself that her emotions were pushed to the very edge of endurance right now. The bigger picture here wasn't that he was stealing an opportunity to cuddle a baby because she couldn't give him one. He was getting to know their niece.

Longing rose in her as she made that connection and a different, more tender kind of emotion filled her, sweet with the layers of reunion with family that had driven her here in the first place. She lifted her head and held out her hands.

"Can I hold her? Please?"

"Of course." He transferred the baby's weight into her arms and Adara nearly dissolved into a puddle of maternal love. "Her name's Evie. Adara, I wasn't—"

She shook her head.

His hand came up to the side of her neck, trapping her hair against her nape as he forced her to look at him and said in a fierce whisper. "I wasn't trying to hurt you."

"I know. It's okay," she assured him, rubbing her cheek on the hardness of his wrist. "I just wasn't expecting it, that's all. I'm not mad."

He cupped the side of her face and leaned across to kiss

her once, hard. "You scared me. I thought I was going to lose you."

She had to consciously remember to hold on to the baby while her limbs softened and her heart shifted in her chest. Every time she thought they didn't have a hope in the world of making something of their marriage, he said something like that and completely enchanted her.

Voices made them break their intense stare into each other's eyes.

"I'm not being a grouch," her brother growled as he emerged from the house carrying his wife in the cradle of his arms. "But you were discharged early because you promised to keep it elevated, so I think you should do that, don't you?"

Gideon moved to pull out a chair so Rowan could slide down onto it, then he offered a hand to Nico. "Gideon."

"Nic," her brother said, completely pulled together after his tearful reassurances to her a few minutes ago. He'd never stopped caring or worrying about her all this time, just as she had for him. She was loved, was worth loving. It was a startling adjustment, like learning she wasn't an ugly duckling but a full-fledged swan.

Could Gideon see the change in her?

He wore a mask of subtle tension as he took his seat. No one else seemed to notice. Nic opened wine and Rowan stole the empty bottle of milk from her baby and handed Adara a burping towel.

When Nic set a glass of sparkling white before her, he smiled indulgently at Adara's attempt to pat a belch out of his daughter. "Looks like you know what you're doing. Do you have children?"

The canyon of inadequacy yawned before her, but Gideon squeezed her thigh and spoke with a neutrality she couldn't manage. "We've tried," he said simply. "It hasn't worked out."

"I'm sorry," Nic said with a grimace that spoke of a man wanting to kick himself for saying the wrong thing, but he couldn't have known.

"Not being able to get pregnant seemed like a horrible tragedy for me at first," Rowan said conversationally. "But we wouldn't have Evie otherwise and we can't imagine life without her. We're so smitten, we're like the only two people to ever have a baby, aren't we, Nic?"

"It's true," he admitted unabashedly while he settled into his own chair and absently eased Rowan's bandaged leg to balance across his thigh. His hand caressed her ankle, their body language speaking of utter relaxation and familiarity with each other. "I don't know what I did to deserve such good fortune."

The fierce look of deep love he gave his wife and the tender way she returned it was almost too intimate to witness, but Adara found herself holding her breath as yearning filled her. *I want that,* she thought, but even though she felt Gideon's fingers circle tenderly on the inside of her knee, she didn't imagine for a minute she'd get it.

The penthouse seemed cavernous and chilly when they returned from Greece. It was after midnight when they arrived after what had been a long, quiet flight.

They'd been through a lot since meeting up at the end of her brother's driveway, so she supposed it was natural they'd both withdraw a bit to digest it all, but the hint of tension and reserve Gideon was wearing bothered her.

They'd made love in the middle of the night and again first thing this morning. It had been wonderful as ever, but afterward, as they'd soaped each other in the shower, things had taken this turn into a brick wall.

Unable to get Gideon's look of paternal tenderness toward Evie out of her mind, she'd pointed out how her brother and his wife made adoption look like the most natural thing in the world.

"They do," he had agreed without inflection.

"It's something to think about," she had pressed ever so lightly. "Isn't it?"

"Perhaps."

So noncommittal.

Adara chewed her lip, completely open to the idea herself, but that meant staying married. Forever. To a man who didn't appear as enthused by the idea of children as she was.

He was such an enigma. Returning to New York was a cold plunge into her old marriage to a workaholic who liked his space and only communicated when he had to—if the scene she entered when she left the powder room was anything to go by.

Paul, their chauffeur, was exiting Adara's room where he would have left her luggage. Gideon was coming back to the living room from his own room, where he would have left his own. He swept his thumb across his smart phone as he gave Paul a rough schedule for the next few days, asking her absently, "Are you leaving early for the office with me tomorrow or do you want Paul to come back for you?"

Back to separate lives that revolved around their careers. She looked at her empty arms as she crossed them over her aching chest. "How early is early?"

He grimaced at the clock. "Six? The time change will have me up anyway."

Her too. "That's fine," she said, then thought, *Welcome back, Mrs. Complacent.* She'd obviously forgotten her spine back in Greece.

Paul wished them a good night and left. Gideon came across to set the security panel, then looked down at her as she stifled a yawn.

"Straight to bed?" he asked.

A bristling sensation lifted in the region between her shoulder blades and the back of her neck. His question was one of the shorthand signals they'd developed in this detached marriage of theirs. He was letting her off the hook for sex.

She was exhausted. It shouldn't bother her, but it left her feeling abandoned and without hope for their marriage, a family, or a love like her brother had found.

"Yes," she said quietly, pulling on her cloak of polite endurance to hide how hurt she was. "It's been a long day and tomorrow will be longer." Smooth out all those rough edges, Adara. Make it seem as if you don't have a heart to break.

"Your place or mine?"

"I—what?" She blinked at him, trying to quell the flutter of sensual excitement that woke in her blood. A little embarrassed by how quickly she could bloom back to life, she murmured, "I'm genuinely tired."

Nevertheless, she seesawed with indecision, longing for the closeness she experienced in his arms, but fearful of how neglected she felt when he drew himself apart from her the way he had since meeting her brother.

"I'm freaking exhausted," he admitted with heartfelt weariness, "but we're not going back to separate bedrooms. Mine," he said decisively, catching her hand to lead her there. "Don't bother moving your clothes. The farther away the better."

"Gideon." She chuckled a little as she stumbled behind him, then was distracted by entering a room she'd rarely peeked into. It was scrupulously clean and not just from the housekeeper doing a thorough job in their absence. Gideon was a tidy man. Living on boats forged that habit, he'd told her once. He didn't like clutter. The decorator's palette for the walls was unmarred by paintings or photos. The night table held only a phone dock that doubled as a bedside light.

He stepped into his closet to set his shoes on a shelf.

"You need to find a few days in the next week to come to Valparaiso with me," he told her as he emerged, drawing his belt free as he spoke, then hanging it precisely alongside the rest.

"You've become very dictatorial in the last few days, do you realize that?" She wasn't sure where the cheeky comment came from, but it blurted out even as her voice tightened along with her blood vessels. He was undressing, shedding his shirt without reserve to expose tanned planes of muscle.

"You used to be a pushover. I didn't have to try very hard to get what I wanted. Now I do."

"Does that bother you?" A pang in her lip made her realize she was biting down as she awaited his answer, habitually fearful of masculine disapproval.

He moved toward her, pants open to expose the narrow line of hair descending from his navel, feet bare, predatory with his tight abs and naked chest and sober expression. His nipples were pulled into tight points by the air-conditioned room.

She tensed against a rush of uncertainty and sexual admiration.

"You were thinking of leaving me because you weren't getting what you wanted. That bothers me very much." He cupped the side of her neck and his thumb pressed under her chin, gently tilting her face up. "We can't meet each other's needs if we don't say what they are, so I'm pleased you're telling me what you want. I'm telling you what I want. I like feeling you next to me and waking up to make love to you in the middle of the night. I need to travel and when I do, I want you to know that no one is in my bed except you."

So he hadn't completely left her, this man who so easily found his way to the deepest recesses of her soul. She swept her lashes down to hide how moved she was.

"What do you want, Adara?"

She practically liquefied into one of those women she often saw following him with limpid eyes and undisguised yearning. Her heart was so scarred and scared she could barely acknowledge what she wanted, let alone articulate it, but she managed to say huskily, "You."

Instantly it felt like too huge an admission, like she was confessing to a deeper need than the sexual ones he had. Unable to bear being so completely defenseless against him, she splayed her hands on his chest and tried to lessen the depth of the admission by saying in a stilted murmur, "I'm not a sexual person, but I want to be in bed with you *all the time.*"

Something inscrutable flashed in his expression, quickly masked by excitement as his chest expanded under her touch with a big inhale.

Adara hid her sensitivity in a sexual advance she couldn't have made a week ago, but their constant lovemaking over the last few days had given her the confidence to lean forward and tease his nipple with her mouth.

He grasped a handful of her hair while his erection grew against her stomach, making her smile as she flicked with her tongue and made him groan with approval.

"I thought you wanted to sleep," he said through his teeth.

"We will," she said, scraping her teeth across to his other nipple. "In a bit."

Gideon checked inside the velvet clamshell box, giving the ring one more critical look. The cushion-cut pink diamond was framed on either side by half-carat white diamonds, two on each side. Like Adara, the arrangement had a quiet elegance that wasn't ostentatious or flashy. It was a rare find that held the eye a long time once you noticed it.

When he'd seen it, he'd thought, *Sunrise. A new beginning.* Then his sailor's superstition had kicked in. *Red sky in morning...*

No, there was no warning here. They were proceeding into the horizon on smooth waters, making this ring the perfect marker for their anniversary in a few weeks. He had considered waiting until the actual date to give this to her, but they had a gala tonight and it seemed the right time for Adara to show off a trinket from her husband.

A good time for him to show *her* off, he admitted to himself with a self-deprecating smirk. A funny pang hit him in the middle of his chest as he tucked the box into the pocket of his tuxedo jacket. Adara was the last person to walk around bragging, *Look what my husband gave me.* He was the one who'd coaxed her into accepting this invitation so he'd have an excuse to give her this ring and seal a deal they hadn't quite closed.

Moving into the empty living room to wait for her, he poured himself a drink and gazed at the lights bobbing across the harbor, disturbed by how insecure he still felt about their future.

If sex was an indicator, he had nothing to worry about. Horny as he may have been as a teenager, he hadn't had access to a female body often enough to be this sexually active. Since Greece, however, he and Adara had been living the sort of second honeymoon every man fantasized about. There shouldn't be an ounce of need left in him, but as he dwelled on waking this morning to Adara's curves melded into his side, and the welcoming moan she'd released when he'd slipped inside her, a flame of sexual hunger came alive in him again.

And it was so good. Not just the quantity, but the quality. Her old inhibitions were gone. She was outspoken enough that he could unleash himself with the knowledge that she'd slow him down if she didn't like it. The sex was a dream come true.

So he didn't understand this agitation in himself, especially when she'd become more open in other ways, making him feel even more special and privileged to wear the label "Adara's husband."

Like yesterday, when he'd swung by her office on impulse at lunch, catching her in a meeting. Through the glass wall he'd watched her hold court, standing at the head of a board table surrounded by men and women in suits, all glued to her words. He'd understood their fascination, hypnotized himself by the glow of—hell, it looked like happiness, damn it.

Adara had paused in sketching diagrams on a smart board to point the tip of her electronic pen at each person as she went round the table, soliciting comments, earning nods and building consensus.

Gideon had stood there transfixed, proud, awed, full of admiration while remaining male enough to enjoy the way her shirt buttons strained across her breasts, just a shade tighter than she used to wear them.

Maybe that wasn't entirely voluntary. She'd said something the other day about eating too much and being too sedentary while they were away. He'd dismissed the comment because who gained ten pounds in less than a week? And even if she had, he was quite happy with her curves, thanks. Studying that ready-to-pop button, he'd been torn between intense desire and the sheer pleasure of watching her work.

She'd turned her head and a flush of pleasure had lit up her expression. She'd bit back a smile, mouthing something about "my husband" to the crowd that turned their heads to the window.

He'd been busted and had to meet a pile of names he'd never remember. It had been worth it. Ten minutes later they had locked lips in the descending elevator and wound up doing a "snap inspection" on the family suite at one of her hotels, skipping lunch altogether.

It was all good. She'd even let him listen in to her calls to her younger brothers when she'd broken the news about looking up Nic. A few beseeching, helpless looks at Gideon while she walked through some difficult memories had kept him close, rubbing her back as she choked through the conversations, but afterward there'd been a level of peace in her that told him she was healing old wounds that had festered for years.

Tell her *your* secret, a voice whispered insidiously in his head.

He slipped his hand into his pocket to close his fist on the velvet box. *No.* It wasn't necessary. They were doing great. Her brother was on the other side of the world, not questioning where Adara's husband had come from. Gideon had dodged any curiosity from that quarter and there was no use rocking the boat.

Even though guilt ate him alive at the way Adara couldn't seem to get enough of watching her niece over the webcam. But what could he say? *Yes, let's allow strangers to dig into my past so we can adopt a baby?*

She hadn't brought it up again, but she didn't need to. It was obvious what she wanted and he couldn't do it.

Assaulted by a fresh bout of shame and remorse, he ducked it by glancing at his watch. It wasn't like Adara to keep him waiting.

Moving to her room where the bulk of her clothes and toiletries remained while their architect prepared renovation plans for a new master bedroom, Gideon was aware of a fleeting apprehension. He rarely checked in on her while she was getting ready. There was something about watching a woman put on makeup and dress to go out that triggered old feelings of being abandoned and helpless. He shook off the dark mood that seemed so determined to overtake him tonight, and knocked before letting himself into her room.

She was a vision of sexy dishevelment in a blue gown not yet zipped up her back. Her hair had ruffled from its valentine frame around her face, curling in soft scrolls around her bare shoulders while her flawless makeup gave her lips a sensual glow and added dramatic impact to the distempered expression in her eyes.

"Problem?" he asked, noting the splashes of color where gowns had been discarded over the chair, the bed, and even the floor. Perhaps they should rethink the room sharing. This kind of disorder could wear on him.

"I told you we were eating out too much. I look like a lumpy sausage in every one of these. This one won't even close and my makeup doesn't match…" She was whipping herself into quite a state.

He bit back a smile, aware that he'd be on the end of a swift set down if he revealed how cute and refreshing he thought this tantrum was.

"Maybe the zipper is just caught. Let me try."

"It's not caught. I'm getting fat." She stood still as he tried to draw the back panels of the silk together and work the zipper upward. *Oh, hell.* This wasn't just a snagged zip, and now he'd done it: put himself in the position of having to acknowledge to his wife that she had gained a pound or two. Might as well go up to the roof and jump right now.

"See?" she wailed when he kept trying to drag the zip upward.

"Honestly, I don't see any weight gain," he insisted while privately acknowledging that spending as much time as he did caressing this body, a small and gradual gain would go completely unnoticed. "You're probably just getting your period. Don't women feel puffy then? You must be due for one."

Even as he said it, he was caught by the realization that she hadn't had one since, well, it would have been before they'd become intimate in Greece. At least a month ago.

He bristled with an unwelcome thought that he dismissed before it fully formed.

While Adara stood very, very still, her color draining away in increments.

Instinctively, Gideon took hold of her arm, aware of the way she tensed under his touch, as if she wanted to reject it.

"I, um, never get back to normal right away after a miscarriage," she summed up briskly, not looking at him while her brow furrowed. Her arm jerked to remove his touch as she shrugged into a self-hug. "You're probably right. It's just a particularly bad case of PMS bloating."

Except she'd also mentioned a few days ago that her breasts were sore because her bra was too tight.

Or tender because of something else?

He could see where her mind was going and it scared

him because he really would lose her if she fell pregnant again.

"I use a condom every time, Adara. Every time." He'd been meaning to book a vasectomy, as permanent protection, but hadn't been ready to take the necessary break from sex.

"I know," she said so quickly it was almost as though she was trying to shut down the conversation before the word could be said, but it was there, eating the color out of her so she was a bloodless ghost refusing to look at him.

"So I don't see how—"

"I'm sure it's impossible," she cut in crisply. "And I'd only be a couple of weeks, not starting to put on weight, but I won't be able to think straight until I'm sure." Peeling the delicate straps of her gown off her shoulders, she let it fall to the floor and stepped out of the circle of midnight blue. Her strapless green bra didn't match the yellow satin and lace across her buttocks, but it was a pretty sight anyway as she walked into the bathroom. "I think there's a leftover test in the cupboard..."

She closed him out, the quiet click of the door a punch in the heart. He rubbed his clammy hands on his thighs, insisting to himself it was impossible.

Even though Adara thought it *was* possible.

And she wasn't happy about it.

How could she be?

Bracing his hands on the edges of the bathroom door, he listened for the flush and heard the sink run. Then, silence.

He ground his teeth, waiting.

Oh, to hell with it. He pushed in.

She'd pulled on an ivory robe and stood at the sink, a plastic stick in her hand. It quivered in her shaking grip.

He moved to look over her shoulder and saw the blue plus sign as clearly as she did. *Positive.*

CHAPTER EIGHT

THE VOLUME OF emotions that detonated in Adara was more than she could cope with. Dark and huge as a mushroom cloud, the feelings scared her into falling back on old habits of trying to compress them back into the shallow grave of her heart.

"The test is old, maybe. Faulty," Gideon said behind her.

"It was the second one in the box from when I tested myself a few months ago." She threw the stick away and washed her hands, scrubbing them hard, then drying them roughly before she escaped the bathroom that was luxuriously cavernous, but way too small when her husband was in it with her.

And she was pregnant.

Again.

Shock was giving way to those unidentified emotions putting pressure on her eyes and rib cage and heart. She didn't want him watching as they took her over and she had to face that *it was happening again*.

"You should go," she said briskly, keeping her back to him. "Make my apologies. Tell people I came down with the flu or something." She was distantly aware of the cold, slippery satin on her arms bunching under her fists, her whole being focused on listening for Gideon's footsteps to leave the room the way she was silently pleading for him to do.

"You're kidding, right?"

"I'm not in the mood to go out right now," she said sharply, grasping desperately for an even tone to hide how close she was to completely breaking down.

"Adara, I'm—"

"Don't you dare say you're sorry!" she whipped around to cry. Distantly she was aware of her control skidding out of reach, but the storm billowing to life inside her was beyond her ability to quell. "Maybe this is all the time we have with our children, but I won't be sorry they exist!"

Her closed fist came up against her trembling lips, trying to stem the flood that wanted to escape after her outburst.

"I'm not going anywhere," he said with quiet ferocity, moving toward her with what seemed like a wave of equally intense emotions swirling around him.

Their two force fields crackled with condensed energy as they met, heightening the strain between them. Adara looked into his face, really looked, and saw such a ravaged expression, such brutally contained anguish, her insides cracked and crumbled.

"Whatever happens, I'm staying right here." He pointed at the floor between their feet. "I won't leave you alone again. This is happening to *us*."

Emotion choked her then, overspilling the dam of denial to flood her with anguish and insecure hatred of this body that didn't know how to hang on to babies. Futile hope combined with learned despair to make her shake all over. She couldn't hold it back, had to say it.

"I'm scared, Gideon."

He closed his eyes in a flinch of excruciation. "I know," he choked out, and dragged her into his protective arms, locking her into the safety of a hard embrace. "I know, babe, I know."

It all came out in a swamping rush of jagged tears. She clung hard to him as the devastating sorrow she'd never shown him was finally allowed to pour out of her. Every hurt that had ever scarred her seemed to rise and open and bleed free, gushing until it ran out the toxins, gradually closing in a seal that might actually heal this time.

As her senses came back to her, she realized he'd carried her to the bed where he'd sat down on the edge to cradle her in his lap. He gently rocked her, making comforting noises, stroking her soothingly.

"Sorry," she sniffed, wiping her sleeve across her soaked cheeks. "I didn't mean to lose it like that."

"Shh." He eased the edges of his jacket around her, cuddling her into a pocket of warmth close to his chest. When she looked up at him, she saw his eyes were red and glassy, his mouth twisted in frustrated pain.

"I wish—"

"I know. Me too." He steadied his lips in a flat line, the impact of his one sharp glance telling her he knew deeply and perfectly and exactly what she wished for.

When his hand moved into the folds of her robe and settled low on her abdomen, she covered it with her own, willing their baby to know that Daddy was here too. Her heart stretched and ached.

Gideon swallowed loudly and drew in a heavy breath, things she felt viscerally with him as she rested her head against his heart. This is love, she thought. The knowing without words. The sharing of both joy and pain.

She sat in stillness a long time, wondering if it was true. Were they both here in this bubble of dawning heart-to-heart connection, or just her? Did he love her? A little?

Gideon swore softly and touched the pocket of his

jacket. "Paul," he explained. "I should tell him we're not going. Is your phone in here?"

"On the dock in the living room."

"Here. You need to warm up." He dragged the covers back from the pillows before rising with her in his arms and neatly tucking her in.

Listless after her storm of weeping, Adara turned her back on his departure and let her eyes close and her mind go blank. She couldn't face that he'd walked out so dispassionately after holding her so tenderly.

She must have dozed because she woke still alone in the bed, but the bedside light was on and someone was rustling in her room. She opened her eyes to see Gideon fitting a hanger into one of her gowns and carrying it into the closet. A tiny smile dawned on her mouth as she surreptitiously watched him housekeep for her. He'd changed out of his tuxedo, which was always a pity because he made one look so good, but pajama pants were fine too. Even when they were obviously crisp and new from a package. Had he ever worn pajamas before tonight? she wondered.

His critical eye scanned the room for anything else out of place before he moved to the door.

Her heart fell. He wasn't going to join her. They were back to separate beds and separate lives.

But no. She heard the distant beep of him setting the alarm, then his footsteps padded back to her. He gently lifted the covers and eased into bed behind her.

She sighed and spooned herself into him.

"Did I wake you? I didn't mean to."

"It's okay. I won't be able to sleep anyway. I've already started thinking about doctor's appointments and taking vitamins and…" She sighed with heartfelt sadness. It seemed like such a futile effort to go through it all again. "…everything."

"I put in a call to Karen, letting her know we want an appointment tomorrow," he said, referring to her ob-gyn.

"Oh, um, thank you." His thoughtfulness startled her. She wouldn't have guessed that he even knew her doctor's name. Snugging herself a little more securely into him, she nuzzled the bent elbow beneath her cheek. "One less thing to worry about." Oddly, she found herself amused again. "Especially because you might actually get me an appointment tomorrow. I'd take whatever they offered, something next week if that's all they had, but no one says no to you, do they?"

"Not unless it's the answer I want to hear."

She snickered and turned in his arms. "Why are you like that?" she asked with sudden curiosity. "What made you so bullish?"

"Having nothing and hating it. You should get some sleep." He rolled back to reach for the light switch.

"Honestly, if I try to sleep, I'll just lie here and worry. Tell me something to distract me. What were you like as a child? Before your mom died," she prompted.

"Scared," he admitted, letting her glimpse the flash of angry honesty in his expression before he doused the light and drew her body into alignment with his. Her robe was bunched, her bra restrictive and the fabric of his pajama pants annoying when she wanted to stroke her bare leg on his.

At the same time, she was caught by the single word that didn't seem to fit with a mother he'd described as "maternal."

"Why were you scared?" she asked gently.

Gideon sighed. "I really don't like talking about it, Adara."

"Mmm," she murmured in old acquiescence, then said

into his chest, "But I told you about my childhood, unhappy as it was, and we're closer for it. Aren't we?"

He sighed and rolled onto his back, arms loosening from his hold on her. "My story's a hell of a lot uglier than yours. I don't know much about my mother except what I told you before. I give her credit for somehow getting us into a rented room by the time she died, but before that, I can remember her leaving me in, literally, holes in the wall. Telling me to stay there until she came back. Can you imagine a woman—a child—trying to keep a baby alive while living on the street? I never felt safe."

"Oh, Gideon," she whispered, reaching her hand onto his chest.

He clasped her hand in his, taking care not to crush her fine bones, but was torn between rejecting her caress of comfort and clinging to it. He was sorry he'd started this, but part of him wanted to lay the groundwork. If his past ever came out, he wanted Adara to understand why he'd become who he was.

"I hate remembering how powerless I felt. So when you ask me why I go after what I want however I have to, that's why."

"How did she die?"

The unforgettable image of his mother's weary eyes staring lifelessly from her battered face flashed behind his closed eyes. He opened them to the streaks of moonlight on the bedroom ceiling, trying to dispel the memory.

"She was beaten to death." By a john, if he'd pieced things together in his mind correctly.

"Oh, my God! What happened? Did the police find who did it? Where were you? Did you go into foster care after, or…?"

"I didn't stick around for police reports. I was so terrified, I just ran." All the way onto a ship bound for America, barely old enough to be in school.

"You *saw* her?"

"I told you it was ugly."

Her breath came in on a shaken sob. "I'm so sorry, Gideon. And you saw that other man, too. Your mentor."

"Kristor," he provided. Kristor Vozaras, but now wasn't the time to explain how they'd come to have the same name. "I knew I couldn't live like that, on the docks where crime is a career and a human life worth nothing. No matter what, I had to climb higher than carrying everything I owned in a bag on my shoulder. Whatever it took, I *had* to amass some wealth and take control of my destiny."

She moved her head on his chest, nodding in understanding perhaps. Her warm fingers stroked across his rib cage and she hugged herself tighter into him, the action warmly comforting despite his frozen core.

"I'm glad you didn't limit yourself," she said. "I've always admired you for being a risk-taker. I've never had the nerve to step beyond my comfort zone."

"Oh, Adara," he groaned, heart aching in his chest as he weaved his fingers into hers. "You're the most courageous woman I know." How else could she stare down the probability of another heartbreak with fierce love for their child brimming in her heart?

Maybe he couldn't control whether or not she kept this baby, but he was going to fight like hell to keep her. *No matter what*.

Adara woke in her old bed and thought for a second it was all a dream. She hadn't gone to Greece, hadn't found closeness with her husband...

Then he padded into her room, half-naked, hair rumpled, expression sober as he indicated the phone in his hand. "Karen wants to know if we can get to her office before the rest of her patients start arriving."

It all came rushing back. *Pregnant*. Fear clutched her heart, but she ignored the familiar angst and sat up, nodding. "Of course. I'll get dressed and we can leave right away."

"Um." Gideon's mouth twitched. "You might want to wash your face."

Adara went to the mirror and saw a goth nightmare staring back at her. "Right," she said with appalled understatement.

Gideon confirmed with Karen and left for his own room to dress.

Their lighthearted start became somber as Gideon drove them to the clinic, neither of them speaking while he concentrated on the thickening traffic and the reality of their history with pregnancy closed in on them.

Nevertheless, as urgently as Adara wanted to self-protect right now, she also really, really appreciated Gideon's solid presence beside her. He warmed her with a strong arm across her back as they walked up to Karen's office and kept a supportive hold on her as they stood numbly waiting for the receptionist, still in her street jacket, to escort them into an exam room.

Karen, efficient and caring as she was, was not pleased to learn Adara had miscarried two months ago without telling her.

Adara drew in a defensive breath, but Gideon spoke before she could.

"Let's not dwell on that. Obviously there was no lasting damage or Adara wouldn't be pregnant again. I'd like to focus on what we can do to help her with this pregnancy."

Karen was used to being the one in charge, but shook

off her ruffled feathers as Gideon's obvious concern shone through.

"I'd like to say there was a magic formula for going to term. Mother Nature sometimes has other plans, but we hope for the best, right? Adara, you know the drill." She handed her a plastic cup.

A few minutes later, Adara was in a gown, sitting on the edge of the exam table while Karen confirmed her pregnancy. The frown puckering her brow brought a worried crinkle to Adara's and Gideon's foreheads as well.

"What's wrong?" Adara asked with dread.

"Nothing. Just our tests are more sensitive than the over-the-counter ones and.... Do you mind? I won't do an internal just yet, but can I palpate your abdomen?"

Adara settled onto her back and Karen's fingers pressed a few times before she set the cool flat of the stethoscope against her skin. "Tell me more about this miscarriage you had. When do you think you conceived that time?"

"Um, late April?" Adara guessed. "I can look it up on my phone."

"So fourteen, maybe fifteen weeks ago?" The cool end of the stethoscope was covering a lot of real estate.

"You're not thinking I'm still pregnant from then," Adara scoffed. "Karen, I know a miscarriage when I'm having one."

"I want you to have a scan. Let's go down the hall."

Gideon's face was as tight as Adara's felt. He held her elbow, but she barely felt his touch, limbs going numb with dread. Something was wrong. Really wrong. Karen's sobriety told her that.

Except that, five minutes later, they were looking at a screen that showed an unmistakable profile of a baby's head, its tiny body lounging in a hammock-like curve, one tiny hand lifting above its head to splay like a wishing star.

Gideon cussed out a very base Greek curse. Not exactly appropriate for such a reverent moment, but Adara had to agree. This was unbelievable.

"Is that a recording from someone else?" she asked, afraid to trust her eyes.

"This is why we put you through those procedures during a miscarriage, Adara," Karen said gently. "We look for things like a twin that might have survived. Given that this one has hung on past your first trimester, I'd guess he or she is exactly that. A survivor. This is a very good sign you'll go to term."

CHAPTER NINE

IF THEY'D WALLOWED in disbelief and shock last night, and tension had been thick on their way to see Karen, it was nothing to the stunned silence that carried them back to the penthouse.

Adara sank onto the sofa without removing her jacket or shoes, totally awash in a sea of incredulity. She was afraid to believe it. They might actually have a baby this time. A family.

An expansion of incredible elation, supreme joy, as if she had the biggest, best secret in the world growing inside her, was tempered by cautious old Adara who never quite believed good things could happen to her. She might have a solicitous husband who felt every bit as protective and parental toward his offspring as she did, but he wasn't in love with her. Not the way she was tumbling into love with him.

Shaken, she glanced to where he stood with hands in his pockets, the back of his shirt flattened by his tense stance, the curve of his buttocks lovingly shaped by black jeans, his feet spaced apart for a sailor's habitual seeking of balance.

"What are you thinking?" she invited hesitantly.

"That I can't believe I let you climb down to that beach in Greece. I've been on you like a damn caveman..." He ran a hand over his hair and turned around. His face was lined with self-recrimination. "I wish to hell I'd known, Adara."

She set her chin, not liking the streak of accusation in his tone. Sitting straighter, she said, "I'm not going to apologize for refusing to see a doctor before today." Even though a lot of things would have been different if she had.

Would she and Gideon have come this far as a couple, though?

And was this far enough?

She clenched her hands and pressed her tightened mouth against her crossed thumbs, trying to process how this pregnancy changed everything. While Gideon had shown no desire to discuss adoption, she had kept divorce on the table. Now...

"It's done anyway," he said, pacing a few steps, then pivoting to confront her. "But moving forward, we're taking better care of you. Both of you. I'll start by informing your brothers you'll be delegating your responsibilities. I want you working four-hour days, not twelve. Travel is curtailed for both of us. Chile will have to wait and Tokyo will go on hold indefinitely. The architect needs to start over and you can't be here through renovations, so we'll have to hurry the Hampton place along."

"Karen said everything is normal, that this isn't a high-risk pregnancy," she reminded, tensing at all he'd said. "I can still work."

"Do you want to take chances?"

"Of course not. But I don't want to be railroaded either. You're acting like—"

Imperious brows went up. "Like?"

"Like it's actually going to happen," she said in a small voice. She watched the toes of her shoes point together.

All of her shrank inward, curling protectively around the tiny flicker of life inside her.

"You just said yourself, it's not high risk." His voice was gruff, but she heard the tiny fracture in his tone. He wasn't as steady as he appeared.

"It's just...to make all these changes and tell people... What if something happens?"

The line of his shoulders slumped. He came to sit beside her, angled on the cushion to face her while he pinched her cold fingers in a tight grip. "I'm going to move whatever mountains need moving to ensure nothing does. We're going to have this baby, Adara."

She didn't look convinced. Her brow stayed pleated in worry, her mouth tremulous. A very tentative ray of hope in her eyes remained firmly couched, not allowed to grow.

Gideon clenched his teeth in frustration that sheer will wasn't enough. "I realize you're scared," he allowed.

"I may not be high risk, but there's still a risk," she insisted defensively.

She was breaking his heart. "I'm not disregarding that. But my coping strategy is to reduce the chances of any outcome but the one I want and go full steam ahead."

"And the outcome you want is...a baby?"

"Is there any doubt?" He sat back, unable to fathom that she'd imagine anything else.

"I asked you what you were thinking and you started talking about architects and Tokyo, like this was a massive inconvenience to your jam-packed schedule."

His breath escaped raggedly. "I'm a man. My first thoughts are practical—secure food and shelter. I'm not going to hang my heart out there and admit to massive insecurities at not knowing how to be a father, or reveal that I'm dying of pride."

Her mouth twitched into a pleased smile. "Or own up

to whether you'd prefer a boy or a girl?" Underlying her teasing tone was genuine distress. Adara would have had more value in her father's eyes if she'd been a male, they both knew that.

That wasn't why he took her question like a lightning rod to the soul, though, flinching then forcing his expression smooth. "I've always wanted a girl," he admitted, feeling very much as if his vital organs were clawed from him and set out on display. "So we could name her Delphi, for my mother."

Adara paled a bit and he knew he'd made a mistake. He could practically see her taking on responsibility for never giving him that.

"Babe—"

"It's a lovely name," she said with a strained, sweet smile. "I'd like it very much if we could do that."

But she wasn't like him, willing to bet on long shots. Her cheekbones stood out prominently as she distressed over whether she could come through for him. He didn't know how to reassure her that this wasn't up to her. He had never blamed her, never would.

"Will you wait here a minute?" He kissed her forehead and stood, leaving to retrieve the ring he'd wanted to give her last night. When he returned, he sat on the edge of the sofa again, then thought better and dipped onto one knee. "I bought this to mark our fifth anniversary, but…"

Adara couldn't help covering a gasp as he revealed the soft pink diamond pulsing like a heart stone of warmth from the frozen arrangement of white diamonds and glinting platinum setting.

"No matter what happens, we have each other." He fit the ring on her right hand.

Her fingers spasmed a bit, not quite rejecting the gift, but this seemed like a reaffirmation of vows. She had been prepared to throw their marriage away a few weeks ago and didn't know if she was completely ready to recommit to it, but she couldn't bring herself to voice her hesitations when her ears were still ringing with his words about his mother. Every time she'd lost a baby, his mother had died for him again. Small wonder he didn't wear his heart on his sleeve.

Given time, would it become more accessible?

He kissed her knuckles and when he looked into her eyes, his gaze was full of his typical stamp of authority, already viewing this as a done deal. The impact was more than she could bear.

Shielding her own gaze, she looked at his mouth as she leaned forward to kiss him lingeringly. "Thank you. I'll try to be less of a scaredy-cat if you could, perhaps, let me tell my mother before calling the architect?"

She glanced up to catch a flare of something in the backs of his flecked eyes that might have been disappointment or hurt, but he adopted her light tone as he said, "I'm capable of compromise. Don't drag your feet."

For a woman battling through an aggressive cancer treatment, as Adara's mother, Ellice, was, the quiet of Chatham in upstate New York was probably perfect. For a man used to a nonstop pace through sixteen-hour days, the place was a padded cell.

It's only one afternoon, Gideon chided himself. Adara had tried to come alone, but he had insisted on driving her. Still reeling over yesterday's news, he already saw that the duration of her pregnancy would be a struggle not to smother his wife while his instinct to hover over her revved to maximum.

Letting her out of his sight when they'd arrived here had been genuinely difficult, but he respected her wish to speak to her mother alone. She had yet to bring up the topic of Nic. Ellice had been too sick for that conversation, but with doctor reports that weren't exactly encouraging, Adara was facing not having many more conversations with her mother at all.

Scowling with dismay at the rotten hands life dealt, Gideon walked the grounds of the property that Adara's father had bought as an "investment." The old man had really been tucking his wife away from the city, isolating her as a form of punishment because he'd been that sort of man. Gideon saw that now. Not that it had been a complete waste of money. The land itself was nice.

Gideon wondered if either of Adara's brothers wanted this place when their mother passed. With only a dried-up pond for a water view, it wasn't Gideon's style. He didn't need a rolling deck beneath his feet, but he did like a clear view to the horizon.

Maybe that was his old coping strategy rearing its head. Each time his world had fallen apart, he'd looked into the blue yonder and set a course for a fresh start. One thing he'd learned on the ocean: the world was big enough to run away from just about anything.

Not that he was willing to abandon the life he had here. Not now.

He stilled as he noticed a rabbit brazenly munching the lettuce in the garden. Bees were the only sound on the late-summer air, working the flowers that bordered the plot of tomatoes, beans and potatoes. The house stood above him on the hillock, white with fairy-tale gables and peaks. Below the wraparound veranda, the grounds rolled away in pastoral perfection.

It was a vision of the American dream and he was exactly like that invasive rabbit, feeding on what wasn't his.

His conscience had already been torturing him before

Adara had turned up pregnant. Now all he could think was that he'd be lying about who he was to his son or daughter along with his wife.

But he couldn't go back and undo all the things he'd done to get here. He'd barely scratched the surface of his past when he'd told Adara he'd started working young. Child labor was what it had been, but as a stowaway discovered while the ship was out to sea, he could as easily have been thrown overboard.

Kristor had put him to work doing what a boy of six or seven could manage. He'd swabbed decks and scrubbed out the head. He'd learned to gut a fish and peel potatoes. Burly men had shouted and kicked him around like a dog at times, but he'd survived it all and had grown into a young man very much out for his own gain.

By the time he was tall enough to make a proper deckhand, Kristor was taking jobs on dodgy ships, determined to build his retirement nest egg. Gideon went along with him, asking no questions and taking the generous pay the shady captains offered. He wished he could say he had been naive and only following Kristor's lead, but his soul had been black as obsidian. He'd seen dollar signs, not moral boundaries.

The ugly end to Kristor's life had been a vision into his own future if he continued as a smuggler, though. Gideon had had much higher ambitions than that. He'd been stowing his pay, same as Kristor, but it wasn't enough for a clean break.

Posing as Kristor's son, however, and claiming the man's modest savings as an "inheritance" had put him on the solid ground he'd needed. Kristor hadn't had any family entitled to it. Yes, Gideon had broken several laws in claiming that money, even going to the extent of paying a large chunk to a back-alley dealer in the Philippines for

American identification. It had been necessary in order to leave that life and begin a legitimate one.

Or so he'd convinced himself at the time. His viewpoint had been skewed to basic survival, not unlike Adara's obdurate attitude when he'd first caught up to her in Greece. He'd been cutting himself off from the pain of losing Kristor in exactly the way he'd fled onto Kristor's ship in the first place, running from the grief and horror of losing his mother.

He couldn't say he completely regretted becoming Gideon Vozaras. At sixteen—nineteen according to the fresh ink on his ID—he'd sunk every penny he had into a rusting sieve of a tugboat. He repaired it, ran it, licensed it out to another boatman and bought another. Seven years later, he leveraged his fleet of thirty to buy an ailing shipyard. When that started to show a profit, he established his first shipping route. He barely slept or ate, but people started to call him, rather than the other way around.

Fully accepted as an established business by then, he'd still possessed some of his less than stellar morals. When he was ready to expand and needed an injection of capital, he started with a man known to let his ego rule his investment decisions. Gideon had walked into the Makricosta headquarters wearing his best suit and had his salesman's patter ready. He'd been willing to say whatever he needed to get to the next level.

He'd been pulled up by an hourglass figure in a sweater set and pencil skirt, her heels modest yet fashionable, her black hair gathered in a clasp so the straight dark tresses fell like a plumb line down her spine. She turned around as he announced himself to the receptionist.

He was used to prompting a bit of eye-widening and a flush of awareness in a woman. If the receptionist gave him the flirty head tilt and smooth of a tendril of hair, he missed it. His mouth had dried and his skin had felt too tight.

Adara's serene expression had given nothing away, but even though her demeanor had been cool, his internal temperature had climbed. She had escorted him down the hall to her father's office, her polish and grace utterly fascinating and so completely out of his league he might as well still have had dirt under his nails and the stink of diesel on his skin.

Three lengthy meetings later, he had been shut down. Her father had refused and Gideon had mentally said goodbye to any excuse to see her again. No use asking her to dinner. By then he had her full background. Adara didn't date and was reputed to be holding on to her virginity until she married.

When she had unexpectedly asked to see him a few weeks later, he'd been surprised, curious and unaccountably hopeful. She'd shown up in a jade dress with an ivory jacket that had been sleek and cool and infuriatingly modest, not the sort of thing a woman wore if she was encouraging an afternoon tryst.

"I didn't expect to see you again," he'd said with an edge of frustration.

"I…" She'd seemed very briefly discomfited, then said with grave sincerity, "I have a proposal for you, which may persuade my father to change his mind, if you're still interested in having him as a backer. May I have ten minutes of your time?"

Behind the closed doors of his office, she had laid out what was, indeed, a proposal. She had done her homework. She had information on his financials and future projects that weren't public knowledge.

"I apologize for that. I don't intend to make a habit of it."

"Of what?" he'd asked. "Snooping into my business or running background checks on prospective grooms?"

"Well, both," she'd said with a guileless look. "If you say yes."

He'd been self-serving enough to go along with the plan. The upside had been too good, offering access to her business and social circles along with a leap in his standing on the financial pages. And Adara had made it so easy. She had not only scripted their engagement and wedding, she'd known her lines. Their marriage had been perfect.

To the untrained eye.

He could look back now and see what a performance it had been on both their parts. From the reception to country clubs to rubbing shoulders with international bankers, they had set each other up like improv specialists, him feeding Adara lines and her staying on message.

And she'd conformed to brand like a pro, elevating her modest style to a timeless sophistication that had put both the hotels and his shipyard in a new class. She'd delivered exactly what she'd promised in terms of networking, opportunities and sheer hard work, putting in the late hours to attain the goals he'd laid out.

She had probably thought that's all he'd wanted from her, he realized, heart clenching. It had been, initially, but somewhere along the line he'd begun to care—about a lot of things. She was an excellent cook and she bought him shirts he liked. Whenever they were about to leave for work or an evening event, she invariably smoothed his hair or straightened his tie and said, "You look nice."

Part of him had stood back and called her actions patronizing, but a needier part had soaked up her approval. It was all the more powerful because he had admired her so much.

Adara set a very high standard for herself. Once he'd

fully absorbed that, he'd begun taking it as a challenge to meet and exceed her expectations. Finally comfortable financially, he'd followed her lead and started helping others, selecting charities with thought for who he really wanted to help, creating foundations that benefited young mothers, street kids, and sailors unable to work due to disabilities.

Meanwhile, pride of possession had evolved into something so deep, Adara's seeming to cheat on him earlier this summer had shaken him to the bone.

It wasn't comfortable to be this invested. Sure he was a risk-taker, but not with his emotions. The way his heart had grown inordinately soft, especially in the last weeks, unnerved him, but he couldn't help the way his chest swelled with feeling and pride every time he so much as thought about his wife.

A screen door creaked, drawing his glance. Pressure filled his chest as Adara appeared on the veranda and lifted a somber hand.

He didn't deserve her or any of this, but he'd do anything to keep it.

Adara's emotions were all over the place and that look of intense determination on Gideon's face as he looked up at her gave her a chill near her heart. He seemed so ruthless in that second, exactly as her mother had just accused him of being. She could clearly see the man who'd said, *Whatever it took, I had to amass some wealth and take control over my destiny.*

But maybe her vision was colored by everything she was dealing with. When she started down the stairs, he met her at the bottom, his scowl deepening as he took in her red, puffy eyes. His arm was tender as he crooked it around her and drew her into his solid presence.

"Pretty rough, huh?"

She began to shake. Until the last few weeks, she'd had to keep her sorrows or worries inside her where they ate like acid. Now she had Gideon. Her mother was so wrong about him. He wasn't cold and heartless like her father. Not at all.

"Can we stay out here a few minutes? I feel like I haven't had air in weeks." Not that the summer heat held much oxygen, but he obliged, ambling beside her as she took a turn around the pond. "This would have been a great place to grow up if my father had bought this earlier. And things had been different," she mused, imagining a swing set and a sandbox.

"If Nic had been your father's, you mean?"

Adara choked on a harsh laugh, voice breaking as she said, "Mom asked me if this baby was yours." Her hand moved to protectively cover their unborn child's ears. "What prospective grandmother has that as a first reaction?"

"*I* don't have any doubt he or she is mine," Gideon said with quiet resolution. "But even if you told me right now that it wasn't, I'd stay right here and work through it with you."

Adara checked her step, startled, thinking again, *whatever it took…* "You wouldn't be angry?"

"I'd be angry as hell, but I wouldn't take it out on you and the baby the way your father tortured you and your mother. I wouldn't push you out of my life to fend for yourself, either."

The way his mother had had to make her own way. Adara's surprise and apprehension softened to understanding. He might have a streak of single-mindedness, but there was a marshmallow center under his hard shell.

"You're a bigger person than me. Maybe it's the miscarriages and fear of infidelity talking, but I don't know if I could stay married if you had a baby with someone else."

"You're not sure you want to stay married, as it is, and the only woman having my baby is *you*."

Adara pivoted away from that and continued walking, startled by the shaft of fear his light challenge pierced into her. It would seem her ability to dissemble around him was completely gone. He knew every thought in her head, every hesitation in her heart.

"My mother said she'd understand if it wasn't yours," Adara said with a sheared edge on her tone, recalling how that conversation had spun into directions she hadn't anticipated any better than this one. Holding on to her composure had been nearly impossible as her mother had tried to find parallels in their two lives. "My parents had had a fight and the engagement was off. That's why she slept with Nic's dad. Olief was a journalist flying back to Europe. She had a layover. It was just a rebound thing. The sort of affair all her flight attendant friends were having. Then my father called and the wedding was back on."

"Even though she knew she was pregnant?"

"I guess paternity could have gone either way. She loved my father so she married him and deluded herself into believing Nic was his."

At least you're not in love with your husband. I've always been proud of you for having that much sense, but children are a mistake, Adara. You have no idea how much power a man has over you once babies enter the picture.

Adara had recoiled from her mother's words, finding it distasteful to be accused of having no feelings for Gideon even though that had been her goal for most of her marriage.

"I wanted her to be happy for us and she just took off on a bitter rant about my father." Hearing her mother refer to her grandchild as a "mistake" had been the greatest blow of all. Her entire childhood, void as it had been of parental pride and joy, had crawled out from under the bed, grim and dark and ready to swallow her.

"She's sick," Gideon reminded her.

"I know, but—" *But you lied to him*, she had wanted to say. Maybe her father wouldn't have twisted into such a cruel man if his wife had been honest from the start.

There was no use trying to change her mother at this point though. Challenging her, arguing and judging, were incredibly misplaced. Her mother wasn't just sick, she was dying.

"We'll do better by our child," Gideon vowed, pausing to turn her into him. He lifted her hand to graze his lips across the backs of her fingers. The ring he'd given her yesterday winked at her.

At the same time, his eyes held a somber rebuke. Gideon was a patient man, but this time he wasn't going to let her avoid his silent question. Even as she absorbed his earnest statement, her mother's voice whispered again, *You have no idea how much power a man has over you once babies enter the picture.*

But she wasn't her mother. There weren't any lies between her and Gideon. The secrets and recriminations that had surrounded her growing up, forcing her to close off her heart out of self-protection, were old news. Their child, unpolluted by any of that, gave her a chance to love cleanly and openly.

This fresh start with this man, who already stirred her so deeply, was a chance to build a truly happy life. If she dared believe she was entitled to it and opened herself to letting it happen. It was a huge leap of faith, but she'd taken one in marrying him at all. Maybe she was putting her heart at deep risk, but again and again he'd proven himself to be a man she could trust.

"We will, won't we?" she said in quiet promise.

Relief and a flicker of deeper emotion was quickly transformed into his predominant mask of arrogant confidence. For a second, he'd seemed moved, which made her heart trip, but now he was his typical conqueror self, nearly smug with triumph—which was familiar and oddly endearing, making her want to laugh and ignore her old self trying to warn her that she might be giving up too much too quickly.

But if she had a soupy, awed look on her face, he wore one of fierce tenderness.

"You're so beautiful." The kiss he bent to steal was as reverent and sweet as it was hard and possessive.

Her lips clung to his as he drew away.

"Don't get ideas," he chided, breaking contact from her look of invitation. "We're cut off until you deliver."

"That's you being overcautious. Karen didn't say we couldn't." She was still aggravated that they'd shared a bed last night but hadn't made love. She was nervous about doing anything to jeopardize her pregnancy, but they'd been making love without consequence until now.

"Karen doesn't know how insatiable we are once we get started. Just do me a favor and don't make this harder than it is."

"Pun intended?" She drifted her gaze down his front to the bulge behind his fly.

"This is going to be a very long pregnancy." He gritted his teeth, making her laugh as he guided her inside for an early dinner before driving home.

CHAPTER TEN

AFTER YEARS OF being the one who micromanaged to ensure everything met her father's impossible standards, Adara was forced to let go and trust others to pull off top-notch work with minimal input. It wasn't easy, but she eased up and was pleasantly surprised by her very efficient teams. Despite her working from home for months, only checking in electronically, they were managing great things without her.

Staying away from the office had a drawback, however. Moving through the ballroom decorated in fall colors of gold, crimson and burnt umber, she couldn't help congratulating people on putting together a brilliant event to celebrate the Makricosta chain's thirty-fifth anniversary. They all reacted with great surprise and when Adara met up with Connie, a woman she'd worked closely with for years, she realized why.

Connie rocked back on her four-inch heels. "Wow, I've never seen a woman as pregnant as you act so happy and outgoing. When I got that big, I was a complete cow."

"Oh, I…" Adara didn't know what to say. Had her personality been frozen for so many years that a bit of friendly warmth was remarkable? Or was she really as big as she felt?

"That's meant as a compliment," Connie rushed to say, glancing with horror at Adara's guardian angel, Gideon.

They'd learned to give each other space in the confines of the penthouse as they worked from home, but tonight he was right beside her, his ripped masculinity nearly bursting out of his tuxedo. He didn't complain about their abstinence nearly as much as she did, but he spent a lot of time expending sexual energy in the weight room. It showed, making his presence all the more electric, while Adara's insecurity ballooned to match her figure.

"It's true," he said with a disturbing slide of his hand beneath the fall of her hair. His touch settled in a light, caressing clasp on the back of her neck, making her follicles tighten. "The pregnancy glow isn't a myth. You're gorgeous."

"I look like the *Queen Mary*," Adara sputtered. Her reports from Karen continued to be good, and weight gain was to be expected, but playing dress-up for this evening hadn't been as fun as it used to be. Her hair had developed kinks, she was too puffy for her rings and wearing heels was out of the question. Growing shorter and pudgier while her husband grew hotter and sleeker was demoralizing. All her excitement in having a date night deflated.

"I only meant that you seem very happy. When are you due?" Connie prompted.

Adara couldn't help brightening at the topic of delivering a healthy baby, her misgivings from early in the pregnancy dispelled by her baby's regular jabs and the closing in of her due date. Nowadays her fears were the natural ones of any mother, most specifically that her water would break while she was in public.

But a few minutes later, when Gideon interjected, "We should start the dancing," and guided her toward the floor, her self-consciousness returned. He must have felt her tension. As he took her in his arms, he chided, "Are you genuinely worried about how you look? Because I was being sincere. You're stunning."

Biting off another self-deprecating remark, she chose to be truthful. "We haven't been going out much, so I guess I wasn't expecting so many stunned expressions at how huge I am. And look around, Gideon. Wait, don't. There are far too many women with teensy waistlines and long legs and—"

"None with breasts like yours. Do you think I've looked anywhere but down your dress tonight? Unless it's at your lips. You're not wearing lipstick, are you? That's all you, ripe and pouty and pink. You're sexy as hell."

Said lips parted in surprise. Everything seemed to taste funny these days, lipstick included, so she'd opted for a flavorless lip balm and yes, had noted that even her lips looked fat. She might have bit them together in an attempt to hide them, but his wolfish fixation on her mouth sent tendrils of delight through her.

With a little moue she said, "Really? You're not just saying that?"

With a low growl, he stopped dancing and claimed her mouth with his own.

The kiss was devastating, making her knees want to fold so he had to tighten his hold on her, shifting her to an angle to accommodate her bump. That tilted her head just enough to seal their lips with erotic perfection.

He didn't keep it to a quick punctuation to prove a point, either. Adara put up a hand to the side of his head, thinking, *People are watching,* but he gave her tongue a wicked tag and she couldn't help letting the kiss deepen and continue.

Oh, this man could kiss.

A cleared throat brought her back to reality with a *thunk* that she felt all the way into the flats of her feet. A woman's amused Irish lilt said, "Don't interrupt them. They're adorable."

"Nic," Adara breathed in recognition of her older brother and his wife, growing hot with embarrassment as she realized what a show they'd been putting on. "Hi, Rowan. It didn't sound like you'd make it."

Her brother and his wife were beyond star power, Nic in a tuxedo and Rowan showing off her lithe dancer's body with an off-the-shoulder figure-hugging green gown.

"Evie got over her cold and we wanted to see you again," Rowan said.

Nic leaned in to kiss Adara's cheek before he shook hands with Gideon.

Something passed between the two men that she couldn't quite interpret and didn't get a chance to study. Having kept up via webcam, she and Rowan had become tight friends and that gave them plenty to talk about. The rest of the evening passed in a blur of catching up while also going through the routine of photo ops and speeches for the anniversary celebration, partaking of the buffet, and finally returning to the penthouse exhausted but still keyed up.

"That went well, don't you think?" she asked Gideon as she removed her earrings. They were enchanting cascades of diamonds commissioned to match her ring. She'd almost ruined her makeup when he'd presented them to her before they'd left earlier in the evening, she was so affected by his thoughtfulness.

Gideon made a noncommittal noise.

"No?" she prompted, alarmed that he might have noticed a flaw she'd missed.

"Hmm? No, it was fine. Perfect. Excellent. I'm a bit distracted. Look, you get ready for bed and I'll be in soon. I'd like a nightcap."

"Oh. Okay." Adara's startled confusion was evident, but Gideon didn't attempt to explain himself.

He breathed a small sigh of relief as she disappeared and didn't see the full measure of bracing whiskey he poured for himself or the rabid way he drained it. Despite the burn that promised forgetfulness, he wasn't able to stop replaying his conversation with her brother.

"I'd like a word," Nic had said when both their wives had been drawn across the room by some fashion marvel.

"Now is fine," Gideon had said, keeping one eye on Adara, premonition tightening his muscles.

"Understand first that I've always felt protective of Adara, even when the only thing she had to fear was a nightmare. Knowing what I abandoned her to, I'm sick with myself for not trying to contact her sooner. I'll be on guard for her the rest of my life."

"Reassuring," Gideon had muttered.

"The way you two were arguing at the end of my driveway wasn't," Nic retorted sharply. "When you first arrived in Greece. Not reassuring at all."

Gideon knew better than to show weakness, but he flinched involuntarily. "I thought she was meeting another man. Tell me how you would react if you thought your wife was stepping out on you."

"She wouldn't. But…" Nic shrugged, seeming to accept the explanation for Gideon's temper that day. "Regardless, I'm a man who collects the facts before he reacts."

Gideon had spilled a dry laugh at that point, enjoying the euphemistic phrase "collects the facts." "You mean you had me investigated."

"I don't have to hire people to do my legwork," Nic said disparagingly.

"No," Gideon snorted, wishing for a drink at that point. He'd known from the outset that Nic could be a threat, but he hadn't expected this. Not now when he and Adara had both found such happiness. "What did you learn?" He surreptitiously braced himself.

"What do you think I learned?" Nic asked, narrowing his eyes. "Nothing. Which doesn't surprise you, does it?"

"Of course it does," he'd lied. "I'm all over the internet."

"Gideon Vozaras is," Nic agreed. "He's never made a wrong move. Some of his early business dealings weren't as clean as they could have been, but that's every scrappy young man trying to make his mark. Those men don't usually appear out of thin air, though."

Gideon had calmly stropped his knuckles on his jaw, trying to disguise that he was clenching his teeth. "I'm fairly protective of Adara myself, you know." He flashed a glance from her laughing face to the vague resemblance of her features in her brother's rigid expression.

The other man wasn't intimidated, but there was a watchful respect. He didn't take the danger of Gideon's temper lightly.

"I can see that things between you are different from the way they first appeared," Nic said. "But secrets destroyed my life. I won't let that happen to Adara."

"It's not secrets that destroy. It's the exposing of them. You really want to do that to her when she's found the first bit of happiness she's known since you were children?" He jerked his chin toward the circle of women where Adara was holding court with a flush of pleasure on her face, allowing another woman to feel the baby kick. "Think about what you're doing, Nic."

"No, you think about it," Nic had retorted sharply. "Do you want to make it easy and give me a name? Tell her yourself before I get there? Because I will."

"You want a name? Start with Delphi Parnassus and happy reading." He'd bit out the words and smoothly extricated his wife from the party, claiming she needed her rest.

"Gideon? Are you all right?" Adara asked him, yanking him back to the apartment where she stood in the bedroom doorway, face clean of makeup. Her hair was brushed into sleek waves. She wore one of his silk shirts, the front crossed over her bulging tummy and pinned by her folded arms. Her bump shortened the shirt, offering such a tantalizing view to the tops of her thighs, he reacted like a drug had been injected into his loins.

"Why are you wearing that?" His voice barely made it up from the depths of his chest.

"I've grown out of all my nightgowns," she said with aggravation. "Do you mind?"

"It's criminal, Adara," he admitted with a scrape in his throat, polishing the last of his drink. "We promised not to tease each other. Let me get you my robe."

She tilted her head to a skeptical angle as he brushed past her. "I wasn't trying to tease. But, be honest, are my legs okay? Because they seem swollen. No wonder everyone was appalled."

Be honest, echoed in his head, but the whiskey was burning through blood that had abstained from alcohol the way the rest of him had been going without his wife. Fear, genuine fear of losing her—not this penthouse or their cruise ship or the other properties they owned—edged out conscience or logic. All he wanted was to hold on to her. Tightly.

"It's been a long night. You should be asleep," he told her when she followed him into the bedroom.

"I had a nap before we left," she reminded, scowling as he shook out his robe and held it for her. "Does it strike you that we act less like a married couple these days than a nanny and her charge? You don't need to dress me."

He patiently continued to keep the robe suspended by the shoulders, inviting her to shrug her arms into the sleeves. "If I treat you like a child, it's only to remind myself that's why I can't have you. You know I'm crazy about you."

"But how could you be? Look at me!" She flashed open the shirt she'd been hugging over her front.

He shut his eyes, but not before he took a mental photograph of creamy skin, nipples dark and distended, lush, plump curves and a ripe round belly with an alluring shadow beneath that was *not* concealed by any satin or lace. She was naked and gloriously fertile.

This was why ancient men worshipped the goddess who provided their young.

"You can't even look!"

"For God's sake, Adara." He hung the robe on its hook and moved into his closet to change, needing the distance or he'd bend her over the nearest piece of furniture and *show* her how badly he wanted her. "If I wanted to sleep with a stick, I would have married one. You've always had a nice round ass and I like it. Frankly, it's better than ever in my opinion. See how hot I am for you?"

He paused in hanging his tuxedo pants over a rod and moved into the doorway, showing her his straining erection barely contained by his boxers. Every cell in his body was primed for her and this fight was only shredding what little control he had left. It didn't help that he was also dealing with Nic's threats, feeling his grip on Adara and their life together slipping away. He wanted to cement their connection with a prolonged act of intimacy, but it wasn't possible.

Adara's gaze went liquid as she roamed it lovingly down his form, wetting her lips as she stared at the shape straining against the molding fabric of his shorts.

"I could—"

"I told you, we're in this together," he muttered, turning away from her offer even though it was like wrenching muscle tissue from his bones. But every time he thought of the way she'd gone down on him to protect this pregnancy in the first place, and that he'd resented not having all of her, he felt like the biggest heel alive.

He *was*.

He finished stowing his clothes and stepped into his pajama bottoms, returning to the bedroom to find her buttoning his shirt up her front, not looking at him.

He sighed, but what could he say?

A few seconds later, the lights were out and that delicious ass of hers was pressed firmly into his lap, driving him insane as she wiggled to get comfortable.

"Can I have your arm?" She lifted her head.

He obliged, sliding his arm under her neck the way she liked. As she settled and sighed, he smoothed her hair back from her ear and rested his lips against her nape. His other hand splayed on her belly and he let out a breath as well.

She was still tense though and it made it impossible for him to relax.

"Don't be angry," he cajoled. "This is only for a couple more months."

"Months," Adara cried, nearly ready to burst into tears of frustration. Feeling his erection against her cheeks didn't help.

"Weeks," he hurried to say, even though they both knew it was eight.

"I'm dying." She covered his hand with hers and drew

his fingers into contact with the wet valley between her thighs. "See?"

It was something she couldn't have even contemplated doing half a year ago, but they'd grown close and honest and sexual. Her body wasn't as visual as his when it came to showing how aroused she was, but she wanted him to know how badly she was suffering. She expected him to pull away and scold her, but he surprised her by burying a groan against her neck and stroking deeply and with more pressure. He explored her with the familiar expertise that always drove her directly to the edge.

Her hips rocked instinctively into his caress, then back into that teasing hardness behind the thin shield of fabric pressed against her bottom. His other arm shifted to clamp around her, clasping one full breast and caging her to the wall of his body while he bit her neck. His hips pushed against her and he pressed two fingertips where she felt it most, pinning her in a vise of sheer delight.

A quicksilver shiver was chased by a shudder and then the quaking poured through her, running like fire between her thighs and suffusing her whole body in sparkling waves of pleasure. The contractions were huge and stunning and incredible. She mindlessly prolonged them by grinding his hand between her legs and rocking her hips against his erection, loving everything about this wildly intimate act.

When the paroxysm receded, she gasped for a normal breath.

Gideon's caressing fingers left her. She protested with a little murmur. Her body wanted more and more and more, but a sweet lassitude filled her too. *Now* she felt sexy and adored.

She also realized her neck stung. Gideon had left a love bite there.

Dazed but determined to keep things equal between them, she tried to turn. He swore and rolled away.

"Don't be mad—" She realized there was also a wet patch on her back. Plucking at it, mind hardly able to comprehend how… "Did you—?"

"Yes," he said tightly. She sensed he was lifting his hips to remove his pajama pants. A second later the pants were dragged from beneath the covers and sent flying across the floor. "What the hell did you just do to me? I haven't done that since, hell, I don't think I've ever lost control like that. It's not funny."

Adara couldn't help the fit of giggles as she sat up to remove his shirt. "I was kinda caught up and didn't realize you were with me. That's nice. I'm glad."

"Yeah, I noticed you were enjoying it. That's why I was so turned on, but I didn't mean to lose it completely. Thank God it's dark. I'm so embarrassed—would you quit laughing?" He threw the stained shirt after the pants.

"I'm sorry," she said, unable to help convulsing with giggles as he spooned her into him again, skin to skin. It felt incredible and she snuggled deeper into the curve of his hot body. "Was it good for you?"

"What do you think? It was fantastic, you brat. How's baby? Did I hurt you? I was holding you pretty tight. Good thing you're not going anywhere tomorrow, with that giant hickey on your neck."

"We're fine. Both very happy." She smiled into the dark, melting as he caressed her belly and nuzzled her ear. "But you're not going to leave those clothes on the floor, are you?" she teased.

He stilled and let out a breath of exasperation. "They're fine till—oh, hell, it'll drive me crazy now you've said it and you know that, don't you?" He flung off the covers and gathered the shirt and pants to throw them in the hamper.

"Enjoying yourself?" he asked as he returned to the bed that was shaking with her laughter.

Adara used the edge of the blanket to stifle her snickers. "I'm sorry. That was mean, wasn't it?"

"Yes, it was," he growled, cuddling her into him once more. They both relaxed. "But you must believe me now. About finding you irresistible?"

"I do," she agreed, sleepily caressing the back of his hand where it rested on the side of her belly. Tenderness filled her and she knew she'd never been this happy in her life. "And I can't help thinking... Gideon?"

"Mmm?" he responded sleepily.

"Are we falling in love?" Her heart stopped as she took that chance. It was such a walk straight off a cliff.

That didn't pay off.

Stillness transformed him into a rock behind her. Her postorgasmic relaxation dissipated, filling her with tension. His breath didn't even stir her hair.

Stupid, stupid, Adara. Hadn't she learned a millennium ago not to beg for affection?

"I'm not sure," he said in a gruff rasp.

"It was a silly question. Never mind. Let's just go to sleep. I'm tired." She resolutely shut her eyes and tried to force herself to go lax, to convince him she was sleeping, but she stayed awake a long time, a thick lump in her throat.

And when she woke in the night, he was no longer in the bed with her.

Gideon stood before the living room windows and saw nothing but his past. A dozen times or more over the years, he'd considered coming clean with Adara. Every time he'd talked himself out of telling her his real name, but this time he wasn't finding an easy way to rationalize keeping his secret.

At first it had been a no-brainer. She'd been all business with her proposal, selling him the upside of marriage in her sensible way. The hook had been deliciously baited with everything he'd ever wanted, including a sexy librarian-style wife. Telling her at that point that he was living under a false name would have deep-sixed their deal. Of course, he'd stayed silent.

His conscience had first pinched him the morning of their honeymoon though. She'd come to the breakfast table so fresh faced and shy, barely able to meet his gaze. He'd been incapable of forming thoughts or words, his entire being filled with excited pride as he recollected how trusting and sweetly responsive she'd been.

"Any regrets?" she'd asked into the silence, hands in her lap, breath subtly held.

"None," he'd lied, because he'd had a small one. It had niggled that she was so obviously good and pristine and unquestioning. He'd soiled her in a way, marrying her under pretense.

He hadn't exactly been tortured by his lie, doing what he could to compensate, even forgetting for stretches at a time as they put on charity balls and cut ribbons on after-school clubs. He had let himself believe he really was Gideon Vozaras and Adara legally his wife. Life had been too easy for soul-searching and when the miscarriages had happened, well, things had grown too distant between them to even think of confessing.

Since Greece, however, the jabs to his conscience had grown more frequent and a lot sharper. Honesty had become a necessary pillar to their relationship, strengthening it as much as the physical intimacy. He respected her too much to be dishonest with her.

And he loved her too much to risk losing her.

God, he loved her. Last night when she'd asked him about his feelings, he'd been struck dumb by how inadequate the word was when describing such an expansive emotion. He'd handled it all wrong, immediately falling into a pit of remorse because he was misrepresenting himself. He *had* to tell her.

And he would lose her when he did.

He could stand losing everything else. The inevitable scandal in the papers, the legal ramifications, the hit to his social standing and being dropped from his numerous boards of directors… None of that would be easy to take, but he'd endure it easily if Adara stood by him.

She wouldn't. Maybe she would stick by a man who came from a decent background, but once he really opened his can of worms and she saw the extent of his filthy start, she'd be understandably appalled. It would take a miracle for her to overlook it.

Yet he had no choice, not with Nic breathing down his neck.

His heart pumped cold, sluggish blood through his arteries as he waited like a man on death row, waited for the sound of footsteps and the call of his name.

Adara didn't bother trying to go back to bed when she woke at six. Swaddling herself in Gideon's robe, she went to find him, mind already churning with ways to gloss over her gaffe from last night. If she could have pretended it hadn't happened at all, she would have, but it was obvious she'd unsettled him. She'd have to say something.

She found him standing at the window in the living room, barefoot and shirtless, sweatpants slouched low on his hips. His hair was rumpled, his expression both rav-

aged and distracted when he turned at the sound of her
footsteps.

He didn't say anything, just looked at her as if the greatest misery gripped him.

Her heart clutched. This was all her fault. She'd ruined
everything.

"It was never part of our deal, I know that," she blurted,
moving a few steps toward him only to be held off by his
raised hand.

He might as well have planted that hand in the middle
of her chest and shoved with all his considerable might, it
was such a painfully final gesture of rejection.

"Our *deal*…" He ran his hand down his unshaven face.
"You don't even know who you made that deal with, Adara.
I shouldn't have taken it. It was wrong."

She gasped, cleaved in two by the implication he regretted their marriage and all that had come of it thus far.
He couldn't mean it. No, this was about his childhood, she
told herself, grasping for an explanation for this sudden
rebuff. He'd confessed that before they married he'd had a
low sense of self-worth. He blamed himself for his friend's
death. He had probably convinced himself he wasn't wor-
thy of being loved.

She knew how that felt, but he was so wrong.

"Gideon—" She moved toward him again.

He shook his head and walked away from her, standing
at an angle so all she could see was his profile filled with
self-loathing. A great weight slumped his bare shoulders.

She couldn't bear to see him hurting like this. "Gideon,
please. I know I overstepped. We don't have to go into
crisis."

"It's not *you* that's done anything. You're perfect. And
I wouldn't do this if your brother hadn't threatened to do
it for me," he said through gritted teeth, as if he was dig-

ging a bullet from his own flesh. "I would never hurt you if I had a choice. You know that, right?"

"Hurt me how? Which brother? What do you mean?"

"Nic. He's threatened to expose me to you, so I have no choice but to tell you myself."

His despair was so tangible, her hand unconsciously curled into the lapels of the robe, drawing it tightly over the place in her throat that suddenly felt sliced open and cold. She instinctively knew she didn't want to hear what he had to say, but forced herself to ask in a barely-there voice, "Tell me what?"

He solidified into a marble statue, inscrutable and still, his lips barely moving as he said, "That I'm not Gideon Vozaras."

After a long second, she reminded herself to blink, but she was still unable to comprehend. Her mind said, *Of course you are.* He wasn't making sense.

"I don't... What do you mean? Who is then?"

"No one. It's a made-up name."

"No, it's not." The refusal was automatic. How could his name be made up? He had a driver's license and a passport. Deeds to boats and properties. His name was on their marriage certificate. You couldn't falsify things like that. Could you?

She stared at him, ears ringing with the need to hear something from those firmly clamped lips, something that would contradict what he'd already said.

He only held her gaze with a deeply regretful look. His brow was furrowed and anguished.

No. She shook her head. This was just something he was saying to get out of feeling pressured to love her because...

Her mind couldn't conjure any sensible reason to go to this length of a tale to escape an emotional obligation. Rather, her thoughts leaped more quickly to the opposite:

that it would make more sense to pretend to love in order
to perpetuate a ruse. The nightly news was full of frauds-
ters who pretended to love someone so they could marry
a fortune.

Her throat closed up and she took a step backward,
recoiling from the direction her thoughts were taking. It
wasn't possible. She was being paranoid.

But she couldn't escape the way tiny actions—especially those taken since she'd asked for a divorce—began to
glow with significance. They landed on her with a weight-
less burn, clinging like fly ash.

I fired Lexi.

*I had self-worth because you gave it to me. People re-
spected me.*

His sudden turn toward physical attentiveness and nonstop seduction. No baby wasn't a deal breaker, he'd said.

But adoption wasn't worth talking about *because that
would require a thorough background check.*

Her heart shriveled and began to hurt. She brought a
protective hand to her belly. He must have thought he'd
won the lottery when she had turned up pregnant and their
marriage was seemingly cemented forever.

*I wouldn't do this if your brother hadn't threatened to
do it for me.*

He would have let her just keep on believing he was
Gideon Vozaras.

"Who are you?" she asked in a thin voice, thinking,
This is a dream. A bad one. "Where did Gideon Vozaras
come from?"

He scowled. "I took Kristor's surname so I could pose
as his son and collect what savings he had. My first name
came off the cover of a Bible in a hotel room." He jerked
a shoulder, face twisting with dismay. "Sacrilegious, I
know."

A fine tremor began to work through her and she realized she was cold. Too bad. There was no cuddling up to her husband for a warm hug. This man was a stranger.

The truth of that struck to her core.

"We're not married," she breathed. Somehow it was worse than all the rest. She was a good girl. Always had been. She'd saved herself for marriage. They'd had a wedding. Her father had finally approved of something she'd done. There were photos of them taking vows. All those witnesses had seen…a joke. A lie.

It was all a huge, huge lie.

Gideon—*the stranger*—flattened his mouth into a grim line. "In every way that matters, I am—"

"Oh my *God*," Adara cried, shaking now as her mind raced through all that this meant. He must have called his bookie and put everything he owned on a long shot when she turned up in his office asking to marry him. What a fantastic idiot she was! "You never loved me. You didn't even *want* me."

"Adara." His turn to take a step toward her and it was her turn to back away.

Whatever it took, I had to amass some wealth…

She remembered exactly how shocked he'd looked when she'd suggested marriage, how quick he'd been to seize the chance. How accommodating and willing to go with the flow of everything she asked, from waiting until the wedding night to keeping separate bedrooms.

She covered her mouth to hold back a scream. And last night she'd had to *beg* him to touch her. She'd had to plead because he'd been avoiding lovemaking—

Humiliation stung all the way to her soul.

"You've been laughing at me all this time, haven't you?" she accused as emotion welled in her. Hot, fierce emotion that made her tremble uncontrollably. "No wonder you fought so hard to stay married. Where would all of this go if we divorced?" She flung out an arm to encompass the penthouse and work space and high living they enjoyed. "Who would half of it go to? Thank God I was pregnant, huh, Gid—" She choked, aware she didn't even know his real name. "Whoever the hell you are."

Gideon's world was dissolving around him, but it had nothing to do with penthouses in the top of a tower. "Calm down," he said, grasping desperately at control, when he wanted to crush her to him and show her how wrong she was. "You're going to put yourself into labor. We can get through this, Adara. Look how far we've come since Greece."

It was a weakly thrown life ring, one that failed to reach her.

"How *far?*" she cried, rising to a new level of hysteria. "I thought we were learning to be *honest*. You might have mentioned this little secret of yours."

"I'm telling you now," he insisted.

"Because my brother extorted it out of you! If he hadn't, I'd still be in the dark, wouldn't I?"

He grappled for a reasonable tone, worried about the way her face was reddening. Her blood pressure wasn't a huge issue, but they were monitoring it. She'd complained of breathlessness a few times and her chest was heaving with agitation.

"We were happy," he defended.

"The mark is always happy when she's well and truly duped," she cried. "How could you do that to me? To anyone? What kind of man *are* you?" She rushed him, looking as if she intended to pulverize him.

He caught her arms and held her off. He didn't care about his own safety. She could pummel him into the dirt if it made her feel better, but she and the baby were everything. If she didn't get hold of herself, she was going to hurt one or the other or both.

She struggled against his hold, but he easily used his superior strength to back her into the sofa, where he firmly plunked her into it, saying sternly, "Calm *down*."

"I have a criminal liar invading my home! I'm entitled to—oh, you bastard! I hate you." She tried to rise and strike at him. "How could you do this? How?"

He forced her back into the softness of the cushions. "You're giving me no choice but to walk out of here," he warned. "I'd rather stay and talk this out."

"And talk me round, you mean." She slapped at his touch. "Get out of here then, you scumbag."

The names didn't matter. The betrayal and loathing behind the words sliced him to the bone. He couldn't bear to leave her hating him like this, but even as he stood there hesitating, she was trying to rock herself out of the cushions and swipe at him at the same time, breasts heaving with exertion.

For her own safety, he couldn't stay. Every step to the door flayed a layer of skin from his body, but he moved away from her, waiting for a pause in her tirade of filthy names to say, "It was never my ability to love that was in question, Adara."

"You should have said it last night when I asked. I might have fallen for it then, but not now, you phony. Get out. And don't ever expect to see this child."

That was meant as a knife to the heart and it landed right on target, stealing his breath and almost taking him back into the fight, but as he glanced back, he could see how pale and fraught she was, obviously going into a kind of shock. He grabbed his cell phone on the way to the elevator and placed a call to Nic as the doors closed him out of his home.

"Get over here and make sure she doesn't lose our baby over this."

CHAPTER ELEVEN

ADARA HAD A very high tolerance for emotional pain, but this went beyond anything she'd ever imagined. Even the news that her mother unexpectedly succumbed to her cancer didn't touch it. Maybe because she'd prepared herself for that loss, she was able to get through it without falling apart, but in truth, she was pretty sure her heart was too broken to feel it.

At least dealing with the funeral and out-of-town family gave her something to concentrate on besides the betrayal she'd suffered. Moving like a robot, she went through the motions of making arrangements while all three of her brothers stood as an honor guard around her.

Nic hadn't been sure of his reception, but she didn't blame him for bringing Gideon's lies to her attention. Nic understood how unacceptable and wrong hiding the truth was. He'd been right to force it into the light.

As for the man she had thought of as her husband, she saw him once. He came to the service, not making any effort to approach her, but she felt his eyes on her the whole time.

After the first glimpse, she couldn't bear to look at him. All she could think about was how easy she'd been for him in every way, screwing up her courage to propose. Giving in to hormones and his deft proficiency with the female body. Feeling so proud to have a man at all, especially one who made women envy her. He'd played on all her biggest weaknesses, right up to his supposed shared pain over the miscarriages.

Here her heart stalled, torn apart by the idea he'd been faking his grief. It was too unfair, too cruel. Was even a shred of what he'd told her about his childhood true?

That thought weakened her, making her susceptible to excusing his behavior, so she cut herself off from considering it. She'd leaned on Theo's wide chest and focused on the inappropriate dress worn by Demitri's date. Leave it to her youngest brother to bring an escort to his mother's funeral.

Her brothers coped in very different ways, but they stayed close, protective in their way, getting her through those first few weeks of loss so she didn't have to dwell on the fact her marriage had been an unmitigated fraud.

But solitude arrived when they went back to work and Nic went home with his wife and baby.

Adara had to say one thing about her fake of a husband. He'd provoked a new sense of responsibility in both her younger brothers. Demitri was still a wild card, but he hadn't missed a single appointment in his calendar since he'd been informed of her pregnancy, and while she wasn't always comfortable with his newfangled marketing campaigns, they seemed to be working.

As for Theo, well, the middle child was always a dark horse, keeping things inside. Epitomizing the strong silent type, he didn't socialize or like people much at all. That's why she was so surprised when he dropped by the penthouse on his way home from the airport, took off his jacket and asked if he could make himself coffee.

"I can make it," she offered.

"Stay off your feet."

She made a face at his back, tired of a lifetime of being bossed by men, but also tired in general. Elevating her ankles again as she'd been instructed, she went back to studying a spreadsheet on her laptop.

"Why are you working?" he asked when he came back to pace her living room restlessly, steaming cup in his hand.

"I'm not checking up on you, if that's what you think."

"Go ahead. You won't find any mistakes. I don't make them."

She lifted her brows at his arrogance, but he only held her gaze while he sipped his coffee.

"We were never allowed to, were we?" he added with a lightness that had an inner band of steel belting.

Her first instinct was to duck. Were they really going there?

An unavoidable voicing of the truth had emerged in her dealings with her siblings once she'd pulled Nic back into their lives. With the absence of their mother's feelings to worry about, perhaps they were all examining the effects of silence, asking questions that might hurt but cleansed ancient wounds.

"No, only Demitri was allowed. And he made enough for all of us," she added caustically, stating another unspoken truth.

Theo agreed to that with a pull of one corner of his mouth before he paced another straight line across her wall of windows. "Which leaves me wondering if I should let you make this one."

Adara set aside her laptop and folded her hands over her belly. "Which one is that?"

"The same one our father made."

A *zing* of alarm went through her, more like a paralyzing shock from a cattle prod, actually, leaving her limbs feeling loose and not her own. She clumsily swung her feet to the floor but didn't have the strength to stand.

"If you're talking about Gid—that man who pretended to be my husband, he *lied*, Theo. That's why our father was the way he was. Because Mother betrayed him. Trust me when I tell you it leaves a bitterness you can't rinse out of your mouth." Her heart ached every day with loss and anger and hurt.

"Our father was a twisted, cruel bastard because he never forgave her. Is that what you're going to do? Punish Gideon and take it out on his baby?"

Adara set her hand protectively on her belly. "Of course not!" She wasn't being that cutting and heartless. Was she?

"Are you going to let him see his child, then?"

She swallowed, unable to say a clear yes or no. The thought of seeing Gideon made her go both hot and cold, burning with anticipation and freezing her with fear that he'd hurt her all over again. She couldn't bear the thought of facing him, knowing how he'd tricked her while part of her still loved the man she'd thought of as her husband. Deep down she knew she couldn't deny her child its father, but the reality of sharing custody with a charlatan was too much to contemplate.

Therefore, she was ignoring the need to make a decision, putting it off until she couldn't avoid it any longer.

"He'll always be in your life in one way or another. Are you going to twist the knife every chance you get? Or act like a civilized human being about it?"

"Stop it," she said, hating the way he was painting her as small and vindictive. He didn't understand how shattering it was to have your perceptions exploded like this. How much like grief it was to lose the man you loved not to an accident, but to duplicity. She rocked herself off the sofa and onto her feet. "Why are you defending him? What do you expect me to do? Lie down and let him wipe his feet on me the way our mother did? He abused my trust!"

"But he didn't abuse you. Did he?" It was a real question, one with a rare thread of uncertainty woven into his tone.

"Of course not," she muttered, instantly repelled by even the suggestion. Why? What did she care what other people thought of Gid—that man?

"You make it sound like you wouldn't have stood for it, but we all hung around for it," Theo pointed out bluntly.

She didn't answer. There was nothing to say to that ugly truth. If she could see her toes, she knew they'd have been curled into the carpet.

"I was scared for you, you know," Theo said gruffly. "When you married him. We didn't know him, who he was, what he was capable of. I watched him like a hawk, and I would have stepped in if he'd made one wrong move, but he didn't. And you..." He narrowed his eyes. "You changed. It took me a while to figure out what was different, but you weren't scared anymore. Were you?"

Adara swallowed, thinking back to those first weeks and months of marriage, when she had been waiting for the other shoe to drop. Gradually she'd begun to trust that the even temper her husband showed her was real. If the ground was icy, he steadied her. If a cab was coming, he drew her back.

And she remembered very clearly the last time her father had touched her in anger, a few weeks after her wedding. She'd been trying to explain why the engineer needed to make changes to a drawing and he'd batted the pencil from her hand, clipping her wrist with his knuckles.

Mere seconds later, Gideon had walked into the room, arriving to take her home.

Her father had changed before her eyes, remaining as

blustery as always, but becoming slightly subdued, eyeing her uneasily as she retrieved her pencil and subtly massaged her wrist.

She hadn't said a word, of course, merely confirmed with her father that they were finished for the day before she'd left with Gideon, but she'd realized she had a champion in her husband, passive and ignorant though he was to his role. As long as she had him, she had protection. Her father had never got physical with her again.

That sense of security had become precious to her. That's why she'd been so devastated when she had thought Lexi had snatched him from her, and now the hurt was even worse, when she knew his shielding tenderness had never existed at all.

"It was in his best interest to keep me happy," she said, voice husky and cold. "I was the facade that made him look real."

"Maybe," Theo agreed, twisting the knife that seemed lodged in her own heart. "In the beginning. But… Adara, I would have done everything I could to help you through this pregnancy regardless of any threats from Gideon. You're my sister. I know what this baby means to you. But the way he spoke to me when he called, that was not just a father speaking. He was worried about both of you. Protective. I've always had a healthy respect for him, but I was intimidated that day. There was no way I was going to be the weak link that caused anything to happen to you or this baby."

"Welcome to my world where you buy the snake oil and convince yourself it works," she scoffed.

He stopped his pacing to stare accusingly at her. "You fooled me, you know. Both of you. I looked at how happy you two were in the last few months and I was *hopeful*. I thought finally one of us was shaking off our childhood and making a proper life for herself. You made me start to believe it was possible, and now—"

"He *lied,* Theo."

"Maybe he had reason to," he challenged and moved to retrieve an envelope from the pocket of his raincoat. He dropped it on the coffee table in front of her. "That's from Nic. He asked me to come through on my way back from Tokyo and bring it to you. I didn't read it, but Nic pointed out that he changed his own name to escape his childhood so he shouldn't have judged Gideon for doing it. Maybe you shouldn't, either."

"He didn't convince Nic he'd married him, did he? He didn't sleep with Nic and make him believe in a fantasy!" He hadn't resuscitated Nic's heart back to life only to crush it under his boot heel. She could never, ever forget that.

"He didn't take over the hotels the way he could have," Theo challenged. "If anything, he kept us afloat until now, when we're finally undoing the damage our father did. He could have robbed us blind the minute the will was read. We all owe him for not doing that. I haven't slept," Theo added gruffly. "Call me later if you want any clarification on that balance sheet for Paris."

He left her staring at the envelope that seemed less snake oil and more snake, coiled in a basket and ready to strike the moment she disturbed the contents.

Throw it in the incinerator, she thought. Theo didn't know what he was talking about. The difference here was that their mother had loved and lied while Gideon had purely lied. He didn't love her. That final, odd comment he'd made about his ability to love not being in question had been a last-ditch effort to cling to the life he had built *no matter what he had to do.*

Thinking of their child growing up in the same hostile atmosphere she'd known made her stomach turn, though. She didn't want to wield her sense of betrayal like a weapon, damaging everyone close to her.

Maybe if she understood why he'd done it, she'd hate him less. Theo was right about Gideon always being connected to her, no matter how awkward that would be. She would have to rise above her bitterness and learn to be civil to him.

Lowering to the sofa, she opened the envelope and shook out the printed screen shots of clippings and police reports and email chains. Through the next hours she combed through the pieces Nic had gathered, fitting them into a cracked, bleak image of a baby born from a girl abused by her stepfather. The girl's mother had thrown her out when she became pregnant. A ragtag community of dockworkers, social services and street people had tried to help the adolescent keep herself and her beloved son clothed and fed.

It seemed Gideon had been truthful about one thing: his mother had possessed a strong maternal instinct. Delphi had been urged more than once to put him up for adoption, but was on record as stating no one could love him as much as she did. While not always successful at keeping a roof over their heads, she'd done all a girl of her age could, working every low-end, unsavory job possible without resorting to selling drugs or sex.

Sadly, a nasty element working the docks had decided she didn't have to accept money for her body. It could be taken anyway. Adara cried as she read how the young woman had met such a violent end. She cried even harder, thinking of a young boy seeing his mother like that, beaten and raped and left to die.

Blowing her nose, she moved on to the account of Delphi's friends from low places doing the improbable: going to the police and demanding a search for Delphi's son. Here

Nic had done the legwork on a trail that the police had let go cold. Taking the thin thread of Delphi's last name, he had tied it to a crew list from a freighter ship dated years later. The name Vozaras was there too, but the first name was Kristor.

A side story took off on a tangent about smuggling, but nothing had been proven. The only charges considered had been for underage labor and somehow that had been dropped.

Adara wiped at a tickle on her cheek as she absorbed the Dickensian tale of a boy who should have been in school, learning and being loved by a family. He'd been aboard a freighter instead, doing the work of a man. No wonder he was such a whiz with all things sea related. He had literally grown up on a ship.

Considering the deprivation he'd known, the loss of his mother and lack of—as he'd told her himself once—anyone caring about him, it was a wonder he'd turned into a law-abiding citizen at all. When she thought of all the little ways he had looked out for her, even before Greece, when he'd do those small things like make sure she was under the umbrella or huge things like finagle her into running the hotel chain despite her father's interference from the grave, she was humbled.

Perhaps he had been self-serving when he'd agreed to marry her, but he'd treated her far better than the man who was supposed to love and care for her ever had.

She'd been avoiding thinking back to Greece and all that had happened since, but she couldn't ignore his solicitude and protectiveness any longer. He could have let her risk her neck climbing down that cliff alone; he could have sent her to her brother's alone. His actions had gone above and beyond those of a man only wanting to manipulate.

And when she recalled the warmth in his smile when

he'd gazed at Evie, the pained longing in him when he'd talked about the loss of their own babies...

Even after that, when they'd been waiting out this pregnancy here, more than once she had glanced up unexpectedly and found a smile of pride softening his face. Half the time his eyes were on her bulging stomach, not even aware she was looking at him. Other times he was looking at her and always seemed to grin a bit ruefully after, as if he'd been caught in a besotted moment and felt sheepish for it.

He couldn't fake all of that. Could he? His shattered control, just from touching her that last night, hadn't been the response of a man who was unmoved and repulsed. He'd been as swept away as she had. Laughing, teasing, pulling her into him afterward as though she was his cherished stuffie.

She swallowed.

Theo was right about a few things. Despite the lack of a truly legal marriage, Gideon had been behaving like a husband and father so well, even she had believed they had a chance for a lifetime of true happiness.

Perhaps they had.

If she hadn't ruined it by throwing him out for daring to reveal the darkest secrets closest to his soul.

She bit her lip, distantly aware of the physical pain, but the emotional anguish was far sharper. It wasn't fair to imagine there had been another time in their lives when they'd been close enough to risk telling each other something so deeply personal. Look how long she'd masked that her father was a brute. If Gideon hadn't followed her to Greece, she might never have told him about that last miscarriage. He'd had as much right to know about their loss as she had to know his name.

Oh, God.

Scanning the scattered papers with burning eyes, she

wondered if he even knew this much about himself. She hurt so badly for him, completely understanding why he'd wanted to escape being the boy who had gone through all this and become someone else.

She hadn't even given him a chance to tell his side of things. She *was* just like their father—a man she had never forgiven for the hurts he'd visited on all of them.

But after acting just like him, she couldn't ask Gideon for another chance. Not when he'd taken such a huge risk and she'd condemned him for it. How could she expect him to forgive her when she'd never forgive herself?

It killed Gideon to do it, but he put together the necessary declaration of his identity and the rest of what was needed to dissolve their fake marriage. Then he had the paperwork couriered to the penthouse.

Adara wasn't taking his calls. The least he could do was make things easier on her. Karen was reporting that everything was progressing fine, but all he could think was that Adara must be devastated by the loss of her mother on top of what he'd done to her. He was eating his heart out, aching every moment of every day, but he couldn't badger her for a chance to explain himself. What was there to explain? He'd lied.

He wasn't her husband.

So why was he personally reframing the apartment below their penthouse, executing the plans his architect had drawn up once they'd decided to stay in the city and expand their living space to two floors, creating a single master bedroom with a nursery off the side?

Because he was a fool. It was either this or climb on the next boat and never touch land again. The option kept tapping him on the shoulder, but for some reason he couldn't bring himself to take it.

He couldn't be that far away from the woman he regarded as his wife.

He stopped hammering, chest vibrating with the hollowness of loss.

Actually, that was his cell phone, buzzing in his pocket.

Setting aside the hammer, he saw the call was from Adara. His heart stopped as he hurried to remove his leather glove and accept the call.

"Babe?" The endearment left his lips as if he was sleeping beside her.

Nothing. Damn, he'd missed it. He started to lower the phone and reconnect, but heard a faint "You said you'd be here."

"What?" He brought the phone to his ear.

"You said I wouldn't have to go through this alone and that you'd be with me every second and the pains have started but *you're not here*. You lied about that too."

Adrenaline singed a path through his arteries and exploded in his heart. "You're in labor?"

A sniff before she gritted out a resentful "Yes."

He threw off his hard hat and safety goggles. "Where are you?"

Silence.

"Adara!"

"In the apartment," she groused. "And you're not."

"Where in the apartment?" he demanded, running up the emergency stairs two at a time to the service entrance. "Don't scream if you hear someone in the kitchen. It's me. Did you change the code?"

"What? How are you in the kitchen? I'm in the bed—" She sucked in a breath.

He stabbed the keypad and the light went green.

He shot through the door, into the kitchen, and strode to her room, ears pounding at the silence. Her bedroom looked like a crime scene with clothes tossed everywhere, nylons bunched on the floor, slippers strewn into the corner, but no Adara. He checked the bathroom.

"Where are you?" he demanded.

"Here," she insisted in his ear. "By the bed."

He'd been on both sides of her bed and rounded it again, but she wasn't there. "Damn it, Adara." He lowered the phone and shouted, "Where *are* you?"

"Here!" she screamed.

Her voice came from the other side of the penthouse. He ran through the living room to his room. *Their* room. A faint part of him wanted to read something significant into that, but when he entered, he didn't see her there either.

Was she torturing him on purpose—?

Oh, hell. He spotted one white fist clinging to the rumpled blanket. Her dark head was bent against the far side of the mattress.

"Oh, babe," he said, and threw his phone aside to come around to where she knelt, bare shoulders rising and falling with her panting breaths. She had a towel around her, but nothing else. Her hair was dripping wet.

"Okay, I'm here. You're sure this is just labor?"

"I know what labor feels like, Gideon."

"Okay, okay," he soothed. "Can I get you onto the bed?" He was afraid to touch her. "Are you bleeding?"

"No, but my water broke. That's why I had a shower." She kept her forehead buried against the side of the mattress. "I'm not ready for this. It hurts. And I'm so scared the baby will die—"

"Shh, shh." He stroked her cold shoulder with a shaky hand. "Have you felt the baby move?"

She nodded. "But anything could happen."

"Nothing is going to happen. I'm right here." He prayed to God he wasn't lying to her about this. Shakily he picked up her phone and ended their call. "Have you called the ambulance? Karen?"

"No." She swiped her eyes on her bare arm, and peeked over her elbow at him, gaze full of dark vulnerability and a frightened longing that put pressure on his lungs. "I just thought of you, that you said you'd be here with me. Where were you? How did you get here so fast?"

"Downstairs," he answered, dialing Karen's personal line from memory. In seconds he had briefed her and ended the call. "She'll meet us at the hospital. An ambulance is on the way."

"Oh, leave it to you to get everything done in one call."

"Are you complaining?" He eased her to her feet and onto the bed, muscles twitching to draw her cold, damp skin against him to warm her up, but he drew the covers over her instead. Sitting beside her on the bed, he rested one hand on the side of her neck and stared into her eyes. "You know me. I won't settle for anything less than the best."

Her, he was not so subtly implying.

Her brow wrinkled and her mouth trembled. She looked away.

Now wasn't the time to break through the walls she'd put up between them though. He reluctantly drew away and stood.

"Where are you going?" she asked with alarm.

"Have you packed a bag?"

"No, but… You're coming with me, aren't you?" she asked as he moved to find an empty overnight case. "To the hospital?"

"You couldn't keep me away. Not even if you had me arrested." She must have wanted to. Why hadn't she? He glanced over and her hand was outstretched to him, urging him with convulsive clasps to return to her side. Her expression strained into silent agony.

He leaped toward her and grabbed her hand, letting her cling to him as he breathed with her through the contraction, keeping her from hyperventilating, staring into her eyes with as much confidence as he could possibly instill while hiding how much her pain distressed him. He hated seeing her suffer. This was going to kill him.

She released a huge breath and let go of his hand to throw her arm over her eyes. "I'm being a weakling about this. I'm sorry."

"Don't," he growled. Her apology made him want to drop to his knees and beg her for forgiveness. He packed instead, throwing in one of his shirts as a nightgown, a pair of her stretchy sweats, her toothbrush and the moisturizer she always used. "Slippers, hairbrush, lip balm. What else?"

Adara watched him move economically through the space they'd shared, demonstrating how well he knew her as he unhesitatingly gathered all the things she used every day: vitamins, hair clips, even the lozenges she kept by the bed for if she had a cough in the night.

"I—" *read about your mother,* she wanted to say, but another pain ground up from the middle of her spine to wrap around her bulging middle. She gritted her teeth and he took her hand, reassuring her with a steady stare of unwavering confidence and command of the moment, silently willing her to accept and ride and wait for it to release her from its grip.

His focus allowed her to endure the pain without panic. As the contraction subsided, she fell back on the pillow again, breathing normally.

"Those are close," he said, glancing at the clock.

"They started hours ago. I was in denial."

She got a severe look for that, but he was distracted

from rebuking her by the arrival of the paramedics. Minutes later, she was strapped to a gurney, her hand well secured in Gideon's sure grasp as she was taken downstairs and loaded into the ambulance.

From there, nothing existed but the business of delivering a baby. As promised, Gideon stayed with her every second. And he was exactly the man she'd always known—the one who seemed to know what she wanted or needed the moment it occurred to her. When the lights began to irritate her, he had them lowered. When she was examined, he shooed extra people from the room, sensitive to her inherent modesty. He kept ice chips handy and gathered her sweaty hair off her neck and never flinched once, no matter how tightly she gripped his arm or how colorfully she swore and blamed him for the pain she was in.

"I can't do it," she sobbed at one point, so exhausted she wanted to die.

"Think of how much you hate me," he cajoled.

She didn't hate him. She wanted to, but she couldn't. She loved him too much.

But she was angry with him. He'd hurt her so badly. It went beyond anything she had imagined she could endure. And then she'd found out *why* he'd lied and it made her hate herself. She was angry most about his leaving her. Living without him was a wasteland of numbness punctuated with spikes of remembered joy that froze and faded as soon as they were recalled. He'd left her in that agonizing state for weeks and...

Another pain built and she gathered all her fury and betrayal, letting it knot her muscles and feed her strength and then she *pushed*...

Gideon stood with his feet braced on the solid floor, but swayed as though a deck rocked beneath him. His son, swaddled into a tight roll by an efficient nurse, wore a disgruntled red face. He wouldn't be satisfied with the soothing sway much longer, not when his tiny stomach was empty. He kept his eyes stubbornly shut, but let out an angry squawk and turned his head to root against the edge of the blanket.

Why that made Gideon want to laugh and cry at the same time, he didn't know. Maybe because he was over-tired. He hadn't slept, his body felt as if he'd been thrown down a flight of stairs, his skin had the film of twenty-four hours without a shower and his own stomach was empty. This was like a hangover, but a crazy good one that left him unable to hold on to clear thoughts. And even though he had a sense he should be filled with regret, he was so elated it was criminal.

"I know, son," he whispered against the infant's unbe-lievably tender cheek. "But Mama is so tired. Can you hang on a little longer, till she wakes up?" He tried a different pattern of jiggling and offered a fingertip only to have it rejected with a thrust of the baby's tongue.

The boy whimpered a little more loudly.

"I'm awake," Adara said in the sweet, sleepy voice he'd been missing like a limb from his body.

Gideon turned from the rain beyond the window and found her lying on her side, her hand tucked under the side of her face as she watched him. The tender look in her eyes filled him with such unreasonable hope, he had to swallow back a choked sob. He consciously shook off the dream that tried to balloon in his head. *Get real,* he told himself, recalling why he was missing her so badly. His heart plummeted as though he'd taken a steel toe into it.

"He's hungry?" she asked.

"Like he's never been fed a day in his life."

Adara smirked and glanced at the clock, noting the boy

was barely four hours into his life. With some wincing and a hand from Gideon, she pulled herself to sit up.

"Sore?" He glanced toward the door, thinking to call a nurse.

"It's okay. He's worth it." She got her arm out of the sleeve of her gown, exposing her swollen breast.

"Do you, um, want to cover up with something?" He looked around for a towel.

"Why?" She drew the edge of her gown across her chest again. "Is there someone else in here?"

"No, just me."

"Oh, well, that's okay then, isn't it?" She started to reveal herself again, but hesitated, her confused gaze striking his with shadows of such deep uncertainty, his heart hurt.

"Of course it's okay." He wanted to lean down and kiss her, he was so moved that she still felt so natural around him. It could only mean good things, couldn't it?

Adara could hardly look into Gideon's eyes, but she couldn't look away. He delved so searchingly into her gaze, as if looking for confirmation they stood a chance, but she'd treated him so badly, rejecting him for being as self-protective as she'd always been. She didn't know how to bridge this chasm between them.

Their son found his voice with an insistent yell and made them both start.

And then, even though she'd had a brief lesson before falling asleep, Adara had to learn to breast-feed, which wasn't as natural a process as some mothers made it look. She wasn't sure how to hold him. Her breast was too swollen for such a tiny mouth.

Their son surpassed his patience and grew too fussy to try. Gideon looked at her with urgency to get the job done as the baby began to wail in earnest.

"What am I doing wrong?" she cried.

"Don't look at me, I've never done it either. Here, I'll sit beside you and hold him so you can line him up— There, see? He's never done it, either, but he's getting it."

She didn't know what was more stingingly sweet: the first pull of her baby's mouth on her nipple or the stirring way Gideon cradled her against his chest so he could help her hold their baby. Adara blinked back tears, frantically wondering how she could be so close to Gideon and feel he was so far out of reach at the same time.

She tensed to hide that she was beginning to tremble, finding words impossible as emotion overwhelmed her. At least she had her back tucked to his chest and he couldn't see her face.

He seemed to react to her tension, pulling away with a grimace that he smoothed from his expression before she'd properly glimpsed it. Standing by the bed with his hands in the pockets of his rumpled work pants, he stared at the baby.

She did too, not knowing where else to look, then became fascinated by the miracle of a closed fist against her breast, tiny lashes, the peek of a miniature earlobe from beneath the edge of the blue cap.

A drop of pure emotion fell from her eye, landing on his cheek.

"Oh," she gasped, drying the betraying tear. "I'm just so overwhelmed," she said, trying to dismiss that she was crying over a lot more than the arrival of their son.

"I know." Gideon's blurred image took a step forward and he gestured helplessly. "I didn't expect it to be like this."

Like this. Those words seemed to encompass a lot more than a safe delivery after so many heartaches.

Adara blinked, trying to clear her vision to see what was in his face, eyes, heart, but all she could think was that she'd screwed up and thrown away something unbelievably precious. Her eyes flooded with despondent tears.

"Please come home," she choked out. "With us. We won't be a family without you and I miss you so much—" She couldn't continue.

"Oh, babe." He rushed forward, his warm hand cupping her face as he settled his hip beside her thigh and drew her into him, pressing hot lips against her temple, her wet cheek, her trembling lips. "I've been trying to think how I'd ever convince you to let me. I'm *sorry*."

She shook her head, burying her face in the hollow of his shoulder as she tried to regain control. "It's okay." She sniffed. "It was never easy for me to tell you about my childhood horrors. I shouldn't have expected you to revisit yours without some serious prodding."

He massaged the back of her head, his chin rubbing her hair. "I didn't want to, but mostly because I knew it could be the breaking point of our marriage. I didn't want that. And not because it would expose me. I didn't want to lose *you*. Does it help at all to know that I've always felt married to you? Maybe it wasn't legal, but it was real to me. You're my wife, Adara."

She nodded. "I am."

He laughed a little, the sound one of husky joy. "You are." He drew back, cupping her face as he looked for confirmation in her eyes. "You are."

She bit her lips, holding back the longing as she nodded. "I am. It's enough."

The radiant pride in his expression dimmed. "Enough?"

"Knowing that our union matters to you. That you want me as your wife. That we can be a family."

He sat back, hands falling away from her. "What are you saying? What does all of that do for you?"

"What do you mean? It's good, Gideon. I want to carry

on as we were, treating this like a real marriage. We don't have to change anything or bring up your past or involve any lawyers. My brothers know why we separated, but no one else does. You are Gideon Vozaras. I'm Mrs. Vozaras. It's all good."

He stood abruptly, his mood shifting to acute dismay. "And why are you staying married to that man? That name?"

"Because—" *I love him.* Her heart dipped. She wasn't ready to put herself out there again and get nothing in return. "There's no point in shaking things up. I read those papers you sent and they say that I have a case to take you to the cleaners, but I don't want that. I'm fine with us being married in a common-law sort of way. No use rocking the boat." There, she was using language he understood.

Or should, but his jaw was like iron as he moved to the window and showed her a scant angle of his profile and a tense line across his shoulders.

"You asked me if we were falling in love," he reminded.

"It was never part of our deal. I can live without it," she hurried to say.

"I can't."

His words plunged a knife into her. She gasped and looked wildly around as she absorbed what it could mean if he wanted a marriage based on love, but was stuck with her—

"For God's sake, Adara. Are you still not seeing what you mean to me?" He was looking over his shoulder at her, incredulous, but incredibly gentle too.

"What?" Her breast was cold and she realized the baby had fallen asleep and let her nipple slip from his mouth. She wished for extra hands as she tried to cradle the baby and cover herself at the same time.

Gideon walked over and grasped her chin, forcing her

gaze up to his. A fire burned in the back of that intense gaze, one that sparked an answering burn in her.

She still wasn't sure, though…

"You're not bound to me legally, but that doesn't matter if I own your heart," he told her. "I want you, body and soul. If there's something standing in the way of your loving me, tell me what it is. Now. So I can fix it or remove it and have you once and for all."

"I—" She almost lost her nerve, but sensed it really was time to let go of the last of her insecurities and be open about what she wanted. Grasp it. Demand it. "I want you to love me back."

She wasn't just wearing her heart on her sleeve, she'd pinned it to the clothesline and wheeled it out into the yard.

A look of unbelievable tenderness softened his harsh expression. "How could I not?"

She slowly shook her head. "Don't make it sound like it's there just like that. I was awful to you. I know that you've lost people close to you and don't want to be hurt again. It's okay that you're not able to love me yet. I can wait." Maybe. She set her chin, determined it wouldn't tremble despite the fact her heart was in her throat.

If only he wasn't so confusing, smiling indulgently at her like that.

"You do love me." He cradled the side of her face in his palm, scanning her face as if he was memorizing it, and she suddenly realized she must look like something the cat had coughed up. Her hair hadn't been washed, she'd barely rinsed her mouth with a sip of water.

Self-consciously she lifted the baby to her shoulder and rubbed his back, using him as a bit of a shield while she worked at maintaining hold of her emotions.

"I love you quite a bit, actually," she confessed toward her blanket-covered knees. "It's not anything like what I feel for the other men in my life. This one included." She hitched the baby a bit higher and couldn't resist kissing his little cheek, even as her soul reached out to his father. "I don't know how to handle what I feel for you. When my father was mean to me, it hurt even though I didn't care about him, but it's nothing compared to how much it hurts when you love someone and trust him and think they don't care about you at all."

"I know," he growled. "Losing someone to death is agony, but it's even worse knowing the person you love with all your heart is alive and doesn't want to see you."

Hearing how much he loved her was bittersweet. She stared at him in anguish, not wanting the power to hurt him that badly, but seeing from his tortured expression that she had. There were no words to heal, only an urge to draw him close so she could try to kiss away his pain.

"I'm sorry. I love you."

"I know, me, too. I love you so much."

Their mouths met in homecoming, both of them moaning as the ache ceased. He opened his lips over hers and she flowered like a plant tasting water. Heat flowed into her. Joy.

Love.

A door swished and a nurse said, "Bit soon for that, isn't it?"

They broke apart. Gideon shot a private smile at Adara as he reached to tie her gown behind her neck.

"And how is our young man? Does he have a name?" the nurse chattered.

Adara licked her lips, eyeing Gideon as she said, "Delphi's not exactly a boy's name, but I thought…Androu?" It was Gideon's real name.

His expression spasmed with emotion before he controlled it. "Are you sure?" he asked, voice strained, body braced for disappointment.

"He's someone I love and want in my life forever. I think, someday, he'd be really proud to know who he was named after."

"I don't deserve you," he said against her lips, kissing her resoundingly, right there in front of the nurse.

Adara flushed and smiled, bubbles of happiness filling her. "We do, you know," she contradicted him. "We both deserve this."

She didn't care that the nurse was smiling indulgently at them even as she took Androu and undressed him so she could weigh him.

"Well, you certainly deserve to be happy. Me, I just demand the best and get it." *You,* he mouthed. *Him.* He cocked his head toward the baby.

"A habit I'm adopting," she said with a cheeky wrinkle of her nose. "I know how possessive you are of the things you've built, too. I'm taking on that trait as well. *Us,*" she whispered, soft and heartfelt.

"Yeah, I'm going to hang on to us pretty tight too," he said in a way that made her heart leap. *"Agape mou."*

EPILOGUE

GIDEON WALKED INTO his home office thinking he really needed to start spending more time in here. It wasn't that things were falling apart. He and Adara had put some great people in place when they'd first learned of the pregnancy. Her brothers were still running things like a well-oiled machine and he should have quit micromanaging years ago, so this was a timely lesson in letting go.

But there was a fine line between delegating and neglecting. Much more lolling about his home, playing airplane with his son and necking with his wife, and he'd be a full-fledged layabout.

Of course, he could blame finishing the renovations, putting in a staircase to the lower floor, painting and furnishing their new private space away from the main floor. That had taken time. There had also been his recovery from minor surgery, but that had really only been the one afternoon on headache pills and he'd been fine.

No, he might be getting up in the night to change diapers, but he wasn't breast-feeding or anemic from childbirth. He didn't have Adara's totally legitimate reasons for shirking work.

He certainly shouldn't be leaving confidential papers lying openly on his desk, whether the workmen were gone or not.

The block letters and signature tabs were a dead give-away that this was a contract, one he couldn't remember even pulling out to review, but— Ah. It was the separation agreement he'd sent to Adara. She must have left it here.

A pang hit him, but it was merely the remembered pain of thinking he'd lost everything and was quickly relieved by a rush of relief and happiness that they'd recovered. Her devotion was as steadfast as his, prompting a flood of deep love for her as he walked the papers toward the shredder. He didn't want this bad mojo in the house, but then he saw she'd signed it. His heart stopped.

Ha. That wasn't her name. Under the statement that began, *I, Adara Makricosta, hereby agree...*, she'd scrawled with a deep impression, *Never,* and added a smiley face.

Quirking a grin at her sass, he decided this was a signed contract in its own right, definitely worth tucking in the safe. Suddenly, work didn't seem important after all. Was she finished feeding Androu? he wondered. They'd had coinciding follow-ups at separate doctor clinics today. He'd returned to find her rocking a drifting Androu to sleep downstairs and decided to see what he could get done here, but...

He turned to find her in his office doorway, the baby monitor in her hand.

"He's asleep?" he asked.

She nodded and came to set the monitor on his desktop. "How did your appointment go?"

"Not swimmingly."

Her eyes widened in alarm.

"That's a joke," he hurried to assure her. "I'm saying there were no swimmers. I'm good. Shooting blanks."

She snorted, then sobered and cocked her head in concern. "You're sure it doesn't bother you? I really was fully prepared to have my tubes tied."

He tried to wave away the same worries he'd been trying to alleviate for weeks, but she kept her anxious expression.

He sighed. "I'd make ten more just like Androu if we could. We both would, right? He's perfect," he said, moving to take her arms in a warm but firm grasp of insistence. "But if we want more children, we can find another way. You can't risk another pregnancy."

"Exactly why I should have been the one having the permanent procedure. What if someday—"

"Are you going somewhere?" he challenged lightly. "I'm not. Therefore, my getting fixed is a solution for both of us. You've been through enough. And this was not a big moral struggle for me. I'm happy to take responsibility for protecting you."

She pouted a little. "Well, thank you then. I do appreciate it."

He caressed from the base of her throat to under her chin, coaxing her to tilt her head up so he could see those pillowy lips pursed so erotically.

"There was some self-serving to it, you know," he admitted, voice thickening with the many weeks of abstinence they'd observed. Now there'd never be any worries for either of them, no matter when or where they came together. And hell, if he hadn't inflicted pain down there to distract himself, he probably would have lost his mind waiting for this moment. "How did *your* appointment go?" he belatedly asked, reminding himself not to let the engine rev too high and fast.

"Oh." Her lashes swooped and her mouth widened into a sensual smile of invitation. "All clear to resume normal activities."

"If you can call how we make each other feel 'normal.'" He backed her toward the desk. "I was just thinking I haven't been spending enough quality time in here."

Her breath caught in the most delightful way, and even though she stiffened in surprise when her hips met the edge of his desk, she melted with reception just as quickly, hitching herself to sit on it. Her hand curled around to the back of his neck and she leaned her other hand onto the surface of his desk, watching without protest as he began unbuttoning her top.

"We do have a nice new bed downstairs that hasn't been used for one of its intended purposes, you know," she reminded in a sultry voice.

"I am quite aware," he countered dryly as he bared her chest and released her bra. Her breasts were bigger, pale and lightly veined, the nipples dark and stiff with excitement. "God, you're beautiful."

"They're kind of majestic, aren't they?" She arched a little.

"They kind of are," he agreed with awe, tracing lightly before he bent to touch careful kisses around her nipples.

"Gideon?"

Her tone made him raise his head. "What's wrong?"

"I know we should savor this because it's been a really long time and we kind of started over with our marriage so this is a bit of a honeymoon moment, but I've really missed making love with you. I thought about walking in here naked. I don't want to wait."

Ever willing to accommodate, he stripped her pants off without another word, taking her ice-blue undies with them. Spreading her knees, he only bothered to open his jeans and shove them down as far as necessary, before he carefully pushed inside her.

Adara gasped at the pinch and friction of not being quite ready, but his hot, firm thickness was the connection she'd been longing for. With a moan, she twined her legs around him and forced his entry, drawing a deep hiss from him.

They fought a light battle, him trying to slow her down, her urging him as deep into her as she could take before she sprawled back on his desk and let him have his way with her.

It was raw and quick and powerful, over in minutes, but they were shaking in each other's arms as they caught their breath. Her vision sparkled and she felt as if she radiated ecstasy.

"You okay?" he murmured as he kissed her neck. "That was pretty primal."

"That was an appetizer," she said, languidly kissing him and using her tongue. Her fingertips traced the damp line through his shirt down his spine. "*Now* you can take me downstairs and show me your best moves."

"You're sounding pretty bossy there, Mrs. Vozaras." He straightened and gently disengaged so he could hitch up his jeans and scoop her off the desk into a cradle against his chest.

"Only a problem if we want different things, and I don't think that's true."

He cocked his head in agreement. "You're so right. Monitor," he prompted, dipping his still-weak knees so she could grab it off the corner of the desk.

She craned her neck over his shoulder as he carried her through the door. "You gonna leave my clothes on the floor like that?"

"Do I look stupid? We're on the clock. He could wake up any second."

She traced his lips with her fingertip. "But if the boat rocks, they'll be thrown all over the place," she teased.

He paused on the stairs. "I am dry-docked and land-locked, sticking right here with you, my siren of a wife. We're on solid ground. Nothing is going anywhere."

"Aw." Touched, she kissed him. It grew deeply passionate. He let her legs drift to find the step above him so he could roam his hands over her naked curves, lighting delicious fires in her nerve endings.

She worked on divesting him, caressing heated skin, leaving a few more articles of clothing on the stairs before she led him below to christen their new bed.

* * * * *

No Longer Forbidden?

I've drafted this First Book Dedication in my head a thousand times, but the one consistent has always been "For Doug."

There are other treasured people I must thank for their encouragement: my awesome parents, my adored sisters and their terrific spouses, my supportive in-laws, and my cousin who wants me to become famous so she can brag about a connection to someone other than those A-listers she already has.

I have to thank my children, of course, for only interrupting my writing time for blood or flood. I especially have to thank them for finding, when they were very little, a way to let me write. They made friends with the most amazing children who possessed the most amazing parents. I very much have to thank their Other Moms and their families for embracing mine.

CHAPTER ONE

NICODEMUS MARCUSSEN rose to shake hands with his lawyer, his muscles aching with tension as he kept his reaction to all they'd discussed very much to himself.

"I know this is a difficult topic," his lawyer tried.

Nic shook off the empathy with a cool blink and a private, *No, you don't*. Nic trusted Sebastyen, but only within the framework of the media conglomerate Nic had fought to run after Olief Marcussen's disappearance. Sebastyen had been one of Nic's first supporters, believing in Nic's leadership skills despite his inexperience. Nic was grateful, but they weren't friends. Nic eschewed close relationships of every kind.

"I appreciate your advice," Nic said with aloof sincerity. Everything Sebastyen had presented was the height of practicality, outweighing any sentiment that might have held Nic back. "It's definitely time to consider it as the anniversary approaches. I'll let you know how I'd like to proceed," he concluded in dismissal.

Sebastyen hovered, appearing to want to add something, but Nic glanced at his watch. His days were busy enough without social chit-chat.

"I only wanted to reiterate that it would be helpful if both next of kin agreed," Sebastyen blurted.

"I understand," Nic drawled, keeping his patronizing

tone muted but heard. It was enough of a butt-out to have the lawyer nodding apologetically and making haste to leave. Nic was quite sure the entire corporation, along with the rest of the world, followed the escapades of the *other* next of kin, but he wouldn't abide open speculation about how he'd gain her cooperation.

The fact was, he already had an idea how he'd accomplish it. He'd been putting things together in his mind even as Sebastyen had been stating his case.

As Sebastyen closed the office door Nic went back to his desk and the courier envelope he'd received that morning. Bills of every description came out by the handful, their disarray as fluttery and frivolous as the woman who'd racked them up. The forget-me-not-blue notepaper was a particularly incongruous touch. He reread the swooping script.

> *Nic,*
> *My bank cards aren't working. Kindly sort it out and send the new ones to Rosedale. I'm moving in this weekend for some downtime.*
> *Ro.*

His initial reaction had been, *downtime from what?* But for once Rowan's self-serving behavior was a convenience to him. Since she hadn't got the message when he'd stopped her credit cards two months ago, he'd confront her and do what Olief should have done years ago. Make her grow up and act responsibly for a change.

Rosedale.

A warm sense of homecoming suffused Rowan O'Brien as she climbed the hill and looked over the sprawling vineyard surrounding the sturdy house of gray stone and mullioned windows. The turreted Old English mansion was out of place against the white beach and turquoise water, pure folly on a Mediterranean island where white stone columns and flowing architecture typically reigned, but it had been built to indulge a loved one so Rowan adored it with all her heart. And here she was free.

She'd sent the taxi ahead with her things, initially frustrated that her finances had stalled to the point where she'd had to take the ferry from the mainland, but the slow boat had turned out to be therapeutic. As much as she'd ached to see the house again, she had needed the time to brace herself for its emptiness.

With a bittersweet throb in her chest she descended to the lawn, ignored her luggage on the stoop and tried the door, half expecting it to be locked and wondering where she'd put her key. She'd left a message for the housekeeper, but wasn't sure Anna had received it. Rowan's mobile had stopped working along with everything else. Very frustrating.

The door was unlocked. Rowan stepped into silence and released a sigh. She had longed to come for ages but hadn't been able to face it, too aware that the heart of the home was missing. Except...

A muted beat sounded above her. Footsteps crossed the second floor to the top of the stairs. Male, heavy steps...

Before she could leap to the crazy conclusion that by some miracle her mother and stepfather had survived, and were here after all, the owner of the feet descended the stairs and came into view.

Oh.

She told herself her reaction stemmed from the unexpectedness of seeing him face-to-face after so long, but it was more than that. Nic always made her heart trip and her breath catch. And—and this was new, since she'd thrown herself at him in a hideous moment of desperation nearly two years ago—made her die a little of abject mortification.

She hid that, but couldn't help reacting to his presence. He was so gorgeous! Which shouldn't matter. She knew lots of good-looking men. Perhaps none combined the blond Viking warrior with the cold Spartan soldier quite the way he did, but marble-carved jaws and chilly, piercing blue eyes were a mainstay among her mother's film and stage crowd.

Nic's looks were the least of his attributes, though. He was a man of unadulterated power, physically honed and confident to the point of radiating couched aggression. Nic had always been sure of himself, but now the authority he projected was ramped to new heights. Rowan felt it as a force that leapt from him to catch hold of her like a tractor beam that wanted to draw her under its control.

Reflexively she resisted. There was no room for quiet defensiveness when she came up against this man's aura. She instinctively feared she'd drown if she buckled to his will, so she leapt straight to a stance of opposition. Besides, he was one of the few people she could defy without consequence. She'd never had anything to lose with Nic. Not even his affection. He'd hated her from day one—something that had always stung badly enough without him proving it on her twentieth birthday by reacting to her kiss with such contempt. She tried very hard not to care that he didn't like her. She definitely didn't let herself show how much it hurt.

"What a lovely surprise," she said, in the husky Irish lilt that had made her mother famous, flashing the smile that usually knocked men off their guard. "Hello, Nic."

Her greeting bounced off the armor of his indifference. "Rowan."

She felt his stern voice like the strop of a cat's tongue—rough, yet sensual, and strangely compelling. It was a challenge to appear as unmoved as he was.

"If you left a message I didn't get it. My mobile isn't working." She hooked the strap of her empty purse on the stairpost next to him.

"Why's that, do you suppose?" he asked without moving, his eyes hooded as he looked down on her.

His accent always disconcerted her. It was as worldly as he was. Vaguely American, with a hint of British boarding school, and colored by the time he'd spent in Greece and the Middle East.

"I have no idea." Needing distance from the inherent challenge in his tone, she slipped out of her light jacket and moved into the lounge to toss the faded denim over the back of a sofa. Her boots clipped on the tiles with a hollow echo, sending a renewed pang of emptiness through her.

It struck her that Nic might be here for the same reason she'd come. She glanced back, searching for homesickness in his carved features, but his face remained impassive. He folded his arms, bunching his muscles into a stance of superior arrogance.

"No, I don't expect you do," he remarked with dry disparagement.

"I don't what?" she asked absently, still hopeful for a sign of humanity in him. But there was nothing. Disappointment poked at her with an itch of irritation. Sometimes she wished… *Stop it.* Nic was never going to warm up to her. She had to get over it. Get over *him.*

But how? she wondered, restlessly tugging away the elastic that had kept her hair from blowing off her head on the ferry. She gave her scalp a rub, rejuvenating the dark waves while trying to erase her tingling awareness of Nic.

"Your mobile stopped working along with your cards," he said, "but the obvious reason hasn't occurred to you?"

"That everything expired at the same time? It occurred to me, but that doesn't seem likely. They've always managed to renew themselves before." She used her fingers to comb her hair back from her face, glancing up in time to see his gaze rise from an unabashed appraisal of her figure.

Her pulse kicked in shock. And treacherous delight. The wayward adolescent hormones that had propelled her to the most singularly humiliating experience of her life were alive and well, responding involuntarily to Nic's unrelenting masculine appeal. It was aggravating that it took only one little peek from him to ramp her into a fervor, but she was secretly thrilled.

To hide her confusing reaction she challenged him, a vaguely smug smile on her face. It wasn't easy to stare into his eyes and let him know she knew exactly where his attention had been. She'd been drilled from an early age to make the most of her looks. She knew she appealed to men, but she'd never caught a hint of appealing to this one. What an intriguing shift of power, she thought, even as their eye contact had the effect of making her feel as though she stood at a great height, dizzy, and at risk of a long fall.

Deep down, she knew she was kidding herself if she thought she had *any* power over him, but she let herself believe it long enough to take a few incautious steps toward him. She cocked her hip, aware that her boot heels would make the pose oh-so-provocative.

"You didn't have to come all this way to bring me new cards, Nic. You seem like a busy man. What happened? Decided you needed a bit of family time?" Again she searched for a dent in his composure, some sign that he craved human contact the way lesser mortals like she did.

His iceman demeanor chilled several degrees and she could almost hear his thoughts. Her mother might have been his father's lover for nearly a decade, but he'd never once thought of Ro as *family*.

"I am busy," he informed her, with his patented complete lack of warmth.

She'd never seen him show affection to anyone, so she ought not to let his enmity bother her, but he always seemed extra frosty toward her.

"I *work*, you see. Something you wouldn't know anything about."

For real? She shifted her weight to the opposite hip, perversely pleased that she'd snared his attention again, even though his austere evaluation was not exactly rich with admiration of her lean limbs in snug designer denim. He just looked annoyed.

Fine. So was she. "These legs have been dancing since I was four. I know what work is," she said pointedly.

"Hardly what I'd call earning a living, when all your performances involve trading on your mother's name rather than any real talent of your own. Next you'll tell me the appearance fee you get for clubbing is an honest wage. I'm not talking about prostituting yourself for mad money, Rowan. I'm saying you've never held a real job and supported yourself."

He knew about the club? Of course he did. The paparazzi had gone crazy—which was the point. She'd hated herself for resorting to it, very aware of how bad it looked while her mother was still missing, but her bank account had bottomed out and she'd had no other choice. It wasn't as if she'd spent the money on herself, although she wasn't in a mood to air *that* dirty little secret. Olief had understood that she had an obligation toward her father, but she had a strong feeling Mr. Judgmental wouldn't. Better to fight Nic on the front she could win.

"Are you really criticizing me for trading on my mother's name when you're the boss's son?"

He didn't even know how wrong he was about her mother's reputation. Cassandra O'Brien had pushed Rowan onto the stage because she hadn't been getting any work herself. Her reputation as a volatile diva with a taste for married men had been a hindrance to everyone.

"My situation is different," Nic asserted.

"Of course it is. You're always in the right, no matter what, and I'm wrong. You're smart. I'm stupid."

"I didn't say that. I only meant that Olief never promoted me through nepotism."

"And yet the superiority still comes across! But whatever, Nic. Let's take your condescension as read and move on. I didn't come here to fight with you. I didn't expect to see you at all. I was after some alone time," she added in a mutter, looking toward the kitchen. "I'm dying for tea. Shall I ask Anna to make for two, or…?"

"Anna isn't here. She's taken another job."

"Oh. *Oh,*" Rowan repeated, pausing three steps toward the kitchen. Renewed loss cut through her. Anna's moving on sounded so…final. "Well, I can manage a cuppa. Do you want one, or may I be so optimistic as to assume you're on your way back to Athens?" She batted overly innocent lashes at him while smiling sweetly.

"I arrived last night to stay for as long as it takes."

His Adonis mask remained impassive. The man was an absolute robot—if robots came in worn denim and snug T-shirts that strained across sculpted shoulders and cropped their blond hair so closely it gleamed like a golden helmet.

"As long as it takes to what?" she asked as she started again for the kitchen, tingling with uneasy premonition as she scoffed, "Throw me out?"

"See? I knew you weren't stupid."

CHAPTER TWO

ROWAN SWUNG BACK fast enough to make her hair lift in a cloud of brunette waves. She was so flabbergasted Nic might have laughed if he hadn't been so deadly serious.

"*You* stopped all my credit cards. And closed my mobile account. You did it!"

"Bravo again," he drawled.

"What a horrible thing to do! Why didn't you at least warn me?"

Outrage flushed her alabaster skin, its glow sexy and righteous. A purely male reaction of lust pierced his groin. It was a common enough occurrence around her and he was quickly able to ignore it, focusing instead on her misplaced indignation. A shred of conscience niggled that he hadn't tried to call her, but when dealing with a woman as spoiled as she was reasoning wasn't the best course. She was too sure of her claim. Far better to present a fait accompli. *She* had.

"Why didn't you tell me you'd dropped out of school?" he countered.

If she experienced a moment of culpability she hid it behind the haughty tilt of her chin. "It was none of your business."

"Neither are your lingerie purchases, but they keep arriving on my desk."

A blush of discomfiture hit her cheeks, surprising him. He hadn't thought her capable of modesty.

"This is so like you!" Rowan charged. "Heaven forbid you *speak* to me. Seriously, Nic. Why didn't you call to discuss this?"

"There's nothing to discuss. Your agreement with Olief was that he would support you while you were at school. You chose to quit, so the expense fund has closed. It's time to take responsibility for yourself."

Her eyes narrowed in suspicion. "You're enjoying this, aren't you? You've always hated me and you're jumping on this chance to punish me."

"*Punish* you?" The words *hate* and *stupid* danced in his head, grating with unexpected strength. He pushed aside an uncomfortable pinch of compunction. "You're confusing hate with an inability to be manipulated," he asserted. "You can't twine me around your finger like you did Olief. He would have let you talk him round to underwriting your social life. I won't."

"Because you're determined my style of life should be below yours? Why?"

Her conceit, so unapologetic, made him crack a laugh. "You really think you can play the equality card here?"

"You're his son; he was like a father to me."

Her attempt to sound reasonable came across as patronizing. Entitled. And how many times had he buckled to that attitude, too unsure of his place in Olief's life? He'd adopted the man's name, but only because he'd wanted to be rid of the one stuck on him at birth. In the end Olief had treated Nic as an equal and a respected colleague, but Nic would never forget that Olief hadn't wanted his son. He'd been ashamed he'd ever created him.

Then, when Nic had finally been let into Olief's life, this girl and her mother had installed themselves like an obstacle course that had to be navigated in order to get near him. Nic was a patient man. He'd waited and waited for Olief to set aside time for him, induct him into the fold. *Acknowledge* him. But it had never happened.

Yet Rowan thought she had a daddy in the man whose blood made Olief Nic's father. And when it had come down to choosing between them two years ago, Nic recalled with a rush of angry bile, Olief had chosen to protect Rowan and disparage Nic. Nic would never forgive her setting him up for *that* disgrace.

"You're the daughter of his mistress." How Olief could want another man's whelp mothered by his mistress but not his own child had always escaped Nic. "He only took you on because the two of you came as a package," Nic spelled out. He'd never been this blunt before, but old bitterness stewed with fresh antagonism and the only person who had kept him from speaking his mind all these years was absent. "You're nothing to him."

"They were lovers!"

Her Irish temper stoked unwilling excitement in him. With her fury directed toward him, he felt his response flare stronger than ever before. He didn't want to feel the catch. She was off-limits. Always had been—even before Olief had warned him off. Too young. Too wrong for him. Too expressive and spoiled.

This was why Nic hated her. He hated himself for reacting this way. She pulled too easily on his emotions so he wanted her removed from his life. He wanted this confused wanting to stop.

"They weren't married," he stated coldly. "You're not his relation. You and your mother were a pair of hangers-on. That's over now."

"Where do you get off, saying something like that?"

she demanded, storming toward him like a rip curl that wanted to engulf him in its maelstrom of wild passion.

He automatically braced against being torn off his moorings.

"How would you justify that to Olief?"

"I don't have to. He's dead."

His flat words shocked both of them. Despite his discussion with Sebastyen, Nic hadn't said the obvious out loud, and now he heard it echo through the empty house with ominous finality. His heart instantly became weighted and compressed.

Rowan's flush of anger drained away, leaving her dewy lips pale and the rest of her complexion dimming to gray. She was close enough that he felt the change in her crackling energy as her fury grounded out and despondency rolled in.

"You've heard something," she said in a distressed whisper, the hope underlying the words threadbare and desperate.

He felt like a brute then. He'd convinced himself that the disappearance hadn't meant that much to her. She was nightclubbing in their absence, for God's sake. But her immediate sorrow now gave him the first inkling that she wasn't quite as superficial as he wanted to believe. That quick descent into vulnerability made something in him want to reach out to her, even though they weren't familiar that way. The one time he'd held her—

That thought fuelled his unwanted incendiary emotions so he shoved it firmly from his mind. He was having enough trouble hanging on to control as it was.

"No," he forced out, trying to work out why he'd been able to hold it together in front of Sebastyen, who was closer to him than anyone, but struggled in front of Rowan. He feared she would see too deeply into him at a time when his defenses were disintegrating like a sandcastle under the tide. He couldn't look into her eyes. They were too anxious and demanding.

"No, there's been no news. But it'll be a year in two weeks. It's time to quit fooling ourselves they could have survived. The lawyers are advising we petition the courts to—" He had to clear his throat. "Declare them dead."

Silence.

When he looked for her reaction he found a glare of condemnation so hot it gave him radiation blisters.

With a sudden re-ignition of her temper, she spat, "You have the nerve to call *me* a freeloader, you sanctimonious bastard? Who benefits from declaring them dead? *You*, Nic. No. I won't allow it."

She was smart to fling away from him then, slamming through the door into the kitchen and letting it slap back on its hinges. Smart to walk away. Because that insult demanded retaliation, and he needed a minute to rein in his temper before he went after her and delivered the set-down she deserved.

As Rowan banged through the cupboards for a kettle she trembled with outrage.

And fear. If her mother and Olief were really gone...

Her breath stalled at how adrift that left her. She'd come here to find some point to her life, some direction. She'd made quite a mess of things in the last year, she'd give Nic that, but she needed time to sort it all out and make a plan for her future. Big, sure, heartless Nic didn't seem to want to give her that, though.

He pushed into the room, his formidable presence like a shove into deeper water. She gripped the edge of the bench, resenting him with every bone in her body. She wouldn't let him do this to her.

"I don't know why I'm surprised," she seethed. "You don't have a sensitive bone in your body. You're made up of icicles, aren't you?"

He jerked his head back. "Better that than the slots of a piggy bank," he returned with frost. "It's not Olief being gone that worries you, but his deep pockets—isn't it?"

"I'm not the one taking over his offices and bank accounts, am I? What's wrong? The board giving you a hard time again? Maybe you shouldn't have been so quick to jump into Olief's shoes like you owned them."

"Who else could be trusted?" he shot back. "The board wanted to sell off pieces for their personal gain. I kept it intact so Olief would have something to come back to."

She'd been aware in those early weeks of him warring with Olief's top investors, but she'd had her own struggles with rehabilitating her leg. The corporation had been the last thing on her mind.

"I've looked for them even while sitting at his desk," Nic continued. "I paid searchers long after the authorities gave up. What did *you* do?" he challenged. "Keep your mother's fan club rabid and frenzied?"

Rowan curled her toes in the tight leather of her boots, stabbed with inadequacy and affront. "My leg was broken. I couldn't get out in a boat to look for them. And doing all those interviews wasn't a cakewalk!"

He snorted. "Blinking back manufactured tears was difficult, was it?"

Manufactured? She always fought back tears when she couldn't avoid facing the reality of that lost plane. Snapping her head to the side, she refused to let him see how talking about the disappearance upset her. He obviously didn't see her reaction as sincere and she wasn't about to beg him to believe her.

Especially when she had very mixed feelings—some

that scared her. Guilt turned in her like a spool of barbed wire as she thought of the many times she had wished she could be out from under her mother's controlling thumb. Since turning nineteen she had been waffling constantly between outright defiance that would have cut all ties to Cassandra O'Brien and a desire to stay close to Olief, Rosedale—and, she admitted silently, with a suffocating squeeze of mortification, within the sphere of Olief's black sheep son.

But she hadn't wished Cassandra O'Brien would *die*.

She couldn't declare her mother dead. It was sick. Wrong. Rowan swiped her clammy palms over the seat of her jeans before running water into the kettle. She wouldn't do it.

"If you want to run Olief's enterprise, fill your boots," she said shakily. "But if all you want is more control over it, and by extension *me*, don't expect me to help you." She set the kettle to boil, then risked a glance at him.

He wore the most painfully supercilious smirk. "I'm willing to forgive your debts to gain your cooperation," he levied.

"My debts?" she repeated laughingly. "A few months of credit card bills?" She and her mother had been in worse shape dozens of times. *"We're in dire straits, love. Be a good girl and dance us out."* Appearance fees were a sordid last resort, but Rowan wasn't above it. "You'll have to do better than that," she said coldly.

He leaned a well-muscled arm on the refrigerator. His laconic stance and wide chest, so unashamedly male, made her mouth go dry.

"Name your price, then."

His confidence was as compelling as his physique, and all the more aggravating because she didn't possess any immunity to it. She wanted to put a crack in his composure.

"Rosedale," she tossed out. It was a defiant challenge, but earnest want crept into her tone. This was her home. This was where Olief would return…if he could.

"Rosedale?" Nic repeated.

His frigid stare gave her a shiver of apprehension before she reminded herself she was being crass because he was.

She tensed her sooty lashes into protective slits as she held his intimidating gaze. "Why not?" she challenged. "You don't want it."

"Not true. I don't like the *house*," he corrected, shifting his big body into an uncompromising stance, shoulders pinned back, arms folded in refusal. "The location is perfect, though. I intend to tear down this monstrosity as soon as it's emptied and build something that suits me better. So, no, you may not have Rosedale."

"Tear it down?" The words hissed in her throat like the steam off the kettle. "Why would you even threaten such a thing? Just to hurt me?"

"Hurt you?" He frowned briefly. Any hint of softening was dismissed in a blink. "Don't try to manipulate me with your acts of melodrama, Rowan. No, I'm not doing anything *to* you. You're not on my radar enough for me to be that personal."

Of course not. And she shouldn't let him so far into her psyche that she was scorched by that. But there he was, making her burn with humiliation and hurt.

"Unlike you, I don't play games," he continued. "That wasn't a threat. It's the truth. The house is completely impractical. If I'm going to live here I want open rooms, more access to the outdoors, fewer stairs."

"Then don't live here!"

"Athens has been my base most of my life. It's a short helicopter or boat trip from here to there. The island's vineyard is profitable in its own right, which I'm sure is the real reason you want your hands on the place, but I'm not going to hand you a property worth multi-millions because your mother slept her way into having a ridiculous house built on it. What I *will* do is allow you to take whatever Cassandra left here—if you do it in a timely manner."

Rowan could only stare into his emotionless blue eyes. His gall left her speechless. Her mind could barely comprehend all he was saying. Rosedale gone? Pick over her mother's things like she was snatching bargains at a yard sale? Give up *hope*?

A stabbing pain drove through her, spreading an ache like poison across her chest and lifting a sting into her throat and behind her eyes.

"I don't want *things*, Nic. I want my home and my family!"

She was going to cry, and it was the last thing she could bear to do in front of this glacier-veined man. It was more like her to go toe-to-toe than run from a fight, but for the second time in half an hour she had to walk out on him.

After hiking the length of the island in heels, her feet refused a visit to all her favored haunts, so Rowan went as far as the sandy shoreline and kicked off her boots. The water was higher than she'd ever seen it, but she usually only swam in summer, rarely came to the beach in winter, and she hadn't been looking at the water when she'd followed Nic down here two years ago.

Wincing, she turned her mind from that debacle—only to become conscious of how grim a place the beach was to visit since her mother and Olief had likely drowned somewhere out there in the Mediterranean. One year ago.

She was starting to hate this time of year.

Starting up the beach, she tried to escape the hitch of guilt catching in her, not wanting to dwell on how she'd asked them to come for her when she'd broken her leg. She hadn't been able to go to them—not physically and, more significantly, because she had feared running into Nic.

Oh, that hateful man! She hated him all the more for having a point. He wasn't *right*, but she had to acknowledge he wasn't completely wrong. She hadn't expected to find her mother and Olief in residence, but she'd wanted to feel close to them as she faced the anniversary of their disappearance and accepted what he'd come out and said: it was very unlikely they would ever come back and tell her what to do.

The rest of her life stretched before her like the water, endless and formless. Until the dance school had kicked her out she'd never faced anything like this. Logically she knew she ought to celebrate this freedom and opportunity, but it looked so empty.

Her life was empty. She had no one.

Rowan drank salt-scented air as she inhaled, trying to ease the constriction in her lungs. Not yet. She didn't have to face all that until the year was officially up. Nic could go to hell with his court documents and demands that she face reality.

As she contemplated dealing with his threats against Rosedale a moment of self-pity threatened. Why did he dislike her so much? His cloud of harsh judgment always seemed directed inexorably toward her, but why? They were nothing to each other. He might be Olief's son, but who would know it? He only ever referred to Olief by name, never even in conversation as "my father," yet he wanted the rights of a son, full inheritance. That egotistical sense of privilege affronted her. She wanted to stand up for Olief if for no other reason than that Nic didn't deserve the position of sole heir. He'd never made a proper effort to be part of the family, and he wasn't looking out for what was left of it: *her*.

Estranged seemed to be his preferred option in any relationship. That wall of detachment had broken Olief's heart. And it made Rowan nervous because it made Nic formidable. Her insides clenched at the thought of Rosedale being torn down. She couldn't lose her home.

Reaching the end of the beach, where a long flat rock created the edge of the cove, she clambered up to a well-used vantage point. The waves were wild, coming in with a wind that tore at her hair and peppered her with sea spray. Barnacles cut into her bare soles while bits of kelp in icy tide pools made for slippery steps in between.

She picked her way to the edge, reveling in the struggle to reach it under the ferocious mood of the sky. Another wave smashed against the rocks under her toes, high enough to spray her thighs and wash bitter swirls of cold water around her ankles before it was sucked back to open water. Uncomfortable, but not enough to chase her away.

Throwing back her head, she sent out a challenge to the gathering storm as if standing up to Nic. "I won't let you scare me off!"

The words were tossed away on a whistling wind, but it felt good to say them. To stand firm against the crash and gush and pull of a wintry sea that soaked her calves before dragging at the denim in retreat.

It wasn't until a third monster, higher than all the rest, rolled in and exploded in a wall of water, soaking her to the chest, that she realized she might not be strong enough to win against such a mighty enemy.

If Rowan thought he'd bring her luggage out of the rain or pour her tea while she stamped around outside throwing a hissy fit, she had another think coming. Nic went upstairs to his office and did his best to dismiss her from his mind.

It didn't go well. That heartbreaking catch in her voice when she'd said, "*I want my home and my family*," kept ringing in his mind, making him uncomfortable.

He wasn't close to his own mother, and after many times hearing Rowan and Cassandra fight like cats in a cage had assumed their relationship was little better than an armed truce. Of course he'd observed over the years that regard for one's parents was fairly universal, and he obviously would have preferred it if Olief had survived rather than disappeared, but he hadn't imagined Rowan was feeling deep distress over any of this. Her anguish startled him. Throughout this entire year, as always, he had tried not to think much of her at all—certainly not to dwell on how she was coping emotionally.

He coped by working long hours and avoiding deep thoughts altogether. Getting emotional and wishing for the impossible was a waste of time. Nothing could be changed by angst and hand-wringing.

Moving to the window, he tried to escape doing anything of that sort now, telling himself he was only observing the weather. On the horizon, the haze of an angry front was drawing in. It was the storm that had been promised when he'd checked the weather report, and the reason he'd come over last night on the yacht rather than trying to navigate choppy, possibly deadly seas today.

A storm like this had taken down Olief's plane. He and Cassandra had been off to fetch Rowan from yet another of her madcap adventures. *She* was the reason Nic had no chance of knowing Olief or grasping the seemingly simple concept she'd bandied about at him so easily: *family*. Rowan might not be the whole reason, but one way or another she had interfered with Nic's efforts to get to

know his father. She had demanded Olief's attention with
cheeky misbehavior and constant bids for attention, interrupting whenever Nic found a moment with the man
and constantly distracting him with her unrelenting sex
appeal. He'd had to walk away from progress a thousand
times. Away from her.

Prickling with antipathy, he unconsciously scanned the
places he'd most often observed her over the years, not
aware he was looking for her until he felt a twinge of confusion when he didn't find her where he usually would. She
wasn't at the gazebo or up the hilltop or on the beach—

He spotted her and swore. *Fool.*

Bare feet had been a bad idea. Rowan couldn't move fast
across the sharp, uneven rocks to outrun the tide that was
coming in with inescapable resolve. She couldn't even
see where she was stepping. The water had come in deep
enough to eddy around her knees, keeping her off balance. With her arms flapping, she silently begged her mum
and Olief, *If you can hear me, please help me get back to
shore alive.*

The response to her plea was the biggest wave yet, visible as a steel-gray wall crawling up behind her with ominous size and strength. Rowan dug in with her numb toes
and braced for impact. Her whole body shuddered as the
weight of the water began to climb her already soaked
clothes, gathering height as it loomed behind her.

She held her breath.

The wave broke at her shoulders and with a cry she felt
herself thrown forward onto what felt like broken glass.
Her hands and knees felt the scrape of barnacles as she
tried to scramble for purchase, but then she was lifted. Her
heart stopped. The wave was going to roll her across these
rocks before it dragged her out to die.

Rowan clawed toward the surface long enough to get a glimpse of Nic running flat out down the beach.

"Ni—" Her mouth filled with water.

Nic lost sight of her as the surf thundered into itself. He pushed his body to the limit, tormented anger bubbling like acid inside him. Questions pounded with his footsteps digging across the wet sand. What did God have against him? Why did he have to lose everything? Why *her*—?

An arm flailed, fighting to stay in the foam that drained off the ledge of rocks. If the retreating wave carried her into deeper water she'd be thrown back into the rocks with the next surge that came in. Rowan fought for her life and so did Nic. He leapt onto the ledge and waded into the turbulence, able to read the terror on her face as she valiantly fought to keep herself from being pulled beyond reach.

At the last second she surged forward enough that he was able to clamp his hand on her wrist. He dragged her up and out of the water, clutching her to his chest as he made for safer ground. The tide poured in with another wave big enough to soak his seat and spatter his back before he reached the sand and finally the grass. He stopped, heart racing with exertion, too close to seeing her die to ease his vise-like grip.

Rowan clung tightly to Nic even as he crushed her, stunned by how close she'd come to being sucked into certain death. She was shocked to the core that he'd arrived at just the right time to help her. Astounded that he'd bothered.

He hadn't hesitated, though. His clothes were as soaked as her own, his heart pounding as loud and rapidly as hers. As her senses crept back to a functioning state she realized how thoroughly she was plastered to him. They were embracing like soulmates.

She lifted her face from the hollow of his shoulder, but his arms remained iron-hard, pinning her to a chest roped with muscle, holding her so close she could smell faded aftershave and sea spray. Warmth crept into the seam of their bodies, spilling a teasing pleasure under her skin wherever their wet clothes adhered.

Gratitude. She tried dismissing it. But it was more. It didn't matter that she'd been here two years ago, very close to this place on the beach, and had received a harsh set down on the heels of experiencing this same rush. Nic was the only man to affect her like this, no matter how often she'd dated or tried to let other men arouse her. Nic had set the bar impossibly high when she'd first begun noticing the opposite sex. She had yet to find anyone who measured up. It meant that his arms were the ones she secretly longed to feel around her. Now he was ruining her even more, because the fit of her body to his was so perfect. The flood of tingling awareness so exciting.

His gaze caught her own and stillness came over him. She mentally braced herself, but instead of fury something hot flickered in his eyes. His expression darkened with a flush that almost looked like— Rowan caught her breath, confused. *Lust*? Impossible. He hated her.

Nevertheless, she could feel an unmistakable male reaction against her abdomen. An answering trickle of desire made her wriggle her hips in embarrassed curiosity.

His arms hardened, holding her still for his penetrating gaze as their mutual reaction became undeniable. He knew she was getting turned on. He was turned on and was forcing her to acknowledge it.

Her mind blanked as her unsteady heart kicked into overdrive. She'd been drunk the last time, and insulated against what had really been happening. The moon behind him had kept his face in shadow. He'd kissed her, angrily, and then had pushed her away as fast as he'd yanked her close.

This hadn't happened. Rowan was a skilled flirt, ever conscious of the power of her sex appeal, but real sexual need had never ignited in her properly. She'd never felt another man's arousal and been intrigued and excited. She'd always kept a clear head and been able to put on the brakes.

Not now. She longed to let Nic support her as she melted in abject surrender.

Panicked by her dwindling willpower, she pushed against his chest. "What are you doing?" she sputtered. The power of his spell glinted like fairy dust around her, disorienting her. Perhaps she'd fantasized from afar too long. She was seeing things that weren't there. Nic had never shown any kind of desire for her. Where had his arousal come from? Why now?

Nic's half-step back was by his choice, not her forceful shove, and now his grim expression held none of the heat she had thought she'd seen. If anything, he seemed vaguely disgusted. A cloak of reserve fell around him, turning him into the distant, condescending man she'd always known.

"I'm saving your life. What were you thinking, climbing out there when the water is this high?"

"Everyone climbs out there," she excused, wondering if she'd imagined that brief press of hard male flesh. Wishful thinking? Hardly. Getting into bed with this man would be like climbing into a cage with a tiger. When she finally slept with someone she'd choose a domesticated housecat. "How was I supposed to know the waves would come up like that? It's never happened before." She crossed her arms, feeling her soaked clothes and wet hair as the wind cut through her. Her chin rattled and she shivered.

"It's called a tide table and a weather report, Rowan."
He kept his gaze locked onto the horizon, his jaw like iron.

"Anyone reading tide tables in their leisure time is in
danger of drowning in boredom. Who *does* that?"

"I checked both before bringing the yacht over yesterday," he said stiffly, barely glancing at her as he added de-
risively, "Anyone who ignores basic precautions deserves
the natural selection that results."

"Then why didn't you let nature take its course with
me today?" she groused. The bottom of the Med sounded
infinitely more comfortable than suffering a lecture while
turning into an ice pop.

A barely discernible flinch was gone before she was
sure she'd really seen it.

His face hardened into an inscrutable mask as he glared
out to sea. "You disappearing along with the others would
look suspicious. I have to keep you alive long enough to
sign the documents I brought. Since I just did you a very
solid favor, you'll comply." His blue eyes came back to her
with freezing resolve.

"Dream on," she retorted, but he was already turning
away, everything in him dismissive of her and sure of his
success.

Annoyed beyond measure, she stayed where she was,
longing to be stubborn. But it was cold out here. Other
sensations were penetrating as well. Her hands and feet
burned along with her knee. The denim was torn out of
her jeans on her bad leg, exposing bloody, scraped skin.
Her palms were rashed raw and cuts on her fingers welled
with blood. The bottoms of her feet felt as if they'd been
branded.

Sickened, she lifted her head to call Nic, but he was
without sympathy, striding away without a backward
glance, his wet clothes clinging to his form as he rounded

the hedge and disappeared. He didn't care if she was hurt. He had his own agenda.

Grimly aware she had no one else to call for help, she gritted her teeth and limped her way back to the house.

CHAPTER THREE

"WHY DIDN'T YOU let nature take its course with me?" Nic was still sizzling when he left the shower, deeply angered by Rowan's remark. She was internally programmed to make flippant, provocative comments, so he shouldn't give her the satisfaction of getting a rise out of him, but today she was under his skin more than ever—and he'd been fighting his attraction toward her since before it had even been sexual.

He paused in hitching a towel around his wet hips, thinking back to those early years when she'd been a nubile sprite, too young for any man let alone one sowing the wild oats of his early twenties. Even so, she'd flitted in and out of his awareness with irritating persistence. He'd been alternately fascinated and annoyed, drawn by her quick wit even while baffled at the way she took it for granted that everyone loved her—especially Olief.

He'd been perversely determined not to fall under her spell, too irritated by how easily everything came to her. At a similar age, Nic had spent his holidays haunting the empty rooms of his boarding school. Olief hadn't wanted his wife to know about his indiscretion, so Nic hadn't entered the man's world until the woman had died and Cassandra had come on the scene. *Her* indiscretion had had an open invitation to spend school breaks in Olief's house. As an afterthought Nic had been asked to join them, but he'd been traveling by then, shedding light on the world's darkest injustices, inexplicably drawn into following Olief's footsteps into hard-hitting news journalism.

When Nic had come to Rosedale after those stints abroad it hadn't been for happy family time. In one way, at least, Olief had understood Nic. Olief had recognized Nic's need to retreat somewhere remote and quiet because Olief had experienced a similar need himself when he'd done that sort of work. The island's tranquility had kept Nic coming here, but the visits hadn't been comfortable—not when Olief showered affection on Rowan and she dominated everyone's attention.

Nic had done everything in his power to ignore and resist her, but she'd still managed to penetrate his shield. He was standing here because of her, wasn't he? Veering from deep insult that she'd actually thought he would leave her to die to stark fear at how close a call she'd had. That near miss unsettled him more than he wanted to admit. He told himself it was its similarity to the other deaths that made his blood run cold, but on the heels of that thought came the recollection that his blood hadn't stayed cold. He'd nearly let nature take its course in the form of raw, debaucherous lust.

His groin tightened in remembrance of the feel of her, the press of her hips.

Idiot. Revealing his weakness had been a mistake. He hadn't meant to, but the cork had popped under the pressure of saving her from danger and finally, after two years of reimagining it, holding her.

Bloody hell—why did she have to feel tailor-made for his form? The perfect height. A slender yet curvaceous shape that could wrap around him without smothering his need for space and autonomy. Her breasts, as natural as

God had made them, had crushed against his chest with nipples so hardened by the cold he'd felt them like pebbles through both their shirts. He clenched his fists, still longing to warm those tight peaks with his tongue until they were both hot all through.

Naked, and burningly aroused, he tilted back his head and struggled against the foe that had been stalking him for too long. He didn't recall when the switch had happened. Sometime between hearing she'd been caught with a boy at school and seeing her climb from the pool at eighteen. Suddenly he'd been unable to ignore her, or the singe in his blood whenever he was around her.

Then she had turned twenty, drunk her way to the bottom of a champagne bottle and, with no other man in the vicinity, turned her wiles on him.

Nic had tried not to let temptation get the better of him. He'd at least gone to the beach to avoid her. She'd followed, determined to get her man.

Nic had rules. Drunk women were never on the menu, no matter how willing they appeared to be. She'd sidled up to him, though, and he'd succumbed to a moment of weakness. One kiss. One warning to a reckless young woman who needed a lesson in putting herself at a man's mercy. One peek through the door into carnal paradise.

And Olief had seen it from the house. He hadn't seen Nic push her away, hadn't heard Nic read her the Riot Act. By the time Olief had reached the beach Rowan had been stumbling her way back to the house, and Nic had finally earned a hard-won moment of privacy with Olief.

It had been punctured by words Nic would never forget. *"What are your intentions, Nic? Marriage?"*

Olief's appalled disbelief, sharp with disparagement, had cut through Nic. It had been more than Olief warning off an experienced man from what he considered an impressionable young woman, deluded as that judgment had been. There'd been a fleck of challenge—as if Olief couldn't believe Nic would dare contemplate marrying into his family; as if he looked down on Nic for imagining it would be allowed. Nic wasn't good enough to be acknowledged as his son. Did he really imagine Olief would accept him as a son-in-law? Where did he get the nerve even to consider it?

It had been worse than humiliating. It had been hurtful. To this day Nic suspected Rowan had set up the whole thing and he wanted to shake her for it.

And yet when he'd had his hands on her today he'd only wanted to feel more of her. He'd seen the glow of arousal seep under Rowan's skin and that had been a fresh, sharp aphrodisiac. The volcano of lust pulsing in him refused to abate now he'd caught a glimpse of answering fire in her, hotter and more acutely aware than he'd ever seen it in her before. Damn it, she was—

What?

He opened his eyes but saw nothing, still blinded by hunger even as a shift occurred in his psyche. She wasn't too young. Not anymore.

Off-limits? By whose standards? Olief's? He was dead, and if he were alive to know how many men Rowan had had, he wouldn't defend her as being inexperienced.

As to marriage—well, Nic didn't want to marry anyone. Especially Rowan. He wanted to slake this hunger and move on with his life.

Nic winced, hearing his rationalizations for what they were, but craving was clawing in his chest, tearing through the walls of resistance he'd kept in place through years of encounters with her. Possibility opened before him with treacherous appeal. What was to stop him? Nothing. There was nothing to keep him from having her. Why shouldn't he? She'd been throwing herself at him for years.

Nic shuddered with physical need and inner turmoil. He never acted on impulse, yet everything in him longed to hunt her down right now and *take*. He shook off wild yearning and reached for self-discipline. Cool logic. Self-respect. He loathed her. Coming to Rosedale wasn't about giving in to an appetite he'd denied for years. It was about gaining what he really wanted: his rightful place as the head of Olief's media conglomerate. Not because he was the man's son, but because he'd earned it.

Nic shrugged into a light pullover and faded jeans, trying to ignore his unrelenting want for Rowan, searching for a clear mind while opportunity hung before him, refusing to be disregarded.

What a profound thorn in his vitals she was. She would never sign those papers if she thought she could string him along by torturing his libido.

His body aching with denial, he gathered his wet clothes and faced the inconvenience of Anna's quitting. Doing the washing and other chores would be a good lesson for Rowan, he decided arrogantly. Perhaps he was looking to punish her after all. She had been tormenting him for years. He was entitled to payback. At the very least she'd learn this wasn't rent-free accommodation.

He was framing exactly how he'd inform her of that when the bloody footprints in the upper hall stopped him cold.

Rowan jerked her head out of the shower spray. *Nic?*

"What the hell? Rowan!" His voice grew louder. The bathroom door opened and he was right there on the other side of the steamed glass, glaring like an angry drill sergeant.

Rowan squeaked in shock and turned her back on him, but she couldn't ignore the fact she was stark naked in front of him. The underside of her skin began to warm even though she was still frozen at her core. She tensed her buttocks, aware her bottom was on blatant display. Since when did he even know which room she used?

Strategically hugging herself, she cried, "Get out of here!"

"What have you done? It looks like a crime scene out there!"

"Oh, did I stain the precious hardwood you're planning to tear up? I'll scrub it once I quit bleeding to death, I promise. Now, get out!"

The door slammed with firm disgust. She sniffed in disdain at his impossible standards and stared at hands that looked worse under the running water. They scorched with protest at the pummel of spray, but they had to be cleaned. Her feet were begging her to get off them, but her leg worried her most. Not the sting on her skin, which was acute enough to make her clench her back molars. No, there was a deeper pain that concerned her. All the walking today hadn't helped. She was afraid to look but had to. No one else would.

Rolling her eyes at her decline into maudlin self-pity, she switched off the shower and dragged a bathsheet around herself. It wasn't as if her mother would be any use in this situation so why bother getting weepy? Olief would have been solicitous, though.

Shaking off wistfulness, still deeply chilled, she closed the lid of the toilet and sat down to pat herself dry. The door swung open again.

"Really?" she demanded, instinctively curling her feet in and closing a hand over the knot of her towel. She was in a high enough state of turmoil without Nic accosting her with his potent male energy every ten seconds. He'd already got her all bewildered on the beach, and then seen her naked in the shower. Sitting on a toilet in a bathsheet, shaking off a near-death experience, put her at the worst disadvantage ever.

He hesitated at the door, but it wasn't with doubt. She had the impression he was gathering himself. Bracing for a challenge.

Odd. She searched his expression for more clues, but he revealed nothing beyond a clinical interest in her hands as he set bandages and disinfectant on the counter. "You scraped yourself on the rocks, I assume?"

"Good work, Holmes. I should have consulted government-issued safe work plans prior to retreating from the tide, I assume?"

A pithy look, then, "It's a wonder your mother didn't drown you at birth. Do you want help or not?"

She grudgingly held out a hand. "I don't even know why you want to help me."

"I don't," he replied flatly, going down on one knee and reaching for supplies. "But I am an adult, and adults take responsibility rather than doing whatever selfish thing they want."

"Is that a dig? Because I'm almost twenty-two. A fully-fledged adult." Even to herself she sounded like a petulant child and, really, reminding him it was nearly her birthday was the last thing she ought to do.

"All grown up," he said, with an ironic twist to the corner of his mouth. Renewed tension seemed to gather in his expression as he smoothed a bandage against her wrist.

"Yes," she claimed pertly. Her pulse involuntarily tripped under his dispassionate caress, making her subtly catch a breath.

His gaze came up sharply, the blue like the center of a flame.

She was transported back to the feel of his arms as they'd stood wet and trembling on the beach, his arousal hardening against her. Heat flooded into her, chasing away the last of her chill, cooking her alive. She should have felt appalled and disgusted, but to her eternal shame she was energized by the crackle of sexual awareness in the air.

"All grown up," he repeated, with flint in his tone, and lifted her hand to press his lips against the bandage, a cruelly mocking glint in his eye.

She flinched and pulled her hand away, even though she'd barely felt the pressure of his mouth. That *so* hadn't been kiss-and-make-it-better!

Derisive amusement darkened his eyes. "No? That's not like you, Ro."

Her heart took a long plunge of disgrace. At the same time she felt herself begin to glow with heated longing and other weakening sensations, even as uncertainty and intrigue muddled her mind. Desperately she reminded herself of how unaffected and ruthless he could be.

"What are you doing, Nic?" she asked, trying unsuccessfully to clear the huskiness from her throat. "Offering a clumsy seduction in hopes of getting what you want out of me?"

"Oh, I'm far from clumsy. I know exactly what I'm doing when it comes to seduction." The hard tone was coupled with a look that might as well have swept the towel from her body and left her as nude as she'd been in the shower.

Had she really wished over the years for him to notice her? *Really* notice her? This was a horribly defenseless feeling! Every single occasion of testing a flirty glance or enticing him with a smile came back to her as mortifyingly obvious behavior that was now giving him the chance to get the better of her.

"You're having a go at me," she accused, as much to remind herself as to let him know she saw through him. "I'm sure other women wither at your feet when you bring your best game, but I'm not one of them. Act solicitous all you want, but I know you don't care. You don't want me. You don't even like me."

He took a moment to smooth a plaster over her second palm, finally asking with detached interest, "Do all of those things have to be in place at once?" He met her gaze with a look of cool consideration.

She pressed her lips into a tight line, stung by the implied agreement that he didn't like her. Yet still wanted her. That shouldn't excite her, but her blood seemed to slow and thicken in her arteries, making her feel hot and full of power.

"Since when did you even think about me before you decided I was in the way of something you wanted?" she managed, trying to ignore the internal signals bouncing with anticipation inside her.

His shoulders went back and his jaw hardened. "One has nothing to do with the other. I may want you to sign some papers, but that has nothing to do with physical chemistry."

"Chemistry that cropped up today of all days?" she scoffed, flushing with anger because her reaction to him had been torturing her forever. "It certainly wasn't there two years ago, was it?" she prodded, thinking, *Shut up, Rowan.*

"You want to go back to that?" With a flash of the tested anger he'd shown her then, he reached forward to cup the back of her wet head and pulled her forward to meet the crush of his mouth over hers.

"N-n-n...!" She almost got the word out, but it turned

into a whimper of surprise, then disintegrated under the assertive rake of his very knowledgeable mouth.

No champagne or the romance of a windswept beach this time. This was raw, unapologetic and incredibly beguiling. He kissed with the same command and purpose that emanated from the rest of his being. *He* was in control. *He* would take what he wanted. Their last kiss and the biting lecture that had followed had been a warning she should have heeded. Nic was a powerful, dangerous man.

Who knew how to level a woman with a kiss.

She brought her hands to his wrist and shoulder, overwhelmed yet helpless to the enthralling press of his lips over hers. There was no fighting him as he took her mouth—not because he was stronger, but because he made it so good. She could practically taste his contempt, his selfish demand that she give up everything to him, but there was skill here, too. A wicked appeal to the primitive in her. He drew her into the kiss even when she knew she shouldn't let herself be drawn.

Her inner being expanded toward him, tendrils of heated pleasure reaching for connection. She moaned, unfamiliar imperatives climbing with primal force in her. This was Nic. He didn't want her. He was messing with her. But this was *Nic*. She'd fantasized about him for years.

The light scrape of his teeth suffused her with heat. The proprietorial thrust of his tongue, the captivating taste of his mouth over hers, stabbed excitement through her, nudging her into a dark world of wild sensations and ravenous desire. Her limbs curled toward him like stems toward the sun, wanting more. It was crazy. Distantly she recognized this possession of her mouth had a purpose: arousal. He intended to take her all the way.

Her heart skipped. She shouldn't let this happen, but she wanted to. And he wasn't a force to be stopped. He reached to her lower back and pulled her hips toward him, forcing her knees to part and bracket his waist. Her shin struck the register. A ringing pain slashed through her wanton stupor, making her jolt in shock. Her towel slipped.

Oh, God, what was she *doing*?

Nic checked the urge to overpower Rowan's recoil and drag her back into the kiss. Into the bedroom or onto the floor. Anywhere. She was flushed, and her breath was stuttering from between glossy kiss-swollen lips. Her eyes were still cloudy with desire, the honeyed taste of her sexual appetite still tangible on his tongue.

The beast ran hard in him, fighting against being steered back into its corral. Nic's chest heaved and the hot coil of pressure behind his fly demanded release. He had one hand braced on the wall and used the other to reach for her jaw, ignoring the mental warnings trying to penetrate his fog of carnal hunger. This time he'd let it happen.

Before he could tilt Rowan back into the direction they'd been headed, her pale expression and the flash of a worried look downward stopped him. She leaned cautiously to examine her leg, her hand pressing the middle of his chest to push him back.

He followed her gaze and the sight froze him. Not the scrape on her knee. That was little worse than a tumble off a bicycle would produce, but the scars down her shin were horrific.

"What the hell?" He sat back on his heels, physical arousal taking a backseat to shock. The depth of her injury, communicated by the crisscross of thin white lines, revolted him. He reached one hand behind her knee and had to school his clenching muscles to take care as he lifted her ankle in the other hand, studying the full extent of the damage.

Her shin wasn't the only issue. She had old scars all over her feet, framing knobbly toes with cracked nails that were only partially healed.

Rowan flexed her foot. "Don't."

"Hurts?" It had to. The marks spoke of repeated injuries.

She snorted. "I've lived with pain at that end of my body for so long I don't even notice it. I don't like anyone looking at my feet." Her lashes swept down in self-conscious dismay. "They're ugly."

"They're not pretty," he agreed, smoothing the pad of his thumb over an old callus, astounded by the time and effort it would have required to form the thick bump. "This is from dancing?"

"We all get them," she defended, and attempted to pull from his grip.

He held on. He hadn't meant to sound so appalled, but he was inexplicably angered. The big scar was bad enough, but at least it was understandable. It had been an accident. These others...

"Why would anyone do this to herself?" he questioned, channeling an unexpected surge of concern into impatience. "I've seen foot soldiers coming off a month-long march with better feet."

She flushed and pushed her damp hair behind her ear. "It's part of the process. They've gotten a lot better since I've been off them."

"Because your leg was broken." He looked again at the long scar. Everything Rowan did was superficial, but suddenly he couldn't be dismissive of what she'd been going through. Her remark about being in constant pain echoed in his head along with her old claims of *"doing the best I can"* to Cassandra's livid, *"How can you not be ready?"*

It occurred to him that his impression of Rowan as a

slacker was largely based on those overheard accusations
that Rowan wasn't trying hard enough. That perturbed
him. He generally formed his own opinions, but he'd been
seeing her with a skewed view to hold her at a distance.
He didn't often mislead himself like that.

"How many surgeries have you had?" he asked, setting
her cut foot on his thigh.

"Three. I'm a little concerned about the pins, actually," she confided hesitantly. "I think they're killing me
right now because they got cold. Does anything feel out of
place?" She bit her lip, the apprehensive pull of her brow
more concerning than her actual words. She was suppressing very real distress.

A chill took him as he carefully felt up and down her
calf. The male in him was aware of lean muscle under
smooth pale skin, and fascinating shadows beneath the
drape of the bathsheet across her thighs. He'd got a too
brief glimpse of her through the steamed walls of the
shower and was dying for a proper study of her form. He
focused on determining whether she'd rebroken something, but that thought filled the pit of his stomach with
ashes—not unlike the defeated fury that had taken him as
he'd run up the beach, afraid he wouldn't reach her in time.

He turned his mind from that raw terror.

"It seems okay. Will you dance again?" He already
knew the answer, and tension gathered in him, resisting
the truth.

She leaned forward to palpate the shin herself, brushing his hands off her calf, remaining silent. He lifted his
gaze from watching her massage her torn muscles. Her
mink lashes formed a pair of tangled lines.

"On tables," she finally replied with a tough smile, "but
not on the stage."

Expecting the answer didn't make it easier to hear. He

was taken aback by a surprisingly sharp stab of sympathy. As a journalist, he'd spent his life asking people for their reactions to events, but he had never asked anyone *How do you feel about that*? He wanted to ask Rowan, but her snarky response grated, compelling him to say, "You never wanted to dance anyway. It was a bone of contention with your mother, wasn't it? Her insisting you go to that fancy school? You must be relieved."

She gave a little snort of cynical amusement and dipped her head in a single nod that left her damp hair hanging. "Yes, I can honestly say I was relieved when they finally admitted I would never get back to my old level and asked me to leave so someone with whole bones and genuine passion could take my spot."

His heart kicked as he disagreed with *anyone* claiming Rowan lacked passion. He was still tingling from their kiss a minute ago. He didn't let the sensation escalate, though, sidetracked by her bitter revelation.

"When *they* admitted?" he repeated. "You wanted to quit and they wanted to rehabilitate you?" He reached for a bandage to cover her knee, aware of his sympathy dwindling. She *was* a shirker after all.

"Madame is a close friend of Mum's. She knew Mum wouldn't want all those years of training to be for nothing, but she also knew as well as I did that I had reached my potential before the accident and that I'd never be good enough. She pushed me anyway, and I tried until my ankle gave out. We finally agreed I was a grand failure and the silver lining was that my mother would never know."

He didn't want to be affected by the wounded shadows of defeat lurking behind her sparking eyes and pugnacious chin, but he was. Rowan might have quit, but because she was a realist about her own limitations, not a quitter. He wondered what else he'd failed to see in her before today.

"If you didn't like dance, why did you pursue it?" he asked.

A brief pause, then a challenging, "Why did *you* go into the same field as Olief?"

It was a blatant deflection from his own question—one that deepened his interest in her motives. He answered her first, though. His reason was simple enough.

"I was curious about him so I followed his work. You can't read that many articles on world events and not feel compelled to discover the next chapter." He shrugged and began patching her other knee. "I wasn't trying to emulate him. Were you? Trying to emulate Cassandra?"

Rowan made a noise of scorn. "Not by choice. Count yourself lucky that no one knew you were related to Olief when you started out. You were able to prove yourself on your own merit and do it because you wanted to. I was pushed into dancing as a gag. It was a way for my mother to stand out, because she had this little reflection of herself beside her. She was allowed to quit when she and Olief got together, but I still had all this 'potential' to be realized."

Nic had never framed his abandonment by his parents as good fortune, but he'd never taken a hard look at Rowan's situation and seen it for misfortune either.

He frowned, not enjoying the sense that he'd been blind and wrong. None of Rowan's revelations changed anything, he reminded himself. He still wanted full control of Marcussen Media. She still needed to sign the petition forms, grow up, and take responsibility for herself—not party her way across Europe at his expense.

Rowan watched Nic's concentration on her fade to something more familiar and removed and suspected she knew why. She dropped her gaze to the bandaged hands she'd clenched in her lap, the fetid crown of disloyalty making her hang her head. In her wildest dreams she had never imagined Nic would be the person to crack this resentment out of her. She'd anticipated taking her anger to the grave, because only the lowest forms of life said anything against Cassandra O'Brien. A good daughter would certainly never betray her mother when she was *gone*.

"Not that I hated her for forcing me into it," Rowan mumbled, trying to recant. "I understood. She was my age when she had me. All she knew was performing, and that sort of career doesn't wait around while you raise a child. She didn't have any support. Her family disowned her when she left to become—*gasp!*—an actress. You have to be an opportunist to survive in that business, and that's what she was trying to do. Survive."

She risked a glance upward and saw that Nic didn't exactly look sympathetic. He was closing off completely to what she was saying, his lip curling in cynical understanding of words like "opportunist" and "survivor."

Rowan clenched her teeth, thinking she would be calling on all the skills Cassandra O'Brien had ever taught her when it came to surviving. That had been the real source of animosity between mother and daughter: the things Cassandra had done to keep them both fed and clothed. The men she'd brought into their home—the homes she'd brought Rowan into. The pressure for Rowan to 'make it' so they had a fallback position if things went south. The fact that when it came right down to it Cassandra had been most concerned about her own survival at the expense of her daughter's happiness, and had alternately been threatened by and quick to exploit her daughter's youth and beauty.

The tenderness of pressure on a cut pulled Rowan back to Nic pressing a bandage into place on the bottom of her foot.

"What are you going to do now?" he asked.

"That's the million-dollar question, isn't it? I'm not exactly brimming with marketable skills."

"Perhaps you should have addressed that as soon as you left school, rather than making a spectacle of yourself with the rest of the Euro-trash."

Ouch. Although a tiny bit justified. She hadn't seen how truly shallow most of her friends were until she'd tried to rely on them as she dealt with everything—not least of which was this utterly directionless feeling of not knowing who she was or where she was going. Her friends had coaxed her to drink her way out of her funk. Something she'd briefly been led into before realizing how quickly she could turn into her father. That had scared her back onto the straight and narrow, but she couldn't believe Nic's attitude toward her bad turn after all she'd told him.

"I had to go somewhere when I was kicked out of residence. I wasn't ready to face this empty house so I stayed with friends. Where else was I supposed to go? To you, *big brother*?"

The warning that flashed in his icy blue eyes spoke of retribution for that label. She took notice, clamping her teeth together and leaning back an inch, not willing to get into a kissing contest again.

His nod was barely perceptible, but it was there, approving of her smart and hasty retreat. That irritated her. She didn't want to be afraid of him and she wasn't. She was afraid of herself and how weak he made her feel.

Sitting straighter, she said defensively, "Perhaps it wasn't the best coping strategy, but I had a lot to deal with."

"It's always about *you*, isn't it, Rowan?" Nic stood and took his time turning over the end on the surgical tape before setting it aside.

Rowan clamped shut the mouth that had dropped open. Had he not just seen with his own eyes how thoroughly she'd been living her mother's life? Fueled by righteousness, she rose hastily—then lost some of her dignity as she had to grapple for her towel. Every point on her body twinged, making her wince.

She braced herself on the wall and demanded, "You really see me as nothing more than a total narcissist, don't you?" It was so unfair.

His eyelids came down to a circumspect half-mast as he pointed out flatly, "Well, you just *had* to have a week in St. Moritz for your birthday last year, didn't you?"

Because she hadn't had the courage to come home and risk facing him after the fiasco the year before—which only added to the colossal self-blame eating her alive.

"And my broken leg put my mother and your father on the plane. Is the storm my fault too?" she asked through lips that were going numb. "Should I have checked the weather on the Med before I let that drunken snowboarder mow me down?"

Nic heard the tortured regret in her tone and recognized it as sincere, but the shriveled, underfed raisin where his heart was supposed to be didn't want to soften toward her. He couldn't afford to let it soften at all. That way led to madness and pain.

He turned away from her, and the tumult she was inciting inside him. His version of Rowan as an immature egocentric needed to stand firm against this more complex vision that was emerging, otherwise he'd be forced to reexamine himself, her, and everything that had transpired between them since day one.

"You think I don't hate myself every day?" Rowan said with a rasp that made him flinch. "Why do you think I refuse to accept they're gone? Maybe you're right, and I do need to show responsibility, but I don't want to be responsible for their being *dead*, Nic!"

A barbed hook seemed to catch at the flesh surrounding his heart.

"Olief made the decision to fly despite the weather," he muttered, unable to stand the weight of guilt she was carrying. "It's not your fault."

"No?" Her thready need for reassurance pulled at him, along with the misery searching for forgiveness in her gaze as he caught her reflection in the mirror.

"No," he affirmed, caving briefly to her palpable anguish. "You'll need your things," he added, seizing the excuse to escape the close atmosphere of the humid room. He needed to get away from her before his barriers against her crumbled any more.

It wasn't until he was halfway down the stairs that he remembered he'd had every intention of forcing Rowan to get out as soon as possible, not help her settle in.

Rowan pulled on leggings and a loose T-shirt from her closet, trying to process the consoling remark Nic had made about Olief choosing to fly. Before she could make sense of it Nic was pushing back into her room and setting his bags on the floor. He straightened and gave her a cursory, masculine once over that made her tingle.

"Let's be clear. This isn't your all-inclusive. I'll give you a few days to gather your belongings, but then you'll move on. While you're here you'll pull your weight with cooking, cleaning and laundry."

She turned her back on him to hide the sting of his sudden return to Lord of the Manor disdain. Without saying anything, she took her time twisting her wet hair into a coil and fixing it with a pair of chopsticks off her dresser-top.

"I came for the anniversary," she informed him stiffly, her insides fluttering with sexual awareness as she considered sharing this house with him. Alone. It could be unpleasant, but she wouldn't be scared off. "Don't even try to pry me out of here before then. I'll shred you to pieces."

His brows lifted and she almost heard his unspoken, *I'd like to see you try.*

Her bravado teetered as she realized he was more than big enough to physically throw her out, and had financial strength on his side, as well. For all her show of defiance, she was fragile as hell at her core. That was why she'd come back to the one constant in her life: Rosedale. She needed a sense of security while she figured out what to do.

"This is the only real home I've ever had, Nic. Maybe you and I aren't related, but this is where we gathered as a family. I need that right now." She kept her tone as steady as possible, refusing to descend into begging. "You can give me that much."

Nic braced an arm against the doorjamb, shaking his head at his bare feet before he lifted his derisive gaze. "I have to question that kind of sentimentality. What do you gain by being here for a day that has no more meaning than any other? They're gone." He wasn't being unkind, just honest—which was more difficult to face. "They're not any more or less gone whether you're here or in London or Antarctica."

Rowan gripped her elbows as she turned, shoulders hunching protectively as she absorbed what a truly unfeeling man he was. "I find it comforting to be here," she excused, hearing the creak in her voice at admitting to what he obviously saw as weakness. "But you can go back to Athens, or wherever you're living these days."

A slow smile crept across his features, completely without amusement. "You wish. No, I'll stay. And I'll even let you stay until the anniversary if you promise to sign your name on the dotted line once you've finished lighting candles in the windows."

"Why do you have to be so disparaging about it?"

"I'm being magnanimous," he defended, straightening into cool civility. "Would you rather I make your stay conditional on your signing right now?"

"Oh, very nice," she said, instantly spitting venom over that sleight of hand. "I knew you were tough, Nic. I didn't know you were ruthless."

"Now you do," he said without acrimony.

"And you expect me to housemaid while I'm here?" Her fists dug into her ribs beneath the pressure of her elbows. "You know it was the evil step*mother* who had Cinderella scrubbing floors and sorting ballgowns all day."

"What would you rather do to earn your keep?" he shot back, swift and lethal. "Demonstrate more of your mother's survival skills?"

"Sleep with you, you mean? Not in this lifetime. Get over yourself!"

His brows shot up and his stance altered subtly to a predatory one full of challenge. Their kiss and her undeniable response was suddenly right here in the room with them. Sexual awareness gathered and sparked. The sheer magnitude of what was being acknowledged, her inability to ignore it, made Rowan's heart race in frightened anticipation. All she could think was, *Oh, my God. Oh, my God. Oh, my God.*

"It wasn't like that with Mum and Olief," she stammered. "She loved him."

"Give it a rest, Ro. I've had mistresses. I know what it's like." His chilly assessment of her figure left a trail of heat over her breasts, down her stomach and up between her thighs. "*Quid pro quo,*" he said with a curl of his lip. "Not love."

His words wrenched at a place between her throat and heart. She didn't examine the source too closely. Part of it had to do with acknowledging all those unknown women who had shared his bed—something she'd never let herself think about too much—but there was a deeper sense of loss in hearing his derision of love.

"Well, I'm not going to have sex with you to stay here," she said, forcing herself to stand up to him even though she was on very shaky legs. Figuratively and literally. Despite his horrid lecture two years ago, she knew not to get into dicey situations with men and this was one of them. Best to get the *no* stated clearly. "I'm not going to let you seduce me into signing those papers before I'm good and ready either."

Her futile training in Paris for once bore fruit, allowing her to walk out gracefully on ravaged feet, her bearing straight and her shoulders proud.

CHAPTER FOUR

SEDUCE HER. IT WAS a challenge no red-blooded man could dismiss, even one whose conscience was as tortured by the prospect as his libido.

Even with the memory of Olief's setdown replaying in his mind, Nic couldn't stop fantasizing about having Rowan. She had essentially agreed to sign the papers after the anniversary, so he didn't need to try persuading her that way, but a carnal voice inside still urged him to seduce her for personal vindication. She deserved some payback for that stunt with Olief, the licentious appetite in him rationalized, not to mention a taste of the wanting and not having that he'd been suffering all these years.

Hellfire, he wanted to end this craving, but as much as he dreamed of taking her to the brink and walking away, he knew if he started something he would finish it.

That was where his hard-earned self-protective instincts kicked in and reminded him not to do anything rash. If you played with fire you got burned, and there was definitely a fire in that woman. Their kiss, the way her mouth had opened and crushed into the pressure of his, wouldn't leave his mind, making him useless behind his desk.

Given that his plans had changed, and he'd now be here a full two weeks, he had spent the afternoon reconfiguring Olief's office space to his own taste so he could work more productively. It wasn't happening. Despite Rosedale being big and quiet, he was intensely aware there was another occupant here.

Forget her, he commanded himself. But there were other distractions. The promised thunderstorm had brought darkness early and was rattling the windows. Hunger gnawed at his belly, reminding him he'd skipped lunch. He needed to approve this project and get it back to the VP while the time change window was still open, though.

Another flash of lightning bleached the windows and a huge clap of thunder reverberated above the house. The lights flickered—then everything went black.

Nic swore at the inconvenience. The wiring here was modern and top-notch. All the equipment was protected with surge bars. The vineyard manager would investigate the outage and report it. All he'd lost was his wi-fi connection and the widescreen monitor. A glance at his laptop in its dock showed the battery light gleaming reliably. Nic opened the lid and the screen came alive with a pallid glow. He flicked his mobile into hotspot mode and was able to retrieve his report and continue making comments.

"Nic?" The flickering yellow of a candle entered the room ahead of Rowan, her face sweetly tinted with warm golden light.

The words *seduce her* tantalized him again. He sat back, thinking, *Do it because you want to.* Such a bad idea.

"Afraid of the thunder?" he taunted lightly.

She set the squat candle in its round bowl on the corner of his desk. "I thought you might be fumbling around in the dark, but of course you're perfectly equipped."

"Thanks for noticing," he drawled, and wondered if that was a blush climbing into her shadowed cheeks or just the flush of impatience women got when a man made an off-color remark. "I'm fine. Working without interruption, in fact." He turned his nose back to the screen to steer himself from temptation.

He still tracked Rowan as she took an idle stroll into the dark corners of the office, pausing at the window as rain gusted against the glass before taking herself to the bookshelf of worn style-guides, atlases, and other reference tomes.

"Use my tablet if you want a novel," he offered. "There are hundreds on it."

"If I have time to read, I have time to practice." She said it like something she'd memorized by rote. "Same goes for television—not that that's an option right now." She came away from the bookshelf with a look that was both disgruntled and lost. "I've already done my exercises. If I work my leg anymore I'll just hurt myself. I was about to start dinner, but the freezer is empty and the power's gone."

"I brought the boat," Nic reminded her, his body involuntarily reacting to the way she moved like a leaf in a stream, meandering in a way that mesmerized him.

"I've had enough of the sea today, thanks." Her aimless path took her to a lamp fringe, which she lightly stroked, making the silk lift and fall in a ripple.

This was so like her—the way she accepted as her due that a room would pause and take notice when she entered. What was it about her that made it happen? he wondered. She was lovely, with her buttermilk skin and sable hair, the sensual softness of her features and the toned perfection of her frame, but that wasn't what gave her such power. There was something more innate, something warm, that promised happiness and fulfillment if she noticed you.

Nic shut down that bizarre tangent of thought. He was not one of those people who fell for charisma, watching and waiting for the next act, aching to feel important because he was touched by her attention.

Irritated with himself, he did what he'd always done when Rowan inveigled herself into his space. He pretended he was ignoring her even though he could practically feel the heat off her body from across the room.

That was his libido keeping her on its scope. He hadn't made much time for women in the last year and his body was noticing.

"Cold sandwiches are fine," he said. "Bring mine here so I can keep working."

"That reminds me. I should have said earlier, Nic." She moved toward him, pale fingers coming to rest like a pianist's on the opposite edge of his desk. The candlelight made her solemn expression all the more wide-eyed and impactful. "What you've done for Olief? Looking after things for him? That's good of you. I'm sure he'd appreciate it."

The unexpected praise turned him inside out. No one had ever suggested he was a good son. Olief certainly hadn't acknowledged him that way—ever—and Nic had long given up expecting him to. Having Rowan offer this shred of recognition was a surprise stiletto through the ribs that slid past his barriers to prick at the most deeply protected part of himself.

For a second he couldn't breathe. The sensation was so real and sharp and paralyzing. Then his inner SWAT team snapped into action and he remembered her using this same gamine face and earnest charm to garner affectionate pats on the head and indulgent approval from Olief. They'd been president of each other's fan club, and now she was obviously looking for a new partner in her mutual admiration society.

"I'm not doing it for him," Nic stated bluntly, angry with himself for sucking up her flattery like a dry sponge.

"But…" Rowan's brows came together and she took

a half step back from the refutation she read in his face. "Who, then?"

"Myself. I've been working my way up since he brought me aboard to launch his web journals on the Middle East ten years ago. It was a merger, actually, since I was already established in the electronic publishing side. I made it clear then that I had ambitions. He hadn't named me as heir, and I wasn't at the top of his corporate succession plan when he disappeared, but it was due to be reviewed and we both knew this is where I wanted to end up."

"What do you mean, he didn't...? Of *course* you're his heir!"

Rowan's certainty made a harsh bubble of laughter rise to catch in Nic's throat. They were talking about a man who hadn't spoken to his son until Nic had walked up to him at an awards gala and said, "*I believe you knew my mother.*"

With fresh rancor, Nic said, "We won't know who inherits until he's been declared dead and his will is read. Perhaps he left his fortune to Cassandra and you?"

With a shake of her head that made loose tendrils of hair catch the candlelight and glitter like an angel's halo, Rowan said, "You're his son. And you can build on what he's already accomplished. Of course he would leave everything to you. Except maybe Rosedale." Her chin hitched with challenge as she gave him a considering look.

"This land was bought as an investment property to be developed. It's never been taken off the books as a company asset," Nic said. "I know that much."

"Therefore you control it as long as you're in that chair?"

"Exactly."

Her narrow shoulders slid a notch, but her breasts lost none of their thrust. For a skinny little thing, she had beautifully rounded breasts. All of her was a little curvier than he remembered. It was nice. Healthy.

"If I *did* inherit everything from Olief, I could fire you."

Her disdainful look down her nose was the kind of entitled sassiness that had always made him want to yank her off her self-built pedestal. He reminded himself not to let her engage his emotions.

"I've spent the last year proving to the board I'm the right man for the job. They're not going to switch allegiance on the whim of a spoiled brat—despite your proven ability to charm older men."

Her chin twitched at the word 'spoiled' before her thick lashes came together and her most impudent smile appeared. "Don't underestimate me. I charm the younger ones, too."

"Yes, you always manage to get what you want, don't you?" he said with chilly disgust. "Until now."

As soon as he said it a vision of her feet flashed in his mind's eye and he heard her again. *I want my family.* The source of hardness in him turned on its edge, pressing at an unpleasant angle against his lungs. He grimaced, wishing for her to be the diva ballerina he'd always found easy to dismiss.

"Am I really that bad, Nic?" Her white hands sifted the air. "Maybe Olief *did* pay my expenses, but developing as a dancer was my *job.* I didn't have time to hold down a real one. And, yes, I did take things too far in the last few months, but it was the first time I'd been free to! I kept waiting for someone to set me a limit and finally realized *I* had to. Everyone goes through that on the way to becoming an adult. You're making out like I'm all new cars and caviar, but what did I ever have that you didn't?"

His laptop timed out, abruptly going black and dimming the room into a place of darkness and shadows. Thunder continued to rumble in the distance, along with the piercing wail of wind and the churn of rough waves against the shore.

"What a loaded question," he muttered, stabbing a key to make the screen come back to life, and rising restlessly at the same time. "What did you have?" he repeated.

He rounded his desk to confront her in the cold bluish glow. He couldn't contain the confused hurt bottled against the spurned rock that was his heart.

"Do you have any idea what it's like to meet your father for the first time when you're an adult? To finally be invited into his home only to watch him fawn over the daughter of his mistress—a girl who isn't even related to him—while knowing he never once wasted affection on his *real* flesh and blood? Now, to be fair, my mother was only a one-night stand—not a long-term companion like your mother—but he knew about me from birth. He paid for my education, but he never so much as dropped by the boarding school to say hello. I came to believe he was incapable of fatherly warmth." He'd had to. It had been the only way to cope. "Then I saw him with you."

Rowan drew in a breath that seemed to shrink her lungs, making her insides feel small and tense. Olief was the one safe, reliable, loving person she could go to without being told to try harder, commit deeper, be better. That was why his disappearance was killing her. She missed him horribly. She loved him.

And apparently Nic felt she'd stolen all those precious moments at *his* expense.

"At least that explains why you hate me." Nic, like everyone, had expected better of her and, like always, she didn't know how she could have been different. All she could do was what she'd always done: apologize. "I'm sorry. I never meant to get between you."

"Didn't you?" he shot back, his feral energy expanding until her skin prickled with goose bumps.

She felt caught red-handed. Her old crush on him sputtered to life in neon glory, making her feel gauche. The memory of today's kiss, which she'd managed to ignore through sheer force of will since entering this room, was released like an illicit drug in her mind—one that stole her ability to think and expanded her physical perceptions.

Betraying heat flooded into her loins while the tips of her breasts tightened. She was hyper-aware of his male power held in tight restraint. For years he'd looked at her with bored aversion. Today he was seeing her, and his gaze was full of the force of his primal nature, accusatory and personal.

And for once she understood his animosity.

The defusing explanation didn't come easily. Her throat didn't want to let the words out. They were too revealing.

"I know I often interrupted the two of you. Please don't judge me too harshly for that." She had wanted so badly to catch Nic's attention. Being in his presence had made her heart sing—not unlike right now, she thought in an uncomfortable aside, burning on a pyre of self-conscious embarrassment. "I wanted to hear your stories," she excused, trying to downplay what a wicked pleasure it had been to eavesdrop on his rumbling voice. His analytical intelligence with such an underlying thirst for justice had drawn her irresistibly. Her fingers tangled together in front of her. "You were traveling the world while I couldn't steal time to climb the Eiffel Tower in my own backyard. Don't fault me for wanting to live your adventures."

"Adventures? I was reporting on civil wars! Crimes against humanity! Those sorts of tales aren't fit for a woman's ears, let alone the child you were then. The only reason I brought them up with Olief was because he'd been there. He understood the line that has to be drawn between exposing the horrors and scaring the hell out of people. You can't do that kind of work without unloading somewhere."

Rowan was struck by more than his words. His eyes darkened and his expression flashed with a suffering that he quickly shuttered away. Her view of his work had always been that it was genuinely glamorous and important, not just appearing that way like her own. His face was splashed on magazine covers, wasn't it? He was no stranger to being a still, compelling presence before a camera. He had accolades galore for his efforts.

There was a toll for bringing forth the stories that held an audience rapt, though. Perhaps she *was* horribly self-involved, since she'd never considered what sorts of anguish and cruelty he'd witnessed in getting those stories. He would have pushed himself because he was a man of ambition, but his opinion pieces revealed a man who wanted to restore peace and justice. That wasn't work for the faint-hearted. If he was tough and closed off it was because he had to be in order to get what he wanted for the betterment of humanity.

Everything in her longed to surge forward and somehow offer comfort, but his body language—shoulders bunched, head turned to the side—shouted *back off.*

She stared down at bare feet that were icy despite the carpet she stood on.

"I always wondered why you were always so…" Aloof? Emotionless? Haunted? "Quiet."

She rubbed her arms, trying to bring life back into herself when she felt chilled to the bone. Her heart ached for him. Of course he would have needed someone to help put all those terrible sights into perspective. She wanted to scroll back time and watch from afar, allowing him the healing he'd so obviously needed.

"I wish you'd said something," she said weakly. "I wouldn't have got in your way with Olief if I'd known how bad it was."

"No?" he challenged, with another shot of that searing aggression.

"Of course not! I'm not so self-centered that I felt threatened by your having a relationship with your own father."

"Then why did you set it up for him to see us on the beach and take a strip off me for it? That was a depth of bitchiness that exceeded even *my* low expectations of you, Ro." His recrimination made her knees go weak.

The tiny thread of hope she'd found and clasped on to, the tentative belief that she was making headway with understanding Nic's reserve and softening his judgment of her, snapped like a rubber band, not only stealing her optimism with a sharp sting, but launching her into an empty space where there was only hard landings.

"Olief *saw* that?" The one person who liked her exactly as she was had seen her inept plea to be noticed and the humiliating rejection that had followed. Rowan wanted to sink through the carpet and disappear. She dropped her cringing face into her hands.

"Oh, give it a rest. The awards committee isn't in residence," Nic bit out.

"I passed Olief on the path, but I didn't think he'd seen us!" She only lifted her mortified face because she was determined to make him believe her. "Do you honestly think I'd want anyone to know I behaved so cheaply? I can hardly face *you*."

"Then why did you do it?" His eyes were cold and measuring, unwilling to accept her protest at face value. "It better be good, Rowan, because he made me feel like a pervert, saying men like me had no business with a girl like you. What the hell does *that* mean? *Men like me?* Too old? Or simply not good enough? Forget finding common ground after that. We were barely speaking."

Her throat closed again. She felt sick with herself. She had to 'fess up or he'd believe forever that she was a tease, and worse—someone who had schemed to hurt him for no reason but a power trip. She couldn't live with that. She wasn't like that at all.

"I…I wanted to," she managed in a strangled whisper, furnace-like heat unleashing in her to conflagrate her whole body. She felt like the candle flame swaying on its spineless wick, all her dignity melting into a transparent puddle beneath her.

"Wanted to what?" he demanded. "Make me look like an opportunist?"

"No!" Rowan pitied every minion who'd ever had to stand before him and explain herself. He was utterly formidable. But his demeanor was the kind of unyielding superciliousness she'd been knuckling under all her life. She was *so* tired of apologizing for being human and having flaws!

"I wanted to kiss you," she blurted with defiance, staring him right in the eye while every nerve ending fried under the responding flash of heat in his gaze. "I was attracted to you. We all have urges," she excused with a shrug, desperate to play it down so he wouldn't know *how* attracted. "I'd had a few drinks. It seemed like a good idea."

For a long time he only stared at her, while the silence played out and the shadows closed in. Just as she began to feel sweat popping across her upper lip he moved closer, studying her so intently her skin tightened all over her body.

"You wanted a kiss bad enough to chase me to the beach for it?"

"Take your pound of flesh if you need it. Yes, I chased

you and, yes, I realize how desperate that makes me seem. It was an impulse. I didn't get out much and it was my birthday." If she kept slapping coats of whitewash on it perhaps he wouldn't see it for the act of lifelong yearning it had been.

"All those years of batting your lashes and trying to get a rise out of me... It wasn't more of that same nonsense?"

She had to drop her gaze then, because it had very much been a culmination of that long, infernal effort to catch his interest.

His hand came under her jaw, forcing her chin up so she couldn't hide from his penetrating glacier-blue eyes. "Because I can forgive a teenager for baiting a grown man, but at twenty you should have known better."

"So you said then, and I wasn't doing that." Impatience got the better of her and she tried to pull away, dying inside as she recalled his angry kiss and his merciless rejection.

His hand moved to the side of her neck, long fingers sliding beneath the fall of her hair so his fingertips rested on the back of her neck, keeping her close.

"And today?" he asked, his tone dangerously lethal.

"Today you kissed *me*." It took guts to hold her ground, especially when she was flushed with self-disgust as she recalled how she'd reacted: as if she still thought kissing him was a good idea. Her nails cut into her palms as she made herself face him and the crushing truth. "Or rather you tried to manipulate me with what mechanically resembled a kiss."

He gave a little snort. "I'm long past the age of playing games. It was more than mechanics. We kissed each other."

He made it sound like something to be savored. When he dropped his gaze to her mouth her stomach tightened. Her whole body tingled and her lips began to burn.

"We started something two years ago that wants finishing."

Her hand came up instinctively to the middle of his chest. He hadn't moved any closer, but she suddenly felt threatened. Her arteries swelled as all her blood began to move harder and faster. "Wh-what do you mean?"

"I'm not blind, Rowan." He glanced down to where her still-bandaged hand pressed against his chest. His strong heartbeat pounded into her palm. "I noticed in the last few years that you weren't a kid anymore. The only thing that stopped me taking what you were offering that night was a certainty that you didn't mean it. If you had…"

She sucked in a breath and jerked back, pulling her hand into her breasts as though his glance at her knuckles had branded them.

Nic folded his arms across his chest, his shoulders hardening. "*Did* you mean it?" he demanded. "Are we finally being honest or still playing games?"

This was moving too fast. "I'm not going to sleep with you, Nic!"

"Because you still want to tie me up in knots for kicks?"

Was he feeling tied up? Insidious heat flooded into her pelvis, licking with wanton anticipation at her insides. He couldn't be serious. She told her feet to run, but they refused. "We can't have some kind of fling and then carry on as if…"

She trailed off, the little cogs in her head making hard, sharp connections that stuck long enough to reverberate painfully in her skull before clicking over to the next one as she took in the way Nic's brows lifted in aloof inquisition.

She was a virgin, not sophisticated and experienced enough to have flings. Nic *was* experienced, though, and when he had flings he carried on just fine afterward because he never saw his partner again. Which was exactly what he intended with Rowan.

How had she not grasped that? He had come here intending to kick her out and never see her again. She'd won a stay of eviction, but after the two weeks were up they would not cross paths again—not unless it was by chance.

She would never see Nic again. Ever. How had she not taken that in?

Because she had subliminally believed that when she was ready she would seek him out. Never once had she thought there would be no Rosedale to come back to— no Nic prowling the grounds where she could put herself under his nose with only minimal risk and wait for him to notice her.

The gray void that was her future grew bigger and more desolate.

"As if what?" he prompted.

She gave a dry laugh, using it to cover the damp thickness gathering in her throat. "I naively thought an affair could make for awkward Christmas dinners in future, but that won't be a problem, will it? I really am saying goodbye to everything I knew and—"

Don't say it. Rowan swallowed and twisted her hands together, trying to rub sensation into fingers that were going numb. "I wish you had some feeling of having a home and family here, Nic. I really do. I'll make us some sandwiches."

She picked up the candle and walked out, leaving him in the glow of the laptop. She didn't see how he stood in the same place long after the device timed out again, silent and alone in the dark.

CHAPTER FIVE

Nɪᴄ ᴡᴀs sᴛɪʟʟ ʟᴇᴛᴛɪɴɢ Rowan's remark eat at him the next morning, and he couldn't fathom why. It wasn't as if he hadn't heard variations of it from other women.

He had concluded over the years that there was a deficiency in him that portrayed him as not needing what others did: a home, family, love. And since he had been denied those things all his life he had learned to live without them. He *didn't* need them. It was a closed loop.

So why did he feel so unfairly judged by Rowan's, *I wish you had some feeling of having a home and family here*? Even if he wanted to be different, he couldn't. The thought of trying to change made his hands curl into fists and a current of nervousness pulse through his system.

"I'm going for groceries!" she shouted from the bottom floor, startling him from his introspection.

Good, he thought, needing a reprieve from the way she upset his equilibrium. "Check the car insurance," he responded in a yell.

"Okay. Bye!"

He let out a sigh, forcing himself back to his desk and the work spread over it, dimly aware of the distant hum of the garage door and then the growl of a motor—

She wouldn't.

Leaping to his feet, he shot open the window in time

to see his vintage black convertible, top down, slithering with the speed of a hungry mamba up the curving drive. Tucking fingertip and thumb against his teeth, he pierced the air with a furious whistle.

The brake lights came on. Her glossy head turned to look back at the house.

Nic pointed at the front steps and met her there a few seconds later. Rowan chirped the brakes as she stopped before him, staying behind the wheel while all eight cylinders purred. Glamorous Tiffany sunglasses obscured half her face, but her mouth trembled in a subtle betrayal of nervousness before she sat a little straighter and gave him a lady-of-the-manor, "Yes?"

"What the hell are you doing?" He hitched his elbow on the top of the windscreen from the passenger side.

"You said to check the insurance. This one is still valid."

"So is the hatchback."

"This is more fun." She pulled out one of her cheeky grins, trying to cajole him into indulging her.

He narrowed his eyes, determined not to fall for her act the way the rest of his sex did. "And you know that *how*?"

Her nose crinkled. "I *might* have taken Black Betty here for a spin once or twice before. But I always fill the tank." The assertive finger she lifted fell. "Today that could be a problem, though. I took the petty cash from the kitchen, but it wasn't much."

"You are utterly shameless, aren't you? I'm speechless." Unaccountably, he had to suppress an urge to laugh.

"Okay. Well, could you...um...step back while you ponder what you'd like to say?"

"Get out of my car, Rowan!"

"Oh, Nic, don't be like that," she coaxed, leaning toward him so the chunky zipper of her flight jacket gaped open and showed him the line of her dark plum scooped-shirt plastered low across her breasts. Pale globes swelled over the top.

"Like what?" He tried not to get distracted. "I know you. You'll start looking at a basket of puppies and won't notice the rain's started again."

But was he any different? A monsoon could blow in at this moment and he'd still be fascinated by *those* puppies.

She caught him looking. He wasn't exactly being discreet, so it wasn't a surprise to lift his gaze and find a smug grin of womanly power widening her lips. In the way of all beauties who recognized the advantage of their appeal, she assumed it was legal tender.

"I'll put the top up at the first spit, I promise." She slipped the car into gear.

He shook his head, as much at himself for revealing his weakness as at her for thinking she had him where she wanted him. "No."

"Look at this gorgeous morning." She gestured expansively at the broken clouds scudding across the brilliant blue sky. Streaks of sunlight bathed the rainwashed landscape in pockets of gold. "Doesn't it make you want to feel the sun on your face and the wind in your hair?"

He never allowed himself to be susceptible to Rowan's appealing enthusiasm. Old reflexes crowded a refusal onto his tongue. *Park the convertible and use the hatchback. I have to work.* Work was the one thing he did care about. It was always there and, since it was all he would ever have, he was making a legacy of it.

But a damp sweet breeze floated across his face, hinting at spring. It turned his mind to the instinctive pursuits of the season—the mating season. His blood warmed with male appreciation of the youthful female smiling up at him with such guile.

Seduce her. The words whispered on the air.

At the very least he should remind her that batting her lashes had consequences.

"Give me the keys," he said on impulse.

"Oh, Nic!" Rowan cut the engine and flung open the driver's door. As he came around to her side, a long thigh in tight green jeans stretched out. Tall boots were planted with firm temper. "Why do you have to be like this? You're just like everyone else who thinks they own my life. *'No, Rowan, you can't possibly have five minutes of enjoying yourself. Take the housekeeper's hatchback because that's what you are now.'* What do you gain from these power trips, huh, Nic? What?"

She stood before him in the V of the open door. The full impact of her tough, piqued magnificence hit him like a truck. He'd thought to play her at her own game, but the stakes were high. It took everything he had to hold out a steady hand.

"I get to drive. Are you going to stand there and sulk or move to the other seat?"

"You're coming with me? To the market?"

Her stunned surprise was mostly hidden by her sunglasses, but he got to watch her elegant chin drop and her glossy lips part. The urge to kiss her edged him into her space.

"Wouldn't you like company? I have my wallet." He felt for it.

She shook back her hair, taking a second to eye him warily. If he hadn't felt the weak sunshine before, he got a full blast of fireball heat as they stood facing each other. The attraction built in exponential waves of silence, bouncing back and forth, compressing with supernova potential for explosion. Excitement for the chase swelled in him like a wind catching a sail.

"Of course."

Her winning smile was meant to disarm and it did.

His abdomen tightened, but when she made an abbreviated move to slip around him he stayed exactly where he was. He wanted her to brush up against him.

The barest hint of nervousness diluted her bravado before she stated airily, "I guess I'll crawl through."

She planted her knee in the driver's seat and offered him a breathtaking view of her wiggling backside while she maneuvered into the passenger seat. Righting herself, she inquired sweetly, "Will you be warm enough without a jacket?"

"Plenty," he drawled, his jeans feeling as snug as hers were. This was insane. "The market and back," he stated as he dropped behind the wheel. "I have a corporation to run."

"I know, and I appreciate you doing this."

Her hand grazed his bare wrist as he turned the key. All the hair stood up on his arm.

"I want us to be friends, Nic."

His insides turned over with the engine. She had to be kidding. Dislodging her touch, he reached across to steal her sunglasses so he could see her as clearly as she saw him. He wanted to watch her comprehend that they'd come too far for any more pretense.

"The extent of the attraction between us doesn't seem to be penetrating for you. We'll never be friends, Ro. People with this much sexual desire between them can't be."

The undisguised stare of masculine intent from Nic started a pull in her belly. Rowan resisted it with a clench of her stomach muscles. Through a night of tossing and turning she'd absorbed that Nic didn't keep his lovers in his life. He was ruthlessly throwing her out of her home. She absolutely shouldn't have an affair with him. But here she was, unable to resist flirting with him when she could see, at last, that she had an effect on him. Insidious thoughts crept in that she might be able to persuade him against his plans for Rosedale if she got close enough to him.

Being close was heady, but frightening. She'd grasped at the let's-be-friends routine to slow things down. He wasn't having it, and the sexual energy between them couldn't be ignored when they were crammed together in this tiny car, her sunglasses dangling from his fingers behind her head. He was caressing her face with his gaze, taking in the telltale bags under her eyes that she'd tried to cover with makeup. She couldn't help dropping her gaze to his mouth and recalling the way those lips had hardened against hers, feasting and appreciating.

The lips in question curled into a knowing smile.

"I—" She became aware of a slow burn inside her, like a fuse that had been lit and was taking its time creeping toward the cache of gunpowder.

"I want you, Rowan." Her sunglasses slid down her shoulder into her lap as his fingers combed her hair over her ear. "I've wanted you for a long time. And knowing you want me too means I have no reason to keep my distance any longer. It's only a matter of time before we satisfy our curiosity."

"Curiosity?" she repeated, her heart trip-hammering as she processed that he'd wanted her for a long time. "You make it sound so…" *Unemotional.* Of course it was pure physical desire for him. It still managed to pierce her with a sweet shot of excitement.

Blinking to ease the sting in her eyes, she shrugged, fighting the urge to turn her lips into his wrist, where his warm hand cupped the side of her head. God help her if she revealed she was motivated by something far more tender than basic earthly appetites.

As a bit of self-protection, she murmured, "You make it sound like you just want to get to the bottom of this."

She waited a beat before she gave him the limpid, *ingénue* blink that would tell him she knew exactly what a *double-entendre* she'd just delivered.

It only took a stunned second before he tipped back his head in a hearty laugh—a rare full-bodied sound that melted her heart. *Thanks, Mum*, she thought with a caustic nod of acknowldgment to the woman who'd taught her the valuable art of flirting. Cassandra had always used it aggressively, to bring a man in line with her wants, whereas Rowan wielded it for defense. But at least it was in her repertoire of skills.

"Well, it would go a long way to easing the tension between us, wouldn't it?" Nic mused as he released her to gun the engine and pull away.

The wind whipped Rowan's hair into her eyes. She slouched into the sheepskin collar of her jacket, but it was more like sinking into the miasma of thrilling emotions filling her. Nic wanted her.

It shouldn't make her tremble like she was six and it was Christmas morning—not when it came with warnings of painful consequences—but all her sexual awareness as a woman was wrapped up in this man. Her adolescent hormones had first been stirred by his solitary masculine figure striding from the surf. As she had matured all her searches for a mate had been a search for Nic's attributes in another man. Of all the kisses she'd experienced none had been topped by the brief, savage touch of Nic's lips on the beach that night two years ago.

Until yesterday.

Peeling a tendril of hair from her eyes, she replaced her sunglasses and then found Nic's in the glove box. He slid them on with the silently efficient way he did everything else. Adeptly. With confidence. With a proprietorial attitude as if he owned the road, knew each curve and how to manipulate it.

Good grief, he didn't have to seduce her. She was doing it for him!

It must be the pending anniversary, she concluded with pensive insight. She'd always had a crush on Nic, but her emotions were exaggerated right now, making her more sensitive and quick to react to any offer of intimacy. She was moving into a state of closure, one that was going to have many fronts if Nic really did expel her from Rosedale and tear it down. Her entire life was being compressed and squeezed through the eye of a needle. Hardly anything of the old life would come with her. Out of desperation she was reaching for anything and everything to hang on to, including Nic.

Especially Nic.

A stuttering sigh ripped through her chest, hidden by the drone of the engine and the rush of the wind. She glanced at him to see if he was tracking her inner struggle.

He kept his attention on the road, his profile starkly beautiful in its intensity, his cheeks still shiny from his morning shave, his mouth the only thing about him that seemed to relax. She longed to trace his mouth with her fingertips.

Maybe she needed to give herself to him in order to get over him once and for all.

Her stomach swooped and her head grew light. The thought of sex with him scared the hell out of her, but her shudder wasn't all trepidation. It was also a delicious betrayal of anticipation. She wanted him.

She forced her hands to uncurl on her thighs, aware that she was kidding herself if she thought sleeping with him would help her get over him. She wanted to go to bed with Nic because deep down she thought maybe, somehow, it would make him *like* her. All night she had tossed and turned, tormented by the mistakes she'd made that had led him to look down on her. She wanted to make up with him. Sleep with him. He was the only man she'd ever wanted to sleep with. That was what it came down to.

But she was a virgin.

And he didn't want anything from the experience but to satisfy his curiosity. He wanted to rock her world and then drop out of it.

Those rather pertinent details filled her with serious misgivings about sliding into bed with him. What would he say? Would it be good? Or awkward and disappointing? Would they be able to part with a sense of closure? Or would it be relief on his side and a mortifying memory for her that tortured her forever?

Would he even want her? Or would he lose interest once he realized she wasn't a sex symbol like her mother?

The fluttering tents of the outdoor market came into view. Nic pulled into the parking lot that was always crowded in the middle of summer, but sparsely occupied today. They drew attention—not just because of the flashy car and the quiet time of year, but because locals knew who they were. It made for a poignant hour of shopping as they fielded questions about the called-off search.

Her Greek was passable, Nic's impeccable, so she let him talk even though what he said took her aback.

"No, we're not planning anything except a follow-up retrospective in select publications and international programs."

Rowan had come to Rosedale thinking to mark the anniversary privately, but if the plan was now to put a final stamp of acceptance on their loss something more definitive was needed: a memorial service and a proper laying to rest.

She was about to bring it up with Nic, but he turned and pressed his hand to the middle of her back, steering her toward the pastry stall. It was a fairly innocuous bit of handling, but she felt as though his chilled fingers reached through the layers of leather and fabric to caress her bare spine. All thought left her beyond an awareness of the cottony scent of his shirt and the muskier warmth near his throat.

He glanced down to see why she'd frozen in her tracks and a moment of electrified tension grew around them like a force field. Nic didn't move, but he seemed to grow bigger, becoming more intimidating and more of a threat to her self-possession. Her heart started to pound hard in her chest. He was only being Nic—sex-god with a hot physique and a way of looking at her as though he knew exactly how completely her senses came alive the second she was near him.

"You're getting curious about me," he accused in a husky scold.

She couldn't help it, despite her qualms. Her palms grew damp and she lowered her gaze to the nearly invisible golden hairs lying flat against the warm skin of his chest where it was exposed by his open collar.

This was a disconcerting experience, being pursued and wanting back. Saying no had always been easy because she had never felt drawn to the men who propositioned her. Suddenly she was susceptible to her own inner weakness and that scared her.

"There's curiosity and there's high-risk behavior," she managed to toss out, retreating a hasty step as a nervous lump formed in her throat. "I'm actually quite choosy. More than you, if the rotation of women on your arm is anything to go by." She kept her tone slightly jaded so he wouldn't guess how genuinely put out and intimidated she was by the extent of his experience.

As she pretended to deliberate between French éclairs and honey-soaked baklava, he came up behind her and requested, "Two of each," from the heavyset baker.

Rowan never allowed herself those sorts of treats, but she couldn't contradict him. Her whole body was paralyzed by the brush of his body against hers.

He waited until the plump woman turned away before saying quietly in English, "And yet I keep getting the impression you've chosen me."

Her knees nearly unhinged. It was too fast, too much of an assumption.

"My hormones might have, but I've given up more than just alcohol and parties. I didn't like not being in control of myself—"

Big mistake. He leaned forward to exchange a few bills for the box of pastries and cut her an eloquent look rife with the anticipation of a challenge.

Her heart took a heavy swing and a dangerous dip. "I'm trying to act like an adult rather than follow silly impulses," she defended. "That should impress you."

"This isn't an impulse. It's an inevitability." Nic couldn't help putting his hand on her again, finding the spot just above her tailbone where her jacket had ridden up.

Her buttocks tensed and a tiny shudder rippled through her before she started back toward the car. Rowan wasn't a fidgety person, but Nic was getting a distinct impression of skittishness. Was it because what she was feeling was stronger than what she thought she could control?

His mind went into a meltdown of smugness and desperation. He'd be damned if he'd admit it was the same for him, though. Part of him already felt defeated at the way he'd let things progress this far, this fast. He told himself he was playing her at her own game, but he was succumbing to exactly what he'd called it: inevitability. A tight coil of desire held him in its grip and all his focus had shifted to having her.

It was a weakness he could only bear if Rowan felt the same. If she didn't... A barbed hook caught at his chest, giving a merciless yank. To reassure himself he set his hand on her thigh once she was seated, stroking lightly to part her knees and press her to make room between her boots for the bag of groceries.

Rowan's leg jerked reflexively and she let out a subtle hiss, her eyes lifting to reveal pupils that went black as a hole in the universe.

Nic deliberately shifted his touch to a gentle caress of her knee. "Did I bump a scrape?" he asked silkily, but with genuine concern. He picked up her hand. "I see the bandages are off." He turned up her palm to see the cross-hatched skin was red and tender, but healing. "Looks better. That's good."

Rowan's fingers trembled revealingly before she quickly tugged from his grip.

"Men are so predictable," she said with an exasperated shake of her head. "You think you hear a dare and now your ego demands you prove something. I've been pressured too many times into doing things I didn't want to do. I won't let you bully me."

"Of course not," he said, oddly affected by how vulnerable she seemed all of a sudden. Beautiful, stubborn, and hesitantly anxious behind a wall of determination. A protective feeling flickered through him, but the fire was still there, always there, raging unceasingly. He let a smile touch his lips as he very gently smoothed her hair behind her ear, taking his time so they could both enjoy the quiet, deliberate caress.

A pretty flush gathered under her cheeks and her lashes fluttered with confusion while her lips seemed to bloom into a plump pout.

"Don't worry, Ro. I understand a woman's need for foreplay. I'm not going to rush you." He almost went for a kiss, but remembered how public they were.

Straightening, he let the wind slice through his shirt and cool his scalp for a moment before noticing the sky was gathering for another downpour. They might outrun it. He was certainly motivated to hurry back.

Nic's stark promise kept replaying in Rowan's head. *Foreplay.* Was that why he grazed his knuckles against her thigh as he shifted gears? And played that music with the sexy Latino beat that echoed the thick pulse of her blood and put a soundtrack in her hips?

He had almost kissed her before he'd rounded the bonnet and climbed in on the driver's side, and despite her plucky talk about holding him off all she could think about was hurtling back to Rosedale. Quiet, secure, private Rosedale. Where they might kiss.

And do more? She didn't know—literally didn't know—what to do.

He pulled up unexpectedly beneath the sprawl of a huge olive tree.

Rowan swung a wary glance at him, both relieved by the reprieve and mildly terrified that he had changed his mind about going home.

"It's starting to rain." He stepped out of the car and pulled his seat forward. "Didn't you notice?" he taunted lightly.

She had no choice then but to offer a vague look into the olive grove and murmur, "Oh, look—puppies."

"You're not funny."

"Sure I am." She left the car and pulled her own seat forward to help him retrieve the removable side windows and canvas top. Her reflexes felt clumsy as she helped him snap and button everything into place, her whole being intimidated by the easy mastery with which he moved.

The patter of rain on the budding branches above them increased as they finished, bouncing through to hit them in fat dollops. They slammed themselves back into the car as the sky opened up. The drumming became a wild rush of sound.

As the windscreen blurred with heavy rain Rowan glanced at him, expecting him to start the car and pull out. In the muted light his blue eyes were charcoal, his body a mass of gathered energy.

"What's wrong?" she asked.

"I can't wait." He leaned across, one hand cupping her cheek as he slanted his mouth in hot possession over hers.

Rowan gasped, parting her lips. Nic took devastating advantage, thrusting past the games and hesitations of their past kisses and slamming them into a new reality of raw seduction. His arm came behind her shoulders, gathering her up and providing a pillow as she yielded. So much had changed between them in the last twenty-four hours Rowan couldn't do anything but give herself over to the flood of desire.

When his tongue touched hers lust struck with blinding ferocity, lighting a fire of aggression in her that made her kiss him back with equal fervor, lashing at his tongue with her own, fueling the blaze of need expanding around them.

She was dimly aware of a soft growl in his throat, that his fingers moved in a gentle caress of her jaw and throat, but she wouldn't give up their kiss. Her hands went into his hair, holding him so she could harden the press of their mouths, inhibitions demolished by how instantaneously he inflamed her. She needed this more than air.

With another feral sound he slid his hand to her breast, boldly sliding beneath the scoop neck of her top and invading the snug cup of her bra.

At the first catch of his fingers across her nipple Rowan released a cry into his mouth, startled by the shot of intense pleasure that bolted directly into the heart of her.

Nic pulled away, watching as he exposed her breast. Rowan thought she ought to be embarrassed, but she wasn't. He wore a reverent look, like her pink nipple was beautiful, thrusting so wantonly. She couldn't help but feel pride as she basked in his ravenous gaze.

Then he lowered his head and took her into the hot velvet of his mouth. A keening sound left her. The sensation was so intense and sustained. Cradling his head in her forearms, she pressed her legs tightly together, trying to ease the ache throbbing between.

He pulled back a little, just enough to jerk open his shirt. "Touch me." He brought her hand to his hot chest, then forced his own between her clenched thighs.

Rowan splayed her hands on his hot damp skin, bombarded by too many sensations: the loving stroke of his tongue against her throat, the rasp of silky chest hair on her raw palms and the stunning pleasure that accompanied the firm cup of his hand where she wanted pressure most.

He kissed her again, short-circuiting her brain. Her hips rose into the press of his palm. She tried to feel all of him: the hair-roughened muscles of his chest, the flat quiver of his belly, the silky smoothness of his spine. As her fingertips quested toward the waistband of his jeans he pulled back again.

"Do you have anything?" His voice was deep and sensual, urgent and ragged.

"What—?" She was so new to this it took a second for her to understand. "Protection, you mean? No!"

"You're not on the Pill?"

"No!"

With a soft curse he fell back in his seat, hands gripping the wheel so hard his knuckles turned white. "That's probably for the best. This car is impossible. What would we do? Lie down in the grass in the rain beside the road? Don't do that on my account," he added, with a covetous look to where she was snapping out of her torpor and rearranging her clothing.

Shell-shocked, she could only tuck, adjust and zip her jacket to her throat. "I didn't mean to let it go that far." How had it happened? What about her little speech about having found a spine against being pressured?

"I shouldn't have kissed you. I knew I wouldn't want to stop." He checked the mirrors, then fired the engine and pulled into the rain, the wipers slapping at full speed in the tiny windscreen. Reaching out to take her hand, he tangled his thick fingers between hers. The tiny stretch was sensual and erotic. He rested their clasped hands on the stick shift.

"It's okay. I have some in my room."

"Some—condoms?" So premeditated. If he'd pulled her to the wet grass a few seconds ago she would have gone without protest, but talking like this allowed reservations to creep in.

"Yes." The curt way he answered and the purposeful way he drove made it sound like they were on their way to pick up an organ transplant.

But his having condoms in his room made Rowan's hand go cold inside the vital grip of his. Did that mean he slept with women at Rosedale? All her insecurities flooded to the fore as she contemplated the scope of his sexual conquests. And she was signing up to be next? How demoralizing!

Twisting free of his grip, she swallowed back sick anxiety that grew all the more troubling when she realized he'd released her because he needed to shift down and make the turn into Rosedale. Seconds later they pulled into the garage. The absence of pounding rain made the interior of the car overly silent—especially once he cut the engine.

Feeling suffocated, Rowan threw herself out of the car, then stopped. She wanted to stomp away in a jealous temper because he'd confessed to having other women, but that would be immature. It wasn't as if she'd believed *he* was a virgin. Maybe it made her heart ache that he treated Rosedale like a brothel, but given the way its owner had caused him to feel left out in the cold could she really expect him to view the house as sacred and special the way she did?

Moodily shifting to the open garage door, she stared through the wall of water pouring off the eaves and hugged herself.

He'd had casual sex with a lot of women. Maybe sex with her would be equally casual for him, but it would mean something to her. Nic, her first, here at Rosedale.

Rowan pressed the backs of her knuckles against lips that began to quiver with vulnerability, edging toward one of the biggest decisions of her life.

"Ro?" Light fingers tickled over her hair, sending a shivery warmth cascading through her. His hand settled warmly on her shoulder.

Rowan turned her head to look up at him, catching her breath at the impact he made on her. He looked into her eyes and she saw a tiny flicker of something, almost a flinch, like he saw something in her gaze that struck past his impervious shell. His hand flexed and hot intent flowed back into his evening-blue eyes, burning out anything else she thought she might have seen.

"Will you come upstairs with me?"

She couldn't speak, but she nodded. His smile, warm and appreciative, softened his warrior features into something so handsome he stole her breath. He took her hand and led her into the house.

CHAPTER SIX

THIS WAS HAPPENING.

Nic's grip on her hand was warm and strong, holding her anchored when Rowan felt she might float away. This was one of those instances so perfect it was like a rainbow on a bubble—enchanting but fragile. She clung to his hand as they climbed the stairs, fearful something would break the spell and cause her tentative euphoria to burst.

When he led her to his door she hung back, trying not to reveal how much tension was gathering inside her.

His gaze searched hers and Rowan felt as though invisible threads looped out to cast around her and back to him, gathering them into a tight, inescapable cocoon. There was such smoldering sexuality in his face she feared for a moment that she was about to be overtaken by him, captured and smothered.

"Second thoughts?" he asked with gruff coolness.

Rowan looked down at the threshold she couldn't bring herself to cross. "Suffering a bit of performance anxiety. I don't want to disappoint you."

Nic surprised her by lifting her hand to press soft kisses on her cool fingers, his lips twitching with amusement. "You've come a long way. Twenty-four hours ago you didn't give a damn what I thought."

Rowan couldn't speak. The truth was too revealing.

She'd always cared. This was just the first time she was admitting it. The back of her throat stung. The moment was huge.

Nic's fingers tightened on hers. "You won't disappoint me," he said. "I've waited too long for this to be anything but completely gratifying." He leaned down and took her mouth in a slow kiss.

She clung to his lips with her own, prolonging the exquisite rightness, letting the soft kiss play out into intensifying rhythms that made her hurt inside. It was so good.

Nic was barely hanging on to a rational thought. Rowan's mouth was petal-soft and she smelled like a warm summer garden: earthy and rosy and fresh. He could feel little tremors striking deep within her as he kissed her. That delicious quiver fed the answering energy prickling under his skin as the taste of her nape was imprinted against his open lips. When she lifted her arms around his neck and pressed closer, delicately clashing into his achingly aroused flesh, his mind exploded.

He tightened his hold on her, reveling in the restless, inciting quest of her mouth. With a groan, he picked her up, never having done anything so feverish in his life. She leapt into a firm bundle against his chest, like she'd done it a thousand times—which he dimly supposed she had, on the stage and possibly for other men.

He ducked the thought, concentrating on how she was light and slender and so much more earnest than he'd expected. *Performer*, he reminded himself, but he responded to her passion all the same, fully involved in their kiss as he carried her into the room.

He should have kept this on neutral territory, he thought dimly, but assured himself that Rowan wouldn't have unrealistic expectations. She'd been around the block.

Setting her on her feet, he pressed her away long enough

to open her jacket. They were both breathing hard, and she shrugged out of the short coat to let it fall to the floor with an impatience he applauded. He wished he could muster a smile of satisfaction, but desire was throbbing in him like an imperative. He threw his own shirt off and kicked away his shoes.

Rowan grasped his arm and bent one leg to unzip her long boot. The second one was released and she stepped out of them, so much shorter than she seemed when her larger than life personality was on full display. This Rowan was…

Vulnerable.

For all her urgency there was a shyness in the way she hesitated with her hands on the snap of her jeans, her pillowy bottom lip caught between her teeth. "Should we… um…close the door?"

Her modesty took him aback, turning over places in him he'd buried under years of jaded enjoyment of women without engaging with them. He had a distant thought to drawl a somewhat tasteless, *Who's going to come in*? but found a shred of a gentlemanly behavior instead. He turned to press the door closed.

And as the click echoed in the silent room the word *gentleman* mocked him. *"What are your intentions, Nic? Men like you…"*

Nic curled a fist against the seam of the closed door, fighting the invasion of the dark memory. He and Rowan had cleared the air. He believed her. They wanted each other; it was as simple as that. This had nothing to do with intentions and futures. It was two adults coming together in mutual desire. Not the sort of thing Olief should have had any disdain for, given the way he'd fathered a child from one mistress and lived in sin for nearly a decade with another.

Rowan had fumbled her jeans open, but couldn't bring herself to peel them down while Nic had his back to her. Having him watch her wouldn't make it easier, but her self-confidence was draining fast as he leaned on the door like that, tension gathering across his naked shoulders. He had such a beautiful back, strong and tanned, powerful muscles shifting as though he was bearing up under a great weight.

"Nic? Are you—?" *Having second thoughts?* She would *die.*

He brought his head up and turned. Desire flared past whatever dark thoughts had taken him for a split second. His avid glance made her feel beautiful even though she wasn't any kind of sex goddess. Her hair was wind-whipped, she wore next to no makeup, and was probably pale with the stagefright that was threatening on the periphery. But he strode forward with purpose and cupped her head, kissing her like he had in the car—like he would spontaneously combust if he didn't do it this second.

It was the reassurance she needed. Grasping his head, she kissed him back with all the passion in her, grateful and excited and swimming in rising desire. When he began to peel up her top she lifted her arms to help him. It landed in a purple stain in the middle of the floor and was quickly topped by her bra.

Nic dragged her close, and the contact of his hard, hair-roughened chest on her breasts undid her. She melted, fingers splaying wide to touch as much of him as possible, while she slowly writhed against his sensuous heat and turned her lips into his throat.

He said her name and swore, then said raggedly, "I'm trying to find a little finesse here, but—" His fingertips swept her spine and shoulderblades before he brought his hands forward and sweetly captured her breasts.

"It's okay. I'm in a hurry too…"

He groaned and his hands gently crushed her curves as he crowded into her, covering her mouth once, hard, before he stepped back and pulled off his jeans. He skimmed his shorts off with them and knocked the crumpled heap away with his foot, straightening before her with feet braced.

A purely female ache of longing clenched deep inside her as she took in his wide chest and taut flat stomach, powerful thighs and even more powerfully thick erection. She swallowed as she measured him with her eyes, intimidated.

Nic opened hands that had curled into tense fists and stepped close to begin easing her jeans down her hips. He loomed tall and potent, his penis brushing her stomach as his mouth touched her shoulder.

Rowan made herself breathe, but it was shaky, and she wasn't getting nearly enough oxygen. As he lowered the clinging denim down her thighs she trembled, wriggling to help him and stepping out of them quickly so she could rush back against him, hiding, but deeply affected. She had never been naked with a man, never touched one like this, and she desperately wanted to give Nic pleasure.

Pressing for a little space, she clasped him lightly and gasped, shocked by how silky he felt. Satin over steel. He seemed to thicken and harden in her tentative hold and his big hand covered hers once, the single stroke a too brief lesson before he peeled her hand away and brought her palm to his mouth.

"I don't want to disappoint you either," he said wryly, and edged her backward, effortlessly levering her onto the bed beneath him.

Rowan couldn't find her voice, too besieged by each tiny sensation she was trying to memorize. Nic's weight beside her on the mattress. His hand massaging her belly as he kissed her again. His tongue stroking over hers so it felt like hot honey gathered between her thighs. His heavy thigh rested across hers, holding still the legs that wanted to pedal in sensual pleasure. The burning rod of his penis was rampant against her hip. She couldn't touch enough of him, couldn't process all the delicious parts of him when her blood pressure was rising in relentless increments.

He slid down a little, his tongue going to her nipple, his knee pressing between her thighs to part her legs. He very lightly stroked the crease where her thighs met plump folds. She grew acutely sensitive under his barely there fondling, her tangled nerve-endings gathering in a storm of greedy hunger. She tried to turn into him, wanting more contact, but he took her nipple deep in his mouth and parted her with knowledgeable fingers.

Pleasure struck like a hammer-blow, making her groan unabashedly. He deepened his caress, stroking and circling, gently invading, then teasing again, repeating the play so the meltdown became a build-up.

"Nic," she moaned, dragging at his hair to lift his head.

He looked at her like he was drugged and swept a hand out. Efficient and quick, he protected them both, then shifted to cover her.

She experienced a stab of nervousness again. Her legs twitched as they parted on either side of his hips. She bent her knees, instinctively wanting to embrace him with her thighs. Every part of her wanted to gather him in. He was so strong and fiercely beautiful with that intense expression on his face, looking down at her like she was the most incredible thing he'd ever seen. Her nipples were shards of crystal that wanted to pierce into him as his chest came down on hers, heavy and firm.

And then he pressed into her.

Rowan caught her breath, startled by the shocking intimacy of the act. It hurt a little, but she was so aroused she didn't care. She ached for the stimulation of pressure and stretching as she felt the thickness of him invade.

"Rowan," he said raggedly, his expression a little bewildered beneath his flush of extreme arousal, "you're—"

"Don't be mad, Nic," she urged, curling her legs around him in a vise-like trap, using her lean strength to pull him in and impale herself a little more. She couldn't help the gasping cry that left her. It felt so extraordinary. "I want this. I want it to be you."

"—so tight," he ground through clenched teeth, demonstrating how strong he was by keeping her from forcing the penetration. He shuddered and gave her an incredulous look. "You *liar*," he breathed, then kissed her possessively while he very, very slowly and oh, so carefully let the weight of his hips settle on her.

And gently, inexorably, his flesh drove all the way into hers.

Rowan tipped back her head and moaned in exultation.

She belonged to him. Now and forever.

Nic kissed her again and again—long, languorous kisses on her lips and sweet caresses down her throat and across her shoulders. Rowan melted under his attention, not realizing how much tension her muscles had gathered until it eased away.

That was when he groaned and started to withdraw, making her protest and cling to him in ways she hadn't realized she could. He came back, body trembling with the effort to discipline himself. It was a control she instantly felt compelled to shatter.

Rowan stroked her hands over his arms and shoulders, lightly raking her nails down to his buttocks. Nic's hips jerked into hers. It hurt, but the friction, the fullness, was so good at the same time. The conflict of wanting to self-protect and yet let him push her toward the pinnacle made her scrape her nails down his back again. He caught her wrists and flattened her hands beneath his, sealing their palms together. With a glitter of pure animal need in his flame-blue eyes he increased the pace, becoming relentless and remorseless, feeding her tension until everything in her began to gather.

It was astonishing. She couldn't hold on, couldn't hold back. "Nic!" She squeezed her legs around him, suddenly feeling the heart-stopping culmination very close. She didn't want it to end! She fought giving in, but wanted it so badly. He kept thrusting and her body clenched on his shaft, as if she could hold him forever. He drew her nerve-endings to their very limit…

And then…

Release.

Everything dimmed for a heartbeat before the cataclysm struck deep within her. Shattering pleasure was carried outward in waves of abject joy. Rowan could only receive him, feeling the writhe of his hard muscles as he released a guttural shout and drove deep. The pulses of his tremendous climax were visceral, playing against her own so they were locked in an exquisite paroxysm. She'd never felt so close to anyone in her life. His name pulsed in her head with the crashing throb of their mutual release. *Nic, Nic, Nic.*

The final sob of ecstasy was hers. For the end that was so beautiful and so unbearable. She wanted to stay joined with him forever, but a final shudder jolted through him and her own climactic pulses began to fade. Still breathing hard, he carefully disengaged and rolled away.

The wordless removal of physical contact smacked her with the savage brutality of casual sex. She'd felt on the edge of a burgeoning beauty, something so profound it filled her chest and made her eyes dampen with happiness.

Having him pull away left her instantly bereft. His back was to her and his feet were bound to hit the floor any second. The door would be next.

Appalled to find herself near tears, Rowan swallowed a pained cry and rolled to her side of the bed, starting to swing her feet off. She could make it to the bathroom before he walked out. It would save a shred of her dignity to not be the one left in the bed.

A thick arm snaked around her and a heavy leg scooped hers back to the middle of the mattress. He was so *hot*. She instinctively pushed her hands against his damp chest where his heartbeat still raced. He carried her hands to a point above her head, trapping them in his own while his massive body engulfed hers in a blanket of hard muscle.

"Wait," he growled, breath still short. "*Why me*, Rowan?"

CHAPTER SEVEN

NIC FELT AS THOUGH he was looking at a stranger—one so beautiful she made his heart lurch. Her eyelids were swollen under a smoky smudge of makeup, her green irises like rain-soaked moss, her lips ripened by his kisses. He pulled back a little for a lengthy study of every flushed curve and trembling muscle.

How in the hell was he the only man who'd ever seen her like this?

Rowan wriggled in muted protest. He was still aroused enough for rational thought to recede and instinct to want to take over. She was so smooth and soft, her warmed scent a soporific drug to his senses. The desire to sink down on her and rediscover every decadent inch of her increased.

His heartbeat elevated, but she stiffened in wariness.

"What are you doing?"

She sounded breathless. Her flat stomach contracted under the weight of his hand while her wrists turned in the light grip of his other hand. Her flexing was a seductive trigger he fought out of self-preservation. This situation didn't make sense and he needed it to.

"I'm admiring this gift you've given me." Her springy curls begged for petting, but he resisted, taking heed of her belligerently angled chin instead.

"You don't have to be so sarcastic about it," she said.

"I'm not trying to be sarcastic. I'm stunned." Winded. Very much in danger of being *moved*. He had to stick to cool analysis or he'd begin attaching meaning to this unique circumstance. He had worried being in his bedroom would make the act too personal, but she had shot things into a realm of intimate sharing that didn't happen often between any two people—most especially between him and anyone.

"How, Ro? There was a boy at school. I heard the stories."

Her lips firmed and her cheeks darkened. "That...didn't work out. I thought I was ready, but I wasn't. I called it off. He was getting dressed when the headmistress found us. Would you let go of me, please?"

He released her and she sat up. Her narrow back seemed very vulnerable. He felt an unaccountable urge to pull her back into his embrace and keep her sheltered against him. A curious lump formed in his chest. She'd been so tight. Exquisite and succulent. Her rippling orgasm had been unmistakable, but her sheath new and small. If he'd hurt her he'd never forgive himself.

"Are you all right?"

"Fine. You?" Rowan flipped the edge of the coverlet up and across her front, dying with self-consciousness. "Shall we have a post-mortem on *your* past, too? Did you get it right the first time, or do you have an inept experience you'd like to share?"

Nic was impervious to the glare she sent over her shoulder. He sprawled as comfortably as any male animal whose appetite had been recently sated. The condom was gone, she noted—with a glance that he caught.

His brows went up while his eyelids stayed heavy.

She prickled with embarrassment, willing to give anything to take back that peek. He was still hard. Had he not been satisfied? The coverlet bunched thickly in her hands as she curled her fingers into apprehensive fists.

"I'm not trying to pry," he said. "I just can't understand how you'd still be a virgin when I've seen you with men I thought were your lovers."

"Who? Dance partners? We're all very familiar. It doesn't mean anything." Kind of like how this act seemed to have no profundity for him beyond a mystery to be solved.

She couldn't believe she had felt apprehensive at the thought of him walking out. This was far worse—sitting naked next to him, insanely aware of what they'd just done, how he'd touched her like he not only owned her but knew her body's responses better than she did, trying to have a conversation.

Her entire world had been flooded with color. A huge bubble of elation had threatened to split her chest. But he didn't need time to savor and process. He wasn't suffering any craving for reassurance. He'd done this a thousand times.

A thousand and one.

"You might have offered a clue," he chided dryly.

"Like what? Can you imagine Cassandra O'Brien's daughter running around wearing one of those 'Proud To Be A Virgin' bracelets? I was happy people thought I'd been with that boy. My school friends quit teasing me. I dated when I could, but my schedule didn't allow for anything long-term so sex never happened."

"I meant you might have said something today." His voice changed, becoming darker and crisper.

She sensed that word *long-term* had done it and swallowed. He didn't move, but she watched a new level of coolness come over him. It made the tiny inch of space between them seem cavernous and the warm room grow cold.

"Why would you throw it away on me?" he asked.

Throw it away. Her stomach clenched. Not exactly a treasured moment. More like taking out the garbage. She hated herself then for not being able to control who she was attracted to. For letting that attraction rule her to the point of waiting half her life for him and then giving herself despite knowing it meant nothing to him.

Yet when she tried to conjure regret all she felt was a stunned ache of poignant joy. It had been the most singularly beautiful experience of her life. She was glad it had been with Nic.

"Do you really think virginity is something precious to be bottled up and hoarded for a special occasion?" she asked with a catch in her voice, trying to hide how deeply stirred she was as she reached back to brace herself on her arm and face him. Her other hand held the coverlet firmly across her breasts and thighs, but she did her best to mirror his nonchalance, affecting only vague interest.

His gaze cut a swift glance at her nude shoulders and exposed knee before meeting hers again. "I guess I wouldn't be a very progressive man if I did, but I imagine you've had other opportunities, so choosing to give it up now— with me—seems odd."

"Why not you?" she challenged, her heart dancing close to a tricky ledge.

His intense look of concentration blanked for a second into a hollow gaze before he shuttered his expression. "Indeed, why not me when any man would do? Why *now* is the real question, isn't it?"

An urge to correct him caught in her throat, but she didn't want to reveal how much she had wanted it to be him. At the same time a stunning insight struck her. Nic had no idea he was special to her or anyone else. She had been told all her life that she was special—so special she had to live up to unrealistic expectations—but he hadn't had that problem. His father had ignored him. What about his mother?

Rowan ached to ask, but prying was out of place. He wouldn't appreciate it, given what a proud, aloof man he was. She let her hair fall forward to hide her frown of empathetic pain.

"I was tired of fighting with you. Fighting that feeling," she confessed, hoping he wouldn't make her tell him exactly how long that feeling had been twisting like a flame inside her. Tossing her hair back, she made a false attempt at flippancy. "And you're the one who thinks I need to grow up, so it's rather fitting for you to be the one to make me a woman, don't you think?"

A disturbing sense of privilege poured into Nic. Plainly this act held a lot less importance to her than it did for him, so he did his best to laugh it off the way she had. "Is that what this was? A coming-of-age ceremony?"

For a second he thought Rowan flinched. A familiar bleak valley threatened to swallow up his brief sense of pride. He tensed, but then Rowan produced a wide smile that was like light breaking over the dark edges that surrounded him, bathing him in reprieve. She cupped the side of his face, leaning close enough to touch a light kiss to his mouth.

"Yes, Nic. You might not be given to sentimentality about these things, but I shall forever look back on you fondly as My First. That's almost as good as whatever you get for being Newsman of the Year, isn't it?"

Always so glib, but her words had a profound effect on him. That *forever look back* ought to be reassuring. He had barely let himself acknowledge the fear that her taking him as her first lover and dropping words like *long-term* meant she expected a relationship. He most certainly was not the man to give her anything like that.

But that *fondly* squeezed feeling out of his incompetent heart. Two days ago he wouldn't have given any thought to parting with animosity between them, but quite suddenly he hoped for something better than that.

She started to pull away and he brought his hand to the back of her head, silky curls crushed under his gentle insistence she stay close.

"I won't forget this either," he admitted.

Which scared him as much as the vulnerable way Rowan caught her lip between her teeth. He closed his eyes against a look that searched for reassurance and drew her forward so he could kiss her, making her release her bottom lip to his own gentle bite and lingering attention to soothe any tenderness he inflicted.

The kiss quickly got out of hand and he groaned, never having come up against anything like this: the desire to make love again so soon after the most intense orgasm of his life, or with a woman so new to it she couldn't.

When she breathed his name against his lips and set a hand on his collarbone he had to let her put space between them.

"Are you saying you won't forget in a good way or a bad way?"

Was she kidding? He glanced down at the raging muscle straining from between his thighs like a compass needle seeking North.

"I know. I'm sorry." Her flush was pure mortification. "I thought it was good for both of us, but—"

"Maybe if you're willing to practice we can do something about it?" he chided facetiously.

Rowan paled and he realized with horror that she'd taken it the wrong way. She tried to bolt from the bed and again he had to grab her, holding tight to her wiry strength while she struggled and slapped at him.

"That was a joke," he insisted, trying to speak over her angry demands to quit manhandling her. He wouldn't let her go, though—not when his heart was bottoming out at how badly he'd misread her sensitivity. "Rowan, listen. *Ouch.*" He swore as he took a scratch down his rib cage before he immobilized her.

"That wasn't funny, Nic!" She was breathing hard, muscles a taut bundle of resistance against his hold, eyes spitting venom. "I know more about practice than anyone, and I'll be damned if I'm going back to trying and not getting it right. For *you.* I'm living for me now—understand? I don't care if it was good for you. It was good for me, so you can go to hell with your *practice.*"

His chest knotted up so tight he could barely breathe.

"It *was* good for me," he insisted, pressing the words into her temple as she turned a stubborn cheek against him. He could see her brow pleated in hurt.

He didn't know how to apologize with the kind of sincerity needed here, and inadequacy threatened to push him out of the room rather than try, but he had learned enough about her in the last two days to realize how deeply it would injure her to think her performance had failed to please him.

"I only meant I want to make love again and I realize you won't want to." He hurried to say it, shifting because he was aroused by their tussle and unable to hide it. He didn't expect anything but a cold shower, though. "You have this insane effect on me, Ro. You always have. I can't help it."

She turned her head to look at him and he began to wobble on a tightrope a thousand stories in the air. He backed onto solid ground.

"I don't know what it is with our chemistry. I had hoped once would be enough." The lie bunched his muscles into aching knots. He had *never* believed once would be enough. "If you let me, I'd be on you night and day to work this out of my system."

Her lashes came down to hide her eyes and he scowled, uncomfortable with how much he'd revealed. He was generally self-sufficient, but now he looked into a bleak future where his frustrating hunger for her might actually be worse, not easier to bear.

"If we were coming together as equals," she said carefully, before she lifted wary lashes, "I'd let you. But not if I don't have the sort of experience to keep you interested."

"You—" she couldn't see the fine tremble in the hand he used to smooth her hair "—are a natural. I'm at the disadvantage. I know how special this is."

"Tell all the girls that, do you?"

"I've never said it to anyone," he contradicted tightly.

"Really?" She rolled into him with a forgiving slither of silken skin and inviting softness, bending his mind away from the alarm bells against making comparisons or revealing how truly exceptional their experience was.

Her pleased smile provoked another zing of warning against feeding her ego and that sense of entitlement to adoration of hers. He didn't want to be a slave to her good graces. But her light hands skimmed over him in deliciously arousing paths, rewarding rather than rejecting, and he quit caring that he was turning into one more ardent fan.

"Me, too. Best ever." She strained to touch her lips under his chin.

With a shaken chuckle and deep reluctance he stopped her. This mood of hers was surprisingly endearing. Gathering her slender fingers in his own, he kissed the scrape on her palm before saying, "You need time to recover. Don't you?"

"No. I like the way you make me feel, Nic. I want to do it again."

The tiny throb of longing in her voice was a golden rope that looped around the root of him and tugged.

He shuddered and gave in, tucking her under him with possessive intent.

One thing about Rosedale, Nic acknowledged later that evening, if you wanted to avoid someone you could.

He'd left her as the sky was starting to darken. Rowan had been on her stomach, nothing but a midnight waterfall of hair and an ivory shoulder. His body had sprung to attention despite the way he'd worked it into exhaustion over hours of lovemaking. He'd forced himself to leave her, partly because he was sure she was tender and partly because he hated how addicted he was becoming.

Becoming? a voice taunted deep in his head. He'd always been obsessed. Now he'd had her it was worse. And he'd *admitted* it to her. That left him deeply uneasy, so he had showered, dressed, come into his office and shut the door.

The memory of Rowan's uninhibited response wasn't as easy to leave behind. At one point she'd kissed her way down his body and murmured, "May I? I've always wondered…" He'd disbelieved she was *that* inexperienced, but the amateur way she'd learned to please him had told him this too was her first time and had nearly undone him.

He glanced at his knuckles, going white where he gripped the arm of his chair. He ought to be working, not reliving Rowan's teasing him beyond bearing before lifting to ride his hips until she was sobbing with rapture.

His laptop hummed with yet another string of emails

hitting his inbox, but he wasn't having much luck being productive and he needed to be. The conglomerate of multi-media interests that Olief had amassed during his lifetime was a demanding operation. If Nic hadn't had this to consume him for the last year, the fruitless search for Olief's plane and its survivors might have driven him to madness.

Lately he'd taken more of his own direction, but he couldn't do it properly until Olief was declared dead and the will was read. Uncertainty hovered around him like the buzz of a mosquito as he considered what it might reveal. He *liked* running things. He wanted to continue to do so. And if it turned out Olief had not named him as his heir…

Nic turned away from the thought, telling himself to be prepared for anything—even that. But it would sting. In the meantime he drew a salary as the interim president by keeping the place running and solvent. He ought to be doing that, not frittering away his time between brooding over things he couldn't change and schoolboy fantasies about Rowan's breasts filling his hands.

Hunger of every kind gripped him. The kind that made him reach to adjust himself in the confines of his jeans and the kind that growled in his empty stomach.

A thought flitted through his mind of taking Rowan down to the ferry landing for a meal. But they weren't dating. He didn't know what they were doing, he acknowledged with a hard scrape of his hand down his face.

Impatient, he flung open the door and was greeted by the surprising scent of… Whatever it was, it smelled delicious. He followed it downstairs.

Rowan hadn't expected her return to Rosedale to be like this. When she'd made the decision to come she'd imagined having the house to herself, perhaps sharing a few light meals with Anna, but mostly taking stock of her life and figuring out her next steps.

She was doing a little of that—or perhaps it was more accurate to say she was absorbing the fact that she was going to have to do some really hard thinking on that front since Nic had cut off her income. Her mind didn't want to pin itself to those sorts of thoughts, though. It was too busy trying to make sense of the passionate affair she'd started with the one man she'd always believed out of reach. She had never imagined this could really happen. Nevertheless, she and Nic had spent hours reading each other like braille text, with his masculine groans of passion filling the air as often as her cries of delight.

Excitement flushed through her as she recalled drawing those sounds from him. At the same time she had to keep reminding herself it was a temporary arrangement. Perhaps he'd given her orgasms at an exponential rate to his own, maybe he'd even admitted that she had *always* had an effect on him, but he'd been the first to leave. She bit her lip, preferring the pain of her teeth over the insecure ache his leaving had caused. Waking with him would have been reassuring. Sweet, even.

"What are you making?"

She squeaked in startlement and almost dropped the whole spice jar into the pot. One glance over her shoulder flashed a million sensual memories through her mind. Her palms began to sweat and she could barely hold the wooden spoon to stir the sauce when she turned back to the stove. Hopefully he'd blame the steam off the pan for the dampness around her hairline.

"Braised beef and roasted vegetables," she answered.

He came to peer over her shoulder, hands settling on her waist. His nearness made her fingers even more nerveless. "Ambitious. Spaghetti would have been fine."

"Oh, you know what they say about the way to a man's heart."

His hands dropped from her waist and she felt a frigid blast move into the space he'd occupied as he moved away.

She made herself laugh, because the alternative was to let his reaction pierce her to the bone. "Apparently we both need to work on taking a joke." She stepped away to reach for her ice water with lemon, using it to ease the constriction in her throat. "The truth is I know my way around a kitchen quite well. One of Mum's nearest and dearests was a French chef. He taught me to put on an evening that allowed Mum to portray the lifestyle to which she aspired." Rowan licked that delicate wording off her cold lips. "So I have one more useless skill in my bag of tricks. I brought in that Bordeaux, if you want a glass." She nodded at the bottle.

"Why is it useless?" He found the bottle opener and cut the wax off the cork.

"Because I don't like cooking to order, and I'm not certified."

He pondered that as he poured a glass and brought out a second one.

"No, thanks," she said to forestall him.

"You don't want any?"

"There's a difference between wanting and needing. I would like a glass. I'm sure it's very nice—look at the year—but I'd rather refuse and prove I don't need it."

"You really did a number on yourself after leaving school, didn't you?"

"You haven't said anything I haven't said to myself," she assured him with a wan smile, recollecting the morning she'd woken with gaps in her memory and a reflection that reminded her too much of her father. It had been a bit of a relief to find her virginity intact, actually.

Turning away from his penetrating look, she removed a tray of hors d'oeuvres from the refrigerator. "To tide you over?" she invited.

He offered a whistle of appreciation at the array of tiny pastries, some topped with caviar and hot relish, all arranged between bites of cheese and colorful olives. Rowan quietly glowed under his approval, pleased she could wow him in this way at least.

"You've never had a problem with alcohol, have you?" She realized she'd never seen him drunk and that it was probably one of the things that attracted her most about him. He epitomized the self-possessed social drinker. "Even with all those horrible things you saw as a correspondent?"

"I don't like inhibiting my ability to control myself or any given situation."

"Oh, there's a surprise!" she said on a bubble of mirth. "You must have given your mother a lot of grief with that attitude." She stole his glass of wine long enough to tilt a splash into the sauce before she stirred it and began plating their meals.

His silence brought her head up.

"I'm sorry—is your mother alive?" she asked with a skip of compunction. "I didn't mean—"

"It's fine," he dismissed. "Yes, she is. And I don't believe I was a problem for her until her husband realized I wasn't his. That's when I was sent to boarding school. I didn't see her after that."

Rowan felt a little shock go through her. Her ears grasped for more, but he didn't expound. With a little frown she concentrated on quickly fanning slices of beef like a tiny hand of cards on the plates. After arranging the vegetables in a colorful crescent around golden potato croquettes, she zig-zagged sauce across the meat, added an asparagus spear decoratively wrapped with prosciutto, dabbed mustard sauce and tiny slivers of cucumber onto it, then a final garnish of a few sprigs of watercress and a radish flower.

"The dining room is set. Can you get the door?"

He followed and held her chair before seating himself and giving his plate the admiration it deserved. "This looks as good as it smells."

"Tuck in." His appreciation suffused her in warmth, but she couldn't shake the chill from what he'd revealed. As he picked up his cutlery, she ventured, "Nic, I can't help asking… Are you saying your mother never came to see you at school?"

CHAPTER EIGHT

THE BEEF MELTED ON his tongue, prepared better than anything any chef he'd ever hired had managed. Nevertheless, it still might have been a slice of his own heart filetted onto the plate, given the way it stuck to the roof of his mouth.

He should have kept his mouth shut. His entire life had been shattered when the truth of his parentage had come to light. It was not something he talked about, and yet it had flowed out uncontrolled with only a sip of red wine to lubricate it. Because he was relaxed by sex? Because physical closeness had fooled him into feeling emotionally comfortable with Rowan?

What to do now? If he refused to speak of it she'd know it was something that still had the power to wring out his insides.

At the same time there was an angry part of him that wanted to take her view of Olief and shake it up, make her see he wasn't a superhero. He was flawed. Or Nic was. He'd never figured that one out—whether it was his parents' deficiency or his own.

"Who was she? I mean, how did Olief know her?"

Her curiosity was not the lurid kind. He might have stood that. No, her brow wore a wrinkle of concern. She had never been ignored, so she didn't understand how any child could be.

Again the deep fear that *he* was the problem pealed inside him.

"He didn't know her. Not really," he said, keeping his tone neutral. "She was an airline hostess. He said it happened as he was coming back from being away in some ugly place."

"Do you think he did that often? Mum was always terrified he'd cheat on her because he'd cheated on his first wife, but— Wait. Don't tell me." Rowan held up a hand, face turning away. "It would kill me to hear that he did."

"I have no idea," Nic said flatly. "He didn't have any other children. I'm quite sure of that. That was the reason he didn't want his wife knowing about me. They tried their entire marriage to have a baby and she couldn't conceive."

The briefest flinch of anguish spasmed across her features, too quick for him to be sure he'd seen it before it dissolved in a frown of incomprehension. "But if he wanted children why didn't he see *you*?"

"He was ashamed of me."

Her eyes widened and her jaw slackened, but she quickly recovered, shaking her head. "You don't know that."

"He told me, Rowan. I asked him that exact question and that's what he said."

"He was ashamed of *himself.* If not, he should have been," she said, with a quick flare of vehement temper.

Her anger, when Olief was like a god to her, surprised him, cracking into and touching an internal place he kept well protected. His breath backed up in his lungs.

"Why didn't your mother do something? Insist he acknowledge you. Or did she? You said he paid for your education?" Rowan pressed.

"He paid for my schooling, yes." Nic set two fingertips on the bottom of his wineglass, lining it up with precision against the subtle pattern in the tablecloth. Every word he released seemed to scald all the way up his esophagus. "She didn't make a fuss because I was her shameful secret, too. She hadn't told her husband that she was already pregnant when they married. When he found out she took what Olief was willing to give her—tuition at a boarding school so they could all pretend I didn't exist."

Rowan had a small appetite at the best of times, but it evaporated completely as she took in the chilling rejection Nic had suffered. He was very much contained within his aloof shell at the moment, his muscles a tense barrier that accentuated what a tough, strong man he'd become, but shades of baffled shame still lingered in his eyes.

Everything in her ached with the longing to rise and wrap her arms around him, to try and repair the damage done, but she was learning. This was why he was always on his guard. He'd been hurt—terribly. Rowan had no trouble believing Olief had wanted to shield his wife, but to hurt a child? His own son?

"How...?" She took a sip of water to clear her thickened throat. "How did the truth come out?" she asked numbly.

Nic pointed at his hair. "My mother and her husband are both Greek, both dark. Babies and toddlers might sometimes have blond hair, but by the time I was entering school and still a towhead, not to mention looking nothing like the man I thought of as my father, it was obvious a goose egg had been hatched with the ducks."

Rowan dropped her cutlery, unable to fully comprehend what he was saying. "So he supported sending you away? After years of believing he was your father? What sort of relationship do you have with him now?"

"None. Once my mother admitted I wasn't his he never spoke to me again." Nic spoke without inflection, his delivery like a newscast.

"You can't be serious."

"He was a bastard. It was no loss to me." He applied himself to his meal.

Rowan cast about for something solid to grasp on to as a painful sea of confusion swirled around her. "You can't tell me that everyone who was supposed to be acting like a parent in your life just stuck you in some horrible boarding school like you were a criminal to be sent to prison."

With eyes half-closed in a laconic, flinty stare, he took a deep swallow of wine. "I didn't mind boarding school. I had the brains and the brawn that allowed a person to succeed there, and I realized quickly that I was on my own so I'd better seize the opportunity. What's in this sauce besides wine? It's very good."

Rowan soaked in the tub, still reeling under the blows Nic had been dealt as a child. He'd barely said another word after his stunning revelations, only cleaned his plate and excused himself to work.

Rowan had almost let out a hysterical laugh as he'd walked away. She so recognized that remote, unreachable man. All those years when she'd heard him described as Olief's estranged son she'd blamed Nic. Nic was the one who showed up at Olief's invitation like he was doing Olief a favor. Nic was the one who never left so much as a spare toothbrush in the rooms set aside for him. Nic was the one who took off for hours in his black roadster, never saying where he was going or when he'd be back.

Olief had so much to answer for.

Rowan was angry with him. Furious. He'd broken something in Nic. The boy had needed his real father to step up when his supposed one had rejected him. Instead Olief's disregard had made Nic incapable of trusting in human relationships. How could Olief have done it? Why?

With a pang, she faced that she'd never know—although

she wouldn't be surprised if it had something to do with the harsh mental toll Nic had mentioned with regard to being a foreign correspondent. Olief had been doing that sort of work then. Perhaps Olief simply hadn't had anything to offer his son.

It still made Rowan ache to reach out to Nic and heal him in some way—not that she imagined he'd let her. If anything, he probably resented letting her draw so much out of him. That was why he'd locked himself in his office again.

Drying herself off, she brushed out her hair and wondered if she should go to him, not sure she could face being rebuffed if he shut her out.

With a yawn, she counted the hours of sleep she'd got last night—not many, as she'd tried to work out ways to talk Nic around to her views on Rosedale. She'd slept after their vigorous hours in bed, but not for long. Once she'd woken to find him gone she'd risen and started work in the kitchen. Now her soak in the tub had filled her with lethargy.

She set her head on her pillow for a moment and picked up her feet. She was a master at catnaps....

Nic nudged open the bedroom door and took in Sleeping Beauty, one hand tucked beneath her folded knees, the other curled under her chin like a child. Her hair was a tumbled mass, her lips a red bow, her face free of makeup and her breath soft. She was as innocent as they made them.

While *he'd* finally given in to the guilty tension swirling like a murky cloud through him and come searching for release. Base, masculine, primordial forgetfulness. His flesh responded to the nearness of hers with a predictable rush of readiness, blood flooding into his crotch so fast it hurt.

Her being asleep was a gift, he acknowledged with sour irony. He hated being so weak as to be unable to resist her. If her eyes opened and flashed at him he'd be lost. If she woke and rolled onto her back—

He bit back a groan and reached for the coverlet, folding it from the far side of the bed until it wafted gently over her. This was better. She was getting too far under his skin with her fancy meals and empathetic speeches. This was supposed to be about sex. That was how he'd rationalized it and it was the only way they could come together.

Rowan's shock this evening perturbed him. She had ideals about family that were completely at odds with his own experience. It worried him, made him think that at some point she'd look to him to reflect some of those values and he simply didn't have them.

Uncurling his tense fists, he moved stiffly to the door, reminding himself that he might want to relieve sexual frustration with Rowan, but he didn't *need* to. He didn't need *her*.

He was on the beach, cold waves lapping at his knees, before he could draw a breath and begin to think clearly again.

Rowan's confusion at waking with the coverlet dragged across her was too sensitive a topic to pick apart first thing in the morning—especially when a nameless agitation made her feel so aware, like her skin had been stroked by a velvet breeze all evening and then it had been too hot to sleep.

Yet it was another windy day of scudding clouds and intermittent rain.

Nic was locked in his office down the hall, not looking for her. Or rather he had come looking and then left without touching her, leaving her heart as skinned as her knee, tight and tender and itchy. Which was juvenile.

The only way to suffocate her sense of irrelevance was to face up to another heartache of equal anguish. She went into the master bedroom and spent a long time with a sleeve held to her cheek, a collar to her nose, whole gowns clutched to her chest.

"You're a little old for dress-up, aren't you?" Nic's voice, rich and cool as ice cream, broke the silence an hour later, prompting a shiver of guilt and pleasure.

Rowan's first instinct was to toss aside the scarf she was tying over her hair and throw herself at him. She made herself finish knotting it in the famed Cassandra O'Brien style, then faced him. "People always tell me I look like Mum and I say thank you. But is it a compliment?"

"She was very beautiful, and so are you—but not because you resemble her."

Rowan blushed, but more because the admiration in his gaze was unabashedly sexual. She swallowed back the silly excited lump rising in her throat, trying to hold her wobbly smile steady as she loosened the scarf.

"What did you come in here for, full of such extravagant compliments? Keep that up and you'll see how much I resemble her when it comes to..." she tilted him her mother's infamous man-eater smile "...encouraging male admiration."

Something fierce and dangerous flashed in his Nordic blue eyes before he strolled forward on predatory feet. "I'm quite aware of how much you encourage it. I've seen you lay on the charm time and again. Why? Are you really as insecure as she was?"

His disparagement didn't allow her for one minute

to think his attitude stemmed from jealousy or posses-
siveness.

Yanking the scarf off her neck with a burn of her nape
and a cloud of painfully familiar sandalwood, Rowan replaced it on the hook beside the mirror. "How am I supposed to know what I am when I've always been told who
to speak to, where to go and how to act?"

She moved away from him, angry and hurt that he was
judging her and, yes, insecure. How could she develop
an identity if her ability to make decisions had so rarely
been tested?

"When Mum sent me to Paris I thought I'd finally be
able to make more of my own choices, but it didn't work
out that way. That was partly my fault, of course. The more
I put into dance, the more I wanted to succeed to prove to
myself I could. It's not easy to walk away from that much
investment. It's like gambling. I kept thinking the next
production would be the one that put me on the front of
the stage, not the back. Mum would finally be happy and
I'd be free to strike out *then*." She hitched her shoulder,
lashed by how nascent and unrealistic that dream had been.

"And when you finally did have the chance you drank
your face off and scared yourself," he said, from where
he'd stayed behind her.

"I did," she agreed with a chuckle of defeated acknowledgment, elbows sharp in her palms and shoulder blades
aching with tension. "The grief and guilt didn't help with
that." She sighed, still ashamed of the way she'd behaved,
but she had to move past it. She was determined to.

She pivoted to offer him a laissez-faire smile.

"So now I'm back at ground zero—the only place where
I sometimes had moments of feeling like I knew who I
was and what I wanted. I'm hoping for inspiration, but it

eludes me. You're a worldly man. Give me advice on what to do with my life."

Rowan's expansion on the picture of a life hemmed in by her mother's dominating personality disturbed Nic. It was such a different upbringing from the fortunate one he'd judged it to be. To keep from dwelling on the struggles that pulled far more empathy out of him than he was comfortable with, he focused on her oblique request, touring his father's suite to see if his idea was feasible.

The rooms sprawling from the southwestern turret of the house were befitting of a billionaire media mogul—expansive and masculine, yet with enough womanly touches to prove one had lived here with him. Nic briefly glanced in the walk-in closet, approving of its size, reassured by contents that were even more extravagant than he'd expected. He detoured out of interest to the well-appointed lounge, with its balcony overlooking the sea, noted the his and hers bathrooms and acknowledged the bed—big as the Titanic.

Rowan watched him with an inquisitive frown. "Have you never been in here before?"

"Never. You?"

"Loads," she said with a careless shrug.

Dismissing a weary *of course she had*, he gave the framed portraits a final considering look. "I think you should sell your mother's things and use the money to get a degree in something practical like business admin."

Rowan's love for her mother might be very much of the dutiful variety, and stained with resentment and angst, but she was appalled by Nic's suggestion. "I can't do that!" she protested.

Nic lifted his brows at her vehemence. "Why not?"

"Mum loved this table and that mirror... You can't just tear down someone's life and make it disappear." Her lingering sense of duty to preserve Cassandra O'Brien's mystique made her balk at the idea completely. "And business admin? Why don't you suggest I become an accountant? Or something really exciting like an insurance actuary? Maybe there's a library somewhere that needs its Dewey Decimal System overhauled?"

"Put it all in storage and wait tables, then." A muscle tightened in Nic's jaw, giving Rowan the crazy impression that she'd injured him. "I don't know you any better than you know yourself," he stated, in a comeback that returned very nicely any wounding she'd delivered. "Given what you just said, this is a decision best made by you, isn't it?"

Nic took on his warrior stance, strong and mute. If he wasn't the product of Thor and Athena she didn't know what he was, all masculine power and superiority.

His confident presence called to the woman in her, but his subtext didn't escape her. He wasn't contradicting her need to move on, and his mention of disposing of her mother's things reinforced his expectation that she'd do so.

Taking a surreptitious breath to ease the panicky constriction in her lungs, she nodded, mulling over what he'd said. "You're right. I need to figure it out on my own. But there is one thing we should plan together." She shoved aside the barbed wires curling around the tender walls of her heart to allow the statement out. "We need a memorial service."

He jerked back his head in immediate refusal. "I don't. Why would you?"

"Everyone does." She hugged herself tighter.

"No. It's a social convention that many subscribe to, particularly if they're of a religious bent, but that doesn't mean you and I have to buckle to it."

"It's not buckling! It offers closure." He couldn't really

imagine she'd sign a piece of paper and that would be it, could he?

Rowan stared at his impermeable expression and got a sick, hollow feeling in her stomach. She was such an idiot. She had thought sleeping with him would change things. Change *him*. Soften his edges and make him feel… something.

Nic shook his head at Rowan's stare of horrified objection, continually amazed by how sentimental she was. His inner core tightened protectively against that weakness. What was nostalgia but revisiting old pain?

"What did you have in mind? You and I reading poetry to each other over a marker on the lawn?" he asked.

"You don't have to be like that about it!" Her sniff of affront was followed by a haughty set of her chin that made him feel about two inches tall. "I thought we'd say something nice to people who care about them in a chapel in Athens."

"Oh, you want a *party*," he said with sudden realization, disgusted with himself for beginning to credit her with more substance. "Why didn't you say so? *No*."

"It's a service!" Rowan argued. "People need one. Aren't you getting emails and phone calls? Their friends are asking for a chance to pay their respects."

"Which they've done," Nic insisted. If he had to field one more empty platitude or soupy look he'd drop *himself* from a plane into the sea. "There is absolutely no reason to drag it all into the limelight again—or is that your goal? Feeling a bit isolated here, Ro? Then *leave*."

Well, that certainly told her how much he valued their time together! Rowan's belligerent chin took his dismissal as a direct hit, pulling in and—she feared—crumpling before she steadied it.

"Is there really nothing in you that feels a need to say

goodbye? Or are you only willing to give Olief as much time as he gave you?" It was a cruel thing to say. He'd spent hours on the search personally, and hiring teams of divers and pilots…

He didn't remind her of all that. He only stared flatly at her. The silence stretched. His stance hardened and his jaw clenched.

Her belly quivered in apprehension.

"I said no." He walked out.

Nic kept his distance for the next several days. If Rowan had lazed around underfoot he might have given her a piece of his mind, but she was actually doing as he'd told her to. She'd made a few trips to the other side of the island to fetch empty boxes. Garment bags had appeared with labels and markers. Every day, when she wasn't leaving him a meal downstairs, she spent hours packing up the master bedroom.

If she had come to *him* he might have engaged, but he would not go looking for her. He was too proud. So proud it made his shoulders ache with hollow pressure. But the way she'd taken everything he'd told her and thrown it back in his face had been a blow. It was a perfect example of why he didn't let people in. He didn't want anyone to have the power to hurt him. If that meant he didn't get the closeness—the sex and laughter and moments of basking in the light of a woman's smile—so be it. Those were things he refused to crave anyway.

And if he had a curious tingling in his chest, almost like he was *missing* her—well, that was pure stupidity. She was right down the hall.

Or was she? He thought he heard a knock and clicked off his shaver.

"Nic?" She was in his lounge. Grabbing a towel off the

rail, he hitched it around his hips and pulled the bathroom door inward.

Rowan was halfway around the sofa, heading toward the double doors that led into his bedroom. She started when he revealed himself, visibly taken aback to find him so close and fresh from the shower, but what did she expect at six-thirty in the morning?

She was in a short robe belted loosely over a torturously short babydoll nightgown. Her warm sleep scent, like almonds and tea, teased his nostrils. Despite going months without a woman on many occasions, he suddenly and acutely felt this recent abstinence.

A flustered blush colored her cheeks and she took a half step back, then held her ground within his reach even though he could tell she was discomfited.

Desire pulsed through him with increasing punches from his strengthening heart rate, reacting to her tousled hair and fresh-from-bed look. He wanted to heave her over his shoulder and carry her to his unmade sheets, but alongside his immediate lust was a pang of surprise at how exhausted she looked. Her eyes were green gems in bruised sockets, her skin thin and pale.

He wasn't exactly sleeping well himself. Every day was a fight to incapacitate his sex drive with punishing workouts. Every night he woke to erotic dreams anyway, heavy and aching to go to her.

Funny how there was no satisfaction in knowing she was suffering too. He shifted his weight so his feet were braced wide, hopeful that his uncontrollable response to her wouldn't become obvious.

"Yes?" he demanded.

She swallowed and ran a hand through her hair, reminding him how silky and thick it was, how good it had felt to grasp a handful of the luscious waves and kiss her until neither of them could breathe.

Her breath sucked in and she said in a rush, "I just heard the ferry horn. It's coming now. I totally forgot they change the schedule on weekdays."

His sex thoughts dissipated under something that made him pull inward with apprehension—even though he didn't know why a change in the ferry schedule was such a crisis she had to burst in here, wringing her hands over it. "So?"

"That means I have to pack and leave now, unless you're coming and want to make other arrangements to get us to the city by two."

His brain stalled on *pack and leave*. The rest penetrated more slowly and didn't make a lick of sense. "What?"

Rowan folded her arms across her chest in a move that was so defensive he instinctively knew he didn't want to be enlightened. She spoke with exaggerated patience that annoyed him further.

"I thought I would have more time to reason with you, but I've just realized I don't. I have to go now. Unless you're willing to have the helicopter come and get us in a few hours? In that case we have all kinds of time to fight."

"About...?" He tensed right down to the arches of his bare feet.

Her mouth pursed before she took a brave breath and stated, "The service."

CHAPTER NINE

"WHAT? SERVICE?"

The way Nic chomped the words made Rowan tremble internally, but it was far too late to back down. She'd known as she set this up that the worst part would be now, when she told him—and there had been a lot of hard parts, not least of which had been finding the money. She'd put off telling him as long as she could, avoiding him, checking that he couldn't overhear her calls. All the way along she'd known she'd need to set aside patience and temper to make him see she was doing the right thing.

Now, though, a mental clock ticked in her head. The ferry's horn usually sounded when it reached the tip of the island. It took ages to empty and reload, so she had at least thirty or forty minutes to get to the marina, but she suspected that wouldn't give her enough time to talk Nic around to her way of thinking.

There wasn't enough time in the world for that. If only he wasn't naked and looking like the biggest, angriest Viking ever to rip off his shirt and go berserk.

"I made it clear we weren't holding a service." That low, livid voice nearly made her knees collapse.

"*We* aren't holding one, are we?" She spoke with admirable civility, keeping the quaver out of her voice. "*I* am.

Courtesy demands I invite you. Could you make up your mind? I have to run if you're not coming."

"How could you?" His fingers curled as if he wanted to close them on her neck.

"Option two, then? We're fighting." Her temper caught like a cat's claw. She might have kept her distance while she made the plans, aware that continuing their sexual relationship while going behind his back would make this betrayal worse, but he had completely ignored her for days! That *hurt*. "Or are you literally asking me how I did it? Because I don't need your permission and I have resources."

"Table dancing?" he derided.

"What else?" she taunted to hide the smart. "Of course in order to earn enough to pay for this big *party* I'm hosting I'll have take off my clothes this time."

Outrage arced from him like an electric bolt, making her jerk as he seemed to rise taller and loom over her. "That had better be a lie."

"What's it to you?" she cried, the words coming straight from the forsaken nights that had piled up in the last few days.

This was the hardest time of her life and he was making it harder with his hot and cold attitude, the exquisite peaks of pleasure he'd brought her to and the pit of dejection he'd left her in. Her incendiary anger carried her forward, resentful words charging off her tongue.

"What do you care if I sell myself on street corners and buy gold-plated urns? I'm just a girl you sleep with when you're bored. I don't rate so much as a good morning or a thanks for lunch or a kiss goodnight!"

An inferno of anger roared in his eyes. *Wrong thing to fight about*, she thought, but his rebuff pained her so deeply she couldn't help herself.

"Maybe if you'd spoken to me I might have told you!"

she rushed on, with a contentious lift of her chin, the burn of humiliation searing through her. "But you didn't even invite me for a spin in one of the guest rooms. What's the matter, Nic? Does sleeping with me make you hate me less?"

He caught her by the upper arms before she saw him move. "What do you want from me? Flowers? Romance? *Caring?* Prepare for disappointment. I'm not built that way. But if you're missing the sex keep talking. I'll accommodate you," he warned.

She could have done a million things: said something cruel, sent her knee into his groin. She wasn't scared by his threat, though. She was aroused. So was he. The hectic flush across his cheekbones, the unsteady rise and fall of his chest and the bulge of his towel filled her with euphoria.

He didn't want to want her, though, and that made her mad. It gave her the power to strike back in the one way she knew would completely undermine his control: she whipped off his towel and threw it to the floor.

"Really?" He backed her into the wall, incredulous.

"What are you going to do about it?" she taunted.

His fierce blue eyes never left hers as his hands shot to her waist, brushing open her robe before descending to her bare thighs in a rough caress. His hands climbed to her hips, bunching the hem of her short nightie over his wrists.

She gasped and jerked at his proprietorial touch, shamefully flooding with heated wetness. It had been *days*! His breath left him in a ragged laugh as he realized there were no panties to remove. He reached to cup her buttocks, sliding his palms to the backs of her thighs beneath the curve of her bottom, and lifted her.

She parted her legs in a practiced leap, arms reaching over his bunching shoulders to brace her weight on him.

Something brazen and fierce was taking hold in her. A knot of anguished loneliness had been building in her and the only way to break it apart was with the hot penetration of her body by his.

She was completely ready for him, whether from her erotic dreams and constant fantasies or because sexual frustration had been at the heart of this fight in the first place. She didn't know. Only knew that she was wet and needy. And when he embedded himself in her with one smooth thrust she cried out in primal fulfillment, locking her legs around his waist with frantic, brazen determination.

He swore and tried to gentle things. She wouldn't let him. His fingers bit into the backs of her thighs as she engaged every well-trained muscle in her body and let her weight deepen his thrusts. Welling emotion was threatening to overflow in her. She wanted to absorb him completely and nipped at his mouth, holding the sides of his head as she sucked hard on his bottom lip.

He leaned them into the wall and pumped harder. Faster. Making her body clench around him stronger and tighter. The crescendo approached. She clasped him in greedy frenzy, determined to bring him over the edge with her as she felt the rushing expansion, both of them tipping, falling, flying...

Nic felt her climax arrive in a powerful clench that nearly took him alive. He let go with an explosion of molten heat so intense his skin went icy. The backlash of pleasure left him too weak to do anything but pin her to the wall, his hips finishing in uneven thrusts. She shivered around him, wringing magnificent throbs from him as he emptied himself into her. Her moans of rapture filled his mouth like spun sugar.

Drained, he stayed leaning on her for long moments, muscles shaking in strain.

Unprotected sex, he thought dimly, and a craven fear unfurled in him—something so apprehensive and insecure he drew in a sharp breath.

At his sudden inhalation Rowan quit playing her hand softly at the back of his neck. Her touch held a tenderness he'd only recognized when she'd moved her hand to his shoulder in a silent request for release. Another clench of loss hit him.

His head felt too heavy to lift. He didn't want to disengage and experience the rush of cool air between them, or watch her nearly crumple because her legs refused to hold her. Chagrin poured through him as he reached to steady her, disturbed by how she trembled and avoided his gaze. "Rowan—"

"If I miss that ferry I'll never forgive you." There wasn't much snap left in her voice. It was more a statement of fact. Weary resignation.

The service. Infuriated anger bled back, but there wasn't anything he could do. Keeping her from it would only make both of them look bad.

"I'll arrange the chopper." He rubbed his face, already dreading the ordeal, his mind split with anger at her for putting him in this position and a more embryonic profound trepidation. She was at the door before he managed to say, "I didn't use anything."

"I know. The timing's wrong. It's fine."

No, it wasn't. Nothing about what had just happened was *fine*.

So that's how babies are made, Rowan thought as she showered, dazed by the primordial way she and Nic had clashed like two cells intent on comingling their DNA.

The fact that pregnancy was impossible should be providing her with a sense of relief, but it only increased the forlorn feeling of isolation that had been eating her all week.

Was that why she'd provoked him? To force his attention when she had been feeling neglected? She'd been so anxious about the tense distance growing between them. Had she just pulled the oldest trick in the female book? Trying to keep him with sex? Dumb idea. He wouldn't hate her any less for goading him into losing control.

Filled with conflicted disappointment, she stepped out of the shower, thankful she couldn't see her wan reflection in the fogged mirror.

Self-pity is not a good look, as her mother would say. *Men are drawn to confidence.*

Right. She had a performance to get through, she thought with a ripple of misplaced hysterical humor. She reached for her makeup case, determined to hide her pained wistfulness from Nic.

His perfunctory knock a few minutes later shattered her efforts at gathering her composure, but he was only informing her they'd leave as soon as she was ready. "We'll dress at my apartment. I need a suit," he said through the door.

"Okay," she called back.

The impersonal exchange burned from her constricted throat all the way into the pit of her stomach. She'd told him the timing was wrong, but that wasn't true. The body was wrong. Underweight. *Infertile*. Not uncommon in her former world of over-training and under-eating. She had never let it bother her, but it suddenly seemed like one more way she fell short, and that was too much to bear when she already felt like he hated her.

Thankfully, Nic didn't seem to want to talk when she eventually faced him. Locking himself away physically wasn't possible, so he did it mentally, acting like the sex hadn't happened. He hustled her into the helicopter on the lawn and waited until they reached Athens to ask about the service. Where and when was it being held? Who was speaking?

She answered numbly, thinking about how anxious she'd been as she made the arrangements, dreading his anger, dreading attending alone. Now it was overshadowed by a chilly tension that had nothing to do with her going against his wishes.

"I tried to keep the press off the scent," she assured him. "Well, as much as possible when the man owned half the world's papers and news stations."

No smirk, just a tic in his cheek. "And how did you pay for everything?"

It occurred to her he might be doing the same thing she was: talking about the service to avoid dissecting this morning. Or maybe he was satisfied with her answer that the timing was wrong and just wanted the service out of the way and her out of his life.

She swallowed, mentally balancing on that ledge of a week ago, with deadly waves threatening to engulf her and no way to get back to where she'd been.

He was leading her to the guest room in his high-rise penthouse. She craned her neck to orient herself. It was a surprisingly soothing expanse of rooms that flowed one into another, surrounding an outdoor pool and a view of the Parthenon that stole her breath. Rosedale must make him feel hemmed in, she realized, and accepted that she'd never win him over on the mansion. Perhaps she should have listened without judging, because she could stay in a place as private and sunny as this penthouse forever.

"My mother's agent is floating me a loan," she answered absently when she realized he was waiting.

"Introduce me to him. I'll repay him."

Her pride prickled. Hosting a service was her choice. She wouldn't let it become his problem. "I've got it. It's not like there's caskets and burials."

"It's my responsibility. I'll take care of it."

"You cut me off because you wanted me to show responsibility," she reminded. "Pay half, if you insist, but I refuse to owe you money. I'll keep my loan with Frankie."

"Don't start a fight you can't win, Rowan."

"I'd rather not fight at all."

"That's funny," he said without a shred of humor, and closed the door.

Nursing anger at Rowan for putting him in the position of owing a stranger for the cost of his own father's service kept Nic from brooding on the disquiet eating a hole in his breastbone. It allowed him to lock his emotions so deeply in his personal dungeon he almost forgot what he was dressing for until he walked into the lounge.

Rowan wore a simple black top over a knit black skirt. Slits in the skirt revealed her high boots and black stockings. Her silhouette, graceful as always, was startlingly slight, making his breath catch. A deep purple scarf held her straightened hair so the length lay in a gleaming line down her right shoulder. She clutched a black pocketbook and opened it when he appeared, walking toward him with purpose as she extracted something.

He tensed, anticipating the hint of sexual awareness that always struck with her nearness, and found himself thrust back to their wild copulation in his lounge. Her invitation might have been more of a dare, but she had participated, welcomed him, taken him in like it was as vital to her as it had been to him. It had been raw and primeval and mind-shattering. He'd never wanted or needed anyone like that before. The culmination had been more than physical. It had been spiritual.

And exceedingly careless of him.

She'd said the timing was wrong, but what if it wasn't? What if it was bang on?

His gut was a cement mixer as he stared at the part in her hair, trying to see into the workings of her mind. What if she fell pregnant? What would she do?

His palms began to sweat.

Her subtle scent invaded his dark thoughts, disguised by a designer bouquet of *grigio* citrus, but he detected the almonds and fresh tea, unique as the rest of her. It was a punch of homespun warmth, gentle and feminine and familiar.

He wanted to reach for her, but the last time he'd done that he'd behaved like an animal. It underlined exactly what he'd told her: he was incapable of true caring.

Guilt hardened in him, stiffening his muscles as he waited to see why she had come so close. Searching for a clue to her motive, he noted that the only adornment on her outfit of unrelieved black was a pair of pins above her heart: one a small emerald brooch that formed a lucky four-leaf clover, the other a familiar insignia—the Marcussen Media four-color shield with an inlaid "O" of white gold.

"How is that a pin?" he asked as he recognized Olief's cufflink.

"I sent them out to be converted." Rowan removed the tiepin he was wearing and replaced it with the matching cufflink inlaid with an "M." She took care to ensure it sat straight. Her nearness, the light graze of her touch between the buttons of his shirt, was like a magnetic interference against his invisible force field, making his self-control shiver and threaten to short. The gesture was so simple and inclusive he felt his throat close over any words he might have found to remark on it.

At the same time he was devastated by the familial connection it symbolized. That wasn't him. He'd been rejected as a son. He'd never make a decent father. His lungs shrank and he began to grow cold.

With a critical eye Rowan scanned his appearance, her hands sweeping across his shoulders, smoothing his lapels, adjusting the kerchief poking out of his pocket.

"Don't." He couldn't bear her touch when he felt so raw.

Her gaze came up. Her mouth still looked bruised, and now so did her eyes. Her vulnerability made his gut clench, sending a spike of regret through him. When he ran his tongue behind his lip he could still feel where her teeth had cut in, leaving a taste of rust. She'd been lost in rapture, but his behavior had still been incredibly crass.

Reckless.

She flinched under his scowl and turned away. "I know you think this is just one more selfish act by a spoiled socialite, but I'm doing it for them. Well, maybe a little for myself." She dropped his original tiepin into her pocketbook. "I let Mum down so many times. I need to give her this at least."

The defeat in her was so tangible, his throat ached as she crossed the room away from him.

"I'm not angry about the service," he blurted.

"What, then?" She drew herself to the full extent of her slender height, seeming to brace herself. She knew. She could see the elephant in the room as well as he could. What they'd done this morning shouldn't have happened.

Could she also see how much he hated himself for putting them in this position? That he wanted to lock his arms around her and beg her not to do anything rash? But he knew it would be better to send her away and let her make her own decision, because he could never be the kind of man capable of involving himself with a woman and their child.

Maybe there wasn't even a baby to worry about. She'd said the timing was wrong.

Shades of regret rose in him, but his ingrained hesitation against emotions—experiencing them, labeling them, acting on them—prevented him from examining that.

The intercom buzzed, making them both jump.

"It's just the car," he managed through a dry throat.

Rowan nodded jerkily and shrugged into her coat before he realized what she was doing. He didn't move forward in time to help her and his hand closed on empty air. It stayed locked in a fist that her sharp gaze detected on her way to the door.

"After this I'll finish packing her things and get out. I promise."

The words scooped into his chest, leaving a gaping space in him. *Grief*, he told himself. For the last year he'd taken refuge from it in work or the gym. His refusal to host a service had largely been an attempt to avoid revisiting the loss.

The choke of sorrow and missed chances had moved into the background of his psyche, though. All his tension and misgivings were rooted in Rowan's behavior right now. She was on the run, and he didn't blame her, but it filled him with anxiety.

The elevator floor dropped away from beneath his unfeeling legs and the blurred city passed before his eyes. He could only clench a hand on the nearest surface and try to hold on to his equanimity while trying to convince himself that facing the memorial service was eating him alive. Not something else.

After this I'll finish packing her things and get out.

His cold fog grew worse when the car slowed outside a low building. Nic finally came out of himself long enough to see how gray her complexion had gone, leaving her makeup as slashes of garish color against her waxen face.

"Are you going to throw up?" He reached for the ice bucket.

"It's stage fright." Her shaking hand went to her middle. "I didn't eat, so nothing to toss. It'll go away as soon as I'm on." She left the car like a ghost rising from a grave, her movements elegant as always, her collected expression niggling at him.

Was she really not the least bit worried? If timing was so reliable there wouldn't be an overpopulation problem. Or had she already made a decision that a baby *wouldn't* happen, no matter what?

He took Rowan's elbow as they climbed the stairs, consciously easing a grip that wanted to tighten with urgency. His heart pounded. *Don't, Rowan. Please don't.*

People were already seated inside—hundreds of them. Once they sat, a man in robes invited them to bow their heads. It was surreal, given his state of mind, but cleansing. This *was* the right thing to do. He should have known, should have trusted that Rowan understood these things better than he did.

As she moved to the podium a few minutes later he noted that she had regained some color, but her eyes were still too big for her face. He watched her with a fatalistic rock in his chest. She was so much better than he was, rising above a difficult childhood like a phoenix, able to sing her mother's praises, warm and beautiful, while he carried only the ashen darkness of his childhood with him, staining everything black.

He had nothing to offer a woman and a child but the same bleak void he'd grown up in. Making her pregnant would be a disaster. He had no choice but to pray it wouldn't happen, yet a torturous want crowded into him. A deep, undeniable ache filled him to be better than he was. Damn Olief for never setting an example or instilling confidence in him when it came to interpersonal relationships. He'd left his son floundering, armed only with a shaky desire to succeed without any skills to back it up.

Rowan's eyes met his as he struggled with his need to be everything his own father wasn't. Her voice cracked and her hand came up to cover her trembling lips. Her self-possession began to fall apart and threatened to shatter Nic's. Purely out of instinct he pushed to his feet, moving to stand beside her. It was like stepping into cold fire. He hadn't meant to put himself in this position. Public speaking didn't bother him, but this was different. He never put his emotions on display, and his intense feelings were just under the surface while a sea of faces stared.

He took Rowan's hand. It was so icy his heart tripped in concern. He closed his fingers tightly over hers. She pointed to a place on the page and he began to read.

"'Olief tried hard to be a father figure to me...'" he began, the words evaporating on his tongue. Olief *had* tried with Rowan, and maybe that was the takeaway lesson. He had to say goodbye to Olief's failings as a father and look forward with his own purpose and approach and simply *try*.

Rowan squeezed Nic's hand with all her might, fighting back the breakdown that had come down on her like an avalanche when she had met Nic's tormented gaze. He was genuinely worried she'd turn out to be pregnant. She'd seen it back at the apartment, had even tried to brace herself for reassuring him how remote a possibility it was, but dread turned like a medieval torture device in her. He'd be relieved and she would be crushed.

The arrival of the car had saved her, but as she'd stood up here, playing the part of the good daughter, all she'd been able to think was that it was her mother's fault she had no periods. Even before the intensity of ballet classes the pressure had been on to mind her calories. Rowan had felt like a hypocrite, talking up the woman she resented deep in her heart. Then she'd looked into Nic's eyes and known he didn't want her to conceive, and with equal fervor knew she wished she *could*.

Yet wouldn't.

It had been too much, and she was clinging to composure by her fingernails.

Nic closed with a few personal words of his own, Rowan swallowed, and thankfully they were able to sit down. But Nic didn't let go of her hand. Maybe that was her fault. Her fingers were white where she entwined them with his. She stared at their linked frozen hands as one of her mother's friends rose to sing an Irish ballad.

The worst was over. She only had to get through the reception in the adjoining hall without betraying her inner tension. As they stood to move through the doors that were thrown open for them she disengaged from Nic's grip. "You don't have to stay," she offered, even though he'd said he wasn't angry about the service anymore.

His dark brows came down like storm clouds, scolding and chilly. "I'll stay."

She felt a lash of fear. A wild impulse to bolt from here whirled through her. *Very mature, Ro.* But there was something resolved in his expression. She sensed a *Talk* looming and wasn't prepared to face it.

"Suit yourself," she murmured, and let herself be drawn by people who were anxious to express their condolences.

Nic wondered if he had imagined her clammy grip on his hand. She was so willing to have him disappear now.

Because she blamed him? She had every right. He was the experienced one—in more ways than one. He shouldn't have taken such a risk with her.

He wished it was as simple as saying she had provoked him, but that wasn't right. Hearing she'd been hurt by his neglect had rattled him. *"Maybe if you'd spoken to me..."* But he'd been afraid to speak to her, afraid she would hurt him again with all that he'd told her. He hadn't liked facing that he was a coward who had avoided her out of fear.

"Does sleeping with me make you hate me less?"

Yes, it did. Which scared him even more and made him profoundly aware of his inability to love. He'd said something crude at that point, infuriated that he could never be what she needed and deserved. The futility of their relationship had struck home and he'd wanted quite desperately, just for a second, to bind her to him in the most irrevocable way possible.

He watched her work the room filled with screen stars, diplomats, business magnates and overgrown titled children. For the first time he didn't see a spoiled girl demanding attention. He saw a young woman who ensured everyone was noticed, greeting individuals affectionately and putting them at ease.

He did his duty, distantly thanking people for coming, but he couldn't help acknowledging what a perfect foil Rowan made for his innately brisk demeanor, brimming with natural warmth and beauty. If their lives became bound by a child—

He refused to let the thought progress, still disturbed by the near yearning he'd felt as he'd contemplated becoming a father while saying goodbye to his own. He tracked down Franklin Crenshaw instead, waiting out the requisite expression of sympathy before nodding at the elegance of the wine and cheese reception.

"I appreciate all you've done. Please send me the bills."

Frankie shook his head. "Rowan made all the arrangements. I only opened an account for her." A rueful smile twitched the man's lips. "But I'm not surprised she's asked you to settle up for her. She doesn't want to owe me, does she?"

Nic slipped into his investigative reporter guise. "Why do you say that?"

"Because she knows how I'll ask her to repay me."

"She can't dance," Nic asserted, instantly protective of her injured leg.

"No, but she can act. Look at her. What a way to spend your birthday," Frankie said under his breath, stealing a glass of wine from a passing tray.

The date struck Nic like a bludgeon, taking his disgraceful behavior this morning to a new realm of discredit. *"Never a good morning or a thank you..."* His insides clenched against more evidence that he failed at interpersonal relationships.

"She's hanging by a thread," Frankie said with pained admiration. "No one else sees it, but when that girl can't find a smile you know she's on her last nerve."

Nic took it as judgment. *He* was the reason her stress level was through the roof.

"I bet she hasn't eaten either," Frankie mused.

With a soft curse, Nic excused himself.

Rowan was wrung out by the time they returned to Nic's suite. She could barely unzip her boots and pull them off her aching feet.

Nic shrugged out of his suit jacket, then poured two drinks—brandy, she assumed. He brought them to her and she did what she had done with the coffee, tea, and plates of food he'd handed her throughout the long day. She set it down on the nearest surface.

He sighed.

"Don't be mad, Nic. I can't do it," she said lifelessly.

"I'm not mad, but we have to talk."

"Not now. I just want this day to be over." She saw him wince, and regretted being so blunt, but the service had been hard enough without the undercurrents between them. He'd never left her side and she was at the end of her rope. "I'm going to bed."

Nic picked up her untouched drink as she walked away, considering going after her. But why? So they could continue battling to keep their emotions in check? He was done with crumpled tissues and weepy embraces. His wall of imperviousness couldn't stand another hit. Ro had it right. Finish the day and start fresh tomorrow.

But his tension wouldn't ease until they'd talked through the various scenarios and how they'd react to them. He couldn't imagine sleeping with so much on his mind and resented her for dragging this out. How could she be so calm about it? Didn't she realize what was at stake? That their lives could be changed forever?

Look who he was dealing with, though. Rowan was the first to turn anything into a joke.

Frustrated, he carried his drink in one hand and tugged at his tie with the other, heading for his bedroom and a fruitless try at sleeping. As he passed Rowan's door he heard a noise. A deep, wrenching sob.

His heart stalled, then kicked in with a painful downbeat. Filled with dread, he slowly pushed the door open. She sat on the side of the bed, one arm out of her shirt, the fabric bunched around her torso as she rocked, keening, her face buried in her white hands.

The jagged pressure that swelled behind his sternum

threatened to clog his lungs. Something between an instinct and a memory pushed him further into the room, even though his feet had gone so cold he couldn't feel them.

He set aside the glass and touched her arm. "Ro, stop."

She clutched at him, face running with makeup. "I'm trying," she choked. "But nothing will ever be the s-same again…"

Her distress threatened his shaky control, urging him to run before his defenses fell completely, but he couldn't leave her like this. *Actress*, he thought and felt like a heel for thinking she wasn't affected by all that had happened today. Of course she was. Beneath the beautiful armor and impudent wit was a scared kid who kept taking on more responsibility than was hers to carry.

It struck him that he'd taken advantage of her when he took her to bed. She'd been at a very weak moment in her life. This was why she'd given herself to him. She was losing the life she'd known and now faced even bigger changes.

"It's okay," he lied, brushing away her ineffectual hands, desperate to sop up his guilt. He never should have touched her. He smoothed her hair, releasing the scarf when he came to it. "You're going to be okay, Ro." His shoulders throbbed with remorse. He stripped her to her undies and eased her beneath the sheet, desperate to tuck her in and close this day for her.

Tomorrow they'd talk. What he needed now was time to come to terms with the injury he'd done her if he'd got her pregnant.

"Don't leave, Nic, please," she pleaded, pressing his fingers to her soaked cheek.

He wavered. She was an iceberg. He compromised by toeing off his shoes and dragging his belt free one-handed, remaining clothed as he moved under the covers. With a tight embrace he tried to keep her shuddering frame from falling apart.

"Just until I fall asleep," she murmured. "Then you can go. I'm sorry."

"No, *I'm* sorry," he said with deep anguish, and soothed the fresh tension that gathered in her. "Shh. Go to sleep. It'll be okay," he lied again, while the possibility of an unplanned pregnancy circled in his mind like a shark's fin. "You'll see."

CHAPTER TEN

Rowan stretched and the hot weight of blankets surrounding her moved.

When she opened her eyes Nic's arresting blue eyes were right there, hooded and enigmatic, fixed on hers. His jaw was smudged with a night's growth of bronze-gold stubble, his hair glinting in the morning sunlight pouring through the uncovered window.

Her breakdown last night came back to her in a rush. The day had been an endurance event of fielding enquiries about her leg and her future. She didn't have any pat answers, and through it all Nic had loomed over her like a giant microscope, seeming to watch her every move.

The tension hadn't let up, so it was understandable that after holding them back all day she had let her emotions get the better of her when she was finally alone. Letting Nic find her at such a low point and grasping at him like a lifeline, however, made her feel more raw and exposed than after the wicked things they'd done to each other in the throes of passion.

Flinching in vexation, she sat up to let her hair curtain her face while she tried to minimize how defenseless she felt. "Gosh, was that *your* virginity I just took? I can't imagine you've spent many nights fully clothed in bed with a female without the precursor of sex. Be honest—not counting this one, how many?"

"She's back," he remarked under his breath, pushing away the covers and rolling to sit on the far edge of the bed. "As it happens, you're not my first," he stated flatly. "I used to let my baby sister snuggle up to me when she'd had a bad dream."

Rowan stared at the wrinkled back of his shirt, barely able to process the information through her sleep-muddled brain. "You have a *sister*? But you said— On your mother's side? Is she younger?"

"And two half-brothers, if you're taking a tally."

No surprise to learn he was the oldest, but the rest stunned her. "That's a big family. Why do you never talk about them?"

His shoulders jerked, then he stood abruptly. Maybe she'd imagined his flinch.

"I don't talk *to* them." He stretched his arms toward the ceiling and his shirt came loose from his waistband while his joints cracked. "My aunt used to bring us together for a week in the summer when she lived in Katarini, but once she moved to America my mother's husband put a stop to my seeing them. He didn't like them coming home and talking about me."

"That's mean!" Rowan's already peeled-thin heart was abraded further by his casual reference to what amounted to outright cruelty. "Your poor mother," she couldn't help adding, sitting in the pool of rumpled blankets and retrospective empathy.

"My poor *mother*?" Nic swung around with a harsh expression of astonishment, arms lowering.

"Well, yes." Rowan shrugged, her hand imperceptibly tightening on the edge of the sheet. "Having to stay married to someone like that. He's probably the reason she didn't see you at school. He sounds controlling."

"She didn't 'have to' stay married to him. She *chose* to. She chose him over me." His flash of rejection was quick and deep, so swiftly snatched back and hidden behind chilling detachment she could only guess how much practice he'd had at stifling it.

Rowan's heart, ravaged by all that had happened in the last week, finished rending in two. She ached to offer him one of those ragged halves, the one beating at a panicky pace, but doubted he'd take it. No wonder he held himself at such a distance. Distance was all he'd been taught.

There weren't any platitudes that could make up for what had been done to him, so she tried to offer perspective.

"What other choice did she have?" she asked gently. "She already had your sister and the boys."

"One boy. She was pregnant with the other," he admitted, one hand rasping his stubbled jaw as though he wanted to wipe away having started this conversation.

"There you go. How does a woman with three children and about to give birth to a fourth hold down a job? Who nurses that baby while she's at work? It sounds like her choices came down to destroying the lives of all her children or just one. I'm not saying she made the right choice, but I don't think she had any good ones. It was an awful position to be in."

"She could have chosen not to get into that position. She married knowing I was on the way." His eyes were so dark they were nearly black. "She could have broken her engagement and asked Olief to support her. For that matter, given they were both committed elsewhere, they never should have made me in the first place!"

Suppressing a stark pang of protest against his never being born, Rowan only said, "Because every pregnancy is planned?" She choked that off, appalled she'd started to go there. She only wanted him to see everyone was human. "It happens, Nic," she rushed on, fixing her gaze blindly on the blurred pattern of the curtains. "Sometimes the choices you're left with are tough ones. Judging by your reaction to my efforts toward you, you're not interested in having a family, so what would *you* do?" she challenged with a spurt of courage. "Marry me anyway?"

It was a less than subtle plea for him to qualify his feelings toward her. He'd been so solicitous, holding her close all night. It made her heart well with hope that something deeper between them was possible.

He'd hardened into something utterly rigid, utterly unyielding. When he spoke, his voice was coated in broken glass. "The greater question is what would *you* do?"

His chilly withdrawal made her insides shrink. She wasn't sure how to interpret his grim question, but his quiet ferocity gave her a shiver of preternatural apprehension. She was convinced he didn't want her to be pregnant, so was he hoping to hear she wouldn't go through with it? He would be vastly disappointed! Her heart hardened like a shield inside her. *Nothing* would make her give up her baby.

"It would be beyond a miracle if I got pregnant so I'd keep it, of course. But don't worry," she charged with barely restrained enmity. "I wouldn't ask you to marry me. My mother's shotgun marriage ruined her life. I'll never repeat *that* mistake."

She threw off the blankets and locked herself in the bathroom, shaken to the bone. She tried to regain control by reminding herself they were arguing about something that couldn't even happen, but when she stood in the shower a few minutes later her hand went to her abdomen where a hollow pang of *if only* throbbed.

"I'd keep it, of course."

There was no "of course" about it, but Nic was reassured that Rowan had said it. Which was crazy. The thought of making a baby with her should be putting him into a cold sweat.

He shifted in the back of the car. He had decided years ago not to have children. Partly it stemmed from spending years in Third World countries. After seeing children savaged by war and famine, their parents helpless to protect or provide for them, he'd concluded that reproducing was irresponsible.

An even deeper resistance came from his certainty that he wasn't built for family life. Every time he'd had the hint of one it had been stripped away—most recently when Olief had flown into that storm. Nic didn't buy into fate, but it really didn't seem he was meant to lead the life of a domesticated man. He'd always been comfortable in that belief. What kind of father would he make anyway, incapable as he was of emotional intimacy?

Rowan would be a good mother, though. Her view of pregnancy was a bit romantic, but it thawed the frozen places inside him. He was reassured. Rowan would show him the way. She was affectionate and playful and knew how to love. His baby would be in good hands because she would love her child even if it *was* his.

The thought caught him by the heart and squeezed. It was such a tiny lifeline, thrown down a well—something delicate and ephemeral in dark surroundings. He wasn't completely sure he'd discerned it. He didn't even have the emotional bravery to reach out and see if it was real. It might not hold. But he wanted to believe it was there.

He glanced at Rowan, his ambivalence high. She'd accused him of not wanting a family and he didn't, he assured himself quickly. The weight of responsibility, the vastness of the decisions and accommodations, were more than he could take. And winding through that massive unknown was a dark line, a fissure. *Him.* The unknown. The weakness. Could he hold a family together or would he be the reason it fell apart?

At the same time he was aware of his heart pounding with… God, was it anticipation? No. He tried to ignore the nameless energy pulsing in him, but he couldn't shake the urge to push forward into the future and see, know, *feel* a sense of belonging after so many years of telling himself to forget what he barely remembered.

He and Rowan were both on their own and surprisingly good together in some ways. He couldn't help wondering if that could extend to parenting a child, making a life together. He could easily stomach waking every morning the way he had today, recognizing Rowan's scent before he opened his eyes. Something had teased at him as he had become aware of her warmth and weight against him. Something optimistic and peaceful. Happiness?

Whatever it was it wouldn't happen, he acknowledged darkly. Her hot statement about shotgun marriages being a mistake had spelled that out clearly enough. She was right; they *were* a mistake. He couldn't even argue that he was good husband material. But her flat refusal to consider marrying him still put a tangle of razor wire in his chest.

She noticed his attention and her hand went to her middle. "Sorry," she said.

They were halfway to the helipad. It took him a second to realize she wasn't referencing a possible baby forming inside her. Her stomach was growling.

"You *still* haven't eaten?"

"You said the car was ready."

"Ready whenever *you* were," he corrected, biting back a blistering lecture on taking care of herself and any helpless beings she might be carrying. "You're a menace," he muttered, and leaned forward to instruct his driver that they were detouring for brunch.

Minutes later they were sitting *al fresco* in the weak winter sun, a little chilly, but blessedly private away from the bustle of hungry diners. He'd ordered a yogurt and fruit cup for Rowan to eat immediately and a proper entrée for each of them to follow.

"I won't get through more than the fruit cup," Rowan warned.

"I'm hungry enough to eat whatever you don't."

"You didn't eat breakfast either? Menace!"

She had her finger hooked in a wedding ring on a delicate chain around her neck. Her mouth twitched behind the back and forth movement as she rolled the ring along its chain. He was inordinately relieved to see the return of her cheeky smile, but still exasperated.

"I'm not eating for two, am I?" he challenged.

She sobered. "Neither am I." She dropped the ring behind her collar.

"You don't know that."

A belligerently set chin and a silent glare was her only reply.

Time would tell, he supposed, dredging up patience, but his hand tightened into an angst-ridden fist. The knife in his belly made a cold, sickening turn as he recalled her rejection of marriage. He steeled himself against the rebuff and ground out, "Yes, by the way, I *would* marry you."

His begrudging statement made Rowan feel like he'd shaken out a trunk of golden treasures and brilliant riches at her feet. But it was all glass and plastic. All for show, with no true value. Numbness bled through her so she barely heard the rest of what he said.

"Don't think for a minute I'd refuse to be part of my child's life."

A choke of what felt like relief condensed in her throat. She wasn't sure why hearing he would be a dedicated parent turned her insides to mush. Maybe because it was a glimmer of the diamond inside the rough exterior. Potential.

She swallowed, but the thorny ache between her breasts stayed lodged behind her sternum. It didn't matter what Nic was capable of if fatherhood was forced upon him. It wouldn't happen. Not with her

Their dishes arrived and she manufactured a weak smile for the waiter, but couldn't unlock her fingers and pick up her utensils.

"I didn't realize your parents were married," Nic said. "Why do you use your mother's name?"

"So no one would find out Mum was married." Her voice sounded a long way off even to her own ears. All she could think was that keeping her mother's secret had been one more accommodation to an overbearing woman whose constant nagging for results had put Rowan in this position: up for the part of Nic's wife and yet not quite qualified.

She ought to tell him she couldn't conceive, but everything in her cringed from admitting it. Even though she could live without making babies. There were other options if she wanted children. She knew that. It was the fact she would never have children with *him* she wasn't ready to admit aloud.

"Is your father alive? Do you see him?" he asked.

Why were they talking about her father? "Yes, of course." Rowan picked up her spoon so she could fill her mouth with yogurt and end that subject.

"Who was he? Why did their marriage put you off it? Was he abusive?"

"Not at all!" Rowan swallowed her yogurt and sat back, surprised Nic would leap to such a conclusion. Perhaps she'd been vehement about what a mistake her parents' marriage had been, but that was how her mum had always framed it. "No, he's just a painter. An Italian."

"So you're not completely without family?" Nic sat back too, wearing his most shuttered expression, not letting her read anything into his thoughts on this discovery.

Rowan licked her lips and her shoulders grew tense. "True. But...um...he's an alcoholic. Not that that makes him less family," she rushed on. "I only mean he's not exactly there for me."

Her helpless frustration with her father's disease reared its head. She rarely mentioned him to anyone, always keeping details vague and hiding more than she revealed. Nic understood that relationships with your father could be complicated, though. That gave her the courage to continue.

"He's an amazing artist, but he doesn't finish much. He's broke most of the time. Olief knew I bought him groceries out of my allowance and paid his rent. He didn't mind. Nic, that's why I did that club appearance. With my leg and everything I hadn't seen my father much, and when I got there—"

She took a deep breath, recalling the smell, the vermin that had taken up residence in his kitchen. Setting down her spoon, she tucked her hands in her lap, clenching them under the table, managing to keep her powerless anger out of her voice.

"It seemed harmless—just one more party and for a good cause." Her crooked smile was as weak as her rationalization had been. "Afterward I realized how easily I could spiral into being just like him and I decided to come back to Rosedale to regroup. I wasn't dancing on tables so I could buy Italian fashions. He needed help."

"You said the marriage ruined your mother's life, but it sounds like it affects you more than it ever did her."

His quiet tone of empathy put a jab in her heart.

"Well, he was my father regardless, and he would have needed my help with or without the marriage. And I do love him even though things are difficult," she pointed out earnestly. "I'm not put off by marriage because he has a drinking problem. Mum just always regretted letting him talk her into making me legitimate, leaving her trapped when she wanted to marry the man she really loved. It made me realize you need more reason to marry than a baby on the way. You need deep feelings for the other person."

His gaze flicked from hers, but not before she glimpsed something like defeat in his blue eyes. Regret. His head shook in subtle dismissive negation—some inner conclusion of dismayed resignation.

A thin sheet of icy horror formed around her heart as she realized she had admitted to wanting to marry for love. There was no shame in it, but she dropped her gaze, appalled that he had read the longing in her and now his hand was a balled up fist of resistance on the tabletop. Everything in his still, hardened demeanor projected that he couldn't do it. Would never love her.

Rowan hadn't imagined he loved her, but confronting the fact that he considered it impossible had her biting back a gasp of humiliation. She blinked hard to push back tears of hurt.

The waiter arrived with their entrées, providing a much needed distraction as he poured coffee and enquired after their needs. At the same time more diners decided to brave the gusting war of spring and winter breezes, taking a table nearby.

They finished their meal in silence.

Nic had locked up when they'd left, so Rowan dug her key from her purse as they came off the lawn from the helicopter pad. She supposed even this quaint touch that her mother had insisted upon—a real key—would go the way of the dodo in whatever high-tech mansion Nic had built.

They stepped into the foyer and both let out a sigh of decompression. Rowan quirked a smile, but the key in her hand dampened her ironic amusement. The jagged little teeth might as well be sawing a circle around her heart. She rubbed her thumb across the sharp peaks, then worked the key off its ring before she lost her nerve.

"What's this?" Nic asked as she left it on the hall table and started up the stairs.

He stood below her, offering her a height advantage she never usually had over him. His thick hair was spiked up in tufts by the wind they'd left outside. She itched to lean down and smooth it.

"I won't need it after I leave." She *had* to leave. She accepted that now. She looked up the stairs, her mind already jumping back into sorting her mother's things. Better that than hanging on to adolescent dreams that could never come true. Nic would never love her. She even understood why he was incapable of it. It was time to move on, no matter how hard and scary.

"Rowan."

His tone stopped her, commanding yet not entirely steady. Height disadvantage or not, he still had the benefit of innate power and arrogance. He still managed to take her breath away with the proud angling of his head.

But an uncharacteristic hesitancy in his expression caused her to tense instinctively.

"If you were pregnant…" he began.

She didn't want this conversation, and tightened her lips to tell him so, but then she realized what he was intimating. She flicked her gaze from the muscle that ticked in his cheek to the bronze key he pinched in his sure fingers.

She felt the blood leave her face. Light-headed, she clung to the rail, trying to hang on to her composure, but it was too cruel of him to hinge keeping her home on something completely impossible.

"If I'm pregnant…what?" Despair gave way to pained affront. The high-ceilinged entryway exaggerated the quaver in her voice with a hollow echo. "I can have Rosedale as a push present? I'm not pregnant, okay? I *can't* get pregnant!"

CHAPTER ELEVEN

THE KEY IN NIC'S fist was hot as a bullet he'd snatched from the air to prevent it lodging in his chest. It was circling from another direction to make a precise hit anyway. His upper body was one hard ache of pressure as Rowan ran up the stairs.

He took a step, helpless to call her back when words were backed up in his throat behind shock. His foot caught on their bags and he stumbled. His legs became rubber, clumsy, and started to give out. He sank onto the stairs, elbows on his knees, and pressed the knuckles of his hard fists into his aching eye sockets.

Had he really let himself think it could happen? He was a fool! Of course it wasn't meant to be if it was for him. His insides knotted in a tangle of sick disillusionment.

He swallowed, his chest so hollow it felt like a gaping wound had been cleaved into it. His reaction was as much a sucker punch as the news. When had he started to care?

He *hurt* for Rowan. For a second, as her defenses had fallen away and she had let him see to the bottom of her soul, she'd revealed such a rend in her soft heart...

The urge to go after her drummed in him. But what could he do about something as absolute and irreparable as infertility?

He rubbed his numb face, dragging at the torn edges

of his control. He was fine with not getting the things that meant something to others. Mostly fine. He knew how to live with it. But it gutted him that Rowan, who openly yearned for a proper family, should be denied something that was such a perfect fit for her. He wished...

But he knew better than to wish.

Slowly he stood and climbed the stairs, every joint rusted and stiff. His goal was the sanctuary of his office and work, but he found himself walking past it like a zombie. He followed noises down the hall beyond the open door to Rowan's suite. The double doors to the master bedroom were thrown open and Rowan was taping a box propped on the bed.

She paused briefly when he appeared, just long enough to betray that she'd noted his appearance before she continued screeching the tape gun.

Nic took in the disarray. Boxes were stacked against the walls. Photographs and knickknacks were moved or had disappeared. He didn't care what she was taking. He didn't have any attachment to any of it. But it hit him how many decisions he'd burdened her with. She was a sentimental little thing. She wore a cheap wedding ring that had sealed an unwanted marriage, for God's sake. Digging through all this couldn't be easy for her. What had seemed like the right thing to do suddenly seemed wrong. Unkind.

He wondered if it was his imagination that she looked as if she'd lost weight since yesterday. It might be the baggy T-shirt over braless breasts, but she looked incredibly slight and fragile.

She set down the tape gun and moved to the corner near the balcony. "Did you know Olief was planning an autobiography?" Her sunny tone sounded forced as she pulled the lid off a box and retrieved a packet of yellowed letters. "These are to his wife, talking about the places he was in. There are other things. Photos, awards, columns. It's interesting stuff."

She held out the letters but Nic didn't take them. All his focus was on Rowan. She was so on edge the air was sharp. Her flash of wary vulnerability when she met his gaze was quickly tucked away as she replaced the letters in the box and closed the lid.

"I thought it might give you a better understanding of who he was," she said with stiff consideration and a never-mind shrug.

Part of him was curious. Of course he was. And he could tell that in offering this up she was looking for a measure of forgiveness. It seemed so unnecessary now. She wasn't the reason he had failed to form bonds with Olief. *He* was. Olief had reached out countless times. Nic had always held himself just beyond touching distance.

He scowled as that hard truth sank like talons into his chest. He didn't know how to be there for someone. He'd never wanted to know because no one had been there for him. So what had he thought to accomplish by coming in here? Raking her delicate heart over the smoldering coals of her lost dream of a family?

The inadequacy that had been smoldering in *him* since she'd admitted she wanted to marry for love licked at him with thicker flames.

"It made me realize I should do the same for Mum," she was saying with a jerky nod at the boxes against the far wall. "Giving all that over to a writer would solve a huge problem I have with what to do with playbills and photos of her with other celebrities—"

"I didn't come in here to take book pitches," he said quietly.

"Well, I don't want to talk about what you did come to talk about, so tell me you'll do it or I'll give it to the competition." Her voice was flat, her spine like a thread of glass—deceptively stiff but innately brittle. "Proceeds to benefit a search and rescue foundation, I think, don't you?"

For a second he knew what other people saw when they looked at him: absolute disengagement. His heart gave a vicious twist inside his chest. He *hated* talking about the failed dreams that lived next to his bones. How could he ask her to show him hers? But he had to know more. He lifted a helpless open palm.

"I had no idea, Ro." It astounded him that he hadn't known. Yes, he might have kept his distance from her through the years, but his ears had always been open, his brain quick to store the tidbits he'd gleaned from Olief. "Did Olief know? Did your mum?"

Rowan's chin jutted out stubbornly in profile before he saw her composure crack with a spasm of pain. She turned away to pick up a handtowel grayed with streaks of dust and wiped her fingers on it.

Rowan couldn't believe she'd blurted out the truth so indelicately. Her stomach was still spinning like a bicycle wheel, burning at the edges when she tried to slow it down. She wanted to make some comment like her sterility didn't matter, but her lungs were wrapped in a tight spool of cord.

"Mum didn't think it was a big deal," she finally managed. She looked through the French doors, beyond the balcony, out to the beach. The tide was receding, leaving kelp on the dark, flat sand. Puffy clouds on the horizon promised a breathtaking sunset. *Thanks, Mum. I didn't get what you wanted and I don't get what I want either.*

"Not a big—? Rowan, what happened?" Nic's tone was outraged, but also bewildered. Worried. Closer.

Rowan's pulse sped up, but she didn't let herself turn around and read anything into his nearness or concern.

With great care she folded the towel, even though it would only be thrown down the laundry chute.

"It's not uncommon for women who don't have much body fat to lose their periods," she said, smoothing the blue nap of the towel. "I haven't had one in years. I've gained a little weight since leaving school, but not enough for things to become normal. It might not ever happen."

She was proud of her steady tone, but his silence encased her organs in ice.

"Mum said kids would ruin my career anyway. I guess I thought she was right. That if I was training and working and traveling I wouldn't make much of a mother anyway. So it was for the best." The words burned like a hot iron rod from the back of her throat to the pit of her stomach. "I didn't let myself think of it much at all, to tell the truth. It was too big and—well, you know how doctors are. Quick to blame me because I wasn't taking care of myself. I felt responsible, but also like I couldn't change anything given the pressure I was under, so I ignored it. But with dance no longer being a part of my life and Mum and Olief gone…"

She sighed and the weight on her chest settled deeper.

"…I'm realizing that I would like a family."

She couldn't help the yearning in her voice. This was the first time in her life that she knew what she wanted, deep down and without a doubt. A blanket of calm settled on her. Not peace. Not relief. She knew she wouldn't *get* what she wanted—not the way she wanted it—but at least she knew what would fulfill her. The relief from fruitless searching allowed her to find a smidge of courage and acceptance.

"Some day," she emphasized with a glance over her shoulder.

A light flush warmed her chest and moved outward to her fingertips. A poignant burn chased it. This was the kind of conversation a couple with a future had, but she didn't want Nic thinking she was begging for one.

"Eventually," she insisted, certain she'd revealed too much as she hugged the towel she held. She tried to cover her tracks and self-protect with a hurried, "When the time and the man are right. Obviously I'm not ready now. I've spent all my life pleasing my mother and I'm still responsible for my father. You've said yourself that I'm immature. I can't even take care of myself. I don't have a home or a job..." She stopped, in danger of sounding pitiful. "And it's not like you want me to be pregnant, is it?" She mustered fake cheer as she made herself face him. "Sure, you would have made the best of it, but do you even *want* children?"

A cold sweat broke out on Nic's spine. Rowan had turned the tables so easily. One minute invoking his deepest empathy, the next putting him on the spot with eyes like deep green velvet, pale cheeks like wind-hollowed snow drifts and a wispy smile of brave fatalism softening her mouth. What heartaches did *he* harbor? she asked so ingenuously.

How could he admit that he would have welcomed a baby with her? It would be brutally hurtful, given what she'd just revealed. And unwelcome. *"When the time and the man are right."* A serrated knife of guilt turned in his gut at how comfortable he would have been trapping her to him. *Him.* A man who could never make any woman happy, least of all one who had been unfairly tied down for too long.

"*Do* you want children?" she asked, her lips barely moving while a horrified shadow of inadequacy condensed in her eyes.

He'd hesitated too long. She was reading his silent torment and coming up with failure on her part. What could he do except offer up the agonizing truth? His jaw opened, but his vocal cords were too thick. His hand turned ineffectually for a second before sound finally emerged from his throat.

"I thought it might be a…second chance." A satanic claw reached out and curled piercing talons into his heart, crushing the organ that had grown tender under Rowan's influence. He instantly wished he hadn't said that. A *second* chance? That was not how it worked. You didn't reinvent your own childhood through your offspring.

"What do you mean?" The dark arches of Rowan's brows slanted into a peak of confused hurt. "A second chance for who? At what?"

Was that tentative *hope* in her eyes?

He couldn't examine it, because this was the foggy morning at boarding school all over again. After this, after Rowan had looked right into him, she'd see what everyone but he saw—the lack. The flaw that had made him a child to be turned from without looking back. He swallowed.

"A second chance for me," he admitted, cringing at how pathetic that sounded. "At having a family."

She looked as bloodless as he felt.

He shook his head in slow negation, all sensation falling away as a rushing sound invaded his ears. "I was fooling myself."

"That's not true, Nic—" Rowan started forward but he froze, lifting hands to ward her off, unwilling to have her touch him when he felt so skinless.

The way Nic threw up a wall of resistance, looking utterly rigid, like a block of stone, stopped Rowan in her tracks. She flashed back to the way he'd clamped down on his wistful sadness when talking of his siblings that morning and her heart tipped out of balance on a hard *oh.* How had she ever thought Nic was detached? He was the opposite. His emotions were so scythe-like he couldn't bear to experience them.

"It doesn't matter," he asserted.

The backs of her eyes began to sting. She hated herself then for working her body into sterility. For provoking him into unprotected sex and letting him think briefly that she could give him what he needed. She *never* could.

A terrifying bleakness filled her. If he had loved her they might have found a workaround on making a family together, but there was absolutely no hope for a future with him now.

Rowan ducked her head and brushed a strand of hair back from her face, revealing a porcelain cheek locked in a paroxysm of disorientation and panic.

What must she be thinking? Nic wondered. That she was relieved not to be saddled with an emotional derelict? That she'd had a lucky break? That what he'd revealed made her so uncomfortable she wanted him out of her space?

"I know I'm not like other people," he said, trying to gloss over his confiding something so personal and implausible. "I observe life. I don't participate in it. Yes, I would try to make the best of things, but my best isn't good enough. Any child I created would only suffer and turn out like me. Emotionally sterile."

"No, Nic. That's not true…"

He rejected her outreached hand with an averting of his head. Her shoulders were sinking in defeat and he wanted to pull her softness into him, beg her to fix the broken spaces in him, but he knew enough about relationships to know that was not what you asked of another person. You didn't burden them with fulfilling you. Either you came into the relationship whole and able to offer something to build on, or you did the right thing and walked away, leaving them intact.

"I should get back to work," he said.

When Rowan didn't say anything he glanced at her.

She was staring with wide eyes, her lips pale in a kind of shock. Finally she offered up a barely perceptible, "Me, too."

He made himself leave, but felt her gaze follow him all the way down the hall.

"You're saying Legal is holding you up?" Nic paraphrased a week later, barely listening to the litany of excuses being offered to him.

"Yes, that's exa—"

"Learn to say more with less, Graeme. That's how this corporation has grown to where it is. Have Sebastyen call me." He ended the call, telling himself to quit acting like every self-important bastard in need of anger management classes he'd ever worked with. He was going on a week without sleep, his appetite shot despite Rowan leaving him hearty stews and tender souvlaki and chocolate brownies that melted on his fingers. He wanted an end to this unbearable tension, but the clock ticking down on his time with her frayed his temper a little more each day.

His laptop burbled with an incoming call. Sebastyen got to the heart of the matter immediately. "We're dragging our feet on several initiatives, waiting on the signing of the petition and the reading of the will. Did you receive the revised documents? Any word on when you'll see forward movement on that?"

Nic glanced at the date on his screen's calendar. He'd been putting off talking to Rowan, knowing it would upset her, but time was running out on that too. He ended the call with Sebastyen and went looking for her.

She was in the breakfast room, where abundant windows around the bottom of the south-eastern turret caught the morning sun and French doors led onto the front court-yard. Bins from the island's thrift store were stacked next to sealed boxes adorned with international courier labels.

"Rowan?"

She jerked, and the look she cast him was startled and wary. They were only speaking when they had to, and every conversation was stiff and awkward. They stared at each other, face-to-face for the first time in days.

Nic wanted to rub at the numb ache that coated his scalp and clung like a mask across his cheeks. His facial muscles felt locked in a scowl. He'd been trying to put her back at a distance, but all he could think was that he'd let her inside him and now there was no way to get her out.

He'd been devastated by her infertility. She wanted a family and something in him desperately wished he could give her one, even though he'd heard her qualifications loud and clear. *The right man. Not now.* His entire being was hollow with the knowledge that even she knew he would ultimately disappoint her.

He took in the growing fretfulness in her eyes.

"What's wrong?" she asked.

"Nothing," he lied, with a pinch on his conscience. "I just need to talk to you about the papers I asked you to sign."

Her back went up immediately. Her knuckles on the pen she clutched glowed like pearls. "I said I'd do it to-morrow. I will."

"That's not it. Legal had to make a change." He took a breath. "After I explained that your parents were still married."

Her brow pleated, but her confused expression quickly gave way to dawning comprehension.

Rowan distantly absorbed what had never occurred to her. The relationship between her parents had been so min-imized the last thing she would have called her father was

Cassandra's next of kin. *She* was her mother's closest relative. But that wasn't actually true and of course Nic was way ahead of her on that.

"Don't—please don't go to my father with those papers." Waiting to sign the papers tomorrow was her one excuse to stay here with him. For him to yank that away would cause a huge fissure to open in her.

"I was only going to offer to do it if you prefer not to," he assured her gently. "But he does have to be the one who signs."

Her heart gave a hard beat. Of course he did. She should have seen that ages ago. But her mind hadn't been on anything but tomorrow—and not for the reason it should be. She was leaving and her heart was breaking. She shook herself back to reality.

"You caught me off guard. Of course I'll take them to him. I should have realized."

He shrugged off her stilted promise with stiff negligence. They couldn't seem to overcome the intimate revelations of a few days ago. It had drawn a line beneath their relationship, leaving it summed up as unworkable. He wanted children. She couldn't give him any. He thought he was incapable of love. She couldn't prove him wrong when he couldn't love *her*.

Did she love him? Yes. Her girlish crush had deepened and matured into something abiding and strong. But so what? She had thought an affair could bring them closer, that she would touch him, draw him out, but she had turned into yet another person who had raised his expectations and then dashed them. He'd never trust in her love.

"While I have your attention…" she began, and then had to clear her throat.

Her abdomen tightened with foreboding. She told herself to quit being so nervous. It wasn't like she hadn't been mentally preparing herself for this. She had been working nonstop on arrangements, determined to finish by Nic's deadline as a matter of pride. She had talked to Frankie, booked travel, and even begun packing her things. She still found herself beginning to shake.

Get a grip, Ro. You knew the end was coming.

Which was the part that was making her fall apart. Dispensing of things was sad, but they were just things. Even the house was something she was gradually letting go of as she accepted that the people she loved would no longer be there to welcome her into it. There was one thing she couldn't face letting go of, though: Nic.

She tucked a strand from her ponytail behind her ear. Her hand was shaking and she saw his gaze fix on it. She folded her arms.

"I'm almost finished, so I should tell you where everything stands. These boxes are going to a theater manager in London who wants to set up a dedicated display in his lobby. A courier is coming tomorrow." Rowan jerked a look to the ceiling. "Mum's gowns are being auctioned. I gave the auction house your PA's details. They'll set up a convenient time to send a team to inventory and pack those properly."

"You're not keeping any?"

She understood his surprise. He knew as well as she did that designers had lined up to custom-make haute couture for Cassandra O'Brien. They were gorgeous one-of-a-kinds—but they were Cassandra's style, not Rowan's.

"Where would I wear them?" she dismissed. "No, they're works of art, so I'll let them benefit an artist by using the money to set up a trust for my father." She glanced warily at him, bracing against his judgment, hurrying to clarify. "So I won't have to resort to tasteless appearance fees or anything like that again."

If she had hoped for an approval rating she was disappointed. He scowled, seeming both thunderstruck and filled with incomprehension.

"You're not keeping *any* of it?"

It being the collection of her mother's possessions, she assumed.

"Well, a few things, of course." She shrugged, pretending it didn't bother her how judicious—ruthless, even—she'd had to be. The boxes for the thrift store were filled with *chotchkies* that had no value but had been in her life as long as she could remember. She would have kept them for her own home if she had had one. "I kept some snapshots and Mum's hand mirror. The dish she put her jewelry in at night. Things like that."

"What about her jewelry?" He leapt on the word. "Auction?"

Rowan pressed her lips together. "I wanted to ask you about that."

"I'm not going to contest ownership, if that's what you're worried about. Olief would have given those things to Cassandra without any expectation of getting them back. If you want to auction them to give yourself a nest egg, do."

"I don't." She tried to suppress the testiness that edged into her. "I'm not interested in profiting from gifts that marked important occasions in their life. Besides, we won't know if they're mine or my father's until the will is read. I just wanted to ask you to take responsibility. I don't have a safety deposit box or anywhere else secure."

His stare grew inscrutable.

Rowan was hugely sensitive to the air of intensity gathering around Nic like dark clouds—especially because she didn't know how to interpret it.

"I've sorted Olief's things as well," she prattled on. "Just recommendations, of course. He has some gorgeous

tuxedos that would fit you with a minimum of tailoring."
She couldn't help stealing a swift tallying inventory of his
potent physique, turned out professionally for telecommut-
ing in a striped button shirt and tie. "I'd love to include the
vintage one with those things going to London if you're
okay with that?"

"Rowan, I told you to *take* what you wanted, not…"
His jaw worked as he scanned the neatly stacked bins and
boxes. "I expected you to identify and keep what amounts
to Cassandra's estate—not disperse everything to charity
and…" He shot his hand into his pocket where it clenched
into a fist.

"I *can't* take much. Where would I store it?"

"But you could sell things for a down payment on a flat
and tuition for a degree. Why would you keep yourself as
broke as you were when you walked into this house? Are
you thinking about your future at *all*? What do you intend to live on?"

She frowned, not liking how defensive he made her feel
for a choice she'd already made. It was a risk, yes, but one
that actually gave her a sense of excitement.

"Frankie has—"

"Do *not* let Frankie exploit you," Nic said, cutting her
off. "I've cleared your debts with him so don't let him
bully you. And don't worry about owing me. Forget that.
Forget the credit cards from before. I was being a bastard
because I was angry. That's in the past. We know each
other better now."

"Do we?" He still thought her capable of selling off possessions for rent the way her mother would have. But she
was taking a real job—one that was temporary, but paid a
weekly wage and would get her on her feet. She was trying to act like an adult while an unrelentingly immature
part of her clung to a rose-hued dream that her efforts at

showing maturity would raise her in his estimation, that somehow he'd begin seeing her with new eyes. Eyes that warmed with affection.

"I know your love for Olief was genuine, Rowan. I believe he was looking out for you in every way he could because he felt as protective as any father." Nic rubbed the back of his neck. Suffering angled across his face as he added, "I think you helped him become capable of experiencing and showing those sorts of feelings because you draw things out of people in a way I never could. I wouldn't even know how to try."

Tenderness filled her. *You do*, she wanted to insist, because he provoked intense feelings of many kinds in *her*. But her throat was filled with the breath she was holding. Was he saying that she'd taught him to experience deeper feelings than he'd ever expected? She searched his troubled brow.

He tensed his mouth, broodingly. "I'm convinced Olief would have made provision for you and your mother. If he didn't he should have, and I'll honor that. What you had before—accommodation, living expenses—I'll go back to covering them."

Her heart landed jarringly back to earth. Rowan reminded herself to draw a breath before she fainted. It came in like powdered diamonds, crystalline and hard. It took her a moment to find words.

"Let me guess. You'll even let me grace your bed while you pay those expenses?" The bitterness hardening her heart couldn't be disguised in her flat, disillusioned voice.

"That's not how I meant it." His shoulders tensed into a hard angle.

"You're going to pay my expenses and *not* want to sleep with me?" she goaded.

His bleak gaze flicked from hers. "I can't say I don't

want you. It would be a lie. The wanting doesn't stop, no matter what I do."

And it made him miserable, she deduced. No mention of love or commitment either.

Rowan told herself not to let his reluctant confession make a difference—especially when he was standing there not even looking at her, his bearing aloof and remote, but her heart veered toward him in hope anyway.

She lifted a helpless palm into the air. "It's constant for me, too, but—"

"Then why can't we continue what we started?" He pivoted his attention to her like a homing device.

"Because I don't want to be your mistress!"

He rocked back on his heels, his jaw flexing like he'd taken a punch.

"I don't want to be *any* man's mistress," she rushed on. "I want a relationship built on equality. Something stable that grows roots. Even if—" Her words were a long walk onto thin ice. She looked down at the pen she had unconsciously unwound so the center of its barrel fell open and parts were dropping out. "Even if it doesn't include children, I still want something with a future."

She looked up, silently begging for a sign that he wanted those things, too.

His eyes darkened to obsidian. His fists were rocks in his pockets.

"You're right, of course," he said, after a long, loaded minute. "All we had was a shelter in a storm, not something that lasts beyond the crisis. I'll never again judge Olief for caving in to physical relief during a low point."

The words impaled Rowan. She nodded jerkily, because what else could she expect him to say? That he had miraculously developed a deeper appreciation for her place in his life? At best he was nursing a sense of obligation toward her. It was the last sort of debt she wanted to make him feel.

"I'm going for a walk." She needed to say goodbye to Rosedale. It was the final item on her to-do list.

"Stay back from the water."

A bitter laugh threatened, but Rowan swallowed it and left.

Rowan caught a lift with the courier in the morning, giving Nic about three seconds to react to her leaving. She walked into his office, said she could save him a trip to the landing and asked where were those papers that needed signing.

No prolonged goodbye. Just a closed door, the fading hum of an engine, then silence that closed around him like a cell. Her scent lingered in a wisp of almond cookies and sunshine, dissipating and finally undetectable.

Nic stood up in disbelief, drawn to the window where the vehicle had long since motored up the track on the side of the hill and disappeared. He had been girding himself for an awkward leave-taking, expecting something uncomfortable in front of the passengers waiting for the ferry. He had thought they'd have a quiet day today, but he'd been sure she'd spend it here. With him.

His limbs felt numb as a graveled weight settled into his abdomen.

Unconsciously he found himself searching the grounds for her lissom silhouette. But she wasn't at the gazebo, or in the swing under the big oak, nor among the rows of grape-vines or even taunting him from the rocky outcropping at the beach. Yesterday he'd watched her wander the estate for hours, often looking back at the house. He'd thought she was waiting to see if he'd join her, but he'd been too disturbed by their discussions in the breakfast room. Too stripped of his armor.

"I don't want to be your mistress."

He hadn't planned any of that: either the offering of a settlement or a continuation of their arrangement. It had come out of the situation as he'd realized she was setting herself up to be destitute. Shame had weighed on him for his arrogance in cutting her off. Rowan wasn't a superficial user. She was too sensitive for her own good, putting other's needs ahead of her own—even people who had deep flaws like her mother and father.

Pushing away from the window, he strode from his office into her room—only to be brought up by the neatly folded sheets on the foot of her stripped bed. He didn't know what he had expected, but it wasn't that.

The night table and dresser top were clear. The closet held only hangers. All the drawers were empty. Even the shower had dried to leave no trace of her. The wastebasket was fresh, the long dark hairs shaken from the floor mat and swept away.

A wild insidious thought occurred that he'd imagined her presence here. The rock music while she had worked, her burbling laugh after a leading remark, the feel of her naked skin against his... His breath turned to powdered glass in his lungs.

She'd given her virginity to him. That meant something, didn't it? She had said she wouldn't forget him, yet...

"Damn you, Rowan!" he squeezed out, instantly needing proof of her existence.

He dragged drawers from their rails and in his impatience tossed their hollow shells to clatter across the hardwood floor. Empty. All empty. With nothing else to throw, he impulsively launched a drawer at the wild-eyed man in the mirror.

His image shattered in a jarring smash that disintegrated into a glinting pile of shards on the floor.

He was losing his rationality, but this was more than a man could bear. He'd dealt with the confusing pain of his father shutting him out and his mother walking away without looking back. He'd even met unflinchingly the gaze of his real father when Olief had looked up from smiling with pride at the girl who wasn't his into the eyes of the man who was.

All of it had devastated him, but this pain was worse.

Driven to the master bedroom, he began overturning boxes. One of them must have photos of her. But they held only Cassandra and Olief, nothing of Rowan. No warmth, no affection, no laughter.

No Rowan.

She had left him.

He'd been abandoned. Again.

CHAPTER TWELVE

N<small>IC'S PA BLIPPED</small> into his computer monitor with a message that the auction house was on the phone. He instructed her to tell them to call back next week, not missing the subtle pause before her assent that silently screamed, *Again*?

Pushing back from his desk, he moved to the window, where he rubbed the back of his neck. His whole body hurt from long work days and harder evenings in the gym. Blinking to clear the sting from his eyes, he tried to take in the view of Athens, but nothing penetrated.

He was too aware that if the auction house was calling the week was up for the demolition team, as well. They'd get the same answer, since he couldn't let anyone into the house while it was in the state he'd left it and he couldn't face going back to clean up.

Nicodemus Marcussen, the man who had looked into the wrong end of a rifle twice, not to mention coming face-to-face with a jaguar and surviving a bout of malaria, couldn't find the courage to do a bit of housekeeping and get on with his life. These days he had a lot of compassion for men like Rowan's father, who drowned in alcohol to numb the pain of being alive.

He cursed and hung his head. *Rowan's father*. She wanted to use the auction money to set up a trust for him. Twelve weeks was too long to put that off. Nic couldn't keep doing it. Why hadn't she contacted him to ask what was holding it up?

Heavy-hearted, he suspected he knew. Drawing his hand from his pocket, he examined the key that seemed to end up in his possession every morning. He'd come to associate its rough-smooth shape and metallic smell with guilt, anger and loss, but he couldn't make himself get rid of it. The key or the house.

Rowan expected him to. Everyone did. The architect had delivered the drawings weeks ago. The builders were being put off as well. Nic was sole heir to everything Olief had owned. There'd been provision to support Cassandra and allow her the use of Rosedale, but the house, as part of Marcussen Media, was his. He had every right to knock it down, but he couldn't make himself do it.

Clenching his hand around the biting shape, he recalled the signed documents arriving that had allowed the declaration of death. The Italian painter's signature had been a shaky flourish in all the right places, but there had been nothing from Rowan. No forget-me-not stationery with a snooty missive demanding Nic sort out her finances.

He'd give anything for the privilege, he acknowledged with a wistful ache in his chest, but after a brief game of financial ping-pong with Frankie he'd had to leave Rowan's modest balance for her to pay off. She didn't want anything from him and it hurt so much he couldn't bear it. But what did he intend with a gesture like that?

Connection, he thought simply. He just wanted to know they were still linked in some way. He was becoming as sentimental about attachment as she was.

The spark of irony glinted in his mind, no bigger than a dust mote catching in a beam of sunlight, but he held his breath, examining it.

When had he last felt like this? Truly wanting someone in his life? He'd grown up wanting Olief in his life, but when the opportunity had finally arisen he'd been too tainted by the years of neglect. He'd held back from letting real closeness develop with his father, certain he'd lose in the long run.

And he had.

Everything in him still screamed that it was dangerous to yearn for love and the indelible link of family, but that was what he wanted with Rowan. He'd settle for scraps if he had to, but he couldn't function under the belief that he'd never see her again. He needed to know that his future contained her.

Even if it doesn't include children, I still want something with a future.

How many times had he replayed those words in his head along with his own response that what had passed between them had been only shelter from a storm? He'd been scared when he'd said it. He could offer her a lot of things, including a secure future, but when it came to love he feared his heart was too damaged. *He* was.

He'd thawed a lot under Rowan's warmth, though. It made him think that maybe, if she could be persuaded to keep seeing him… But he was getting ahead of himself. She might not want anything to do with him.

A yawning chasm opened before him as he contemplated going to her and putting his soul on the line. But it wouldn't hurt any more than he was hurting right now. At least he'd know.

And, damn it, he was not a helpless six-year-old any longer. He was a man who knew how to fight for what he wanted. He would do anything to have her back in his life. To *keep* her in his life.

The decision made him suck in a breath that burned. A

flame of something he barely recognized came to life inside him. Anticipation of relief from pain. *Hope*.

Wherever she'd gone, he'd find her and bring her back to where she belonged!

Rowan watched the little girl appear and disappear between the heavy coats of the bustling street, her face a picture of frightened despair as Ireland's ever-present rain drizzled into it. Her voice, clear and agonizingly uncertain, lifted in a shaky plea. Everything in Rowan wanted to run to her. She was overwhelmed with compassion for this waif who'd lost everything.

Until a man in a modern trenchcoat, his dark blond hair foreign in a sea of black Irish peasant cuts, strode from between the carriages and ruined the scene.

"Cut! What the hell?" someone yelled. "Security!"

"Nic!" Stunned to recognize him, Rowan rushed forward, shock making her stumble. "It's okay, I know him," she assured the men in the red shirts charging forward.

Her whole body trembled in crazed reaction. He looked so good! But tired. His face was lined with weariness, breaking her heart. And he was *annoyed*. He glared at the assistant director when the woman tried to take his arm.

"Come with me, you crazy man." Rowan grasped Nic's wet sleeve and led him away, glancing back at her charge to say, "You're doing great, Milly. I'll be right back."

Little Milly beamed with pride, then stood dutifully still as Makeup approached.

Rowan dragged Nic into a friend's trailer and tried to catch her breath. It was impossible when he filled the space with his dominant presence and masculine scent. Everything about him hit her with fresh power: the authority he projected, the stirring energy he radiated into the air. The sexual excitement he sparked in her with the simple act of falling into her line of vision.

Oh, that physical pull was so much worse now she knew how incredible it was to lie with him. All of her wanted to fall forward and kiss, hold, caress, *be* with him.

She tried to conquer it, tried to quell the shaking and hold on to control. Tried to find her equilibrium and act like a rational human being when he'd just knocked her back after three months of learning to live without him.

"What are you doing here?" she asked with growing defensiveness. "And like that? If someone barged into your board meeting you'd have them arrested."

"Not if it was you." He narrowed his gaze on her mouth. "Why is your accent so strong?"

The sound of his voice, the leading words he'd said, made her heart lurch. She could barely stay on her feet. "Living here does that. And I'm teaching that girl to speak like a native so they won't crucify her for being American. I'm her dialogue coach."

Nic ran a hand across his hair, then dried it on his thigh. "Frankie said you were on a film set in Ireland. I didn't know if that meant you were acting… Can we go somewhere to talk?"

Seriously? She bit down on her lip, shocked by how badly she wanted to go anywhere with him, but self-preservation reminded her to keep her feet on the ground. "We're in the middle of a scene," she pointed out with forced patience.

"Do you like this job?"

His penetrating gaze had an effect that was nothing less than cataclysmic. She had missed those blue eyes, that stern expression, the way he looked at her like he really wanted to hear what she had to say.

"I do. I get to tell people off if I think they're pushing

Milly too hard and she's a doll. I'm not sure what will come next. Frankie's looking into an Italian film. But for the moment I have a roof over my head." She tried to make it sound like it was all sunshine and roses, not hinting at how badly she'd been missing him.

"About that… A roof, I mean." He cleared his throat and his hand went into his pocket. "I've done a few things." The mixture of arrogance and sheepishness in his tone made Rowan tense.

"What things?" she asked with low-voiced foreboding.

His hand came out of his pocket and he set a key next to where she was involuntarily clutching the edge of the sink. Recognition hit in stages as she processed the bronze shape, the familiarity of it, the way its sharp angles seemed worn down—and the possessive longing and sense of privilege it inspired only now, after she'd given it up.

"What—?" She couldn't believe he'd come all this way to tell her the house was rubble. That would be too cruel.

"It's yours, Ro."

"Rosedale?" The magnitude of the gift was too much. She had to clap a hand to her mouth to keep her suddenly wobbling chin from falling off. At the same time the tears that filled her eyes stung with loss. She couldn't face that big, empty house without him in it. "I can't," she choked.

"You'd rather I destroy it?" He reached for the key.

She was quicker, snatching it up and holding it in a protective fist against her heart, realizing when she caught the glimmer of smug satisfaction in his eye that he'd been bluffing. He was far quicker than her when he wanted to be.

"Why, Nic? Something in Olief's will?" She couldn't believe it.

He dismissed that with a brief movement of his head. "No, this is my decision. Olief made provision for your mother, but left everything to me. And you must have seen a copy of Cassandra's will by now?"

Rowan hitched her shoulder, dismissing it because it was exactly as she had expected. Gowns and empty purses. Jewelry she didn't want to sell.

"About the gowns—I've had emails," she began with a concerned frown.

"I know. I've…done something else. I went to see your father."

"What?" Dread poured into her, making her want to sink through the floor and disappear. One pained word came out. *"Why?"*

"Cassandra was meant to be taken care of, and he was still married to her. It seemed right to make sure there was something in place for him. Don't look like that, Ro. It wasn't bad. I liked him. I see where you get your sense of humor. And I was there first thing in the morning, so he was relatively sober," he allowed with a diffident shrug. "I've purchased his building, so rent will never be a problem again, and hired a caretaker to go in every day. A man who will cook and clean and has a background in addiction rehabilitation. We had a heart-to-heart, your father and I, about losing parents and that maybe you don't need to face that again any time soon. I don't know if it will make a difference, but…"

"That's incredibly generous, Nic," she said to his shoes. "I'll pay you back—"

He took a firm hold of her jaw, his warm thumb covering her lips to still them as he drew her face up so he could look into her eyes. The impact of his touch, his closeness, the deep eye contact was earth-shattering.

"Don't you dare."

"But—" She was coming apart inside, fighting the urge

to shift her lips into his palm and kiss him. "I don't want to owe you," she whispered.

"You don't want to be my mistress. I know that. None of this comes with a catch. I'm not trying to buy you, Rowan. I just want to know you're looked after, not breaking your leg or—" A completely uncharacteristic agitation seemed to grip him. He took his hand from her face to rub it over his own. "I want to know you'll be at Rosedale sometimes and I might have a shot at seeing you, that you're not out of my life forever."

"You want to see me?" A very fragile hope, one she'd had to tamp down on a million times, began to twine up from the depths of her heart.

He reached into his pocket, drawing out a small velvet box that he set next to the sink with almost confrontational determination. "I want to marry you."

Rowan was so stunned she reflexively backed away until her legs hit the edge of the bench and she sat down in a clumsy heap, her head falling into her hands as she tried to deal with all he was throwing at her. The key dug into her closed fist. Too much to process. Now a *ring*?

"All right, just *see* me," he rushed out gruffly. "That's enough. Just be in my life, Rowan. Even if it's like it used to be—a few times a year. Whatever you want. Just don't make me live with this loneliness that hits every time I think of that house without you in it. I can't go near Rosedale, but I can't knock it down and obliterate the only good memories I have."

"Nic..." Her voice didn't want to work, catching and quavering in her throat while her icy fingers shook against her numb lips. Her heart pounded as though she'd been running for her life and now she was cornered. Not safe, but maybe...just maybe...

"Do you love me?" she risked.

His face tightened and started to close, but before he could withdraw into the unreachable man she could only dream of from afar Rowan threw herself at him, wrapping anxious arms around his rain-dappled coat and big, unyielding body.

"You don't have to say it. This is enough."

"I want to say it," he said tightly, as though struggling with a great burden.

She squeezed him tighter. "It's okay. It's enough that you're here. I love you. I always have." Joy flooded through her as she finally admitted it to herself, to him—

Hard hands caught her upper arms and pushed her away. He held on to her, but his incredulous and furious expression scared her. "You've *always* loved me?"

Oh, she'd made a terrible, horrible miscalculation— opening her heart like this and assuming a bit of nostalgia on his part was anything like the soaring love she felt. Sickened, she could only stand there dumbfounded.

"Then why did you leave me?" he asked in a voice of abject despair.

Shock gave way to a slam of relief, followed by heart-rending regret.

"You can't just rip a man apart like that," he rebuked.

"But you hated me for years. You only asked me to stay as your mistress," she reminded him with a spark of offense. Her pique crumpled as her view of a shared future with him struck a brick wall. "And since I can't give you a baby, and you want one—"

He groaned in a release of frustration and despair, hauling her against him under his wet overcoat and into the shelter of his warmth and strength. "I have been fighting letting you under my skin every second of my life. I knew you'd destroy me if I did, and you have. I hate trying to live without you, Ro. I *need* you in my life. And, yes, I will always wish we could make babies together. But we'll make our family whatever way we need to. If it's only us, that's enough. *I love you.*"

His arms crushed her, making it hard to find enough breath to talk, but she wouldn't have it any other way. She was shaking so hard she needed him to hold her up.

"I didn't mean to hurt you. I didn't think I could," she managed.

"You can, Ro. More than you know."

Because he cared. He was letting down his guard for her and she recognized what a sacrifice he was making. She silently swore a vow of duty to protect, never wanting to hurt him again.

His mouth found hers and they kissed with a reverence anointed by salty tears. His hand in her hair was possessive and cherishing, his other hand gently stroking to meld her curves indelibly to his hard angles.

The door to the trailer opened and a male voice cursed. "Get your own room." The door slammed.

Rowan choked on a laugh as they broke apart in surprise, breathless and blinking to see through her wet lashes.

"I've missed this smile," Nic said, with a tender knuckle against the corner of her mouth. "But I agree with whoever that was. What are we going to do? I want to marry you *now*."

"Are you sure?" His urgent determination lifted her heart into the stratosphere, but she forced herself at least to try to be sensible. "We can see how things go—have a long engagement. You and I…we have our clashes."

"We're both too headstrong not to. But I'd rather have a ring on your finger as a promise that we'll work it out."

The deep tenderness in his eyes turned everything in her to liquid heat, but she heard something else in his tone that touched her even more deeply. Implacable determination. He wanted a seal on this deal and no room for her to back out. Nic wanted her. Forever.

With a trembling smile, she held out an equally trembling hand. "Okay, then. Yes, please, I'd love to marry you, Nic. I love you."

He drew in a sharp breath, like he was taking the words into him. His hands shook as he opened the velvet box and worked the ring onto her finger. "I only brought this to prove my intentions were honorable, never expecting you'd actually say yes…"

It was a perfect fit, but the dazzling diamond and its band of emeralds almost made her start crying again. "Not trying to buy me, huh?" she joked, in an effort to hold on to her composure.

"Go big or go home alone." Nic's grin was rueful. He offered her the key to Rosedale.

Rowan tucked it into his breast pocket, giving it a little pat. "You hang on to it. This is a package deal. I don't want the house unless you're in it."

His chest rose as he took a big breath, and they both nearly fell into another passionate embrace.

Rowan made herself check her watch. "Help me show a bit of responsibility here. There's a few hours of filming left. Then we can go back to my flat. It's not much, but I have a feeling you won't be looking at anything but the bedding."

"I won't be looking at anything but *you*."

EPILOGUE

Eight and a half months later...

NIC NEVER CLOSED his door against Rowan, but with workers running table saws and nail guns at the bottom of the stairs while he was trying to work he'd not only closed his door, but started thinking about disappearing to Athens.

Rowan wanted to oversee the renovations, however. If she wouldn't come with him, he wouldn't go. It wasn't his idea to change things, but she was insisting on finding a middle ground between keeping what they both loved about Rosedale while opening up the design more to his preference. Since that would make Rosedale very much *theirs*, he approved.

"Nic?" She pushed in with a confused frown, giving the door a baleful glance as she closed it behind her.

"I couldn't hear myself think with the noise—are you all right?" He was always completely attuned to her moods. Both of them were still capable of putting on a facade around others, but they read each other like a book and Rowan was not herself at this moment.

He scanned her slender figure, stopping where her hands were wringing out the cordless phone like a wet towel. Her face was pale, her eyes wide with shock, her bottom lip caught abusively between sharp white teeth. She was shaking.

Stark concern lifted him onto his feet with instinctive readiness, adrenaline piercing his system like an injection of drugs. "What happened? Who was that?"

"We're in labor," she said, with a sudden beaming smile that instantly became slushy with trembles.

That was supposed to be a joke, he recognized, but his brain wasn't computing humor when the implication was so huge.

"That was the agency?" His knees almost buckled.

If a crowd had rushed in here and hefted him high, touting him as a hero, he wouldn't have been more shocked, elated or proud. Part of him had felt like it was a losing cause to chase adoption. The background interviews hadn't been easy for him. He'd opened up for both of them, to give them this chance, but he couldn't change the fact that he was perceived as a very distant man. The more they'd talked about what they might be able to offer a child, however, the more he'd wanted one. He hadn't been sure he'd even pass muster as a prospective father—now this?

Rowan was nodding and grinning, her brimming eyes spilling happy tears onto her cheekbones. "They have a baby girl. Her mum was killed by a landmine and she was injured. She needs to stay in hospital for a couple of weeks, and will need a number of surgeries over the next few years, but—"

"Us," he said, staggering his way from behind his desk to reach his wife in a lurch. "She needs us."

Rowan nodded, sobbing as she threw her arms around his neck, "Nic, I'm so happy!"

"I didn't think I could be happier than I already was," he choked, lifting and crushing her to him, trying to absorb her lithe frame into his bones. "God, I love you. Look what you're doing to me. Turning me into a father!"

She took his face in her hands and looked at him in the undisguised way that always made his heart bottom out. "You are going to be the most amazing father. I can't wait to see it."

He teared up, and swept her in a scoop against the racing pound of his heart, stumbling to the sofa so he could sit with her in his lap and stroke her shaking body with his shaking hands.

"My whole life is better with you, Rowan. Thank you for loving me."

Rowan was so deeply happy and in love it was more than she could contain. Wiping her damp cheeks, she laughed helplessly, "I can't stop crying and I want to kiss you!"

"Did you have the sense to lock the door?" In one powerful twist he had her gently sprawled beneath him, his weight braced over her. He paused, hand massaging her flat abdomen. "Can we do this in your delicate condition? Being in labor and all?"

She let out a peal of appreciative laughter. "Better hurry before we have a baby stealing our attention."

"When you put it like that, I think I'd better take my time. I want to give you all the attention you deserve." He covered her smile with a reverent, loving kiss.

* * * * *

COMING NEXT MONTH FROM

HARLEQUIN *Presents*®

Available December 17, 2013

#3201 THE DIMITRAKOS PROPOSITION
Lynne Graham

Tabby Glover desperately needs Greek billionaire Acheron Dimitrakos to support her adoption claim over his cousin's child. His price? Marriage. But as the thin veil between truth and lies is lifted, will this relationship become more than in name only?

#3202 A MAN WITHOUT MERCY
Miranda Lee

Dumped by her fiancé *via text,* Vivienne Swan wants to nurse her shattered heart privately...until an intriguing offer from Jack Stone tempts her from her shell. He is a man used to taking what he wants, and Vivienne is now at his mercy!

#3203 FORGED IN THE DESERT HEAT
Maisey Yates

Newly crowned Sheikh Zafar Nejem's first act is to rescue heiress Analise Christensen from her desert kidnappers and return her to her fiancé...or risk war. But the forbidden attraction burning between them rivals the heat of the sun, threatening everything....

#3204 THE FLAW IN HIS DIAMOND
Susan Stephens

When no-nonsense Eva Skavanga arrives on Count Roman Quisvada's Mediterranean Island with a business arrangement, Roman's more interested in the pleasure she might bring him. Perhaps Roman could help her with more than just securing her family's diamond mine...?

HPCNM1213RA

#3205 THE TYCOON'S DELICIOUS DISTRACTION
Maggie Cox

Forced to rely on physio Kit after a skiing accident confines him to a wheelchair, Hal Treverne has no escape from her intoxicating presence. But unleashing the simmering desire beneath her ever-so-professional facade is a challenge this tycoon will relish!

#3206 HIS TEMPORARY MISTRESS
Cathy Williams

Damian Carver wants revenge on the woman who stole from him, and her sister Violet won't change his mind...until he needs a temporary mistress, and Violet's perfect! But sweet-natured Violet soon turns the tables on his sensuous brand of blackmail....

#3207 THE MOST EXPENSIVE LIE OF ALL
Michelle Conder

Champion horse breeder Aspen has never forgotten Cruz Rodriguez, so when he reappears with a multimillion-dollar investment offer, Aspen's torn. She may crave his touch, but his glittering black eyes hide a deception that could prove more costly than ever before!

#3208 A DEAL WITH BENEFITS
One Night with Consequences
Susanna Carr

Sebastian Cruz has no intention of giving Ashley Jones's family's island back, but he does want her. He'll agree to her deal, but with a few clauses of his own—a month at his beck and call... and in his bed!

YOU CAN FIND MORE INFORMATION ON UPCOMING HARLEQUIN® TITLES, FREE EXCERPTS AND MORE AT WWW.HARLEQUIN.COM.

HPCNM1213RB

REQUEST YOUR
FREE BOOKS!

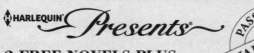 HARLEQUIN® *Presents*~

 PASSION GUARANTEED SEDUCTION

2 FREE NOVELS PLUS
2 FREE GIFTS!

YES! Please send me 2 FREE Harlequin Presents® novels and my 2 FREE gifts (gifts are worth about $10). After receiving them, if I don't wish to receive any more books, I can return the shipping statement marked "cancel." If I don't cancel, I will receive 6 brand-new novels every month and be billed just $4.30 per book in the U.S. or $4.99 per book in Canada. That's a saving of at least 14% off the cover price! It's quite a bargain! Shipping and handling is just 50¢ per book in the U.S. and 75¢ per book in Canada.* I understand that accepting the 2 free books and gifts places me under no obligation to buy anything. I can always return a shipment and cancel at any time. Even if I never buy another book, the two free books and gifts are mine to keep forever.

106/306 HDN FVRK

Name _____ (PLEASE PRINT) _____

Address _____ Apt. #

City _____ State/Prov. _____ Zip/Postal Code

Signature (if under 18, a parent or guardian must sign) _____

Mail to the **Harlequin® Reader Service:**
IN U.S.A.: P.O. Box 1867, Buffalo, NY 14240-1867
IN CANADA: P.O. Box 609, Fort Erie, Ontario L2A 5X3

**Are you a current subscriber to Harlequin Presents books
and want to receive the larger-print edition?
Call 1-800-873-8635 or visit www.ReaderService.com.**

* Terms and prices subject to change without notice. Prices do not include applicable taxes. Sales tax applicable in N.Y. Canadian residents will be charged applicable taxes. Offer not valid in Quebec. This offer is limited to one order per household. Not valid for current subscribers to Harlequin Presents books. All orders subject to credit approval. Credit or debit balances in a customer's account(s) may be offset by any other outstanding balance owed by or to the customer. Please allow 4 to 6 weeks for delivery. Offer available while quantities last.

Your Privacy—The Harlequin® Reader Service is committed to protecting your privacy. Our Privacy Policy is available online at www.ReaderService.com or upon request from the Harlequin Reader Service.

We make a portion of our mailing list available to reputable third parties that offer products we believe may interest you. If you prefer that we not exchange your name with third parties, or if you wish to clarify or modify your communication preferences, please visit us at www.ReaderService.com/consumerchoice or write to us at Harlequin Reader Service Preference Service, P.O. Box 9062, Buffalo, NY 14269. Include your complete name and address.

HP13

SPECIAL EXCERPT FROM

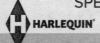 HARLEQUIN®

Presents®

Read on for an exclusive extract from
THE DIMITRAKOS PROPOSITION, the sensational
new story from Lynne Graham!

* * *

TABBY looked up at him and froze, literally not daring to breathe. That close his eyes were no longer dark but a downright amazing and glorious swirl of honey, gold and caramel tones, enhanced by the spiky black lashes she envied.

His fingers were feathering over hers with a gentleness she had not expected from so big and powerful a man, and little tremors of response were filtering through her, undermining her self-control. She knew she wanted those expert hands on her body, exploring much more secret places, and color rose in her cheeks, because she also knew she was out of her depth and drowning. In an abrupt movement, she wrenched her hands free and turned away, momentarily shutting her eyes in a gesture of angry self-loathing.

"Try on the rest of the clothes," Acheron instructed coolly, not a flicker of lingering awareness in his dark deep voice.

Tension seethed through Acheron. What the hell was the matter with him? He had been on the edge of crushing that soft, luscious mouth beneath his, close to wrecking the non-sexual relationship he envisaged between them. Impersonal would work the best and it shouldn't be that difficult, he reasoned impatiently, for they had nothing in common. She cleaned up incredibly well, he acknowledged grudgingly,

HPEXP1213-1R